TANGLED LIVES

ALSO BY STEPHANIE HARTE

Risking it All
Forgive and Forget

TANGLED LIVES

Stephanie Harte

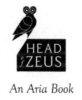

An Aria Book

This edition first published in the United Kingdom in 2020 by Aria,
an imprint of Head of Zeus Ltd

Copyright © Stephanie Harte, 2020

A CIP catalogue record for this book is available from the
British Library.

ISBN: 9781035905492

Typeset by Siliconchips Services Ltd UK

Aria
c/o Head of Zeus
First Floor East
5–8 Hardwick Street
London EC1R 4RG

www.ariafiction.com

For my husband, Barry and my children, Sarah and James. Thank you for spurring me on when I felt overwhelmed and for always believing in me.

I

Gemma

It was three o'clock in the morning, and I couldn't help noticing that everything was unusually quiet on the Golden Mile. Since moving to Puerto Banús, a thriving resort that boasted numerous nightclubs and late-night bars, we'd become accustomed to the throb of the after-dark playlist that continued until the small hours. My eyes were closed, but I lay awake, listening to Nathan's steady breathing. I suddenly became aware of somebody climbing the stone stairs below our penthouse apartment. The sound appeared amplified in the darkness – or was it because my senses were heightened that made the echoing seem especially disturbing?

When the footsteps stopped outside our front door, my eyes sprang open, and panic gripped me with an iron fist. Recently, I'd been having a recurring nightmare that someone broke in and kidnapped my baby in the middle of the night, while Nathan and I were sleeping. But I could see

Luca's chest rising and falling in the Moses basket next to our bed, so I knew he was safe.

'Nathan, wake up,' I whispered, shaking my husband by the arm. He stirred at the sound of my voice, but he was still in the depths of sleep, so I shook him again, harder this time.

'What's up, Gemma?' Nathan's sounded groggy. Removing his hand from under his pillow, he rolled over and looked at me.

'There's somebody outside.' Clutching the covers in terror, I slid further down in the bed.

As Nathan's dark eyes registered what I'd said, he threw back the quilt and swung his long legs out of bed. I reached over and put my hand on his bare shoulder before he had a chance to stand up.

'Phone security; please don't go out there,' I said.

After Alfie Watson and his team were arrested in Boulogne, Nathan and I decided we'd move to Spain until the dust settled. Although the authorities had said they were confident they had caught the men responsible for the robbery at the Antwerp Diamond Centre and were not looking for anyone else in connection with the heist, we felt it was too risky for us to go back to British soil at the moment. One of the reasons we'd chosen to buy this ultra-modern luxury apartment was for the safety aspect. It was situated on the top floor of a three-storey building inside a gated community with a concierge and round-the-clock security. It had its own lift, so why would somebody bother to climb all those stairs?

Nathan's dark hair flopped forward when he reached under the bed and pulled out a baseball bat. 'Stay here,' he said. As he crossed the white marble floor of the hallway, we heard the footsteps retreating down the staircase. Nathan flung open the front door, but the intruder was long gone.

I was eager to hear what he had to say. He wouldn't be able to dismiss my concerns this time. How would he explain the presence of somebody outside our door? 'I suppose I just imagined hearing those footsteps running down the stairs, did I?' I said when Nathan came back into the bedroom.

'It was probably just kids.' Nathan yawned and slipped back into bed.

'At three o'clock in the morning?'

He tucked a strand of my dark brown bob behind my ear before kissing the top of my head. 'Go back to sleep, Gemma.'

'I won't be able to, not with somebody lurking outside our apartment.'

'Whoever it was isn't there now.' Nathan pulled the quilt over himself and rolled onto his side. Pulling me towards him, he draped a protective arm over me.

Despite my husband's reassurance, I knew I wouldn't sleep for the rest of the night. I was on edge, so my anxious state of mind wouldn't allow it. There's nothing like a bit of sleep deprivation to lower your mood and allow self-indulgent paranoid thoughts to fill your brain. It didn't matter how many times Nathan told me there was no evidence we were under threat, the eerie feeling of someone watching my every move had become part of my daily life. It never left me and occupied my thoughts day and night. It was an unnerving sensation, but Nathan was convinced it was all in my mind. As far as he was concerned, there was nothing to worry about; I was just imagining it. He was probably right.

Since Luca's birth, I'd been on edge; my emotions were out of control. Nathan was sure the change in my behaviour was because I was adjusting to life with a new baby, but I thought there was more to it than a case of the baby blues. Although that would account for some of my symptoms, it didn't explain why I'd developed a fear of being watched all the time. I didn't know if it was an irrational fear brought on by anxiety or if my sixth sense was right.

Either way, something was amiss. I didn't imagine the incident just now outside our apartment, no matter what Nathan said. As it played on my mind, I knew I'd have trouble sleeping, and if I managed to drift off, I'd dream I was reliving the nightmare.

No wonder I'd found myself travelling down this dark path. Our lives would never be the same again. When you lived through a traumatic experience, it did strange things to a person; you couldn't expect everything to return to normal in an instant, could you? The memory of Alfie setting the yacht ablaze to destroy any evidence it contained, even though he knew Nathan and I were still on board, haunted me. He had been willing to burn us alive to stop himself being linked to his crimes. I couldn't get my head around that fact. I had been pushed to the edge and felt like I was unravelling. My sanity was fraying at the seams.

I didn't like feeling weak and out of control. I'd always been the strong one in our relationship, but these days I had to lean more and more on my husband for emotional support. That was something that didn't sit comfortably with me. I valued my independence too much.

I was seventeen when I met Nathan on the beach at Southend. We were childhood sweethearts. People said we were too young to marry, but nothing would keep us apart. He was my soulmate. My world fell to pieces when our marriage hit rock bottom, but since I'd become pregnant, it was back on track, and our relationship was stronger than ever.

Being a mother for the first time was hard work. I was struggling without a close network around me. Nathan had been a fantastic help, doing chores and everyday tasks to take some of the strain off me, but that hadn't stopped me feeling overwhelmed at times. Reeling from exhaustion and fluctuating hormones, I'd found myself being sucked into a dark place. A place I was reluctant to visit, in case I couldn't find my way out again. I kept reminding myself that this was all new to me, so I shouldn't be too hard on myself. But I'd always been my own worst critic.

Nathan had found it difficult growing up without his father around, and in the past, he'd struggled with commitment issues and insecurities. Because of that, he wanted Luca to grow up with two loving parents and never experience the pain he went through.

2

Nathan

The day Gemma showed me the little pink line on the pregnancy test, it brought a tear to my eye. It was a fantastic feeling knowing my wife was expecting our first child, but I also couldn't help feeling a little sad. I wanted to share the news with my family, but I'd been estranged from my mum since I'd found out she'd lied to me about my dad. She'd let me grow up thinking Dad had abandoned me. I never understood why he'd do that to me, and it filled me with insecurity.

Mum had paid the ultimate price for keeping her secret from me. It had damaged our relationship, and I wasn't sure we'd ever recover from it. We hadn't spoken in over a year. I'd thought about picking up the phone and putting an end to our argument on several occasions, but I wasn't sure I was ready to forgive her yet. Because of what she'd done, I was thirty-three years old, and I'd never met my father. She'd cut him out of our lives when I was a baby, so I'd been denied a relationship with him. That had a powerful effect on me. My upbringing had undoubtedly left its mark on me. I'd battled demons all my life.

Since Gemma first told me she was pregnant, I'd had a sudden urge to find my father. I was curious to find out about the man I never knew. I wanted to contact him and hear his side of the story. I hoped it wasn't too late for us to start building bridges.

I'd spent an unsuccessful year trying to locate Gareth Stone, but rather than diminishing, my desire to find him had intensified. It crossed my mind that he might have changed his name, and be living under an alias. That could explain why I hadn't managed to track him down. I didn't want to consider a different possibility; there was a chance he might be dead. I couldn't bear to think about the fact that we might never get the chance to meet and make memories. I had to stop myself from grieving the role he never got to play.

I knew I wouldn't be able to rest until I found out the truth, so I decided to use a people-tracing service. They contacted me yesterday to tell me they had an address and phone number for Gareth Stone.

3

Gemma

Nathan was sitting on the balcony, in his favourite sheltered spot, out of the wind and in the sun, when he broke the news to me. He wanted to go back to England. I felt the hairs on the back of my neck stand up. I didn't want to return to the eye of the storm.

Since he'd learnt the truth about Gareth, and now that he was a father himself, Nathan had been preoccupied with meeting his father. My husband had waited more than thirty years for this opportunity. Wanting to trace your biological parent is a completely normal thing to do. I knew he was desperate to meet Gareth, so I couldn't be the one to stand in his way. I just wished we could get on a plane like normal people and be in England in a couple of hours, instead of embarking on a three-day trek. We had Alfie to thank for that. Exposing us to a life of crime meant we now had to live under the radar, and airports had far too much security for us to negotiate.

Nathan had already made the travel arrangements. I was

slightly peeved that he hadn't consulted me first, but that was typical of my husband. He'd always been impulsive. I can't say I was overjoyed at the thought of an eleven-hour drive from Marbella to Santander, followed by a twenty-four-hour ferry to Portsmouth before a two-hour drive to London. The journey was not for the faint-hearted, especially with a four-month-old baby in tow.

Breast milk is about ninety per cent water, and the doctor told me it was important to drink plenty of fluids to stay hydrated. But I wouldn't be able to do that unless I developed a bladder of steel before we left. I knew what Nathan was like, once he got behind the wheel of a car – he was like Cruella de Vil. He wouldn't stop for anything. Nathan dismissed my concerns and assured me it was a better option than having to drive through Spain and France to get to the Eurotunnel terminal.

'I know you want to avoid the long drive, but just think about this for a minute: it's January, Nathan. How will Luca cope on a twenty-four-hour crossing if the sea's really rough? I think we should travel by car in case the weather's bad.' I could see my husband was excited by the prospect of finally meeting his dad, so I didn't want to rain on his parade, but despite my best efforts to bite my tongue, my words came out in a nagging pitch.

Nathan brought his dark eyes back to mine and smiled. 'You're overthinking this. Luca will be fine. He sleeps most of the time anyway.'

I flashed my husband a look of disbelief. 'Only a man who wasn't breastfeeding could make a statement like that! I think the dark circles under my eyes tell a different story.'

Nathan reached towards me, caught hold of my hand

and kissed it. 'I'm sorry, Gem, I shouldn't have said that. I was only joking. Do you forgive me?'

'That depends...'

Nathan pulled me down onto his lap and wrapped his strong arms around my shoulders. 'Look, if you're that worried about the journey, we can stop at Aranjuez and spend the night there.' Nathan flashed me his bright, white smile before he continued with his sales pitch. 'It's halfway between Marbella and Santander, so it's only five hours away.' My husband looked deeply into my green eyes before he continued. 'Where's your sense of adventure gone? It'll be fun, Gemma.'

'Don't you think you should phone your dad first and let him know we're coming?' I said, putting my arms around his waist.

'There's no need.'

Nathan's dark eyes didn't meet my gaze. He seemed put out by my suggestion. I knew there was no point saying any more. My husband had made his mind up. By the look on his face, it was clear he didn't want to talk about it. This wasn't up for discussion. Nathan had a habit of keeping his emotions bottled up. I could tell something was bothering him. Even though he wanted to see Gareth as soon as possible, it was obvious Nathan wasn't sure how he was going to react. It wasn't every day your long-lost son turned up on your doorstep. It must have crossed his mind that Gareth might reject the idea of a reunion before it could even get off the ground.

Nathan had decided without any real consideration that the element of surprise was the best tactic to use here. I couldn't help feeling uneasy about the situation. Purely from a selfish point of view, it was a long way to travel if we were going to find a closed door at the end of it. But who could blame Gareth if he reacted like that? Turning up on his doorstep out of the blue was a risky thing to do. That pretty much summed up my husband though – he was a born risk-taker.

For me, the thought of leaving Spain was like a double-edged sword. On the one hand, it would be a blessing. I didn't feel safe here at the moment. I was on edge all the time. Either my mind was playing tricks on me, or somebody was watching me. If we went away, in theory, that should stop and then I might be able to relax. But on the other hand, returning to the UK could be a huge mistake. Would we be able to remain undetected once we were on English soil? I couldn't help thinking it was too soon to go back. Thanks to my current state, whichever way I looked at it, neither option was desirable. I was being ruled by fear.

4

Nathan

I knew I hid my true feelings where my dad was concerned. I made out it didn't bother me that he wasn't in my life. That wasn't true. Since Gemma had become pregnant, I'd become obsessed with finding him, and now that I had, I couldn't let my fear of rejection stop me in my tracks this time. The sooner we got to England, the sooner this feeling of uncertainty would be over.

I'd resented my dad from an early age because I hadn't known the truth. Now I was desperate to make up for lost time. Not just for my sake, I wanted Luca to have a relationship with him too. Becoming a father had changed my life, and it now occurred to me that I wasn't the only one who'd suffered when my dad was cut out of my life. He had also been cheated out of fulfilling his role by the experience. We were both victims.

I went to every doctor's appointment with Gemma. I held her hand during labour and felt utterly helpless, watching her writhing in pain. She went through hell, but she didn't once take it out on me. She was so brave. When she finally delivered our son, and I heard his first cry, it was the best sound in the world. The time came to cut Luca's umbilical cord. I was given the honour. I was overcome with emotion and proud to say I shed a tear. Childbirth was a humbling experience. Gemma had just given me the most incredible gift. As I held my son in my arms, I felt a renewed appreciation for women, especially my wife.

I couldn't wait to start our lives together as a family. But the joy was tinged with sadness as it made me realise just how much my dad and I had missed out on. It also highlighted the fact that since I'd been on bad terms with my mum, it had left a gaping hole in my life. My wife had been trying to get me to make peace with Mum since we'd found out Gemma was pregnant. Gemma wanted me to phone my mum and share our exciting news with her. She thought it was the perfect opportunity for us to try and rebuild our relationship. But I was adamant I didn't feel ready to talk to her. I wasn't denying Mum had invested a lot in my childhood, but if she wasn't prepared to admit that she'd let me down, by cutting Dad out of our lives, I didn't know where we could go from here.

As the wronged party, I felt it was my mum's place to make the first move. She needed to initiate the repair. That seemed like a tall order. It was easy to see where I got my stubborn streak from.

5

Three days after leaving Puerto Banús, my husband wiped the palms of his hands on his jeans as he stood outside a terraced house in Crofts Way, before he finally plucked up the courage to knock on the door.

'Nathan.' Gareth's blue eyes widened when he saw his son standing in front of him.

'Hello, Dad.'

I sat in the front seat of the car with the window open so that I could hear their conversation while giving them some space. The two men stood in the doorway for a long time, locked in a wordless embrace.

Gareth pulled back from Nathan and held him at arm's length. 'I'd given up hope that this would ever happen. All those wasted years. I've missed you so much.'

'I've missed you too, Dad.'

'You'd better come in. We've got a lot to talk about.' Gareth opened the door wide and invited Nathan inside.

Nathan gestured towards the black Jeep with Spanish

plates that was parked opposite the house, then he signalled for me to join them. I got out of the car, opened the back passenger door and carefully manoeuvred the car seat that contained my sleeping son, through the open doorway.

Nathan crossed the road to help me with the baby and all the paraphernalia that now accompanied our every move. He kissed my cheek with his soft lips before taking the carrycot from me.

'I'm Gareth, pleased to meet you.' Nathan's father held out his hand, but the greeting seemed too formal, so I reached up, put my arms around his shoulders and hugged him instead.

'Pleased to meet you, I'm Gemma, and that is your grandson, Luca,' I replied, looking over my shoulder.

'Luca.' Gareth nodded. 'That's a nice name. It shows you're proud of your Italian heritage. I bet your mum approves.' Gareth smiled and as he did the skin around his eyes wrinkled.

The corners of Nathan's lips curved into a smile, but he didn't reply. He obviously didn't feel comfortable admitting that he wasn't on speaking terms with Rosa and he looked decidedly awkward, but Gareth didn't seem to notice. He was too busy coming to terms with the situation. He'd not only come face to face with his long-lost son, but he'd also discovered he was a grandfather. That didn't happen every day of the week.

'Come inside. This calls for a celebration.' Gareth slapped Nathan on the back of the shoulder.

Nathan couldn't have hoped for a better reception, and I was delighted that for once, his gamble had paid off.

'Take a seat, and I'll fix us a drink.' Gareth pointed

towards a brown leather sofa on the far side of the minimally furnished room. 'I haven't got any champagne, but I've got a nice bottle of single malt. Will that do?'

'Yes,' Nathan and I both answered.

'I wasn't sure if you'd recognise me,' Nathan said when Gareth handed him a tumbler containing a generous measure of whisky.

'When I opened the door and saw you standing there, I knew you were my son. You're the image of your mother.'

Nathan did look a lot like Rosa; they had the same colouring, dark hair and dark eyes, but I could see Gareth in him too. Even at sixty-two, he was a handsome man, tall and slim with a full head of greying hair and a neatly trimmed beard. Although Nathan had Rosa's mouth and nose, he had his father's jawline and had also inherited his height and build.

'I'd always thought Nathan looked like his mum as well – he was blessed with olive skin and Italian genes – but now that I've seen the two of you together, I can see you share definite similarities. He certainly didn't get his height from his mother.' I laughed.

'That's true,' Gareth agreed. 'Rosa was tiny, but she could be a little firecracker if you upset her.' A smile spread across his face as he remembered his ex-wife with fondness. 'So who does this little fella take after?' Gareth asked as he looked at his blue-eyed, blond-haired grandson.

'I'm not sure. I suppose time will tell,' I replied, as the conversation carried on around me.

'I still can't believe I've finally met you after all these years. I often wondered how you were doing and what your life was like.' Gareth downed the drink in his glass. 'Do you mind me asking what made you look me up?'

Nathan inhaled a long, slow breath. 'Let's just say curiosity got the better of me,' Nathan replied. 'But you weren't easy to find. You seemed to have disappeared off the face of the earth. In the end, I had to get professional help.'

Gareth raised his eyebrows and tilted his head to one side. 'I'm sorry you had to go to so much trouble, but I like to keep a low profile. Thank God for your persistence. I hope you're not disappointed.'

'Of course I'm not,' Nathan replied. 'I couldn't have hoped for a better welcome.'

Gareth was surprised we'd travelled all the way from the Costa del Sol by car with a tiny baby. I could see his happiness was tinged with sadness. The last time Gareth saw Nathan, he wasn't much older than Luca. He hadn't laid eyes on his son in more than thirty years. I couldn't begin to imagine what that must feel like. I was estranged from my family, but that was my choice. Nathan and Gareth's separation had been forced upon them, and they couldn't undo the past no matter how much they wanted to.

'Did you know I'd been inside?' Gareth asked before he took a sip of his drink.

Nathan nodded. Father and son sat opposite each other in the living room, locked in eye contact. The silence in the room was palpable, and an awkward tension spread between the two men.

'Do you know why I got sent down?'

'Mum said you attempted to rob a Securicor van.'

'So she told you the truth then. Fair play to her.'

Nathan bit the skin on the side of his nail while he thought about how to reply. 'To be honest, I only found out recently.'

I was glad to see Nathan had chosen to be diplomatic. I knew he still hadn't come to terms with Rosa's decision to lie to him. He didn't feel like she deserved his loyalty, and I wondered if he'd tell his father that she'd let him live his whole life believing that Gareth had left her for another woman.

'It's so good to see you, son. Now tell me all about yourself. Tell me everything I've missed out on,' Gareth said, changing the subject. I couldn't help noticing his words had a bitter edge to them.

6

Nathan

I was so glad I'd finally had the opportunity to meet my dad. It had opened my eyes to lots of things. But more than anything, it made me realise the importance of honesty. Although Jethro Watson had set my mum and dad up, if she had been truthful about it, instead of hiding it from me, we may have been able to avoid this situation. Keeping secrets was never a good thing. They always came back to haunt you.

Gemma was constantly fighting my mum's corner. She'd worked tirelessly to try and pave the way for us to reconcile and phoned her every Sunday to keep her in the loop. Tempting as it was to blame Mum for everything that had happened, I knew that wasn't fair. She had suffered as well and was as much a victim as the rest of us. The Watsons had well and truly deceived my parents. Mum and Dad were pawns in the game, and they had been powerless to stop the events that unfolded.

Now that I had a son of my own, getting even with the

men that kept Dad and I apart for more than thirty years seemed more important than ever. Jethro wanted to be with my mum so badly he set my dad up and destroyed our parent and child relationship before it had even begun. That was something we would never get back. The Watsons robbed me of a normal childhood. What right did they have to change the course of my life? I wouldn't forgive or forget what they'd done to my family.

I was slightly older than Luca when my dad was sent to prison, so I had no memories of him at all. I wouldn't want to be in that position. I couldn't imagine my life without Luca in it. Becoming a father was one of the best things that had ever happened to me, but Jethro had deprived my dad of that incredible experience. I would never let anybody come between myself and Luca.

7

Gemma

Gareth had insisted that we stay with him instead of checking into a hotel, which was an incredibly kind offer, but if I was honest, I'd rather Nathan hadn't accepted it. Luca still woke several times in the night, and I was worried he was going to disrupt the whole house.

'When are we going to introduce Rosa to her grandson?' I said when Nathan and I were alone in our room.

Nathan pushed his hands into the pockets of his jeans and avoided my gaze.

'Don't you think it's about time you put your argument behind you? Why don't you phone her and tell her we're staying with your dad in London?'

Nathan pulled a face. 'I don't think that's a good idea.'

Now that we were back in England, I'd tried to persuade Nathan to make peace with his mum, but he was having none of it. So I called Rosa when I woke the next morning to see if she was free to meet up. Rosa had been like a mother to me. I wasn't going to fall out with her even though Nathan had. I'd phoned her every week since we'd moved to Spain to keep the lines of communication open.

'It's lovely to hear from you. How is Nathan?' The delight in Rosa's voice was evident.

'He's fine.' I wished I could hand the phone to my husband, but I knew what his response would be.

'Why are you in London?'

'Nathan's managed to track down Gareth. He lives in Whitechapel now.' My news was met with stony silence. 'Are you still there, Rosa?'

Another tense silence followed before Rosa's reply. When she finally spoke after a lengthy pause, she raised her voice. 'I'm begging you not to meet up with him, Gemma. He will only bring trouble your way.'

Nathan was staring into my eyes. I didn't want him to know what his mum had said. It would only make their strained relationship worse, and anyway, it was too late to listen to Rosa's advice.

'When are you coming home?' Rosa asked.

'I'm not sure.' I delivered the lie as convincingly as I could. I just hoped Rosa wouldn't suspect anything. Nathan and I never intended to return to Southend, but I couldn't tell my mother-in-law that. She would ask too many questions. 'We're staying with Gareth at the moment.'

'Mark my words, nothing good will come of this.'

'What did she say?' Nathan asked when I'd ended the call.

My husband's question gave me a glimmer of hope. If he didn't care about his mum he wouldn't be interested in what she had to say, would he?

'She was over the moon to hear we're in London. I'm going to introduce Luca to her later. Are you sure I can't convince you to join me?'

Nathan glared at me for making the suggestion. 'I'd rather pull my teeth out with a pair of rusty pliers.'

'Don't be like that.' I reached forward and caught hold of my husband's hand. 'She'd love to see you.'

'I'm sorry, Gem, but I don't want to see her.'

Nathan was in one of his man-child moods. The spoiled brat side to his personality quite often reared its ugly head if things didn't go the way he wanted them to. Much as I loved him, he could be exhausting, and I wasn't sure I had the patience to deal with him right now. Being a new mother was taking its toll on me, and the sleepless nights had sapped my energy levels.

'It's a shame you're being like this. You two used to be so close.'

Nathan shrugged. 'Well, we're not any more. People change.'

I could tell Nathan was putting on a front. I knew he missed his mum even if he wasn't prepared to admit it. Rosa would be so disappointed that Nathan was refusing to back down. I knew she wanted to make peace with him more than anything.

'You of all people should understand what it feels like to have somebody cut out of your life. I shook my head and glared at my husband. 'I know you want to get back at your mum for hurting you, but this has got to stop. You're being cruel, Nathan.'

I'd arranged to meet my mother-in-law at Whitechapel station, close to where Gareth was living. I didn't feel comfortable venturing too far without Nathan. As I approached the entrance, I saw her waiting on the pavement, wrapped up against the cold. Letting go of Luca's pushchair with one hand, I waved over to her. I was secretly relieved that she'd arrived before me.

'Gemma, it's wonderful to see you.' Rosa held out her arms and wrapped them around me.

'It's good to see you too.' Nathan didn't realise how lucky he was to have such a wonderful mother.

'So this is my grandson. What a beautiful little boy. He has the face of an angel.' Rosa leant into the pram and placed a kiss on each of Luca's cheeks.

Luca gave his grandmother a toothless smile.

'You've changed your hair. You're still a beautiful woman, but it's a shame you cut off your long, glossy locks. They were your crowning glory.' Rosa reached up and touched the ends of my dark brown bob.

'I've got my hands full with Luca at the moment and it's much easier to look after. Anyway, it's only hair. I can always grow it back at a later stage,' I replied, brushing off my mother-in-law's remark. Rosa was a straight talker, and her honesty made me feel a tinge of sadness. I hadn't wanted to chop off my hair, but my safety had to come first.

'I'm sorry, Gemma, I didn't mean to upset you,' Rosa said, a look of concern spreading over her face as she patted my hand.

'You haven't,' I replied. I didn't want Rosa to know she had unintentionally knocked my confidence.

'It really suits you, but you look so different with short hair. I almost didn't recognise you for a minute.'

'You're not the first person to say that.' I smiled; that was music to my ears.

'I was hoping Nathan would join us today.' I saw Rosa's eyes mist over.

I didn't want to hurt her feelings, so I considered making up an excuse. But my mother-in-law was no fool. Rosa had a knack of extracting the truth, so she'd see straight through it. There was no point trying to cover for him.

'I hoped so too, but I'm afraid he's still digging his heels in.'

Rosa struggled to hold back her tears. Anyone could see she was heartbroken that she'd fallen out with her son. It was every mother's worst nightmare. But until Nathan was ready to come round, the best thing she could do was give him some space. She knew exactly what he was like. His stubbornness was legendary.

'Let's go and get a coffee.' –

Rosa linked my arm as we walked along the pavement. 'This place looks nice,' she said, stopping outside a small independent café called Lorenzo's. It was the perfect place for a catch-up, and thankfully there were plenty of customers for us to blend in with.

Rosa pushed open the glass door and the heady scent of freshly ground coffee wafted towards us. I wheeled the pram to the back of the shop, and we took a seat at a round table in the corner. After unclipping Luca from the harness, I handed him to Rosa.

'I'll get this,' I said. 'Cappuccino and a slice of coffee and walnut cake?'

'Yes, please.'

Old habits die hard, I thought as I went to the counter to order.

Rosa was desperate to know how long Nathan and I would be staying in England, but I couldn't answer her question when I didn't know myself. She was devastated that her son still wouldn't speak to her. Rosa wanted to see him more than anything before we went back to Spain. I promised to help pave the way to their reconciliation.

'If anyone can get my son to see sense it's you, Gemma. He adores you,' Rosa said. She reached across the table and covered my hands with hers.

I looked into her pleading eyes for the longest moment before I replied. 'I'll do everything I can.' I tried to reassure my mother-in-law but we both knew what Nathan was like. He had a stubborn streak that was a mile wide. Putting things right between them was going to be an uphill battle.

'I bet Gareth has tried to poison Nathan against me.' Rosa bowed her head so that I wouldn't see the tears in her eyes, but they were impossible to hide.

'You might not believe this, but your ex-husband has only had good things to say about you. He's been encouraging Nathan to make up with you.'

Rosa's lips curved into a smile, and she tilted her head to one side. 'Now that does surprise me.'

I knew if Rosa slagged off his dad in front of Nathan, it would drive a deeper wedge between them. 'I honestly think being on good terms with Gareth would help you build bridges with Nathan.

I could see Rosa considering my suggestion, but she didn't reply, instead, we spent the next couple of hours chatting about Nathan and Luca and the joys of motherhood. Rosa had waited a long time for this moment, so she was going to make every second count. It was such a pity Nathan wasn't here with us.

'Children are the greatest gift in life,' Rosa said, planting several kisses on Luca's cheek. He giggled in delight. 'The sound of this baby's laughter has made my day. Enjoy every minute you have with him because, in the blink of an eye, he'll be a grown man.'

Rosa passed Luca back to me, and I couldn't help noticing that her eyes had misted over again, so I leant towards her and placed my hand on hers to offer some comfort. Not being on speaking terms with Nathan was breaking her heart. I was doing what I could to help them repair their relationship. I was sure it was possible, but it would take time and patience for them to get there. Rosa attempted to smile as a tear rolled down her cheek. My heart bled for her. She looked distraught. I wished I could do more to help.

'You have to make a lot of sacrifices when you're a mother, but the joys far outweigh all the difficulties.' Rosa's lip quivered.

Rosa spoke from experience; if anyone knew how hard it was to raise a child, it was her. She'd had to bring up Nathan on her own since he was Luca's age. The thought of being a single mother terrified me, but she'd done an incredible job. I was embarrassed that this was how my husband repaid her. Even though she hadn't said anything, I could tell she was devastated that he hadn't bothered to come and see her today.

8

Nathan

Gemma knew how I felt about my mum at the moment.
She'd lied to me, and I still didn't feel ready to forgive
her. The fact that my wife had ignored my feelings and taken
our son to see her anyway was hard for me to swallow.
Talk about double standards. I would never try to influence
Gemma the other way around. She hadn't spoken to her
family for over a decade, but that was her decision, and I'd
never interfered. It wasn't my place to. I wish she'd show
me the same respect.

The idea of Gemma and my mum conspiring against
me had added more stress to an already-stressful situation.
I never thought I'd be in this situation. Mum and I had
always been so close. It was us against the world while I
was growing up. I'd adored her. But she'd betrayed me,
and now I wasn't sure I wanted to have a relationship with
a person who could hurt me that badly. Even if we did
manage to come back from this, you couldn't rush these
things. Hurt took time to heal. An estrangement was messy

and emotional for everyone involved. The fact that our relationship had changed suddenly and unexpectedly only added to the problem.

In an ideal world, both my parents would be in my life at the same time. Knowing how my mum felt about my dad, I couldn't see that ever being a possibility. But if I had to choose between them, at this moment in time, I would definitely choose my dad. There was no contest.

9

Nathan

Dad put his mug down on the pine table. He pushed his chair back, stood up and went to switch the kettle on. 'Do you want a cup of tea?'

'No, thanks,' I replied.

'Why didn't you go with Gemma to see your mum?' Dad asked.

I shrugged my shoulders and let out a long sigh. 'I didn't fancy it.'

'I would have thought you'd have been desperate to see her after all this time. Is everything all right between the two of you?'

'Things have been better.'

'Don't be too hard on her, Nathan,' Dad said, and his expression softened.

'It's hard not to feel bitter. She cut you out of my life.'

'I know she did, but that doesn't mean you should do the same thing to her. If I can forgive your mother, you should be able to.' Dad leant back in his chair and folded his arms across his chest.

I let out a loud sigh before I changed the subject. 'Mum didn't like talking about what had happened between the two of you. That's one of the reasons I started trying to trace you. I wanted to hear your side of the story.' I didn't want to have to admit that, up until now, I'd had no time for the father I thought had abandoned us, so I decided not to mention it. The man sitting opposite me was nothing like the person my mother had described.

Dad clasped his hands together at the back of his neck. 'It all happened such a long time ago, I don't know where to start.'

'Mum said that when the guard refused to hand over the money, you shot him. Is that true?'

Dad placed his elbows on the table, interlinked his fingers and let out a long breath. 'Yes, it's true. It's not something I'm proud of, but it happened, so there's no point trying to deny it. One stupid decision cost me my wife, my child and my freedom. I'll regret that day for the rest of my life.'

This was the first time I had given any thought to how much my father had suffered being behind bars for all those years. I knew how difficult life had been for myself and Mum; she'd struggled to bring me up alone, and for that I respected her. But she should have told me the truth instead of letting me believe a lie. If Mum had let me visit my father while he was inside, life might have been easier for all of them.

'Prison life is hard, and I didn't adapt well to it. Being locked up took its toll on me.' Dad locked eyes with me, and I noticed that his face suddenly appeared drawn.

'I know, Dad; this hasn't been easy for any of us.' My shoulders slumped as if I was carrying the weight of the world on them.

'Everything changed in the blink of an eye after I got sent down. My life was on a downward spiral. I'd unintentionally hit the self-destruct button.'

I listened while Dad relived his past. It was interesting to hear his side of the story; the devastation my father had felt being parted from us mirrored Mum's and my experience.

'It took me a long time to accept what I'd done.' Dad's voice cracked with emotion as he continued to talk. 'I was young and stupid, and I'll regret it for the rest of my life.' What I did to you and your mum will hurt me forever.' Dad ran his thumb and forefinger back and forth along his beard-covered jawline.

Growing up thinking one of my parents had abandoned me had a powerful effect on me. It had filled me with insecurity and shaped my character. I hadn't realised until now that Dad felt we had abandoned him too. Knowing that Mum could have prevented the situation by letting me have contact with my father, while he was locked up, was something I would never be able to understand. How could you do that to your child? She had no right to come between a father and his son. Even though my mother had explained her reasons for cutting Dad out of my life, I couldn't get my head around them, and I felt fresh resentment for her rise within me.

'I used to lie in my cell, feeling like I was suffocating. I can't begin to describe how awful it is to be locked in a confined space, trying to kill time. I couldn't make sense of what my life had become. The worst part of it was, I'd created this situation myself, and that tormented me day and night.'

I looked into Dad's hollow eyes and saw how much he had suffered. If Mum hadn't been forced into coming clean, we might never have met. Secrets destroyed relationships. But even after what she'd done, my mother was still playing the victim. People like Mum were experts in blame-shifting and denial. No matter what the circumstance was, you would never hear them say they were sorry for their words or actions. The more my father spoke, the more complicated the story became and I struggled to process all the different emotions that were swirling in the air around me.

'Time passes slowly when you're inside, but eventually the days do turn into weeks, weeks turn into months, months turn into years, and years turn into decades.'

I didn't know what to say as Dad continued to paint the grim picture of life behind bars.

'When you're in prison, you have to find ways to occupy yourself. It's boring sitting for hours on end with nothing to do. You spend a lot of time thinking about why you're in there in the first place. I should never have agreed to do the job for Jethro Watson.' Dad's eyes misted over as he spoke.

Mum had never told me what drove my father to attempt the robbery. He must have been pretty desperate to do something so reckless with so much at stake. But I didn't like to ask. I just hoped in time he would feel comfortable enough to tell me.

10

Gemma

After seeing Rosa onto the train, I began making the short walk back to Crofts Way, where Gareth's house was situated. I was only metres from the front door when a black Mercedes with tinted windows turned into the road and pulled up at the side of the kerb. The sight of the car sent my pulse into overdrive, and a sudden sensation of fear washed over me. The car was exactly the same as the one Alfie used to drive. But it couldn't be Alfie behind the wheel. He was in prison, wasn't he?

When the electric window slowly dropped, my heart skipped a beat. The urge to run was so strong, but I stood frozen on the spot. My legs wouldn't move no matter how much my brain willed them to. I looked in the pram at my baby peacefully sleeping, blissfully unaware of the danger we were in. The back passenger door opened, and a tall, fair-haired man, dressed in a dark grey suit stepped out onto the pavement. I wished I hadn't ventured out without my husband now. As he stood next to me, I gripped the handle of the pushchair so tightly, my knuckles turned white. My heart pounded against my ribcage as I waited for him to make a move. I stared into his blue eyes, wondering what he was going to do.

After what seemed like an eternity, he spoke. 'Hello, Gemma.' The man's voice was exactly like Alfie's and the sound of it made my heartbeat go into overdrive.

I'd never seen this man before in my life, but I knew it was Jethro Watson. As illogical thoughts filled my head, I felt panic rise within me. I struggled to concentrate. I didn't know what to do. I'd had a bad feeling about this trip before we left Spain, but Nathan had convinced me that everything would be OK. Now I was questioning my decision to come back to England. If we'd stayed in the Costa del Sol, this wouldn't be happening.

I knew I needed to face my fear and stay strong, but my strength seemed to have deserted me when I needed it the most. I was like a deer caught in the headlights, paralysed by fear. It was the kind of moment that although you knew you'd witnessed it, your brain rejected it. My mind wouldn't allow me to believe what I'd just seen. Without saying a word, I began pacing towards Gareth's front door. Surely Jethro wouldn't try to harm us in broad daylight, would he? As I hurried away, Alfie's dad's laughter echoed in the street around me.

Outside the front door, I glanced over my shoulder to check that he hadn't followed me, then with trembling hands, I tried to locate the key in my handbag. I rifled through the contents, but couldn't put my hand on it until finally, my fumbling fingers found it buried at the bottom. I put the key in the lock, but it wouldn't turn. Tears sprang into my eyes when I heard footsteps on the pavement. To my relief, Nathan opened the door. I burst into the hall and slammed the door behind me.

'What's going on, Gemma? You look like you've seen a ghost.'

I was too shocked to speak. There was a difference between thinking you were being watched and being confronted in the street by a stranger. I stood shaking in the hallway with tears streaming down my cheeks. Nathan peeled my fingers from the handle of the pram and pushed it down the narrow hall and into the living room. I followed behind him sobbing as I walked.

'I could have told you this would happen.' Nathan shook his head. 'I knew it was a bad idea to go and see my mum. That's why I didn't want to go with you.' Nathan couldn't hide the irritation in his voice.

I took a seat on the sofa and tried to compose myself before I spoke. 'This has nothing to do with Rosa.' I took a tissue out of my pocket and dried my eyes on it.

Nathan sat down beside me and draped his arm around my shoulder. 'So why are you crying?'

'I've just seen Jethro Watson. He was outside the house in a black Mercedes,' I blurted out.

Anger flashed across my husband's face at the mention of his name. Nathan didn't think twice. He'd always been fiercely protective of me. He leapt off the sofa and charged towards the front door. When he flung it open, the street was deserted. So he ran down the middle of the road, then turned onto the high street looking for the car, but there was no sign of it anywhere.

The minute I saw that Mercedes pull into the road, it

triggered a memory within me, and even before Jethro stepped out onto the pavement, I sensed something awful was about to happen. The sight of the car had reminded me of a time I'd rather forget. While we'd been working for Alfie, we'd been travelling in a Mercedes just like Jethro's when we'd been involved in an accident. The Swiss police had stopped us at a checkpoint because they wanted to search the car before they'd allow us to pass into Germany, so Tommy – Alfie's driver – had sped away. He'd been trying to shake off the wailing sirens after the police gave chase, but he rounded a sharp corner too quickly, and the car swerved and almost tipped over.

I'd had constant nightmares about that journey and would often wake in a cold sweat, imagining the car spinning out of control. Nathan and I were lucky neither of us had been killed.

When Nathan returned a few moments later, he closed the door behind him and attached the safety chain. He walked back down the hallway and into the living room. His footsteps were heavy on the laminate flooring.

'Are you sure it was him? I know you said you thought you'd seen Jethro but how can you be certain?' Nathan's dark eyes scanned my face.

'I'm positive it was him.'

'But you've never even met him before.'

'I'm not making this up, Nathan.'

'I never said you were. It's just I don't understand why you're so convinced you've seen somebody you've never met.'

'Alfie is the image of him, only a younger version.' I felt a shiver run down my spine, and I fixed my husband with a panicked stare.

Nathan reached forward and took hold of my hand. It didn't matter how much he tried to reassure me that Jethro didn't know what I looked like – the man spoke to me by name. So he was wasting his breath.

Nathan held me at arm's length and studied my face. 'Start at the beginning and tell me exactly what happened.'

'I was walking home after I dropped your mum off at the station.' My eyes began to well up again, so I dabbed at them with the crumpled tissue.

Nathan caught hold of my trembling hand when I'd finished drying my eyes. 'Everything's going to be OK. Do you think you can continue?'

I nodded my head and took a deep breath. 'I'd just turned into Crofts Way when a black Mercedes, like the one Alfie used to drive, came around the corner and stopped right near me. Jethro got out of the car and came over to where I was standing.' Nathan threw his arms around me and held me close. I buried my face in his chest and began to sob. 'We should never have come back; it was too dangerous.' I pulled away from my husband and looked up at him with a tear-stained face.

'Don't cry, Gemma, everything will be OK,' Nathan soothed.

'Do you think we should go and stay in a hotel?' I asked.

Nathan shook his head at my suggestion.

'Why not?'

Nathan pulled me towards him and wrapped his arms

around me, so I buried my face into his chest and gripped the fabric of his T-shirt.

'Please don't cry.' Nathan kissed the top of my head before he continued speaking. 'There's nothing to be scared of.'

'But Jethro's stalking me. Please can we go and stay somewhere else?'

'Honestly, Gem, there's no need. You'll be safe here. Dad and I will see to that.'

A vision of Alfie's burly henchmen breaking into Gareth's house in the middle of the night sprang into my mind. I pulled back from my husband and looked at him with puffy, bloodshot eyes. 'Well, I don't feel safe, not now that Jethro knows we're staying with your dad. I feel like a sitting duck.'

II

Gemma

I'd thought I was going insane imagining someone was watching me, but I wasn't delusional after all. Nathan was convinced I couldn't separate fact from fiction and was suffering from paranoia. Knowing my husband didn't believe me, only made matters worse. But this situation was real. I now had evidence that justified why I'd felt this way. It wasn't all in my mind.

My fears and secrets had spun a web around me, and I was trapped at the centre with no way out. I was all over the place. It was fair to say, I'd been off-kilter for some time now. I felt stressed, and that was having an adverse effect on my emotional stability.

Motherhood wasn't as easy as it was cracked up to be. I'd read too many glossy magazines while I was pregnant, featuring new celebrity mums. They made the process look effortless, so I'd developed a rose-tinted view of what it was going to be like. The reality was, I was tired to the point of exhaustion, and my body was depleted of energy. That had affected my mood. I didn't like to admit it, but I was struggling to cope.

My wonderful husband had been a tower of strength since Luca had been born. He'd sat with me in the middle of the night while I was breastfeeding to offer me his support, instead of snoring his head off on the pillow next to me like some men do. He was also doing the household chores so that I wouldn't become overwhelmed by everything. Nathan had taken to fatherhood like a duck to water, and much as that delighted me, it also made me feel like a failure.

12

Gemma

'How are you feeling, Gemma?' Nathan asked when he came back into the bedroom.

I was lying on the bed, staring into space. At the mention of my name, I looked towards my husband and met his cheerful gaze with expressionless eyes.

'I thought I'd give you some time alone. Dad and I have been catching up.' Nathan crossed the room, leant forward and kissed the tip of my nose.

'How's everything going?' I asked before swinging my legs around and perching on the edge of the bed.

'Dad was telling me what it was like in prison.'

'It sounds like he's really opening up to you.' I smiled. I knew how much Nathan wanted this, and I was genuinely happy for him.

'I'd thought so too, but then all of a sudden, just as the conversation was getting interesting, Dad clamped his mouth shut. He literally stopped talking mid-sentence and changed the subject. There's nothing more frustrating than somebody half telling you something, is there?' Nathan walked over to the window and looked down at the small backyard before turning around to face me.

'Give him a chance. You only came back into his life yesterday after a thirty-three-year absence. If Gareth isn't ready to talk, you'll have to respect that. There's no point pushing it.'

'You know what I'm like – I'm impatient. Now that I've finally got to meet him, I want to make up for lost time.'

'I'm sure Gareth does too.' The corners of my handsome husband's mouth turned down, so I got off of the bed and walked towards him. 'Don't be sad,' I said before I threw my arms around his waist and squeezed him tightly. 'The three of us turning up out of the blue is probably a bit overwhelming for him.'

I offered to make dinner, so the two men could talk. They sat opposite each other at the small pine kitchen table while I rustled up spaghetti carbonara. It didn't take long before the conversation got around to Jethro Watson. I felt the hairs on the back of my neck stand up at the mention of his name.

'Revenge is long overdue. I had to rot inside because that bastard set me up,' Gareth said.

'We've both got scores to settle. What Jethro did changed the whole course of our lives,' Nathan replied.

I couldn't believe what my husband had just said, after everything we'd been through. My heartbeat quickened as I listened to their conversation almost in a trance. A suffocating feeling of helplessness came over me. I wanted to shout out and make them see sense. They were talking about Jethro Watson, not Phil Mitchell. What had got into Nathan? Had he forgotten this man had a reputation for being a prominent figure in one of the criminal underworld's most powerful families? In the Watsons' world, money and intimidation talked. How could my husband and father-in-law possibly make Jethro pay for anything? The idea was toxic to me, so my nervous system was on high alert.

I needed to talk to Nathan about Jethro and make him see sense before it was too late. I wanted to tell my husband to stop being ridiculous. Trying to get even would end up damaging our family, not his, but for some reason, I couldn't find the right words. It was human nature to hold a grudge and want payback, but surely Nathan realised that would come at a high price. A price that I was not willing to pay. We all needed to learn to let go of the past and move on. My temples began pulsating the more I thought about it. I could feel a tension headache starting and was tempted to go and lie down, but I knew I'd have to stay until they finished their conversation.

'I got sent down for twenty-four years. That's a long time,' Gareth continued.

'I know it is, and because you went to prison, we all suffered.'

Rosa lost her husband, and Nathan grew up without ever meeting his father. He'd thought Gareth had abandoned them. Now that he knew the truth, he wanted Jethro to pay. Was I the only one who was thinking straight? Nathan's judgement of the situation was seriously impaired if he thought he could do something awful to Jethro and get away with it. I wanted to stay as far away from the Watson family as possible. I knew I should never have let Nathan persuade me to come back to England.

All this talk of revenge was making me stressed. I wasn't expecting either Nathan or Gareth to forgive Jethro for what he'd done, but two wrongs didn't make a right. If they insisted on going after him, we'd be watching our backs for life. Men like Jethro had long memories and were happy to wait patiently for the right moment to present itself before they retaliated. That was the nature of the game, and nobody knew that better than Nathan.

When the people-tracing company located Gareth, and Nathan suggested going to London to meet his father, unannounced and uninvited, I didn't know what to say. He could get the door slammed in his face if he turned up on Gareth's doorstep without any warning. I was genuinely scared that Nathan might be rejected, and I wasn't sure he'd be able to cope with that. For all we knew, his dad could have married again and have another family who didn't know Nathan existed. It could have been a potential powder-keg situation, like a scene from a Jeremy Kyle show. Instead, the emotional reunion was like something out of a Hollywood movie. While I'd sat in the car and watched them come face to face, I'd had to fumble in my pocket for a tissue. Their meeting had brought a tear to my eye, and a lump had formed in my throat. I'd been so relieved they were off to a good start.

Although some people might have been suspicious of Nathan's intentions, I knew he didn't have an ulterior motive and wasn't after anything, other than a chance to try and get to know his father. He wasn't looking for money, a bone marrow transplant or an organ donation. He just wanted his father in his life, or at least that was what I'd thought. I hadn't expected my husband and father-in-law to have this shared lust for revenge, and it made me question if that was what had been driving Nathan to find his father in the first place.

Naively, I'd thought they would spend this time catching up on the thirty years they'd missed out on. I hadn't expected them to start plotting to bring down the gangster they held responsible for their forced separation. I wasn't suggesting it would be easy watching someone get away with what they'd done to you, but in this case, it would be madness to try and do anything about it.

Jethro Watson was part of a notorious crime family, and only a fool would mess with a dangerous trigger-happy gangster like him. The phrase, let sleeping dogs lie, came to mind.

13

Gemma

Now that I knew Jethro was watching me, it suddenly crossed my mind that maybe he was the intruder outside our apartment the other night. Nathan said I was being ridiculous when I'd suggested that to him. But I didn't care what he thought; somebody had been outside our door. Although he was adamant about it, Nathan couldn't say for certain it wasn't Jethro as he hadn't seen the person. He'd been quick to dismiss the idea, but how could he be so sure? By the time he'd opened the front door, the person had disappeared into the night.

Nathan was convinced it was just kids outside our apartment. I found that hard to believe. Admittedly, groups of young people often congregated in the parks or down by the marina for want of having no better place to hang out. They weren't up to anything dodgy; it was all perfectly innocent. But I'd never come across teenagers hanging about in our apartment complex in the time we'd lived there. The security guards would have moved them on if they'd tried to loiter in the grounds. Also, there had only been one set of footsteps, so Nathan's theory seemed flawed. Whoever paid us a visit at three o'clock in the morning, was alone and had a sinister motive.

'I know you've had a fright, but there's bound to be a perfectly logical explanation for what happened. You had a chance encounter with a stranger. Don't let your imagination run away with you.' Nathan squeezed my hands and looked into my eyes. 'Jethro isn't following you. It's just a case of mistaken identity.'

That was easy for Nathan to say, but he hadn't experienced the paralysing fear I had when I bumped into Alfie's dad in the street. My husband might think I'd mistaken Jethro for someone else, but I knew I hadn't. What I didn't understand was why Jethro had come face to face with me? Maybe he had a message from Alfie. I had to stop panic from ripping through me. No good would come from trying to second-guess the situation.

I didn't want to lie low inside the house, waiting for Jethro to make his next move. But, on the other hand, I felt so traumatised by the sight of him that now I was terrified to go outside. Peering tentatively out of the front window, I half expected to see Jethro's face pressed against the glass. The thoughts inside my head were running riot, so I made a mental note to myself to stop watching horror films.

'I'm scared, Nathan.' I wrapped my arms around myself for comfort.

'I know you are, but try not to worry.' Nathan put his finger under my chin and tilted my face towards his.

Dread rose up inside me. 'We should never have come

back to England. The Watsons are going to come after us, aren't they?'

I could tell Nathan had grown tired of this conversation from the tone of his voice. 'Alfie runs the family business, not Jethro. He retired years ago. Alfie's in prison, so how's he going to come after us?'

An idea suddenly popped into my head. Maybe Jethro had come out of retirement while Alfie was behind bars. That was a feasible explanation. I couldn't understand why Nathan was so relaxed about the situation. We'd experienced first-hand what these men were capable of. They were no strangers to violence. I'd have to try and put this out of my mind for now, or I'd end up overthinking the situation.

'What are we going to do if Alfie wants the money we took from the yacht?'

Nathan frowned, then he began biting the skin at the side of his nail.

'I can't go through the stress of being in debt to Alfie again.'

My husband stared at me for a moment before he replied. 'Has it occurred to you that you might have jumped to the wrong conclusion? Alfie told you to keep it, remember? Nobody's mentioned the money, have they? You've got this idea in your head, and now you're going into meltdown over it.'

I thought about what Nathan had said. He was right, Alfie hadn't asked for the money back, but if he did, we wouldn't be able to pay up, and then we were going to be in his debt again. That was something we'd promised ourselves would never happen after we broke free of him. How could we have done something so stupid?

'Do you think Alfie knows we've spent some of the money?'

'For God's sake, Gemma, give it a rest,' Nathan snapped.

But I couldn't let it go. 'Please, just answer the question.'

'How could he possibly know?' Nathan softened his tone.

'What if he's been having us watched? I told you I'd felt like I was being stalked for months now, but you dismissed my concerns. That could explain why Jethro turned up today. If Alfie wants the money back and we can't pay, he could force us to work for him again. I can't do it.' Tears sprang from my eyes, and I began to tremble with fear.

'Listen to me; nothing like that is going to happen. I promise you. You need to put these ideas out of your head, or you'll end up making yourself sick. You're worrying about nothing.' Nathan put his arms around my waist, pulled me towards him and held me tightly.

14

Gemma

As I lifted my son's carrycot into the car, I noticed a black Mercedes pull up in front of our Jeep and my pulse quickened at the sight of it. The back passenger door opened and Jethro stepped out onto the pavement.

'Hello, Gemma,' the tall blond man said.

I looked up at him with terror-filled eyes and willed myself not to cry. I didn't want him to know I was scared, but that was easier said than done. Panic raced through my veins as he fixed me with his blue gaze. Why had I let Nathan convince me it was safe for me to go out without him?

'There's no need to be scared. I won't hurt you as long as you do what I say.' Jethro smiled. He used a gentle tone to deliver the threat.

I held my breath and stopped myself from hyperventilating, as I attempted to process what was happening.

'Don't make a fuss, get in the back of my car and bring the baby with you.'

What the hell was I going to do? My mind went blank. I knew the last thing I should do was get in the car with Jethro. But there wasn't a soul around on this usually busy street. Where were the Great British Public when you needed them the most? Whitechapel had suddenly become like a ghost town. I kept hoping Nathan would come bursting through the front door and help us, but he didn't. Judging by the look on Jethro's face, my stalling tactics weren't working. I had just run out of time, and that gave me a sinking feeling.

'I wouldn't stand there for too much longer if I were you; patience is not my strong point.'

I knew that wasn't true. Jethro had waited years to get back at Rosa, but I didn't want to call his bluff.

'Please don't do this.' I stood on the pavement staring at Jethro, hoping to appeal to his better nature.

'Time to go, Gemma. Either you carry the baby, or I will.'

As Jethro's words echoed in my head, I knew there was no point resisting any longer. I lifted the car seat with a trembling hand while grabbing Luca's changing bag with the other.

'Now that wasn't so difficult, was it?' Jethro smiled as he guided me away from the Jeep.

As we approached the Mercedes, the driver's door opened, and the unmistakable frame of the bear-sized man climbed out. It was Knuckles. What was he doing here? He walked around the car and opened the passenger door. The huge man took the handle of Luca's carrycot from me, placed my son on the front seat and fastened the seat belt around him. I didn't want to be separated from my baby, but before I could protest, Jethro opened the back door and, placing his hand on the small of my back, he pushed me gently but firmly onto the leather chair.

The Watson family had a reputation for being violent and dangerous, and nobody in their right mind messed with them. Even though I was petrified, I had to stay strong. It wasn't the right time to show weakness, so I forced myself to face my fears head-on. I took a deep breath to calm my nerves and then I spoke. 'Where are we going?'

'All will be revealed in good time.'

A shiver ran down my spine. Alfie used to say that.

As Knuckles started the engine, my mind began to race. I went cold like someone had walked over my grave and then panic set in. Adrenaline coursed through my body, sending my pulse racing and making the palms of my hands sweat. Fear washed over me when the Mercedes turned onto the high street and reality set in. Nathan wasn't coming to rescue us; he didn't know we'd been taken.

A knot formed in the pit of my stomach. I stared out the window with wide eyes when, after what must have been about three quarters of an hour, Knuckles turned off the main carriageway and drove the car along a quiet road, bordered by high hedges and spindly trees. We were in Epping Forest. This area had been the setting of many an unsolved grisly murder. It was the perfect place for a hit-man-style execution if that's what Jethro had in mind for us. Any moment, I was expecting him to produce a hood and handcuffs and bundle me out of the car so that he could put a bullet through the back of my head.

There was something undeniably eerie about a quiet

country lane in the fading afternoon light. Bare branches scraped at the blacked-out windows like ghostly fingers as we passed along the narrow track. I had to muster every ounce of strength I had to stop myself from crying out. I didn't want Jethro to know I was scared because that would only heighten his enjoyment of the situation. I'd learnt that lesson from Alfie, and it wasn't one I'd forget easily.

As we travelled deeper into the forest, I wondered where Jethro was taking me. I knew there was no point asking; he wasn't going to share the details of this white-knuckle ride with me. While I studied the scenery along the winding lane, hoping I'd see a recognisable landmark, my mind drifted to my husband. Had Nathan realised we were missing yet? Even if he had, he was never going to be able to do anything about it. He'd never be able to find us. My brain struggled to process that thought as a fresh surge of terror rose up within me, and once again I found myself wishing we had never come back to England.

Just when I thought the journey would never end, Knuckles pulled up next to a high ivy-clad wall that was so thickly covered with foliage it blended into its surroundings. He waited in front of a set of wrought-iron gates until they opened fully before he drove the Mercedes through them. At the end of the long gravel drive was a huge detached house. You could have easily missed its secluded location, nestled within the forest, if you hadn't known the mansion was there. How could such an imposing building be invisible from the road?

'Welcome to my home,' Jethro said.

I jumped when the gates clinked behind us as they closed shut. The sound was like the cell door closing on an inmate.

That was exactly how I felt. I was Jethro's prisoner, and he wasn't going to let me go until he was ready to. I knew I had to remain calm. Men like Jethro could smell your fear, and if he was anything like Alfie, the more terrified he thought you were, the more powerful it would make him feel.

The Mercedes crunched along the gravel drive and came to a stop outside an enormous brick-built double-fronted residence. It was common knowledge that the London underworld was awash with cash and Jethro's home only highlighted this fact. Under any other circumstances, I would have been delighted to have had the opportunity to spend time at a beautiful property like this, with its manicured lawns and landscaped gardens. But I hadn't been invited here as a guest; I'd been forced to come against my will.

Knuckles stepped out of the car and opened the back passenger door. Jethro gestured for me to get out.

'What about Luca?'

Jethro laughed. 'You didn't think I was going to leave him here on his own, did you? What do you take me for, Gemma, a monster? Knuckles is going to bring the baby.'

The house was in the middle of nowhere with no immediate neighbours. A perfect spot really for a man like Jethro. He could come and go as he pleased with no prying eyes watching him. But the fact that the mansion was so isolated wasn't good news for me.

The sound of Jethro's leather shoes reverberated in the air around us as he climbed the stone steps of the property and stood outside the set of oak doors. My eyes were drawn to the glass above them. The name Darkwood Manor was embossed on it. While he waited for us to join him, he placed his hands into the pockets of his dark navy suit and surveyed his kingdom. It was vast. Three raised terraces like the ones you'd see at a stately home overlooked the front aspect of the house.

Jethro opened one of the heavyset doors and stepped into the hallway. As he did, the light bounced off the polished white marble floor. Knuckles followed him, carrying Luca in his car seat, and I brought up the rear. Although I already had high expectations, the house exceeded them the minute I crossed the threshold. The enormous space was tastefully decorated and the epitome of luxury.

Jethro turned right and walked into the living room where a real fire roared in the feature fireplace. The room felt warm and cosy with its solid wood flooring, deep purple walls, and matching velvet furnishings.

'Put the baby down over there, Knuckles, and get Gemma a drink,' Jethro said as he played the part of the charming host.

Knuckles placed the carrycot down on a thick aubergine-coloured rug before walking to the back of the room. He opened up a set of double doors and revealed an oak-beamed area that was set up as a miniature pub complete with beer pumps and a fully stocked bar. An exposed brick wall on one side gave the room a rustic appearance. The other three walls were painted foxglove pink and matched the upholstery of the tall stools that stood in front of the panelled bar. It reminded me of a gentlemen's drinking club, but the pink hue gave it a feminine touch.

Knuckles reached up and took a large glass down from the hanging rack. 'Do you want a gin and tonic, Gemma?' he asked.

I thought about having a soft drink so that I could keep a clear head but decided against it because I hoped the alcohol might help to calm my nerves. 'Yes, please.'

'Mr Watson is a bit of a connoisseur and has quite a collection. Is there any particular one you'd like?' Knuckles asked gesturing to the enormous selection on the glass shelves behind him.

'I don't mind – surprise me.' After the words left my mouth, I wished I hadn't said them. It probably wasn't a good idea to tell a gangster to surprise you.

Knuckles reappeared carrying two glasses. The tumbler contained an amber-coloured liquid served on the rocks, the other, a balloon glass held a vibrant purple drink garnished with a sprig of lavender and a twist of lime peel.

'Parma violet gin and elderflower tonic,' Knuckle said as he handed me the glass. He had given Tom Cruise a run for his money with his bartending skills.

'Thank you.'

I reached forward and took the glass from him. If it tasted half as nice as it smelt I was in for a treat, I thought as I lifted the fishbowl-like glass to my lips. When I inhaled the sweet aroma, it momentarily took me back to my childhood. As I swallowed a sip of the floral-flavoured liquid, something crossed my mind. If Jethro was a gin aficionado, why was he drinking a dark spirit?

'Take a seat, Gemma,' Jethro said.

Putting my glass down on a side table, I cautiously lowered myself into the luxurious armchair closest to the fire and hoped my knees wouldn't begin to shake now that my full weight wasn't resting on them.

Luca had been asleep since our ordeal began, but now he

was starting to stir. When he began to cry, I lifted him out of his car seat and put him up on my shoulder, rubbing his back to see if I could soothe him, but I knew it wasn't going to work – my son was hungry. I wished I hadn't accepted a drink now. But thankfully, I'd only had one mouthful.

'I need to feed him,' I said when Luca's crying intensified.

I began pacing backwards and forwards across the room to try and pacify my baby while I thought about how to deal with my predicament. Breastfeeding in public had always been a contentious topic for me, and I had no desire to strip off in front of everybody.

'Take Gemma up to one of the guest bedrooms so that she can have some privacy,' Jethro said. Thankfully he must have realised without me having to say anything.

I bent down and picked up Luca's changing bag. After slipping it over my free shoulder, I followed Knuckles out of the room and across the marble floor of the hallway. Holding on to the polished rail with one hand, I climbed the grand sweeping staircase that curved back around on itself. Knuckles' huge frame padded along the pale-grey-carpeted corridor before he opened a door and stepped into a vast bedroom with a dressing room and en-suite bathroom. Against the far wall was an enormous circular bed covered in lilac silk bedding and scatter cushions in complementary shades. To the side of this, double doors opened out onto a spacious terrace that overlooked the beautiful gardens. Opposite the bed was a large window seat, positioned to make the best of the dual aspect view.

Once Knuckles had left the room, I moved a plump feather cushion into the corner of the seat. Leaning back against it, I made myself comfortable so that I could feed my son.

I was reluctant to go back downstairs after Luca finished feeding, but I knew if I didn't, it was only a matter of time before Jethro came and found me.

When I stepped back into the living room, I was surprised to find nobody was there. With my son in my arms, I wandered into the bar area to have a look around. There were so many unusual bottles housed in optics and displayed on glass shelves. I was mesmerised by them. Jethro clearly liked the finer things in life. His collection contained spirits I'd never seen before, let alone tasted.

'Hello, Gemma.'

I jumped. The familiar voice, which came from behind me, startled me. I hadn't noticed anybody when I'd walked into the room. Turning on my heel, I struggled to keep my composure when I saw Alfie sitting in a winged chair in the far corner. This was my worst nightmare. What the hell was he doing here? He was meant to be in prison. My heart began pounding as my fingers instinctively tightened around my son, dozing contentedly on my shoulder. While we stared at each other, neither of us moved a muscle. Now it was all starting to make sense; the drink Knuckles had poured earlier wasn't for Jethro, it was for his son.

15

Alfie

People measured success in a variety of ways. If you counted money and power as status symbols, I considered myself a high achiever. But if the importance of your life depended on you having a deep and meaningful relationship, I would be at the bottom of the pile. I'd always maintained that money could buy anything, but I was well aware it couldn't buy love. Not the kind of love that Gemma and Nathan shared.

I'd reached a point in my life where I wanted a loving partner by my side. Not one who was after my money, but somebody who was genuinely interested in me. The problem was there was only one woman I wanted as the future Mrs Watson. She was a tall, slim brunette with beautiful green eyes. I'd never known attraction like it before. My feelings hadn't changed towards Gemma in the time we'd been apart. If anything, they'd intensified. Absence does make the heart grow fonder. She meant the world to me.

I was besotted with her. Loving her came naturally to me; it was as involuntary as breathing.

I wished Gemma loved me the way I loved her. I knew the feeling wasn't mutual; Gemma didn't give a shit about me. I meant nothing to her, and that was hard for me to come to terms with. To save myself from needless heartache, I should accept that nothing more would happen between us and let her go. I knew I wouldn't be able to do that.

Our paths had crossed again, so I was going to make sure I kept her close. Right now, Gemma was scared of me. I saw the fear in her eyes when she looked at me. I wasn't proud of that. But I could be charming when I wanted to be, and if I didn't try to rush things, Gemma would come to realise she'd be much better off with me than the loser she was currently married to. The problem was, the two of them looked happier than ever. I'd have to make sure I did something about that.

16

Nathan

Several hours had passed before I realised Gemma hadn't returned from the supermarket. I checked the time on my watch before I looked out the front window. Noticing that our Jeep was parked outside with the back passenger door open, I went outside to help her with the shopping. As I approached the car, I could see she wasn't there. When I looked inside, I noticed Luca's carrycot was missing. Slamming the door closed, I rushed back to the house.

'Gemma and Luca have gone,' I shouted as I burst through the front door.

Dad put his newspaper down on the kitchen table and came out into the hall. 'What do you mean?'

'The car's outside, but there's no sign of either of them. By the looks of it, Gemma never made it to the supermarket.' I began chewing the side of my nail before pulling my mobile out of the back pocket of my jeans. After locating Gemma's number, I hit dial. The phone began to ring, and when it finally connected to her voicemail, I left a message.

'Gemma, where are you? Phone me back as soon as you get this message.'

Dad and I stood in the hallway staring at each other for what seemed like an eternity. Every second was like a minute as time ticked by so slowly. 'I feel completely helpless.'

'Try not to worry. I'm sure everything's all right.'

Dad offered some words of reassurance in an attempt to ease my suffering, but they provided little comfort. I dialled Gemma's number again, and it connected to her voicemail. 'Please phone me as soon as you can.' I tried to keep the worry out of my voice, but it was impossible to disguise. My distress was palpable.

'This doesn't make any sense. Why would Gemma take off without telling you where she was going? I wish I could suggest something, but for the life of me, I can't figure it out,' Dad said.

I knew Gemma was emotionally unstable at the moment and was struggling to get out of the dark place she was trapped in. Would that make her act so unpredictably? Unless there was another explanation. A sense of dread engulfed me. 'I bet Jethro Watson's taken them.'

'Why would he do that?'

'I don't know, but Gemma was worried about it. I shouldn't have been so quick to reject the idea. She was convinced she'd seen him the other day when she came back from visiting Mum. But I thought she'd just imagined it.'

'I find it hard to believe that Gemma could have bumped into Jethro around here.' Dad tilted his head to the side and studied my face.

'I didn't believe it either. Gemma hasn't been herself recently. She's finding the demands of motherhood overwhelming and has been paranoid that somebody's watching her,' I offered by way of explanation before I cast my eyes to the floor. I was embarrassed that I hadn't taken my wife's concerns more seriously. Her anxious behaviour was so out of character for her. She was normally so strong. 'But if Gemma was right, Jethro was outside your house.'

'Why didn't you tell me this before?' Dad stared at me as concern filled his blue eyes.

I let out a long breath and forced my hands into the front pockets of my jeans. 'I didn't think it was important. She spends so much energy worrying about anything and everything that sometimes for my own sanity, I have to switch off from it.' That sounded terrible because I loved my wife more than anything.

Dad ran his fingers over his grey beard. 'Jethro wouldn't normally show his face around this area, so if he's turned up out of the blue, it is a bit suspicious, I have to admit.'

I clasped my hands behind my head. 'What am I going to do? They could be anywhere by now. This is all my fault. I wish I'd listened to her.'

'It's not your fault, so don't beat yourself up about it. Try not to worry. We'll find them.' Dad attempted to reassure me, but as he looked into my troubled eyes, I knew what he was thinking. If Jethro had taken my wife and son, their lives could be in danger.

17

Gemma

The last time I'd heard Alfie's voice was when he'd given the order to torch the *Lady Nora*. He knew Nathan and I were trapped on the yacht. At the time I'd thought we were going to be burned alive. The flashback seemed so real; my heart began pounding inside my chest, and for a moment, I was sure I could hear the crackle of the fire and smell the thick acrid smoke that had filled the air around us. It was suffocating. The trauma had caused me such emotional distress that it made it hard to resume my everyday life. I'd been psychologically scarred by the experience and had relived it vividly on a daily basis for months. Even now, the anxiety the event left me with made me question whether I'd ever feel safe again. I had been to the darkest place on many occasions, and I didn't want to go back there again.

The next few moments passed by in slow motion. Alfie sat in front of me dressed in a smart grey suit, sipping Jack Daniel's with a smug smile on his face while my world began crashing in on me. I couldn't think straight; my head was spinning, and I felt disorientated as a million thoughts bombarded my brain.

All the effort we had made to stay under the radar had been for nothing. I should have realised Alfie couldn't be trusted, and the fact that he'd given me his word that he wouldn't come after us didn't mean anything.

The sense of impending doom had been looming over me like a dark shadow for months now. I would lie awake at night, watching Luca sleep, worried that if I closed my eyes for a second, he might choke or die of sudden infant death syndrome. You name it, I imagined it. I was scared that everything and anything might put my son in danger. The thought of somebody coming into my room in the middle of the night and taking Luca away from me was a constant fear.

Nathan was convinced I was being paranoid when I'd told him I was worried that somebody was going to harm or steal our baby. Why was I being so irrational? Surely that wasn't normal. My husband had put my unease down to the fact that I was sleep-deprived. I'd never experienced tiredness like it. I'd thought I was going insane. But that was before I realised Alfie was a free man.

As I battled to keep my panic within, my lungs tightened. But this wasn't the time to show weakness; if I did, Alfie would use it against me. I had to be strong for Luca's sake and put my barriers up. If I didn't show any emotion, Alfie wouldn't know what I was thinking, I reasoned. *Take a deep breath and stay in control,* I told myself.

Alfie was leaning back in the chair with his legs spread wide apart, and as his eyes scanned every inch of me, they lit up. When he smoothed back his blond hair with the palm of his free hand, I caught a glimpse of the holster inside his open jacket. Alfie looked me over as if I was for sale. I clenched my teeth together to stop myself from saying something; it would only make matters worse. The intensity of his blue gaze was unrelenting, and my heartbeat speeded up in response to it. I could see Alfie was enjoying the effect his visual interrogation was having on me.

'You're looking well. Short hair suits you. But then again, you'd look good in a paper bag, wouldn't you, Gemma?' Alfie said as charismatic vibes radiated from his body.

But instead of making me go weak at the knees, Alfie's compliment made my stomach flip over, and bile began to rise. The rancid taste it left behind in my mouth was so unpleasant; I knew there was a good chance I might actually vomit. I flashed him a look of disgust. I didn't want him to flatter me. The man made my skin crawl.

'I see you've been working on channelling your inner ice queen since I last saw you.' Alfie's face broke into a broad smile; he was delighted that he'd made me feel uncomfortable.

I didn't know how to respond. He was impossible to read. At the moment, Alfie was oozing charm from every pore, but he had a violent temper that he could unleash in the blink of an eye. His unpredictability terrified me, so I couldn't afford to say the wrong thing. I wasn't in the habit of backing down, and usually had no trouble speaking my mind. But for once, I decided to keep quiet.

'It seems like the cat's got your tongue, Gemma.' Alfie stood up, walked over to the bar and placed his glass on the counter. 'And to think you used to be so mouthy. Where's your feistiness gone? It was one of the things I liked about you.'

'People change, Alfie,' I replied, glaring at him.

'That's better. I can see a bit of it returning. There's a look of pure hatred in your pretty green eyes.'

Alfie threw his head back and laughed. He was highly amused by his observation, but I maintained a stony silence as he approached me with a self-assured swagger. The way he dressed and carried himself exuded power and confidence. When Alfie walked into a room, everyone sat up straight and took notice. Alfie grinned then reached across and kissed my cheek. As the smell of his aftershave wafted over me, I turned my face away from him. I wanted to put some distance between us.

Alfie positioned himself so that he was standing right in front of me, then fixed me with his blue eyes. 'Enough of the pleasantries, let's get down to business. You have something that belongs to me.'

Now he had my full attention. Alfie continued to stare me straight in the eye to gauge my reaction. I could feel the pulse in my neck throbbing against my skin and hoped it wasn't noticeable. 'You said we could keep the money.'

'Did I?' Alfie tilted his handsome face to one side.

'I distinctly remember you telling me I'd earned it.' I fired the words straight into his face. I was going to have to stand my ground on this. I knew we couldn't pay him back the full amount we'd taken.

The smirk on Alfie's face made me feel sick. 'I don't remember saying that.'

'You did, and you promised you wouldn't come after us.' I turned away. I didn't want Alfie to see the tears that were threatening to spill from my eyes.

'And you believed me?'

A lump formed in my throat as I fought to hold back my tears. Nathan and I had been so happy living in our dream apartment, thinking that we'd put our time with Alfie behind us. How could we have been so stupid?

Alfie was standing so close to me, I could feel his breath on the side of my neck. He took hold of my elbow and turned me around so that I was facing him. My heart began pounding when he leant towards me so that he could get a closer look at Luca, and my grip instinctively tightened around my baby.

18

Nathan

I put my head in my hands as I sat at the kitchen table. How the hell was I going to find Gemma and Luca? I didn't know where to start. I had no idea if Jethro had taken them or not, and I couldn't exactly phone the police and file a missing persons report, could I?

Dad sat opposite me, deep in thought. He was doing his best to support me, but I could see by the look on his face he was worried sick.

'This might be a stupid suggestion.' Dad paused for a moment before he continued to speak. 'But I know where Jethro lives.'

My eyes widened, and I searched my father's face. 'You do?'

'Yes, but I don't know if it will be any help. Jethro might not have taken them.' Dad didn't want to give me false hope.

'It's got to be worth a try. Do you have the address?' I asked, grabbing my jacket from the back of the kitchen chair.

'No, but I can take you there.'

Dad took his keys out of the bowl on the hall table, and we climbed into his Blue Ford Mondeo that was parked outside.

'Does he live far from here?' I asked when my dad started the engine.

'About an hour away. Less, if the traffic isn't heavy.'

As I sat in the passenger seat, I wondered what we were going to do if Gemma and Luca weren't at Jethro's. There was a good chance we wouldn't find them there. But where else could we try? We had to start somewhere, and Jethro's house was as good a place as any.

Dad put his foot down once we were on the dual carriageway to try and save time. 'Keep an eye out for speed cameras,' he said as the car raced along the tarmac.

It was dark by the time we turned off the carriageway, and onto the quiet country road that led to where Jethro lived in Epping Forest. Dad killed his speed as we travelled along the winding lane that was only wide enough for a single car in some places.

'Are you sure it's down here?' I asked when I looked out the window and took in our remote surroundings.

'Yes. It's a long way from the main road. If I remember rightly, the house is down here somewhere. You won't be surprised to hear it's well hidden from public view.'

Dad stopped the car after several minutes to get his bearings. There were no street lights, and everything always looked different in the dark, didn't it? Dad reckoned the place was hard enough to spot on a clear summer's day, let alone on a gloomy evening in January. He drove on at a snail's pace, peering out of the windscreen that kept threatening to mist up.

'What's wrong?' I asked when he stopped at a junction.

'Jethro's place isn't as far as this. I must have driven past it.'

Realising he'd missed the house, Dad tried to turn the Mondeo around in the narrow space, and after many attempts, he succeeded. Then he inched the car along the winding lane, scouring the darkness as he drove. We were out in the middle of nowhere. I couldn't believe anyone lived out here. There was nothing around us but dense forest. It felt very isolated and cut off from civilisation, but that would suit the Watsons down to the ground.

'There it is,' Dad said when he spotted the ivy-covered perimeter wall that blended in so well to the landscape.

'Are you sure this is it? It doesn't look like there's anything behind that wall.'

'Trust me; I've been here before. This is Jethro's house.' Dad stopped the car in front of the wrought-iron entrance.

'How are we going to get in?'

'That's a good question.' Although Dad knew the location of Jethro's remote mansion, gaining access to it would be easier said than done. It was an impenetrable fortress.

'There's a buzzer on the gate, but we need to think about whether we should use it or try to get in another way. I'm not sure Jethro's going to answer the door and welcome us in with open arms.'

The trees that surrounded the house had blocked out any natural light hours ago, so we decided it would be better to ring the entry system, rather than try to break in, as we wouldn't be able to see what we were doing in the darkness.

'Did you say you'd been here before?'

Dad nodded. 'Yes, but it was a long time ago.'

I raised my eyebrows. 'I'm surprised to hear that. Was it a social visit or had he kidnapped you too?'

'I'll tell you about it another time. It's a long story.'

Dad got out of the Mondeo and walked across to the iron gates. He pressed the intercom and waited for a response. Nobody replied. Just as Dad was about to press the button again, the heavy gates began opening. Dad got back in his car and turned towards me. We looked at each other, but neither of us spoke. Dad drove the car through the access gate into the mature gardens that shielded the house from the road. As soon as we began driving towards Darkwood Manor along the private driveway, motion detector lights switched on at ground level to light the way. The Mondeo's tyres crunched along the gravel and came to a stop outside the front of the house. Jethro stood in the entrance of the double doorway waiting for us.

'Let me handle this, Nathan,' Dad said when we got out of the car and began to climb the steps at the front of the property.

'Long time no see,' Jethro said. 'I'd like to say it's a pleasure, but we both know that would be a lie.'

'Likewise,' Dad replied.

'What brings you to Epping Forest at this time of night?' Jethro asked, and a slow smile spread across his lips.

My eyes blazed with fury. I didn't bother to hide how I felt. 'Don't act all innocent. You know why we're here.'

'Nice to meet you too, Nathan.' Jethro grinned and stepped back from the doorway. 'You'd better come inside.'

Jethro turned and walked into the hall and his footsteps echoed on the white marble floor. He led the way into the living room, past the roaring fire and into the bar. Although he hadn't confirmed that he'd taken Gemma and Luca, he hadn't denied it either.

'Get these gentlemen a drink, will you?' Jethro said.

A bear-sized man walked into the room and took up position behind the counter. 'What's your poison?'

I stared at him with eyes like saucers. Either Knuckles had an identical twin, or he wasn't behind bars like he was meant to be. I put that thought out of my head. I had more important things to deal with. 'I don't want a drink; I want to see my wife and son.' I hadn't come here to make small talk, so I struggled to keep a lid on my volcanic temper.

Jethro took a step towards me and got into my personal space. Then he pointed his finger at me. 'Don't come into my house and start making demands. Count yourself lucky I even opened the door to you.'

I knew if I wanted to see my family again, I'd have to do what Jethro said, and much as I was desperate to know that they were safe, it was obvious Jethro was playing a game. He wasn't going to let me see Gemma and Luca until he was ready to. All I could do was bide my time and be patient. But patience had never been my strong suit.

Knuckles handed Dad and I bottles of Stella Artois then he fixed Jethro a large Monkey 47 gin and tonic. Jethro gestured for us to take a seat in the corner of the bar at a round table that overlooked the floodlit landscaped gardens and cascading terraces.

'So how's life been treating you?' Jethro asked and the corners of his mouth lifted into a smile.

A flash of anger crossed my face. I could see what Gemma meant now. Not only did they look alike, but Jethro also had the same smug way about him that Alfie did. He was toying with us, relaxing back in his chair while he held court. I felt like jumping up and grabbing him by the throat. I could picture myself with my hands around his neck, tightening my grip until he proved to me that my wife and son hadn't come to any harm.

'Life's good,' Dad replied. His words had a bitter edge to them.

'Glad to hear it.'

Jethro raised his glass but didn't clink my dad's. Instead, the two men locked eyes and studied each other with thinly veiled contempt. The hatred between them radiated into the room and was almost palpable. You wouldn't need to be told the history; anyone could sense from the tension that was filling the room that the two men were age-old enemies. It was obvious their feud ran deep. Bitterness still reigned between my father and Jethro, I thought, as I watched their frosty exchange. They were eyeballing each other like a couple of cowboys did before they engaged in a shootout. Years of pent-up animosity circulated between them. Their resentment for each other couldn't be more obvious; it was as plain as day. Dad had every right to feel bitter towards Jethro; he set him up after all. Their feud had raged on for a long time; the bad blood dated back decades.

'Let Gemma and Luca go, and I'll take their place,' Dad said.

I could tell by the tone of his voice, the taste of revenge

was on his lips, but he hadn't come here to talk about the past and settling old scores. Dad just wanted to find his grandson and daughter-in-law and was prepared to swallow any thoughts of retribution, at least for the meantime, in return for their safety. I shot my dad a worried look and Jethro began to laugh.

'That's very noble of you, Gareth,' Jethro replied before taking a sip of his gin. 'But I'm afraid trading places isn't an option I'm prepared to consider.'

'I'm not leaving here without my wife and son.'

Jethro smiled and took another sip of his expensive gin. 'I don't think you're in a position to make demands do you, Nathan?'

I put the bottle of Stella down on the bar and stormed out of the room. 'Gemma, where are you?' I shouted at the top of my voice.

The loud sound resonated around the hall and must have startled the baby. When he started to cry, it alerted me to their position in the mansion. My footsteps echoed as I ran down the marble staircase to the basement area, passed the games room, home cinema and swimming pool. When I entered the conservatory at the back of the house, my mouth fell open. What the hell was Alfie doing here?

'I wondered how long it would take you to find us.' Alfie threw me a look of disgust before smoothing down his blond slicked-back hair.

The tension in the room was tangible as we locked eyes and glared at each other.

I didn't answer Alfie but rushed to my wife's side. 'Are you OK?'

I looked into Gemma's beautiful green eyes. She didn't

need to say a word. I knew she was terrified, so I leant down and kissed her on the cheek before I took Luca out of her arms. His crying stopped instantly, and he beamed up at me. Alfie glared at us with a look of pure hatred in his blue eyes.

'Ahh isn't that sweet. Your white knight has come to the rescue.' Alfie's words seemed to suck the air out of the room.

I'd always been extremely protective of Gemma. I wasn't sure why I felt the need really because she could definitely kick someone's arse if the occasion arose. Right on cue, Gemma shot Alfie a disapproving look, which made him laugh. I put my arm around my wife's trembling shoulder to comfort her, but it did little to ease her suffering.

19

Gemma

I hadn't said anything since we'd returned to Gareth's terraced house. I was at a loss for words. I wasn't sure what was making me feel withdrawn and claustrophobic. Was it was the small space I found myself in after visiting Jethro's enormous mansion, or the realisation that there was no escape from the situation? Whichever it was, the walls felt like they were closing in on me. So much had happened in the space of a few hours, and I couldn't make sense of any of it.

There were few things worse in life than feeling trapped, and that was exactly how I felt at this moment in time. Alfie wanted his money, so he was going to back us into a corner, no doubt subjecting us to severe psychological distress along the way. He loved to play games, and this was by far his favourite type: predator versus prey.

Alfie had got us right where he wanted us, and I had to admit I was overwhelmed by the situation. It was like being locked in a dark room without any source of light.

I didn't know what to do for the best. When we'd broken free from Alfie, Nathan and I had promised ourselves we would never get into a position like that again, and yet, here we were. Why had we been so naive? We should have known we couldn't trust him to keep his word.

'I was so worried when I realised you were missing. How did you end up at Jethro's house?' Nathan asked, and his words derailed my train of thought.

When my husband sat down on the sofa beside me, he reached for my hand. His dark eyes searched mine while he waited for me to speak.

'While I was putting Luca in the Jeep on my way to Asda, Jethro's car pulled up in front of me. He got out and told me he wouldn't hurt me as long as I did what he said.' My voice broke as I finished my sentence, and tears began streaming down my face.

'It's OK, Gemma, don't cry.' Nathan pulled me towards him and cradled me in his arms. 'This is all my fault. If I'd gone shopping with you, none of this would have happened.'

Gareth appeared in the doorway with a mug of sweet tea. 'Here you go, Gemma, drink this, darling. It'll make you feel better.'

I pulled back from my husband and tried to take the drink from Gareth, but my hands were trembling too much.

'Thanks, Dad,' Nathan said. He took the tea out of his hand and put the mug down on the side table.

'I'll look after Luca, so you two can talk.' Gareth picked up the car seat containing the sleeping baby and walked out of the room, closing the door behind him.

'I was so scared, Nathan. I thought something terrible was going to happen to us.'

My husband held me tightly as his lips covered mine before he pulled back and whispered into my ear. 'You're both safe now.'

'What the hell's going on? Alfie and Knuckles are meant to be in prison.'

'I know they are, but don't worry about that now. You should go to bed and try and get some rest, Gemma; you look exhausted.' My husband gently ran his fingertips along the dark shadows under my eyes and wiped my tears away with the pad of his thumbs.

20

Nathan

'I don't understand how Alfie walked away from a prison sentence. It doesn't make any sense.' I sat down at the kitchen table opposite my dad. 'It was all over the news when he got arrested with his men in Boulogne.'

Dad stood up from the table and walked across to the fridge. He took out two bottles of Budweiser, opened them, and before he sat down again, he handed one to me. 'Maybe they didn't have enough evidence to prosecute him.' Dad took a swig of his beer before wiping his lips on the back of his hand.

I shook my head. That couldn't be the case. 'He was caught with fifty thousand pounds' worth of cocaine. Interpol reckoned they'd been trying to infiltrate the gang for years.'

'I'm sure they had, but it's always difficult for the authorities to convict the kingpin.'

I was sceptical about my dad's explanation and wished

Gemma and I had followed the case now instead of presuming Alfie's arrest would lead to his conviction. The police had so much evidence we didn't think for one minute Alfie would be able to worm his way out of doing time. In hindsight, that was naive of us.

'I believe you, and if it had been anybody else apart from Alfie Watson, the police would have locked them up and thrown away the key.'

'So how come he's not behind bars? Do you think Jethro broke him out of jail?'

'I doubt it. Alfie's from a powerful family. My guess would be that he wasn't locked up in the first place. Guys like him are untouchable. Alfie is the undisputed king of the London underworld since Jethro handed him the baton.'

Dad could be right. Alfie always had considered himself above the law. Once we'd seen Alfie and his men get arrested, Gemma and I thought we had finally broken away from them. We were desperate for a fresh start and wanted to put the time we'd spent with Alfie behind us, so we closed the door on him completely. Out of sight, out of mind. I was kicking myself for not keeping an eye on the proceedings now, but it was easy to avoid the press coverage of his trial. We were living in Spain and were too busy concentrating on rebuilding our marriage to bother watching the English news.

Come to think of it, perhaps it was Alfie who had been watching us in Spain. Gemma had been convinced that somebody was stalking her, and I'd dismissed her concerns repeatedly because I hadn't realised Alfie Watson was free to walk the streets. Even if he had been sent down, a man in his position had people working for him on the outside. Alfie's team might be few in numbers, but they all displayed unquestionable loyalty to their boss. Their fear of Alfie guaranteed they wouldn't be stupid enough to double-cross him like we had. No wonder Gemma was terrified; I hardly recognised her any more. She'd become a nervous wreck.

'Did you ask Gemma what happened?' Dad stood up from his chair and went to get two more beers out of the fridge.

I shook my head. 'No, she was too distressed to talk about it.' I knew I had to tread carefully; anyone could see Gemma was teetering on the edge.

Dad passed me a bottle and then bowed his head. 'I hope Jethro didn't take Gemma and Luca to get back at me. There's been a war raging between our families for years.'

'I know, Dad, but I don't think Jethro's the one we have to worry about.' I stood up, placed my hands behind my head and stretched out my neck.

'What makes you so sure? Jethro was the one who took them, wasn't he?' Dad searched my face for the answer to his question.

'I know he did, but he was probably following Alfie's orders.' I dropped my hands and cracked my knuckles.

'But why would Alfie take them?' Dad questioned, his blue eyes full of concern.

It was a long story and not one I wanted to go into. I'd come to England to get to know my father; I didn't want the Watsons to dominate the time we had together. I sat back down at the table, picked up my bottle of beer and started peeling the label from it. I didn't want to tell my dad that Gemma and I had taken Alfie's money when he'd torched his yacht, knowing we were trapped inside it, and now he wanted that money back.

21

Gemma

No relationship can be sunshine and roses all the time, but since my encounter with Alfie, I found myself increasingly withdrawing from Nathan as I battled to overcome the depression I was experiencing. I felt like nobody understood what I was going through, not even my husband, the person closest to me. That seemed strange as he always assumed the role of my best friend, confidant and emotional support-giver.

It was difficult to explain. I was experiencing a type of loneliness that couldn't be cured by spending time around others. The only way I could deal with it was to retreat inside myself. But in the process, I'd ended up distancing myself from the very person who was trying to help me. I knew I was pushing my husband away, but I couldn't seem to stop myself from doing it. Why do we try to hurt the ones we love the most?

Life had been good while we were living in Puerto Banús. Nathan and I had spent an idyllic year locked in our own little bubble, blissfully happy together like we were newlyweds again. We couldn't keep our hands off each other. We'd agreed to put our relationship first after a rocky couple of months derailed our marriage, and it nearly ended in divorce. Everything was going well between us. We were back on track, so when I discovered I was pregnant, it was the icing on the cake.

Considering Nathan had sat on the fence for years about starting a family, it was amazing to see him with Luca now. He was embracing fatherhood and was determined to be involved in all aspects of Luca's life. He'd come a long way from the man who was scared he wouldn't make a good father because he hadn't had a role model. He'd been worried about nothing; Nathan was a brilliant dad, and that made me love him even more if that was possible.

Nathan and I both had difficult childhoods. My relationship with my family was non-existent. I knew how much that hurt even though I pretended it didn't. Now that I was a mother, I sometimes found myself wishing I had a relationship with my mum. But that was a pipe dream. It was never going to happen. Even before we fell out, we didn't have a natural mother and daughter bond. Despite what I'd like to believe, the female of the species isn't hardwired to love her offspring. My mum didn't possess any maternal warmth, and she was the last person I'd go to in a crisis or share a secret or a problem with.

I envied the bond other women had with their mothers, especially now that Nathan and Rosa were estranged. Since Nathan and I had been a couple, Rosa had been like a mother to me, and I missed her company and that of my surrogate Italian family. Nathan's relatives were amazing, and they had welcomed me with open arms and showered me with unconditional love and kindness, feelings that were quite alien to me. In the beginning, they'd made me feel at home even though I was a stranger and now that I was part of their family, I knew they would always be there for me, through thick and thin. I loved the traditional values they held. Rosa always said her family was the most important aspect of her life, and I couldn't agree with her more. I wouldn't trade Nathan and Luca for the world.

My family could learn a lot from the Italian culture. Rosa was warm-hearted and generous, whereas my parents cut me off because they were disappointed in my choice of partner. They didn't approve of Nathan and thought he was a liability. My parents told me that if I married him, they would write me out of their will. What kind of people would do that to their child? That was the last time I ever saw them. I haven't had any contact with them since that day. Even though at times that was painful, nothing I did was ever good enough for them. It might seem like an extreme measure, but closing the door on our toxic relationship had a positive effect on me.

Looking back, I feel that experience honestly changed my life for the better. They'd done me a huge favour. I wished I'd cut contact with them sooner. I could have saved myself a lot of heartache.

Because we'd both had difficult childhoods, we shared common ground. We both wanted everything in our son's life to be perfect. Neither of us wanted him to grow up the way we had. We believed that if we established a strong parent–baby bond right from the start, it would set Luca up for healthy relationships throughout his life. We were both determined to get this right. Nathan had managed it, but the irrational thoughts that were taking up so much space in my head meant I wasn't able to access the small piece of rational mind that was available. There was a big difference between being protective towards my son and smothering him. It was essential that I got the balance right for everybody's sake.

In the past, I'd been plagued with feelings of inadequacy. My deep-seated fear of failure and not being good enough had always been bubbling under the surface, no matter how many times Nathan bolstered my sense of self-worth. Now that it had been triggered again, I felt like I was drowning. I couldn't see anything but the waves and the water. I was in danger of going under.

I was scared of what was about to happen. I wanted to take Luca and run, but deep down, I knew there was no point. Alfie had eyes and ears everywhere. It wouldn't matter where I went, he would come and find us. Nathan and I thought we'd covered our tracks and left him no leads when we moved to Spain. Life was good while we'd thought we'd vanished into thin air. But in the back of my mind, I'd known all along that something wasn't right. Somebody had been watching us. If I tried to run away, I was going to spend the rest of my life looking over my shoulder. Living the life of a fugitive would play havoc with my nerves, and at this moment in time, they were frazzled enough. Waiting for Alfie to make his next move was torture. He was taunting me with his silent presence. Fear dominated every aspect of my life.

I was still trying to come to terms with the fact that Alfie wasn't behind bars. How could he be a free man? I knew he'd always considered himself bulletproof, but the police had finally caught up with him and arrested him. That wasn't something I'd imagined; I'd seen it with my own eyes. Interpol had named Alfie Watson as the gang leader and high-profile member of an international drug-smuggling ring that they had been trying to infiltrate for years.

Nathan and I thought the case was clear-cut, so we hadn't bothered to follow his trial. It would have been torturous, and we'd been through enough already. In a desperate bid to move on from the traumatic experience we'd been through, we'd decided to have a news blackout. The media only ever reported on stories that were depressing or shocking anyway, so we wouldn't be missing much. Our time with Alfie had taught us that it could be extremely stressful reading about yourself in the paper or seeing your image flash up on TV and we'd endured enough stress to last us a lifetime. We'd thought ignorance was bliss until we found out the truth.

For the last few days, I'd been constantly watching the clock. I hated playing the waiting game, but that was how this business worked. Alfie wanted to make this as agonising for us as possible, and his tactic was working. The passing of time was a powerful tool. While I waited for the dreaded moment to arrive, my confidence was being chipped away. I'd become a prisoner in my own home as the ticking clock dominated every detail of my life. As the stress intensified, it was impossible to get things into perspective. I couldn't see a way out of this situation.

My mobile began to ring on the bedside table, and the sound of it made me jump. With fumbling fingers, I swiped at the screen to answer the call. Alfie spoke before I had a chance to say anything.

'Hello, Gemma. Aren't you going to venture out today?' His voice was filled with vengeful delight. I could picture him with a smug look on his face, and it made anger rise up within me.

He wanted me to know he was watching me. 'Leave me alone, Alfie.' My words came out sharply; I couldn't help it. The man had put me through hell.

Alfie didn't answer, and the phone went dead.

22

Gemma

'Gemma, come out here now and bring the baby with you,' Alfie shouted at the top of his voice while banging on the front door with his fist.

Nathan, Gareth and I exchanged worried glances. It was almost midnight, and we were just about to go to bed when our unwelcome visitor had turned up. When I didn't answer, Alfie began pounding on the door once more. The whole street must have been able to hear the commotion. Tears sprang from my eyes. Alfie was terrifying when he acted like this. I knew I didn't have a choice. I'd have to do what he said.

'Nathan, I'm scared.' After looking into my husband's eyes, I glanced over to where Luca lay in his Moses basket, with his arms above his head, fast asleep, oblivious to the drama unfolding around him.

'Don't be. We're not going to let Alfie anywhere near you.' Nathan walked out of the living room and down the hall. He was just about to open the front door when Gareth put his hand on his shoulder.

'Let me deal with this,' Gareth said, stepping in front of his son.

The sound of the gunshot resonated around the hall as the bullet entered the house. I stood in the living room doorway, holding on to the architrave with my mouth open. It all happened so quickly, one minute we were drinking tea, and the next, all hell had broken loose. I watched helplessly from the other end of the hallway as my father-in-law fell to the floor with blood pouring from his leg. The still-smoking barrel of the gun, sticking through the letterbox, was only inches away and was pointing ominously at him.

Gareth had scrunched his eyes closed to try to block out the pain. He was writhing in agony on the laminate floor when the front door burst open. Alfie stood in the entrance, dressed in a charcoal grey suit. It was dark outside, but a street light shone brightly behind him. He still had the revolver in his hand as his tall frame stepped over Gareth's crumpled body before he pushed past Nathan, who was crouched at his father's side, trying to stem the bleeding with his bare hands. There was so much blood coming from the wound; it ran between Nathan's fingers. The once-white walls were covered in tiny splatters; it had gone everywhere.

When Alfie paced down the hall towards me, he trod in Gareth's blood and left a trail of red footprints behind him. Nathan didn't attempt to stop him; he was too busy trying to help his father.

'Where's Luca?'

I looked at him with wide eyes as I backed myself into

the corner. I wanted to drop to the floor and curl into a ball, but what good would that do?

'Gemma, where's Luca?'

I could see the gun in Alfie's hand, and it sent a shiver down my spine. I couldn't answer him. I was too shocked to speak. Instead, I stood staring at him, trembling like a leaf. The colour drained from my face, and I felt my breath catch in my chest when Alfie turned away from me and walked into the living room where my baby was sleeping.

He looked over his shoulder at me and laughed. Seeing me white-faced delighted him. Alfie undid the button of his suit and put the gun back into the holster concealed inside his jacket. He bent down and undid the clips that attached Luca's bassinet to the stand. As he gently lifted the cradle, I sprang across the room to stop him. Placing my hands on the handles, I tried to pull it away from Alfie, but his grip was too tight.

'What do you think you're doing?' I shouted. If Alfie thought I was going to stand back and let him take my son, he had another thing coming.

Alfie repositioned the cradle so he could hold the straps with one hand, then he reached forward and grabbed the sleeve of my jumper tightly. Turning on his heel, he pulled me from the room. I tried to make myself as heavy as possible by digging my feet into the floor, but Alfie trailed me along behind him with ease. As we approached Nathan, he jumped up from his father's side and tried to block Alfie's path, but Knuckles was waiting outside the front door, so he came to his boss's aid. The huge man stepped into the hallway, and using the butt of his gun, he hit Nathan on the back of the head.

My husband hit the floor with a thud, and it shook me to the core. I screamed at the top of my lungs, but nobody was going to come and help us. The high-pitched noise woke Luca, and he began to cry. Alfie passed the basket containing my wailing son to Knuckles. Alfie's minder walked over to the Mercedes, opened the front passenger door and placed Luca on the leather seat.

'When we go outside, I don't want to hear a sound out of you, do you get my drift?' Alfie was standing so close to me, I could feel his breath on my cheek. 'Don't speak until I tell you to.'

I didn't answer him, but I nodded, so he knew I'd understood the order. Dry-mouthed fear had taken my voice again. I tried to hold back my tears as I stepped over the bodies of my husband and father-in-law lying in the narrow hallway. A feeling of nausea came over me, and I thought I was going to be sick. I was now at the mercy of this cold-blooded killer. There was no telling what he might do. The thought of that sent my pulse rate soaring, and my head started to spin.

I looked up at Alfie with panic-filled eyes. The man was a lunatic; there was no disputing that. 'Please don't take us away,' I begged. A feeling of helplessness washed over me, and I couldn't hold the tears back any longer. They began streaming down my face.

Gareth's rented two-bedroom house in Crofts Way was situated just off the high street. I couldn't help noticing it was unusually quiet tonight. In fact, it was more than quiet; it was completely deserted. Under normal circumstances, I would have expected the sound of a gun firing in a residential area to have drawn a crowd, even in the East

End of London, but there wasn't a soul to be seen. I suppose with Knuckles' huge frame standing guard outside the front door as a deterrent, anyone who might have been curious to see what was happening had decided to stay away for their own safety. There wasn't a single curtain in the road twitching.

The appalling crimes that Alfie had just committed hadn't produced a single witness apart from myself that was. How was that even possible in a busy London suburb? I knew it was no coincidence. Alfie was well known in the area, and anybody with any sense would stay well out of his way unless they were looking for trouble. If anybody attempted to cross him, he would take on the role of judge and jury and determine the unfortunate person's fate. He had a reputation for dishing out such brutal punishments that only a fool would be prepared to step out of line.

As Alfie bundled me into the car, I felt an agonising pain in my chest. But it wasn't a physical pain, it was an emotional one. Having to leave Nathan and Gareth behind, not knowing what was going to happen to them, was tearing me apart. Would this be the last time I'd see my husband and father-in-law?

23

Gemma

'Take a seat in here, Gemma, and Knuckles will get you a drink,' Jethro said, leading me towards a dark purple armchair in the corner of the living room next to the fireplace.

'I don't want anything, thank you,' I replied, trying to hold back my tears. My head was throbbing; I'd been silently crying since we left Gareth's house. I was on edge. I knew I was at breaking point, but I'd have to pull myself together, put on a tough exterior and adopt an empowered frame of mind. If I was going to take on the Watsons, I'd need to regain my mental strength, but at this moment in time, that would be easier said than done.

Knuckles brought Luca's carrycot in and put it down by the side of my chair. He was fast asleep, but I lifted him out anyway and held him in the crook of my arm. I wanted to keep my son close to me.

I tried to hide in the shadows, as I watched Alfie striding

around the bar area with a tumbler of neat Jack Daniel's clenched in his hand.

'What's the matter, Alf? It's obvious something's bothering you by the way you're behaving.' Jethro lifted a cut-glass gin balloon to his mouth and took a sip of his drink.

'The fuckers wouldn't let me in, so what was I meant to do?' Alfie glared at his father before looking down and swirling the drink in his glass.

Jethro let out a slow breath like he was blowing away his frustration. Alfie was expecting his dad to read between the lines and work out for himself what had happened this evening. But even in the violent circles they moved in, I doubted very much he would guess what Alfie had done.

'You're going to have to elaborate. I'm not a mind reader, Alf.'

'I fired my gun through the letterbox to scare them, and I ended up shooting Gareth in the leg.'

Jethro rolled his eyes. 'Couldn't you have forced the door in instead?'

So it wasn't just me who thought Alfie's behaviour was insane even by his standards. Jethro thought it too. Only a psychotic lunatic would do a thing like that. What kind of man puts a gun through a person's letterbox and fires a shot when there's a baby in the house just because they didn't open the door?

'I didn't intentionally shoot the bastard. I didn't realise he was behind the door. My eyes don't penetrate solid spaces,' Alfie said in a sarcastic tone.

'I thought I told you to keep your nose clean.'

Jethro might not be visibly in charge of the firm any

more, but he was definitely still the head honcho behind the scenes. It was eye-opening to see the dynamic between father and son. Alfie wasn't the one who called the shots after all.

'I dealt with the situation the way I saw fit. It isn't up for discussion.' Alfie knocked back the drink in his glass and turned to look out of the window.

You could feel the friction between the two men. Alfie looked like he was going to explode any minute. Even though he had his back to me, I could tell by the way he was standing. He was holding himself in a rigid stance, and his shoulders were tense. I wondered if he was going to have a full-blown outburst. I'd seen a few adult temper tantrums in my life, but I never expected to witness Alfie throwing one.

Jethro didn't attempt to pacify him or engage him in conversation. Instead, he ignored his son and continued sipping away on his gin. I knew Alfie was a mummy's boy. He hadn't approved of the way Jethro had treated his wife, and they had a difficult relationship because of that. The strain was plain to see. They weren't trying to hide it from anyone. They were behaving like two alpha males battling against each other for the top spot. Any minute now I was expecting them to start beating their chests like two rival silverback gorillas.

'I don't know what gets into you sometimes. I told you to keep a low profile, not put yourself in the spotlight,' Jethro continued after a long pause. He opened the button of his blue suit jacket and took a seat on one of the bar stools. 'You can't start shooting people through their letterboxes without bringing attention to yourself. We're not living in the Wild West, Alf.' Jethro shook his head.

Alfie turned around and locked eyes with his father, but he didn't reply. His silence sent a very clear message to me. I'd never seen him behave like this. It wasn't in his character to back down, yet he was accepting his dressing-down. I wouldn't have believed it if I hadn't seen it with my own eyes. It was obvious he respected Jethro because he hadn't attempted to interrupt him once in the time he'd been speaking. If I hadn't been so scared, the exchange between the two men would have been fascinating to watch. It surprised me because although Alfie portrayed himself as head of the family, he was still very much under Jethro's control. Alfie wasn't the organ grinder, he was the monkey. Watching their exchange reminded me that no matter how old we are, we will always be children to our parents.

I tried to evaluate what was going on. Had Jethro come out of retirement since Alfie's arrest? Or had he always been there in the background, giving out the orders, while keeping himself a safe distance away from the action? It would be the sensible thing to do and would explain why it was so difficult for the police to put the kingpins behind bars. They never got their hands dirty. That was something I'd accused Alfie of before. While he was more than happy to keep away from some areas of the business, he couldn't resist getting involved in the violent beatings the firm dished out. At the back of my mind, I wondered if that might become his downfall. Well, a girl could dream, couldn't she?

Jethro got up from the bar and walked over to where Alfie was standing. 'You've got to rein it in, son. You're becoming a liability. Do you want to end up behind bars?'

'That's not going to happen.' Alfie turned to face his

father then he laughed, not because he was amused by Jethro's comments – it was an act of defiance.

Jethro's blue eyes bored into his son's as he drove the message home. 'Don't make the mistake of thinking you're above the law.'

A huge smile spread across Alfie's face as he listened to his dad's ear-bashing, but Jethro wasn't put off by Alfie's cockiness and carried on regardless.

'How many times do I have to tell you? Don't be the one to dish out the punishment. We employ people to do that. Keep your hands clean, Alf, otherwise the cops will be sniffing around you like flies on shit.'

As Jethro continued to nag, Alfie's attitude worsened. He took a packet of cigarettes out of the inside pocket of his suit jacket and placed one in his mouth.

'If you want to smoke that go outside,' Jethro said. 'I thought you'd given up that disgusting habit.'

'I have.'

Alfie rolled his eyes and took the cigarette out of his mouth. Then he walked over to the bar and put his empty glass down on the counter, tossing the cigarette next to it. Jethro followed him, and the two men stood side by side, inches apart, staring at each other.

'You don't need to resort to violence, Alf. Your reputation on the street is fearsome. People are terrified of you.' The tone of Jethro's voice softened momentarily.

'They've got good reason to be.' A slow smile spread across Alfie's face, and his arrogance returned.

'You'll be destroyed by your own ego if you're not careful.'

Alfie let out an audible breath. 'You can stop the lecture now, Dad. I've got the message.' He walked behind the bar and refilled his glass, then swallowed the amber liquid in two gulps. His expression changed as it passed down his throat and into his stomach. No doubt the Jack Daniel's left a burning sensation behind.

I listened to the conversation with interest as I perched on the edge of the seat with Luca in my arms. He hadn't stirred since we got here, but I wasn't going to put him down. I wanted to hold him close for comfort and to make sure he didn't come to any harm. I had to protect my son at all costs. I had a gut feeling that if I could get Jethro onside, maybe this business with Alfie could be resolved peacefully. My instinct was telling me to trust it. Jethro seemed like a reasonable person. He was nothing like I had expected him to be. Either the stories I'd heard about this softly spoken man had been greatly exaggerated, or he'd mellowed considerably over the years.

'Knuckles, can you arrange for the doctor to go to Crofts Way and clean up Alfie's mess? The last thing we need is for Nathan and Gareth to turn up at A&E, one of them with an unexplained gunshot wound and the other a severe concussion.'

'What's with the sudden concern over Gareth Stone anyway? I thought you hated the man?' Alfie asked.

'I do. You know there's no love lost between us. The man's a bastard. Always was, always will be.'

'So why are you sending the doctor to see him? He might have bled out by now.' Alfie clenched his jaw to stop himself from saying any more.

I felt fresh tears spring to my eyes as Alfie's words slowly registered in my brain. There was nothing I could have done to help Gareth or Nathan, but that was hard to accept.

'You're missing the point. I don't give a shit about what happens to Gareth, but we can't just leave two bodies in the hallway and hope nobody notices.'

Jethro's words shocked me. I'd thought he had more compassion than Alfie. Being difficult to read was a trait that both the Watson men possessed.

'I've got a better idea. Knuckles could go back to Gareth's place and find out what's going on.'

Alfie's right-hand man was filling the doorway with his eyes fixed on me.

Jethro lifted his hand to silence his son. 'We won't call the doctor for the minute. Let's wait and see what happens first. If Gareth and Nathan are OK, it won't be long until they're knocking on my front door. But next time I send you to do a job, make sure you follow my instructions. I managed to get Gemma to escort me to Darkwood Manor without having to resort to violence, didn't I?' Jethro paused and glared at Alfie. 'I expected you to do the same.'

'If she'd come out of the house when I asked her to, none of this would have happened.' Alfie fixed me with a death stare, and I felt myself burrow deeper into the plush chair. I suddenly had a horrible feeling my name could end up on the missing list.

24

Nathan

'What the hell happened?' I asked when I started to come round.

'Knuckles knocked you out with the back of his gun,' Dad replied, hobbling over to me.

I had no memory of being hit. Lifting one hand to the back of my head, I examined the sizeable lump that was forming with my fingertips. Only a few minutes had passed since Alfie left, but it felt like he'd been gone for hours. I couldn't think straight as I attempted to retrace the event in my mind. One moment I was trying to stop the gangster from taking my wife and child, and the next thing I knew, I was waking up face down on the floor. I was still groggy and slightly disoriented, and it took me a moment to get my limbs to move before I managed to stand up.

Although Dad was up on his feet, he couldn't disguise the pain he was in. It was written all over his face. When Alfie had fired the gun through the letterbox, the bullet zipped through the air, and the piece of hot metal sliced past Dad's leg, grazing the side of his thigh. It had pulled chunks of skin and flesh off his leg before embedding itself in the wall. Fortunately, his injury was relatively superficial. It looked a mess, but in the grand scheme of things, he was lucky to be alive. The wound had bled profusely, but if the bullet had penetrated his thigh bone, he could have bled to death. Alfie's reckless behaviour could have had serious consequences.

'We need to get you to the hospital – you've lost a lot of blood.'

Dad looked down at his blood-soaked jeans. 'No way, they'll ask too many questions. The sooner we go after Alfie, the better.'

For selfish reasons, I was glad my dad had suggested that. There was no telling how much danger Gemma and Luca were in and if we'd had to go to the hospital first, it could have delayed us for hours. There was a good chance they would have admitted Dad, and I didn't think I'd be able to find my way back to Darkwood Manor without him.

'Are you sure?'

Dad nodded. 'It hurts like hell, but I'll be OK.'

I paced down the hallway to the kitchen and opened up the drawer next to the sink. Taking out a clean cotton tea towel, I went back to my father. 'We can't go anywhere until I've done some basic first aid on you.' Even though I was keen to get to my wife and son as soon as possible, I wasn't prepared to risk Dad getting an infection from the dirty wound. It needed urgent medical attention.

I tied a tea towel tourniquet around my father's thigh. Taking hold of Dad's arm to support him, I led him into the sitting room. His mobility had been affected, and he was hopping along like a three-legged dog. 'Do you think you can sit down?'

Dad winced and scrunched his eyes closed as he lowered himself onto the sofa.

'You'd better take those off,' I said, pointing towards Dad's jeans. 'I'll get you something to change into.'

I ran up the stairs two at a time and reappeared moments later with a clean pair of jeans and a first aid kit that I'd grabbed from the bathroom cupboard.

Applying direct pressure with a piece of gauze to the wound, I lifted Dad's leg up onto the armrest of the sofa to elevate it and help stop the bleeding. Dad gritted his teeth and drew a sharp intake of breath. He was barely able to tolerate the pain.

'I'm sorry. I know it hurts.'

'Just do what you have to do.' Dad forced out the words; he was writhing in agony.

After a couple of moments, I was able to take the gauze off and clean up the wound. Using the largest dressing in the first aid kit, I placed it over the open flesh. It wasn't a scene for the squeamish, and I had to stop myself from freaking out while I treated him. Just when I thought I'd won the battle, blood began to show through the self-adhesive fabric dressing, so I placed several more on top. That seemed to do the trick.

I grabbed my keys and helped my dad get into the Jeep. Jumping into the driver's seat, I sped off in the direction of Darkwood Manor. There wasn't much on the road at this time in the morning, and we soon arrived outside the wrought-iron gates of Jethro's mansion. Before I even got out of the car, the gates started to open. The Watsons had been expecting us. Gravel sprayed from the tyres as I drove towards the house. Jethro was standing on the steps, with his hands in the pockets of his bespoke suit, waiting for us.

'That's a relief,' Jethro said as I got out the car and went around to the passenger's door to help my dad. 'I'm glad to see you're both in one piece after your run-in with Alfie and Knuckles.'

'Your concern is touching,' Dad replied as he inched his way out of the passenger seat.

A smile lit up Jethro's face. 'I think you've misunderstood what I meant. I'm not concerned that you're injured. I'm glad you survived the bullet because I haven't finished making you suffer yet.' Jethro looked down his nose as he spoke.

25

Gemma

'It's time we had a little chat, Gemma,' Alfie said as he strode around the huge conservatory that spanned the width of the house.

Alfie gestured over to where Knuckles stood filling the doorway, so the huge man stepped outside and closed the glass door behind him.

'What do you want to talk about?'

I looked over Alfie's shoulder and took in the view of the floodlit landscaped grounds. Darkwood Manor was the kind of house people dreamed about visiting. But every time I came to the remote location, with its impenetrable security system, it scared me to death. I didn't feel like a guest, I felt like I was a prisoner, being held against my will. I was sure Alfie would be delighted if he knew how unsettled the surroundings made me.

Instilling fear in others was Alfie's favourite pastime. He'd earned his position as an underworld boss using a combination of violence, intimidation and control, and would stop at nothing to get what he wanted. I'd read about the brutality used by the men in these organisations. It was incomprehensible. Torturing people was a regular occurrence. They thought nothing of threatening to pull out a person's fingernails as a way of extracting information from them, and if they weren't satisfied with the answers to their questions, they'd get one of their heavies to carry out the threat. I looked down at my hands as they lay in my lap, wondering if I was going to suffer the same fate.

'Are you surprised the police let me go?' Alfie smiled, but the usual twinkle in his blue eyes was missing.

Surprised didn't begin to explain how I'd felt. I wasn't going to tell Alfie I couldn't believe my eyes when I'd seen him in the bar, sipping on a Jack Daniel's. It was fair to say I was gobsmacked, and my world had come crashing down around me. I locked eyes with Alfie. I was more than curious to know why he was free, but I was never going to ask him what happened. I knew him better than that. If he realised I was interested, he'd never tell me about the circumstances that saw him walk away from the charges against him. Although the police had arrested Alfie and his team, for some reason, they mustn't have been able to make the convictions stick. In the blink of an eye, I'd lost faith in the law and the justice system.

The Watsons must have more than just corrupt detectives on the payroll if Alfie had evaded prison. How anyone could walk away after masterminding the heist at the Antwerp Diamond Centre, where one hundred million dollars was taken from safety deposit boxes, was beyond me. Let alone everything else the police had on him. They had discovered thirty fake passports belonging to Alfie and his men hidden inside the safe when they searched the burning wreckage of the *Lady Nora*. Then further inspection of the craft revealed hundreds of packages of cocaine stashed inside two holding tanks. The drugs had an estimated street value of fifty thousand pounds a kilo. Interpol had been trying to infiltrate the international drug-smuggling ring he was involved in for years. He was also wanted in connection with money laundering, arms sales and the trafficking of stolen vehicles amongst other criminal activities.

The charges went on and on. Alfie should have been locked up for life, and yet here he was, larger than life, standing in the room opposite me. I knew full well if Nathan and I had been arrested, we wouldn't have been released without charge. Alfie would have sacrificed us to save his own skin.

'Are you sure you don't want to know how I got away with it?'

My curiosity finally got the better of me. 'I can't even begin to imagine how you didn't get sent down. You must have had some legal team!'

Alfie smirked. 'It wasn't as easy as you'd think. The French police were refusing to extradite us to Britain, so it was touch and go for a while. They took some convincing, but once we got them onside, everything started to fall into place.'

Having a reputation like The Godfather clearly carried a lot of weight. As I tried to get my head around the injustice of it all, I felt my lips break into an involuntary smile. Anytime I was uncomfortable, I suffered from the ever-present threat of inappropriate laughter, but now definitely wasn't the right time to lose control. Thankfully, Alfie was too wrapped up in his story to notice.

'I didn't get off that lightly. The case against us should have collapsed before it made it to court, but the bastards made me stand trial.'

Alfie seemed outraged by that. Anyone would think he was an innocent man.

'Knuckles and myself were acquitted, but the rest of the team are doing time until we win their appeal.'

Alfie rarely ventured out without his entourage of henchmen. Even though the sheer size of Knuckles was intimidating, he wouldn't normally work alone. I'd been wondering what had become of Frankie, Tommy, and Johno – the other members of Alfie's team – now I understood.

I raised an eyebrow. Alfie was so sure of himself. 'How do you know you'll win the appeal?' I couldn't hide the sarcastic tone in my voice.

'Our legal team will see to it. Besides that, we've got the judge onside this time.'

I glanced up at Alfie as he finished talking. He had my full attention now, but the intensity of his gaze was unnerving. 'They had so much evidence against you.' I shook my head. I probably shouldn't have said that, but the words tumbled out of my mouth before I could stop them.

'They did, didn't they?' Alfie threw his head back and laughed. 'No wonder the press found it so unexpected when the judge released myself and Knuckles due to lack of evidence. It took years for the police to arrest us, but it only took a few hours for a jury to declare us not guilty on all counts. Unfortunately, the rest of the guys weren't so lucky. But that's the trade-off. Somebody has to go down for the offences.'

All of this was beginning to make sense. Nathan and I

should have realised that Alfie would never be locked up because there would always be a loyal employee who would be willing to do time for him.

'It's not so bad. I make sure my guys are well compensated for their trouble. They receive all the benefits going while being detained in prison, thanks to the prison officers we have on the payroll.' His face showed a flicker of a smile as he stared into my eyes.

No wonder Alfie was never worried about being arrested. I remember him telling me, that he got away far more than he got caught. I'd just been given an insight into how things work in the power-rich criminal underworld. Was there nothing that money couldn't buy?

Alfie must have had some legal team to be able to persuade the judge to drop the charges against him. No matter how much I thought about it, I couldn't get my head around it. Alfie explained that it was a simple process. His highly skilled defence team somehow managed to convince the jury that the evidence the police had on Alfie and Knuckles was inconclusive. With their involvement in the crimes in question, they were found not guilty and released from custody. It didn't bear thinking about and made me wonder how many other serious offenders were roaming the streets.

'We very rarely get arrested, let alone have to stand trial.' Alfie laughed. 'Somebody seriously ballsed up this time.'

It was one thing for the authorities to accuse Alfie of something, but it was a different matter entirely trying to prove it. Nathan and I should have realised he paid off the police to ensure he stayed untouchable. But Alfie's way of life was all new to us. We had no idea how things worked in the underworld.

It made me feel ill to think high-ranking officers would be happy to turn a blind eye to his criminal activities and go against their professional ethics, in return for money. That was bad enough, but I hadn't realised they'd have the whole legal system, including jurors, lawyers and judges accepting bribes. The level of corruption was mind-blowing. Was there anyone out there with enough morals not to end up on the Watsons' payroll?

'Anyway enough about that. Let's get down to the real reason I invited you here today,' Alfie said before he swaggered across to where I sat perched on the edge of the cream sofa. 'Like I said the other day, you have something that belongs to me, and now it's time to give it back.'

26

Alfie

The doctor removed the temporary dressing before he examined Gareth's thigh. 'You've had a lucky escape. The femoral artery isn't damaged, and you've walked away from the experience relatively unscathed with essentially a surface wound. But there is still a chance you could get an infection. If that happens, you will need to get medical attention. Mr Watson can contact me to arrange this.'

'If you put guns in the hands of crazy people, things like this are bound to happen,' Gareth said once the doctor had left the room.

Fury flashed across Dad's face, and to my surprise, he jumped to my defence, even though he'd told me in no uncertain terms earlier, that he thought my behaviour was reckless.

'Don't you dare say that about my son.'

'It's true. He's a nutcase.' Gareth clenched his jaw while he glared at Jethro.

'Alfie only intended to scare you.'

Dad brushed off the comment, but Gareth wasn't prepared to let the matter go.

'He could have killed me. What did I do to deserve that?'

'I wish I could forget Levi as easily as you have.'

Colour rushed to Gareth's face and his fingers balled into a fist. I thought he was going to punch my old man and I was ready to spring into action. He deserved to get a serious kicking after what he'd said about me. But somehow the cheeky fucker managed to hold his hand down by his side and suppress the desire to lash out.

'Levi and I were good friends. I had nothing to do with your brother's death. How many times do I have to tell you that?'

Gareth turned his steely blue eyes on to my dad, and the two men stared at each other. The tension from their long-running feud filled the air around us.

'So you keep saying,' Dad replied. 'But no matter how many times you deny it, I still don't believe you. I was only eighteen when my brother was killed and if it takes me the rest of my life to get even with the person responsible, then so be it.'

Dad rarely spoke about his older brother. He'd been traumatised by my uncle's untimely death. He'd told me the only way he could deal with the pain was to block out the memory. But I could see being face to face with his old enemy had made his desire for revenge build inside him once again.

'Is that a threat?' Gareth asked, squaring up to my dad.

'No, it's a promise.'

'Did you take Gemma and Luca to get back at me?' Gareth's words were met with stony silence. He shook his head and let out a long breath. 'We've been over this a thousand times before and I've never once changed my story.' When Gareth spoke frustration crept into his tone of voice. 'If I was lying, you would have tripped me up by now.'

Nathan tilted his head to the side. The bitter feud between the Stones and the Watsons had raged on for decades and had many layers. It was obvious he was curious to know the background. But he was being kept in the dark. Only hearing half the story was so frustrating and would be pure agony for him. The thought of that made my day. I'd take any opportunity to make Nathan suffer.

27

Nathan

People always said that Gemma and I had a unique connection. You could almost feel the chemistry between us when we made eye contact with each other from across the room. We had been childhood sweethearts and shared something more profound than love. Gemma understood me on so many levels. We put our relationship first and were each other's top priority. We brought out the best in each other. Gemma and I had an 'us against the world' attitude.

I knew right from the start of our relationship that Gemma was a keeper. She was amazing. I always tried to make sure she knew how much she meant to me. Even more so since we'd almost split up. I never thought that would happen to us. I learnt a valuable lesson from the experience. It taught me never to take my wife for granted.

I never thought Gemma would battle depression and anxiety. She was usually the strong one in our partnership, and even though I was doing my best to support her, she kept shutting herself away. That was only making things worse. Anyone who had been on the receiving end of the silent treatment, especially when you had to try and guess what you'd done wrong, would sympathise with the way I was feeling. I could only presume that Gemma was pissed off with me for insisting we come back to England because she was refusing to enlighten me.

This form of emotional manipulation was incredibly effective. I hated it. It left me racked with guilt, and the longer it went on, the harder it was to deal with. I was at my wits' end. No matter how much I tried, I couldn't seem to get through to her. She'd withdrawn into her own world.

Gemma was keen for Mum and I to reconcile. She'd been increasingly vocal about it since we'd arrived in England and had been chipping away at my reluctance to make peace. But even if I wanted to, I wasn't sure how to go about healing our frosty relationship after all this time. Then again, if putting an end to our argument would make my wife happy, maybe I should consider being the bigger person and open up the lines of communication to try to work things out. Desperate times called for desperate measures. Even though my stubborn side was reluctant to admit it, I could see where Gemma was coming from. It didn't seem right that Mum was being excluded from Luca's life, but it was hard to make the first move.

If I did call my mum, I'd need to choose my words carefully. There was no point in me phoning her if I still had both barrels loaded. It wasn't only about what I said, how I said it mattered too. I'd have to let go of all the pent-up anger I'd been holding on to. As we wouldn't be face to face, I didn't want my voice to come across in a rage-filled tone. That would do nothing to help the situation.

I paced backwards and forwards in the living room, trying to pluck up the courage to make the call. I knew it was the right thing to do. It was long overdue, but the stubborn voice in my head kept trying to talk me out of it. I couldn't put it off any longer. I had to do this for Gemma. It was time to let go of my resentment.

'Mum, it's me.'

'Nathan, how lovely to hear from you.'

I could tell Mum was surprised that I'd called her out of the blue and the emotion in her voice began tugging at my heartstrings.

'I can't tell you how happy you've made me.'

A sob escaped from Mum's lips. Hearing the sadness in her voice was a wake-up call and a real turning point for me. I knew it was time to start building bridges. She had done her best to bring me up on her own and had always given me everything she could. I wanted her to be part of my life again.

'I'd love to see you. Can I take you out for lunch?'

I was sitting at the table facing the view of the seafront when my mum walked into Padrino's. The traditional Italian restaurant in Westcliff-on-Sea was close to where she lived, and we'd visited it many times before, so I knew she'd be happy with my choice.

I pushed back my chair when she approached the table and stood up. She was dressed in a black knee-length coat and looked effortlessly elegant with her dark hair swept into a low bun. I stooped to kiss her on both cheeks and couldn't help noticing that she was trembling.

Mum sat down opposite me. 'You're looking well. How have you been?'

'I'm good, thanks. You're looking well too.'

At first, our conversation was a bit stilted but that was hardly surprising. We spent a while making small talk and stuck to safe topics like the weather and the food on the menu. I wasn't sure whether to bring up our argument or brush it under the carpet and pretend it had never happened. It was a difficult call. The last thing I wanted to do was kick off the hostility again.

'I've missed you, Nathan,' Mum blurted out before she reached over the table and took hold of my hand.

'I've missed you too, Mum.'

'We always used to be so close. I never wanted to fall out with you.' Tears glistened in my mum's dark eyes.

'I know. It's been a horrible time for all of us.'

It felt good to be able to open up to Mum after all this time, and I was glad I'd made contact with her now.

'I shouldn't have lied to you about your father. It was wrong of me to tell you he'd left us to set up home with another woman. I should have told you he'd been sent to prison. But I didn't know what to do for the best. I only kept it from you to protect you from getting hurt.'

Even though I didn't agree with what she'd done, I knew deep down she'd had my best interests at heart.

'If only I'd told you the truth as soon as you were old enough to understand, we wouldn't have fallen out over it.' Mum covered her lips with shaking fingers. Her words were filled with regret. 'I'm so sorry. I hope one day you'll be able to forgive me.'

Mum couldn't hold back her tears any longer. I could see

she was devastated that she'd upset me and her suffering was difficult to watch.

'Please don't cry. It's time we put this behind us and moved on with our lives. I don't want us to be on bad terms any more.'

Mum looked up at me and dabbed her eyes with a tissue. 'Oh, Nathan, you don't know how happy that would make me.'

I shed a silent tear and wiped it away with the back of my hand before smiling at her.

When we'd finished our meal, Mum and I stood outside the restaurant locked in a wordless embrace. As I held her tiny frame close to mine, all the unexpressed hurt and anger seemed to seep out of me. We hugged for the longest time before we reluctantly said goodbye.

I wasn't sure how Dad would feel about seeing his ex-wife again after all these years, but there was only one way to find out.

'I'm worried about Gemma. The more I try to talk to her, the more she pushes me away. Would you mind if I asked Mum over sometime? She might be able to help. They've always been very close.'

'Of course not,' Dad replied without any hesitation.

Now that Mum and I were on speaking terms again, I wanted to see as much of her as possible, to make up for lost time.

'Can you come over to Dad's house tomorrow?'

At first, my question was met with silence. Mum was reluctant to accept the invitation. She'd divorced my dad while he was serving his prison sentence, and she hadn't seen him since. Even though she was putting up a protest, I knew Mum would change her mind if I told her that Gemma needed her help. When I explained that Gemma could do with some motherly advice, Mum eventually agreed. Gemma was the daughter she'd never had, so she would do anything for her. They adored each other.

Dad opened the front door. 'Rosa, you're looking well. Please come in,' he said, breaking the wall of silence that had existed between them for over thirty years.

Mum was well dressed as always, and her dark hair was swept into a loose bun. Her petite, curvy frame stepped over the threshold and into the hall. She looked up at Dad as he towered over her and took in his features before she spoke. 'I see you've grown a beard,' she replied.

Dad smiled and the skin at the corners of his steely blue eyes crinkled. He ran his fingers along the greying hair that covered his jawline. 'Do you like it?'

Mum's face puckered, and she refrained from answering.

'I'll take that as a no then, shall I?' Dad laughed.

A smile spread across my face, and I felt my shoulders drop in relief. My parents were being civil to each other. Would wonders never cease? This was going better than I'd expected, and hopefully, Mum's visit would bring Gemma out of the dark place she was currently visiting.

'Hello, Nathan,' Mum said, changing the subject. Her eyes lit up at the sight of me. When she got close enough, she reached up and kissed me on each of my cheeks in turn.

'It's good to see you,' I replied. I threw my arms around my mum and hugged her tightly.

'Where's my favourite grandson, then?'

I led Mum into the living room where Gemma was feeding Luca. I hadn't told my wife I'd arranged for my mum to visit. I wanted it to be a surprise.

'Hello, Gemma,' Mum said. 'I hope you don't mind me dropping in to see you. I was just passing.'

I'm sure Gemma knew that wasn't true, but she didn't seem to care. She looked happy to see her mother-in-law. Mum took a seat next to her and stroked Luca's head before planting kisses on both of Gemma's cheeks.

'I'll go and make some coffee,' I said. I'd have to make myself scarce to allow Gemma to open up.

Mum patted Gemma's hand. 'So how have you been getting on?' she asked as I closed the door behind me.

I stood in the hallway, leaning against the wooden panel. I knew I shouldn't be eavesdropping on their conversation, but I was desperate to hear what Gemma was going to say.

Gemma let out a huge sigh. 'Not so good. I always knew that I worried more than most people, but I've turned into a neurotic overprotective mother. I know I'm doing it, but I can't seem to help myself.'

'That's a natural reaction. It's a mother's role to worry about her child,' Mum said, doing her best to reassure Gemma. 'As doting parents, sometimes we over-dote. We're all guilty of that from time to time. When Nathan was little, he had me wrapped around his finger. In fact, he still does.'

★

'Let me walk you to the station,' I said when Mum was about to leave.

She linked my arm when we stepped onto the pavement, and a smile spread across my face when she looked up at me.

'Thanks for inviting me over.'

'You're welcome. I'm so glad I'm managed to persuade you to come.'

Mum cast her eyes to the floor. 'I wasn't trying to be difficult, but I was worried about having to face Gareth after all this time.'

'I'm sure you were, but it was fine, wasn't it?'

Mum nodded. 'Nobody else, apart from you, would have been able to talk me into this.' Mum patted my arm.

My mum had made a huge sacrifice by coming here today. I knew it had been difficult for her, but she'd made the effort because she was trying to put things right between us.

28

Gemma

Rosa hadn't been honest with me when she'd said she was just passing Gareth's house today. It wasn't really a big deal; it was a little white lie. But it was a lie all the same. I knew damn well that wild horses wouldn't have dragged her here unless Nathan had intervened.

Don't get me wrong, nobody was more delighted than I was that Nathan and Rosa were back on speaking terms. You could have knocked me down with a feather when my husband told me he'd taken his mum out to lunch. By all accounts, their reunion had been an emotional one and having spent hours talking things through they'd put their argument behind them.

I was sure Nathan had reached out to his mum because he knew I was finding it difficult to juggle the demands of a small baby. Although I was certain his intentions were good, he'd just made me feel like a failure.

Nathan was fantastic with Luca. He had been a hands-on dad since day one. But we weren't living in the Dark

Ages, so why shouldn't my husband change the odd nappy? I found it difficult to accept that everybody thought Nathan was amazing for taking an active role in Luca's life. Whereas it was expected of me, and I wasn't a natural. I knew I was underperforming. Presumably, that's why Nathan had felt the need to round up the cavalry behind my back. But, instead of making things better, he'd made me see red. The more I thought about it, the angrier I was becoming.

Because Rosa had skirted around the truth when she came to see me earlier, I'd responded by immediately putting my guard up. I wasn't stupid and could see right through their plan. Although Nathan had enlisted Rosa to help me, he'd made matters worse and undermined my confidence. I felt embarrassed that I was struggling to do something that should have come naturally to me. So when my mother-in-law asked me how I was getting on, I wasn't going to tell her the real reason I was on edge. I followed her example and told her a lie.

29

The following afternoon we were treated to an unexpected visit from Alfie.

'We're a bit short-staffed at the moment, as Tommy, Johno and Frankie are being detained by Her Majesty and we could do with an extra pair of hands,' Alfie said, relaxing back on the sofa in Gareth's living room. 'I want you to assist Knuckles with a spot of debt collecting, Nathan, in lieu of what you owe me.'

'Thanks for the offer, but if it's all the same to you, I'd rather not.' Nathan began biting his nails.

Alfie smirked, then threw his head back and laughed. 'You're hilarious, Nathan. You crack me up.'

'I wasn't joking,' Nathan replied with a deadpan expression on his face.

'You double-crossed me, so now you owe me. Hand over the cash you stole from me if you don't want the baby to come to harm.'

Alfie's words stung as they penetrated my brain.

Threatening my baby was a low blow even for a depraved gangster like him. This situation had nothing to do with Luca. Nathan and I had taken his money. I shook my head in an attempt to banish the thought, but it kept floating around in my mind.

'I don't think you're in any position to refuse, do you?'

'I'll pay you back, but I'm not working for you again.'

'I don't like repeating myself, but perhaps I didn't make myself clear: once you join the firm, you're in it for life. I can't let you go because then I'd have to trust you to keep our secrets.'

'You know they're safe with me.'

Alfie watched myself and Nathan exchange glances. It went without saying if the police asked questions, becoming deaf, blind and mute was the only option. If you wanted to see another birthday, it wasn't a good idea to snitch on a gangster.

I felt my blood run cold, and my heartbeat quickened. Alfie's words hit me like a steam train. I could feel them ringing in my ears. As Nathan and I stared at each other, a muscle twitched in my husband's jaw. We'd used some of Alfie's money to pay for our dream apartment, so we weren't in a position to say no to his demands. Nathan didn't want to work for Alfie, but until we paid back what we owed, he didn't have a choice. Alfie had taken hold of our lives and was about to shred them to pieces while we stood by and watched helplessly.

Nathan's shoulders drooped as he accepted his fate. We were trapped, and Alfie was about to exploit the situation. There was no way out for the foreseeable future, and so the cycle continued.

'You can play the role of the mediator. You haven't got the presence to be an enforcer,' Alfie said to belittle Nathan.

Realising my self-control was a limited resource, I clamped my mouth shut. I decided to stay silent and not tell him exactly what I thought of him. That was better left unsaid. But my throat felt like it was on fire as I struggled to keep the tirade within. I decided to direct a bitter glare at Alfie instead of giving him a piece of my mind.

'Is something the matter? You've got a face like a slapped arse, Gemma.' Alfie smiled.

Fury began to bubble up inside me, but I knew it wouldn't be wise to unleash it on Alfie, even though I was seriously tempted to. The way Alfie stood staring at me made me nervous. He was waiting for me to speak, but I couldn't trust myself not to say the wrong thing. His blue eyes scanned over every inch of me with such intensity; I felt my pulse quicken in response. He was studying me like a spider watching a fly.

'So that's sorted then, Knuckles will pick you up at midnight tomorrow, Nathan. This isn't a nine-to-five job.' Alfie got to his feet and sauntered out of Gareth's house.

30

Gemma

How could I stop Alfie from hurting my child when my confidence had disappeared almost overnight? Every time I looked in the mirror, I saw a failure staring back at me, instead of the strong woman I once was. I had to shed the insecurities that were weighing me down before they took over my life. Deep down, I knew I was stronger than I thought I was, I'd proved that to myself before. But Alfie's threat had caused crippling fear to spread rapidly inside me like a cancer. Perhaps if I channelled that fear, it would give me the push I needed to find my strength again.

Luca was a helpless baby, so keeping him safe was bound to be my main priority. I was a protective lioness, so it went without saying that I would shield my son from anything harmful. What sort of mother would I be if I couldn't do that?

Alfie liked to play games. It suddenly occurred to me that his remark was intended to torment me. But I couldn't afford to let him get inside my head and overpower me. If he took control of my mind, the battle between us would be over. I mustn't show any vulnerable emotions, or Alfie would feed off of my weakness.

Alfie had used our child as leverage to ensure that Nathan and I followed his orders. He knew we wouldn't put Luca in danger. It disgusted me that he was prepared to stoop so low to get what he wanted.

You would have thought trafficking drugs and extorting money from innocent people would become tiresome after a while. It wasn't as if the Watsons needed the income to live on. They were running a business empire that had been passed down from generation to generation. It hadn't just appeared out of thin air; they'd built it up over the years. The Watsons had worked hard to achieve their position, gobbling up their competition and everything in their path.

In Alfie's line of work, you had to earn your status. You didn't become a respected underworld boss by chance. The role required one hundred per cent commitment. If Alfie's dominance was ever called into question, he would be happy to beat the shit out of his rivals to reinforce his power over them. It was a ruthless world. I wished Luca didn't have to be a part of any of this. If I could, I'd wrap him in cotton wool and let him grow up in a bubble away from the danger.

31

Gemma

Dressed in Gareth's only suit, the one he wore for weddings and funerals, Nathan paced up and down the living room, glancing up at the clock every ten seconds or so. He was clearly agitated while he waited for Knuckles to arrive. Hearing a car pull up outside at midnight, he walked over to the window that looked out onto the street. Knuckles was just about to get out of the driver's door.

'I'd better go,' Nathan said, without making eye contact with me. He straightened his tie and dusted something invisible off the front of the black jacket before walking out of the door.

That was the first thing Nathan had said to me all day. He'd stayed out of my way because he hadn't wanted to discuss the situation we were in again. I wanted to run after my husband and beg him not to go, but the atmosphere between us was frosty and awkward, and I was experiencing the sensation of a huge weight pushing down on my chest. It had me pinned to the spot, and I felt like I couldn't move.

I was incredibly concerned for my husband's safety. I didn't want Nathan to work for Alfie; it was too dangerous. The problem was, we didn't have another choice, so I had to let him go.

When the front door closed, tears welled up in my eyes, but they were a useless by-product. They couldn't change the situation. It frustrated me that the slightest thing seemed to set me off at the moment. No doubt that was a result of my fluctuating hormones. My emotions were all over the place, rising and crashing like ocean waves.

When we'd made the decision to take Alfie's cash out of the safe before we left the burning yacht, we thought we had planned our escape carefully. We were only going to have one chance to pull it off, so we couldn't afford for anything to go wrong. Although at the time I'd felt uncertain, I focused on something Alfie had told me to give me the strength to see it through. You should never expect to get caught. Otherwise, you lined yourself up to fail.

With that thought firmly planted in my head, Nathan and I disappeared into the night. We never expected to see Alfie again. We were going to do our best to stay under the radar and use his money to finance a new life for ourselves. We deserved it after what he'd put us through. But sometimes even the best-laid plans end up failing.

I genuinely thought we'd left the dramas of our time with Alfie behind us after we settled in the Costa del Sol. In hindsight, I should have known better. If Nathan and I hadn't trusted Alfie to keep his side of the bargain, we could have given him back the money, and we wouldn't be in this position now.

My mind was in turmoil. I'd been taking my frustration

out on my husband, and that wasn't fair. Since we'd become parents, I'd discovered Nathan had vast resources of patience I never knew he had. He had been incredible with Luca and a tower of strength to me. If something happened to him tonight, I'd never forgive myself for being such a bitch to him. I wished we'd made peace before he'd left. But I'd been out of sorts all day. There was an undercurrent of trouble in the air. Something didn't feel right, but I couldn't put my finger on it.

As I sat on my own in the living room, mulling things over, I bitterly regretted not trying to stop him now. I loved my husband more than anything.

32

Nathan

An enormous wave of guilt washed over me and smothered me. I felt like I was drowning and had to stop myself from gasping for breath as I stood in the bedroom of the unfortunate man who owed Alfie money. The man couldn't disguise the look of terror on his face when he opened his eyes and saw the outlines of Knuckles and myself in the doorway. At this stage, all the man knew was that he had uninvited guests, but he was about to find out why.

Knuckles and I stood side by side in the shadows, as he rhythmically swung a baseball bat backwards and forwards, catching it in his huge hand. The whooshing sound the metal made as it glided through the air penetrated the tense silence.

'Mr Watson has sent us here so that you understand what will happen to you if you try to take the piss out of him. This is a taste of what's to come if you're late with the repayment again.'

I delivered the ultimatum as I'd been instructed to, and as I did, the man sat up and backed himself into the headboard. Wide-eyed with terror, the colour drained from his face and perspiration broke out on his forehead. As the threat registered, his Adam's apple went into overdrive.

Alfie always carried out business of this nature in the early hours of the morning, knowing his victim would find being woken in the night by the presence of intruders terrifying and that the intimidation would work twice as well. It was Alfie's calling card. I remembered it only too well. A vision of Knuckles swinging the very same baseball bat at the end of Gemma's and my bed brought an unpleasant memory flooding back into my mind. I could relate to this situation only too well, and that made me feel uneasy. I had been in this man's shoes not so long ago. Now I had become Alfie's messenger boy, and one of the people sent to collect his debt. The thought of that left a bad taste in my mouth.

Under normal circumstances, intimidation would be enough to drive the message home, without us having to resort to violence. But Alfie had decided the man had taken liberties and needed to be taught a lesson, so this wasn't going to be a verbal warning. Knuckles approached the bed and pulled back the covers. The naked man instinctively curled himself into a ball on the mattress. Crippled by fear, he lay motionless waiting for the punishment he knew was coming his way.

Dragging him to his feet, Alfie's henchman squared up to his prey. Knuckles towered over the middle-aged pot-bellied man, who quivered like a human jelly as his toes sank into the beige shag pile carpet. Knuckles began swinging the bat backwards and forwards again, catching it in his hand.

He was going to take his time to dole out the beating, to intensify the man's panic. The victim's naked state stripped him of any dignity he might have had while he waited for Knuckles to deliver his fate.

The man begged for mercy after Knuckles struck him with the bat. I felt myself flinch. It would be a long time before I'd forget the sound of his ribs cracking when the metal made contact with his skin. Knuckles ignored the man's pleas and delivered a series of brutal blows, repeatedly hitting him across his back. My blood ran cold as I watched Knuckles beat the poor man into a pulp. There was nothing I could do to help him. If I didn't do exactly what Alfie instructed, I would be the next in line.

Unable to take any more, the man fell to his knees and began weeping like a baby. Then, fearing for his life, he lost control of his bladder. I heard his pee hit the carpet before the undeniable scent of urine wafted into the air.

Knowing that he'd made the man incontinent with fright put a smile on Knuckles' face. 'That's the sound that strikes fear into the heart of every dog owner. Go and clean yourself up, you disgusting piece of shit,' he said, before we retreated from the room.

33

Gemma

Nathan and I had become ships that passed in the night due to the unsociable hours he was working. Alfie was exploiting Nathan's role as general dogsbody to the maximum. We'd hardly clapped eyes on each other in days.

Nathan seemed to be taking the demands of his new role in his stride, but I was struggling with it. I didn't know if it was the stress of the situation, or the lack of sleep that went hand in hand with having a baby that was to blame for the way I felt. Either way, every time Nathan went out on a job with Knuckles, I wondered if that would be the last time I'd see him. It was a dangerous line of work, so there was more than a chance he'd end up six feet under. Despair took on a battle with anger inside my head and left my mental state teetering on the edge. I was in danger of losing the plot if I didn't get a grip.

Nathan was officially nocturnal and slept for much of the day. Alfie was taking advantage of that and kept turning up at Gareth's house unannounced. To help Luca and I pass the time, while my husband was resting, he'd insist on taking us out.

'If Nathan worked regular hours, we wouldn't need to tiptoe around the house all day,' I said, unable to keep my thoughts to myself as I pushed Luca's pram around the deserted park.

Alfie smiled. 'You've just given me a good idea, Gemma. I could always offer Nathan a job at our casino. That's open during the day.'

Up until that moment, I hadn't realised the Watsons owned a casino. Panic coursed through my veins. Even though working in the casino wouldn't have been nearly as dangerous as some of the things Nathan had been doing, it would be a disaster. Nathan had a gambling addiction that he struggled to keep under control, so the temptation would be too great for him. It would be like giving an alcoholic a job in a pub. I hoped Alfie wouldn't carry out his threat and exploit Nathan's vulnerability. Even if he didn't already have a gambling problem, it would be easy to develop one if you worked in that environment.

The look on my face must have said it all. Alfie knew he'd got under my skin. I didn't know how to respond without making matters worse, so I decided to say nothing.

'Maybe I'll give him a trial on the blackjack tables. He knows the rules of the game, so becoming a dealer would be a piece of piss for him.'

Alfie had pushed me too far. I stopped walking and stared at him for a moment. Before I could stop myself, the palm of my hand raised. The sound of my slap echoed through the air. I watched Alfie's reaction. He flinched when my hand made contact with his skin. I'd left a red, throbbing mark on his cheek. The look of anger in his glare spoke volumes. I had succeeded in momentarily wiping the smug smile off his face, but at what cost? What the hell was I thinking of?

'You shouldn't have done that, Gemma.' Alfie glared at me with poorly disguised fury in his eyes. 'You have a real anger management issue. You've got to overcome the impulse to lash out, or that temper of yours is going to land you in trouble. I've got a good mind to press charges against you.' Alfie smiled, but the twinkle in his blue eyes was missing.

My heart pounded against my ribcage as I tried to calm myself down. Why had I let Alfie get to me? No matter how tough the situation was, and no matter how much he was trying to wind me up, I shouldn't have let Alfie realise how much he was affecting me.

Even though I didn't want to, I knew I had to say sorry. But when I went to speak, my brain didn't want to co-operate, and nothing came out of my mouth. Finally, between gritted teeth, I forced myself to apologise and begged Alfie not to give Nathan a job at the casino. I didn't want him to abuse the situation because I knew the temptation would be too much for Nathan. When I finally managed to get my words out, they left a bitter taste behind.

'I like watching you grovel; being subservient suits you. You should try it more often.' Alfie winked. 'If I agree to your request, how are you going to repay the favour?' Alfie flashed me a smile that left me in no doubt what he was implying. The way he scanned every inch of my body with his piercing blue eyes made me uneasy.

I was skilled at picking up his not so subtle hints by now, so he didn't need to undress me with his eyes. Tempting as it was to give him a piece of my mind, I knew that would be a stupid thing to do. I'd have to tread carefully. I couldn't afford to bruise his ego at this stage. I needed to make sure I didn't forget my manners.

Alfie was an expert at coercing an unwilling person into doing what he wanted when he wanted. Playing mind games was one of his favourite pastimes, so if I was going to compete with him, I'd need to learn everything there was to know about manipulation. Alfie was a master of exercising dominance and control, and in my present emotionally wrecked state, I was no match for him. My strength had deserted me when I needed it most, but Alfie didn't need to know that. He'd prey on my weakness if he had the slightest idea.

'How's your sex life these days?' Alfie asked out of the blue.

His question startled me. 'I don't think that's any of your business.' I tried to get the words out as fast as possible before my nervousness gave me away. I could feel heat spreading across my face.

'I can tell by the way you replied that it's non-existent.' Alfie laughed. 'I thought as much.'

I attempted to stare him down, but the intensity of his eyes made me feel too uncomfortable, so I decided to look away. I was too flustered to put him in his place.

34

Gemma

On the journey home, I could feel an argument brewing. Nathan had been given a rare day off, so the whole family had taken a trip to Asda of all places. The fact that we hadn't gone on a day out somewhere had got my back up to start with, and then I'd had to listen to my husband prattling on to his dad about anything and everything. I knew they had a lot of catching up to do, but trying to summarise the events of the last thirty-plus years in a couple of hours was impossible. Nathan had barely come up for air since we'd left the house and his verbal diarrhoea was winding me up.

As I sat in the back of the car next to Luca, tension began building up inside me. I could feel my blood pressure rising by the minute. The closer we got to Crofts Way, the more agitated I was becoming. Once we were back at Gareth's place, I decided to leave Nathan and his dad to it. Maybe if I had some space, I might be able to calm down a bit.

'I'm going to put Luca to bed,' I said, making an excuse to take myself off.

About ten minutes later, I heard footsteps climbing the stairs, and I let out an audible sigh. It was bound to be Nathan. He'd never been good at reading signs. Even when I spelt it out to him and told him I needed some me time, he couldn't seem to help himself; he wouldn't leave me on my own for more than a couple of minutes. Just because we were married, it didn't mean we needed to be constantly glued to each other's side. I had always been a very independent person, and that wasn't about to change any time soon.

I suppose it was my own fault for not being direct enough, but you would have thought he would have detected the frosty tone in my voice when I spoke to him in the kitchen. I didn't bother to try and hide the fact that I was pissed off with him. This was Nathan's first day off in ages, and instead of taking our son somewhere nice we'd trawled the aisles in the supermarket. It was a riveting way to spend time. Gareth deserved a gold medal for his enthusiasm as Nathan pointed out all of his favourite things as we passed them on the shelves.

Nathan poked his head around the door, and our eyes met. I felt ready to explode at the sight of him; his presence suddenly made me feel claustrophobic.

'Are you OK?'

I nodded. Considering we'd been together all our adult lives, my husband still couldn't read me. Right now, the fact that I needed some space had gone completely over his head.

'What are you doing?' he asked, leaning against the

doorframe with his hands stuffed in the front pockets of his jeans.

'What does it look like? I'm changing Luca's nappy,' I snapped as I stated the obvious.

'Don't speak to me like that.' Nathan folded his arms across his chest and gave me his well-honed wounded look. The one he'd perfected over the years. He'd taken my barbed comment to heart. 'You've been in a funny mood all day. You're obviously spoiling for a fight. You keep trying to start an argument with me for no reason.'

Leaving my son dozing in the centre of the bed, I stood up and glared at my husband. 'So let me get this straight, you don't think there's a reason why I'm annoyed with you?' I shook my head.

'I can't think of anything off the top of my head.' Nathan shrugged his shoulders then his face lit up as if a light bulb had gone off in his brain. 'Time of the month, is it?' His words had a sarcastic edge to them.

I felt my blood boil. I took a deep breath and tried to control my temper, but it was impossible. 'Don't come out with a stupid comment like that when you can see I'm stressed out of my mind. Go away, Nathan. I came up here so I could be alone. You're suffocating me.'

'What the hell have I done?' Nathan put his hands on his hips and stared at me. Then he began chewing the inside of his bottom lip. 'I can't win, can I? If I didn't come to see if you were all right, you'd accuse me of not caring. But when I check up on you, I get told I'm smothering you.'

We'd been trying to speak in hushed tones, so as not to disturb Gareth or Luca, but it's difficult to argue with somebody and whisper at the same time. The more heated our debate became, the more the volume rose until we were interrupted by knocking on the bedroom door. Nathan walked across the floor and opened it.

'That's enough, you two. This isn't achieving anything,' Gareth said as if Nathan and I were a couple of children fighting over the last scoop of ice cream.

I was mortified. Our escalating voices had made Gareth feel the need to step in to try and prevent an unresolvable standoff developing between us.

'Neither of you are in the right frame of mind to be having this discussion. Why don't you sleep on it, and talk it over in the morning instead?' Gareth said, hoping to nip the pointless argument in the bud.

My father-in-law had done a good job attempting to be the mediator, and now he looked incredibly awkward as he stood in the doorway, caught in the middle, waiting for one of us to respond.

'I'm sorry we disturbed you,' I said, feeling guilty that an innocent person had needed to get involved in our heated interaction.

I was embarrassed that Gareth had to intervene and be the voice of reason. He was trying to be diplomatic and defuse the volatile situation with the skill of a bomb disposal expert. Only a brave man would take on that heroic responsibility.

'It's OK, but do me a favour and let it go for now.' Gareth closed the door behind him.

My father-in-law was right; we needed to let things calm down. If we didn't, we'd run the risk of reigniting the argument. Inside I was still raging, and my emotions were out of control, threatening to erupt at any minute. I wished I could snap out of my bad mood and go back to normality. But it wasn't as simple as that. I was stubborn, and once I'd lost my temper, it would take time for me to let go of my anger.

I lifted Luca off of the bed and placed him in his cot. Thankfully, he'd slept through the whole slanging match. When I turned around, Nathan had stripped down to his boxer shorts. Without making eye contact with me, he pulled back the quilt with a theatrical flourish and disappeared under the covers. He'd burrowed so far down only the tips of his dark brown hair were visible on the pillow. I had to stifle a laugh. He could be so dramatic at times.

I couldn't get tonight's events out of my head, so I waited as long as I could before I got into bed beside my husband, making sure I stayed on my side of the imaginary line that had been drawn down the middle of the mattress. I hated going to bed on an argument, but neither of us wanted to be the one to make the first move and apologise. We weren't at the stage of calling a truce and extending an olive branch yet. That wasn't something either of us was prepared to do. But we were staying in Gareth's house, so for tonight, I was prepared to put our disagreement on hold. I'd have to try and keep a lid on my pent-up anger. It wasn't fair of us to make Gareth feel uncomfortable in his own home.

Nathan lay on his side with his back towards me, pretending to be asleep, but I knew he was as awake as I was. I had a horrible feeling that with Alfie back in our lives, our relationship might begin to fester again. I knew fretting about that wouldn't help the situation, but I was guaranteed to lose sleep over it. It would keep me awake tonight.

At some point, I must have drifted off, but I woke with a start after I experienced a terrifying nightmare. I'd had a flashback to the dangerous world I thought we'd left behind, and now the back of my hair was coated with sweat as it clung to my skin, like seaweed on a rock after the tide goes out.

Fearing for my son's safety, I looked over at the cot. Luca was lying on his back with his arms above his head in a peaceful slumber. I let out a slow breath. It was going to be another long night. In an attempt to calm my troubled mind, I focused on Nathan's steady breathing. I closed my eyes again, but now I was too frightened to go to sleep. The stress was taking its toll on my mental, emotional and physical health. I hated the way Alfie had appeared back in our lives and was dictating the path we had to walk down. I knew we would never be able to clear the debt because Alfie didn't actually want his money back, he just wanted to control us.

35

Gemma

While Nathan was accompanying him on company business, Alfie insisted Luca and I wait for them at Darkwood Manor. I complained bitterly and tried to dig my heels in, but he wouldn't take no for an answer.

'Nora had the most beautiful red hair and blue eyes,' Jethro said with a wistful look on his clean-shaven face. 'She was like a little doll, tiny and petite, with skin like porcelain. Alfie and my girls adored her. She was a fantastic mum.'

I wondered what else Jethro was about to divulge, so I bit down hard on the side of my lip, while I waited for him to continue. Alfie had always maintained that Jethro didn't love his mum. He'd told me Jethro never gave a shit about Nora the whole time they were married because he was in love with Rosa, but that wasn't coming across. He was talking about Nora with such fondness.

The blond-haired, blue-eyed man looked good for his

age. I'd say he must be about sixty but looked considerably younger. He was just starting to go grey. Several silvery strands were visible at his temples and judging by the condition of his skin, he was definitely a man who moisturised.

He'd been given the job of entertaining me while the others were out. I didn't have any complaints so far. Jethro was being a charming host. I was sitting on a high stool in front of the blue pearl breakfast bar while he made us coffee, with the skill of a barista, from a stainless steel machine that wouldn't have looked out of place in Starbucks. I sat mesmerised as he poured coffee beans into the machine and watched as it effortlessly ground them into a fine powder. The aroma was heavenly. Jethro selected the coffee from the touch screen, pressed a button and produced a café-quality drink in a matter of seconds. He handed me the clear glass mug containing a layered latte.

'Thank you,' I said. I was seriously impressed. It was almost too nice to drink.

Jethro smiled when he saw the look on my face.

'Nora was a cracking girl, really,' Jethro continued in his softly spoken tone. 'But unfortunately, we weren't well-suited. She was kind and gentle, but she was weak-willed. That was her downfall. Nobody finds a doormat attractive, do they?' Jethro sighed.

I would have thought the egotistic, self-centred Watson men would have been first in the queue to dominate their partners as they both loved to have complete control over situations. But I was wrong. Jethro and Alfie both liked a strong woman who would stand up to them. I found that surprising really because in the male-dominant world that gangsters inhabit, most of the men still thought they lived in the Dark Ages. They treated their women like possessions.

In a way, I could understand why they would do that. Their partners had been acquired through material means and not because of the things they had in common. These men selected gold-digging trophy wives. The women weren't looking for a genuine romantic connection either. They wanted the best that life could offer them without having to lift a manicured finger, so that suited them down to the ground. In return, the kingpins ensured their wives always felt inferior to them. They were only good for bearing children, satisfying their man's every whim and turning a blind eye to their indiscretions, of which there were many.

I couldn't imagine having a partner like that. Nathan was a modern man and treated me with respect and as an equal, not a slave. Whereas the alpha males of the underworld thought it was acceptable to metaphorically drag their woman around by the hair while beating her with a club, caveman style, if she dared to be disobedient. The sacrifice the suffragettes had made when they chained themselves to railings had been lost on this particular sector of the population.

The sound of Jethro's voice broke my train of thought. 'Nora lacked the qualities I looked for in a partner. She was too predictable, and when something's predictable, it bores me. I love a bit of mystery.'

Jethro and Alfie were like two peas in a pod. Not just in looks, but also in personality.

'There was no doubt in my mind that Nora loved me,

but that didn't stop me resenting her. When she was stupid enough to get herself pregnant, my dad forced me to marry her.'

What a sexist thing to say, I thought. Alfie didn't magically appear in Nora's womb without any intervention from Jethro. He got her pregnant. I was tempted to point that out but stopped myself at the last minute in an act of self-preservation. Although I hadn't witnessed it first-hand, I was pretty certain Jethro had the same explosive temper as Alfie. It probably wasn't the right time to tell him some home truths.

'It's no wonder I resented her. Nora and I weren't exclusive. Well, not as far as I was concerned. I was happily sowing my wild oats.' Jethro smiled, and his blue eyes twinkled at the memory. 'I was a young man and only interested in one thing. I wanted to have sex with as many women as possible, until she tried to clip my wings and trapped me.' The thought of that made his smile fade.

I looked at Jethro with a puzzled expression on my face. Why did he resent Nora so much? She hadn't insisted he married her; his father had.

'Nora might have forced me to put a ring on her finger, but I promised myself the day we got wed, that was the only thing of mine she was going to have. She would never have my heart. Nora knew I was never going to be faithful to her. I made no secret of my extramarital activities.'

As Jethro rambled on, I had to stifle a yawn. Not because I wasn't interested in hearing his life story, but the lack of sleep was catching up with me, and it was so warm in the kitchen I had to battle to keep my eyes open. The Aga was pumping out heat at a furious rate. Even the shot of caffeine I'd had wasn't keeping the tiredness at bay.

Attempting to shake away the drowsiness, I got up from my stool and walked across the marble tiles to where Luca lay sleeping in his carrycot over by the full-length windows, that overlooked the vast gardens. It was all I could do to stop myself pressing my face against the cold windowpane as I pretended to check on my son. I couldn't help wondering why Jethro was telling me all this. Before I even had a chance to sit back down, the details of his married life continued to spill out of his mouth like the final confession of a man on death row.

'Nora had a miserable life with me. I put the poor girl through hell. She drank to escape from her problems. Back then, I was a womaniser. I'm ashamed to admit, I was with one of my whores on the night Nora died. Alfie was only fifteen, and the poor little sod was left to deal with everything because I was out with some slag.' Jethro's eyes glazed over as he talked about his wife's death.

I straightened my posture. Now Jethro had my undivided attention. I couldn't hide the look of surprise on my face. Up until this moment, I hadn't realised Nora was dead. I presumed they were divorced. Alfie hadn't mentioned that his mum had died when he'd told me about his family. I suppose it wasn't the sort of thing you dropped into everyday conversation though.

Despite Alfie being hell on two legs, all of a sudden, I unexpectedly found myself feeling sorry for him. Losing his mother at a young age was bound to have had a profound effect on him. Not that I was making excuses for his behaviour, and I wasn't claiming to be a psychiatrist, but some of Alfie's issues must have stemmed from the things he'd experienced in his childhood.

'Oh my God, that's awful. What happened?'

'Nora collapsed at home while I was out. Alfie phoned for an ambulance, and she was taken to the hospital, but she died shortly afterwards.'

'I'm so sorry to hear that.' I genuinely meant what I'd just said. that. 'The loss of a parent is a great blow to anyone, but it's especially hard for a child to come to terms with,' Jethro said. 'It's something that stays with them for the rest of their life.'

Jethro looked gutted, and if the circumstances had been different, I would have walked around the island and given him a hug.

'Initially, the doctors thought Nora had suffered a heart attack, but a post-mortem found that she'd died from liver disease as a result of her excessive drinking. What a waste of a young life. She was only thirty-three.' Jethro shook his head. 'The outcome of the autopsy shouldn't have surprised me; Nora used to drink vodka out of a mug for breakfast!'

My eyes widened. The story was becoming more tragic by the minute, and thanks to my overactive hormones, I felt tears prick at my eyes. It wasn't my place to cry, but this was a real tear-jerker, and I was having trouble holding the sadness inside.

Nora was thirty-three when she'd died; she was a year older than me. My thoughts turned to Luca. I couldn't imagine being in her position. I wouldn't want somebody else raising my baby and taking on the role of his mother.

'The kids were so young. They never got over losing their mum. Her death affected them very badly. They couldn't understand why it had happened.'

Jethro seemed at ease opening up to me, but I wasn't sure I wanted to hear any more in case it clouded my judgement. I was already in a depressive state, and the more I listened to the tale of woe, the more emotional I was beginning to feel. I'd always been a sucker for a sob story.

'As you get older, you see things differently. I'm not proud of the way I treated Nora. At the very least, she deserved my respect, but while she was alive, she never got it. She let me walk all over her. If she'd have stood up to me, things might have been different.' Jethro shook his head. 'I'm not making excuses for my behaviour. I can't justify why I treated the mother of my children so appallingly that she drank herself to death.' Jethro cast his eyes to the floor.

The man was a skilled storyteller. He was definitely going to have me in tears in a minute if I wasn't careful. I was desperate to change the subject onto something more light-hearted, but it wasn't going to be easy making small talk with an ageing gangster I clearly had nothing in common with. Before I could think of anything to say, Jethro's monologue began again, so I strapped myself in and prepared for the bumpy ride.

'Having to live each day with regret is a terrible thing. The way I treated my wife weighs heavily on my conscience. If Nora hadn't got pregnant with Alfie, I don't think we would have ended up together, and although I didn't appreciate her at the time, if we hadn't got married, I wouldn't have Alfie and my two beautiful girls, Danielle and Samantha.'

The sound of muffled voices and the front door slamming announced Alfie's arrival and put an end to our conversation.

36

Jethro's words played over in my head. To say I was shocked that the Watsons had such a large skeleton in their closet was an understatement. The family came across as being the kind of people who had everything – and they did in terms of material possessions. But no amount of money could prevent bad things from happening to someone.

I would never have imagined that their lives had been blighted by such tragedy. Alfie had never mentioned that his mum was dead. But he kept his cards close to his chest, so I shouldn't have been surprised that he didn't talk about it. It obviously still caused him a great deal of distress, and if he showed his emotions that would make him vulnerable. Alfie would never allow anybody to see him like that.

I felt a sudden sense of guilt that I had no contact with my parents, but that was out of choice, not circumstance. I was sure Alfie would have given everything he owned to have his mother back. The thought of that made a lump form in my throat. It made me realise there was a lot more to Alfie than met the eye.

Alfie hadn't had an idyllic childhood after all. He might have grown up in the lap of luxury, but that hadn't stopped him from experiencing tremendous heartache. Now I could understand the deep-seated resentment he held for Jethro. No wonder there was friction between them. Alfie blamed his dad for his mother's death, and although Jethro didn't pour the alcohol down Nora's throat, it was his behaviour that was the cause of her excessive drinking, so he should take some responsibility for it. It wasn't as though her drinking was a secret. Why the hell didn't he try to stop her?

I couldn't help wondering what kind of a man Jethro was. He saw what his behaviour was doing to his wife, and yet he didn't bother to change it. Instead, he continued to torment her until the poor woman took her last breath. No wonder he felt guilty. The memory of how he treated his wife would never stop affecting him. He would always have it on his conscience, and so he should.

37

Alfie

Joshua Clarke or Curly, as I liked to call him, was the bald-headed manager of our nightclub, Sherlock's. The huge venue was spread over three floors. People flocked to it every day of the week. The club was full of wannabes and spotty teenagers trying every trick in the book to get laid. Situated in West India Quay, Sherlock's was just a stone's throw from central London. It was a prime piece of real estate, and thanks to its waterfront location, it was worth a small fortune. It was the place to be seen, and you were almost guaranteed to spot a celebrity or reality TV star if you ventured into the VIP area.

The ground level contained a huge dance floor and a large well-stocked bar area, which stretched across the entire width of the room. Around the perimeter, were free-standing columns filled with thousands of tiny bubbles that changed through a whole spectrum of colours in time with the music on the dance floor. Every inch of the room was covered with seizure-inducing strobe lighting and LED ceiling and wall panels.

A black-carpeted sweeping staircase in the far corner behind the DJ booth led to the first floor. An illuminated circular cocktail bar, surrounded by high-backed bar stools, stood in the centre of the room. Tables with colour-changing bases were positioned around the rest of the floor space in an open-plan arrangement to make the most of the glass-panelled viewing gallery.

The top floor, reserved for VIP guests, only had table service available. This level was sectioned off into intimate booths and private rooms. The bucket-style seating and walls were covered in silver crushed velvet fabric. Huge crystal-encrusted mirrors hung behind the black sparkly quartz bar, and above the matching tables.

I'd spent a small fortune doing this place up when I took over running the business from my dad. Needless to say, he wasn't impressed with the cost or the final result. But my dad had old-fashioned taste, so I hadn't expected him to like it. I tried to explain that sometimes you have to spend money to make money. You couldn't charge punters top dollar to get into a club if it didn't look the part. The money I'd spent had turned out to be a wise investment. The refurbishment had paid for itself ten times over, and the firm had been able to lose surplus cash along the way.

My first encounter with Curly, a crack cocaine dealer, was when he started his one-man distribution network close to the border of my patch. Realising the Jamaican crime lord wasn't part of a rival gang and was operating alone, I made him a proposition he couldn't refuse.

Curly was six feet four inches tall and had biceps of steel.

I looked slight in comparison to him. Because of Curly's sheer size, I had originally recruited him as hired muscle, but he was wasted in the role of a door supervisor, and he soon rose up the ranks. He was now in charge of the day-to-day running of the club. Curly's background in narcotic distribution made him an obvious choice for the position. I supplied the stock and Curly controlled the drug market that operated within the club, selling the cocaine via a team of resident dealers who mingled with the masses as they carried out dance floor transactions.

My large team were intentionally young and roamed the interior of Sherlock's with small amounts of coke so that if they were unfortunate enough to run into an undercover cop, they wouldn't get nicked for a serious crime but would be let off with a caution. The golden rule was they mustn't carry so much cocaine for them to be classed as a dealer. So far, this tactic was working. Sherlock's nightclub drug trade was booming. I maintained a heavy security presence on the door, and my bouncers carried out physical searches to ensure drugs didn't make their way through the doors. If people wanted gear, they had to buy it inside, not bring it with them like a kid sneaking sweets into the cinema.

I had zero tolerance for people smuggling illegal substances into my club. Only drugs bought on the premises could be consumed within its walls. But clubbers had to play by my rules and not be too blatant in the way they took the gear. As long as they were discreet, my staff would be happy to turn a blind eye. If not, they'd be out on their ear. I couldn't afford to be raided and lose my licence over a punter's drug use.

When Dad was running the club, it was swamped with independent dealers that the door staff sanctioned for a backhander. The bouncers were on to a nice little earner. If they found drugs on a person at the door, they would confiscate them. Then they would sell the confiscated item to the dealers, who resold it on the dance floor. The chances were if your drugs were taken off you at the point of entry, an hour later, you were probably buying your own gear back from a dealer. The thought of that brought a smile to my face.

Back then, ecstasy was the drug of choice. It was cheap and readily available. But when a spate of ecstasy-related deaths hit the headlines, a media frenzy followed. The police traced the dangerous batch of tablets back to nightclubs, so Dad came down hard on anyone found dealing at Sherlock's, and he banned the consumption of illegal substances altogether. The clampdown was necessary; he didn't want the club to be shut down by the authorities because a drug user happened to be unlucky enough to take a fatal dose inside Sherlock's walls.

After I took control of the club, I decided a change of tactics was in order. In some ways, I agreed with Dad. I didn't want to risk bad press if any of our clubbers were hospitalised after taking dodgy pills or other substances, but I didn't want to be left out of the action either. Supplying cocaine to clubbers was a lucrative business, and for some, its consumption was as essential as alcohol to ensure they had a good night out. I felt we needed to move with the times and was frustrated by my dad's attitude. He didn't think it was a good idea to reintroduce drugs to Sherlock's after all this time.

I forged ahead with my plan, regardless of my dad's feelings. Either he wanted me to run the business, or he didn't. Dad had promised to give me control of the reins, but the problem was, he wouldn't let go of them. My idea was as safe as houses. I'd figured out if I controlled the supply, I could guarantee the product. I knew for a fact that Vladimir Popov only trafficked quality merchandise. High-quality cocaine was a status symbol. I had no intention of peddling cheap rubbish. I wouldn't stoop so low as to flog tablets at five pounds a pop in my club, no matter how much demand there was for them, so Dad had nothing to worry about.

Drugs were a dominant part of the nightclub scene and could be obtained quicker than ordering a round of drinks. In the VIP area, guests consumed the gear in a private booth. They would pass the plate holding the lines of white powder around the table like port at a fancy dinner party. Groups of friends and colleagues felt comfortable openly hoovering up the coke.

On the ground floor of Sherlock's, where discretion was required, the disabled toilet was the favourite haunt of drug-takers. The club had a distinct lack of wheelchair users, so to utilise the large space, Curly had come up with an ingenious suggestion. Horizontal mirrors were installed in the cloakroom area, so customers had a surface to cut their cocaine on. They could take the coke in the privacy of a locked room rather than on public display in the ladies and gents toilets. Judging by the amount of white residue we found after closing time, his idea had been a resounding success.

38

Nathan

Charlie Miller could have easily passed as a member of a boy band with his platinum blond hair and porcelain-veneered smile. To the untrained eye, Curly looked like his minder, not his boss. Curly used to be Charlie's dealer before he gave up freelancing and started working for Alfie. When Charlie's habit became too expensive for him to maintain on his allowance from his father, Curly suggested he join the team. Alfie welcomed him into the fold with open arms.

Champagne Charlie, as he was affectionately known, wasn't your average gangster. The glossy-haired playboy was well-dressed and mild-mannered. He was more familiar with hanging out with aristocrats and multi-millionaires than people in the criminal underworld. His previous profession as an events organiser worked as an ideal cover for his new activities. Nobody would ever suspect that this public-school-educated young man would be involved in anything illegal. Charlie Miller had led a charmed life. He'd been born with a silver spoon in his mouth. Charlie was the son of an eighties yuppie; his father had made millions on the stock exchange.

Charlie's upbringing couldn't have been more different from Jamaican Yardie, Curly, or the team of men working the door who hailed from the local council estates. But somehow he blended in with everybody. The main thing that distinguished Charlie from the rest of the workforce was his toff's accent. It was nothing like the cockney twang of the door staff, and if you weren't aware that the official language of Jamaica was English, you'd be forgiven for thinking Curly was speaking a local dialect. I found him incredibly difficult to understand. Maybe Alfie should consider sending him to elocution lessons, then he could learn to speak like Charlie.

Charlie's private education had provided him with access to a multitude of well-heeled society chums. He had contacts in the right places. Since he'd started working at Sherlock's, he had brought some seriously wealthy clubbers with a passion for cocktails and cocaine through the doors of the nightclub. By organising parties for VIP guests, Charlie expanded Alfie's clientele with non-restrictive budgets overnight and reinforced the fact that the posher you were, the more drugs you took. Thanks to the boom in Sherlock's business, Charlie could do no wrong in Alfie's eyes.

I had been given the lofty position of general dogsbody since I'd been working for Alfie. I'd had to turn my hand to a variety of different roles in recent weeks, and tonight, I was making my debut appearance at Sherlock's.

I was watching the door, barely visible behind two huge doormen dressed all in black. They were checking the IDs of potential punters to ensure the clubbers were of legal age to enter and were dressed appropriately. Counterfeit designer trainer-clad feet would not be allowed to cross the threshold of Sherlock's.

Alfie detested chavs. He didn't want people like that in his club. They would lower the tone of his classy establishment, so he wanted them weeded out at this stage. They might be dressed head to toe in expensive brands, but they'd bought the items down the market and not in the genuine stores. He maintained people like that did indeed have a distinctly nasty smell about them, and would contaminate his club's interior. Once a customer was deemed fit for entry, I'd been given the job of scanning randomly selected people with a hand-held security metal detector. The body search was designed to check for knives and weapons.

'I've been supervising you for the last twenty minutes, and I'm confident you've got the hang of the wand now. I need to pop down to the office. Will you be OK on your own for a bit?' Charlie asked.

'Yeah, no problem, mate,' I replied.

'If you ever get bored of working at the club, you could always get a job at the airport.' Charlie smiled, then slapped me on the back, before leaving me in charge.

I watched Charlie walk across the dance floor and disappear into the crowd. It was happy hour, so Sherlock's was packed with eighteen-year-olds dressed in tiny miniskirts and skyscraper heels and young men who were barely old enough to shave.

'Where's Charlie?' Curly asked when he came into the foyer.

Charlie had been in the back office for about half an hour, but I didn't want to get him into trouble, so I didn't tell Curly that. 'He's gone for a slash,' I replied.

'When he comes back, ask him to go up to the VIP area.'

I peered through the glass panel of the office door and saw Charlie sitting behind the desk with a rectangular mirror and a tiny plastic bag in front of him. I watched as he tipped a small amount of the contents onto the hard surface. He crushed the rocky clump, then cut it into two lines with a credit card before snorting the fine powder through a tightly rolled twenty-pound note. Charlie's drug of choice was also his namesake. He wasn't just an occasional user; he was hopelessly addicted to the white powder. He snorted the coke firstly into his left nostril, then into the right. Inhaling deeply, he closed his eyes while he experienced the familiar rush. A few minutes later, Charlie opened his eyes and wiped his finger across the reflective surface, to clean up the last traces of white residue, then he rubbed it into his gums, so as not to waste any of the treasured substance.

I blew out a breath. After what I'd just witnessed, I decided to leave Curly's message undelivered and go back to the door and wait for Charlie to return of his own accord.

★

The young men seemed surprised when the door staff waved them through as Sherlock's had a reputation for having an over-the-top door policy. Usually, a line of security guards checked a person's ID before they were permitted entry to the club, but there were only two bouncers on duty tonight, and they had both been distracted by a scantily clad hen party from Toxteth. The women were moaning because they'd been queuing up in the cold for the last half an hour and due to the amount of alcohol they'd already consumed, they were starting to become rowdy.

I gave the teenagers, a cursory glance. Seeing as the bouncers were unbothered by the two young men, I decided not to scan them with the hand-held detector either.

Alfie and Knuckles arrived at the club just after eleven. They made their way up to the first floor, and Alfie stood on the balcony, master of his own kingdom, surveying the dance floor when he noticed two young men dressed in dark clothing working their way around the crowd.

'Look at those cheeky fuckers,' Alfie said, pointing out the two bearded men. 'I mean, who the fuck wears the hood up on their jacket in a club? It's two million degrees centigrade in here. Talk about drawing attention to yourself.'

'What do you want me to do with them?' Knuckles asked.

'Tell Curly to get them away from my punters and take them to my office.'

By the time Curly got hold of the young men, they had already sold their gear, and were sitting on one of the leather sofas, beers in hand, stretched out as if they owned the place. They hadn't even had the good sense to leave after they'd shifted their baggies. Instead, they'd stayed behind to soak up the atmosphere. Curly frog-marched them to Alfie's office to interrogate and search them.

'I've confiscated the wad of notes and the knives the teenagers were carrying, boss,' Curly said. 'They finally admitted, after some persuasion, that they work for the Albanians.'

'Where the fuck is Charlie?' Alfie asked, getting up in my face.

'He's in the back office,' I replied.

Charlie was still savouring the moment when Alfie, Knuckles and I walked into the room. He blinked, startled by the intrusion, but the cocaine had made his eyes water, so it took him a moment to focus. Alfie's eyes were drawn to the discarded credit card lying on top of the mirror and Charlie realised he'd been busted. While grinning like a lunatic on day release from an asylum, Charlie reached forward and took a tissue out of the box on the desk. Keeping eye contact with Alfie, he dabbed at his dripping nose.

'Two guys from a rival firm were dealing drugs on my dance floor while you were in here getting wasted.' Alfie wasn't impressed.

The blood drained from Charlie's face. There was no point offering Alfie empty excuses; Charlie knew they wouldn't wash with him. The only thing he could do was apologise profusely. 'I'm sorry, mate; I fucked up. What more can I say?' The blond man stood up and steadied himself on the desk.

'There's plenty more you can say. You could attempt to explain yourself, and don't call me mate; I'm no friend of yours.'

Alfie fixed Charlie with a death stare, and the young man looked taken aback. Alfie's words came as a shock to him. Up until now, he'd always been the boss's golden boy.

'What you do in the privacy of your own home is your business, but you don't take drugs on my time.' Alfie might be happy to be a distributor, supplying dealers who in turn supplied users, but he had zero tolerance for people in his inner circle taking drugs. He was well aware of Charlie's habit, but he chose to ignore it, so he didn't want it flaunted in front of him. 'You've disappointed me. Didn't anyone ever tell you not to bite the fucking hand that feeds you?' Alfie was fuming.

'I'm sorry, Alfie, I've honestly only been in here for a couple of minutes. I thought everything would be OK. I left Nathan in charge...'

Alfie put his hand up to silence Charlie, so he left his sentence unfinished. 'And look what happened. The man's a complete cretin. He let two foot soldiers armed with knives into my club. They could have caused carnage. That bastard couldn't organise a piss-up in a pub.'

The atmosphere in the room suddenly changed. I felt myself snap and I lunged forward, but Knuckles threw his huge arm across my chest and stopped me in my tracks. I was furious, and it showed. My nostrils flared as anger simmered inside me. I'd always had a temper and knew I could explode at any minute.

Alfie looked over his shoulder, locked eyes with me and

smiled. 'What's the matter? Have I hit a nerve? Sometimes the truth hurts, doesn't it?'

I clenched my jaw to keep my mouth shut. Tempting as it was to get into an argument, I knew I shouldn't. If Alfie hurt Luca in response to my outburst, I'd never forgive myself. I had to will myself to keep a lid on my temper. But it was difficult. Having to stand in a room full of people while Alfie belittled me was hard to stomach. Alfie seemed content to ignore the fact that the door staff had waved the boys through in the first place, so technically, it was their fault. But as usual, he laid the blame firmly at my feet. I was going to have to carry the can.

'Get back on the door, Charlie, and don't let me catch you doing a row of sherbet soldiers again or I'll be forced to let Knuckles do a spot of DIY on your features. He's a dab hand with power tools and a blowtorch.' Alfie raised an eyebrow.

Charlie nodded to acknowledge he'd understood, then lowered his eyes to the floor before he walked out of the office and went back on the front door.

Alfie, Knuckles and I made our way to a private booth in the VIP area where a bottle of Cristal was waiting on ice.

'Who do those cheeky fuckers think they are? They're barely old enough to order a pint, and they waltz into my club, tooled up, and start selling right under my nose. They deserved to get a serious hiding. If word got out about this, it would damage my reputation. I'm not about to let that happen.'

Alfie was raging; he couldn't understand what had possessed the Albanians to try and muscle in on his territory. Knuckles opened the champagne and passed Alfie a glass. He looked like he could do with a drink. Alfie raised his glass and drained it. Then signalled to Knuckles for a refill.

Alfie sipped at his drink for some time before he spoke. 'I'm going to have to send a message loud and clear to the Albanian boss and the wider community that only a fool shits on his own doorstep.' Alfie put his empty flute down on the table before he stood up and pulled down the sleeves on his navy suit jacket. 'Right, Knuckles, it's time to teach those little wankers that Nathan let in a lesson. We'll show them what happens when you fuck with the Watsons.'

Alfie stood in the doorway of his office staring into the terrified boys' faces. 'We're going to give you two a lift home. It's way past your bedtime, and I need to pay your boss a visit.'

Alfie gestured to Knuckles, and the huge man walked over with the grace of Frankenstein's monster to where the boys sat side by side on high-backed chairs. Standing behind them, he grabbed the teenagers by their jackets at the scruff of the neck and pulled them onto their feet.

'Should I come with you?' Curly asked. He'd been sitting on the edge of Alfie's desk, with his arms crossed over his chest, keeping watch over the dealers.

'No, we'll take it from here. As of now, you're officially relieved of your babysitting duties,' Alfie replied.

Curly smiled and exposed his gold front tooth.

★

Somebody's head was going to roll for the fuck-up tonight, so it might as well be mine for a change. I wanted to point out that I wasn't solely responsible for the cock-up. Charlie should have been supervising me instead of getting wasted on company time, and the boys had also got passed the two minders on the door. But I was the one Alfie wanted to blame, so there was no point trying to talk my way out of it.

In all fairness, it was my first night on the door. How was I meant to know those two harmless-looking boys were part of a rival gang? They just looked like regular teenagers to me. But Alfie was never going to let me forget it. In his eyes, the damage had already been done.

Alfie was in no mood to listen to excuses. As far as he was concerned, because of my stupidity, the teenagers had got away with dealing drugs right under his nose. They'd made a fool out of him, and now somebody was going to have to pay. Given my lack of options, I did the only thing I had the power to do. I took the ear-bashing like a man. Receiving a daily dressing-down from the boss had become part of my job description. Initially, I'd wondered if he was trying to break my spirit, but it was more likely that Alfie was just entertaining himself at my expense.

The ball was unquestionably in Alfie's court. It wasn't as though I could hand in my notice or file a formal complaint with the human resources department, so I'd just have to get on with it. But I didn't find it easy to turn the other cheek. I'd inherited my short fuse from my mum. Being quick-tempered was a curse. Biting my tongue didn't come naturally to me, but I was going to have to learn to control my rage while I was around Alfie. He liked to push my buttons because he knew he'd get a reaction out of me. I'd have to stop being so predictable.

In some ways, working so closely with Alfie was a good thing; it was teaching me how to exercise self-control.

39

Alfie

The Mercedes had only just cruised past the four chimneys of the iconic London landmark, Battersea Power Station when Knuckles turned down a pothole-ridden alleyway littered with debris. It was clearly a magnet for fly-tippers. The derelict industrial estate was a million miles away from the elegant Art Deco Grade II listed building. Driving slowly to avoid damaging the car, Knuckles parked up outside unit twenty-two.

'What a shithole,' I said, peering out of the tinted window at the dingy-looking lock-up.

The vast warehouse, located in Wandsworth Business Park, was in a serious state of decay. At least half of the original cast-iron window frames were boarded up and the ones that weren't had broken panes of glass. The smog-stained, red-brick exterior was covered with colourful graffiti, and well-established plants grew out of the gutters.

I got out of the car and approached the double loading

doors. Nathan and Knuckles followed closely behind, flanking the two young men we were returning. As I watched Knuckles steer the teenagers, dressed in black hooded jackets and low-slung jeans towards the door, I wondered how scum dressed like that had even been allowed to step over the threshold of Sherlock's. I made a mental note to give the door staff a serious bollocking when I got back to the club.

I placed my hand on the peeling paintwork of the door and pushed it forward. As it opened, I turned over my palm and brushed off the red flakes that were left behind on my skin. I had to clamp my lips shut when the musty smell in the cavernous room hit me at the back of the throat as I stepped over the threshold. I'd never smelt anything like it. The decaying aroma mingled with the scent of excrement to produce a terrible combination that assaulted my senses. My leather shoes echoed around the room as I crossed the concrete floor. It was covered in pigeon shit, from the multitude of feathered creatures that were residing within the warehouse's four walls.

Three men were playing cards, sitting on plastic chairs gathered around a filthy table. The bare bulbs that hung from the ceiling did an inadequate job of lighting the dingy space. When I walked into a room, everyone stood up. That was the level of respect I commanded, but these men barely even acknowledged my presence. They were a different breed.

I stood and observed the gang dressed in cheap nylon tracksuits for a moment. They were grubby and didn't look like they'd washed in weeks. They could have clambered out of the back of a lorry having just clawed their way out of poverty for all I knew.

'I'm not going to pretend to know how things operate in Albania, but in this country, firms have set boundaries, so unless you want a turf war on your hands, keep your dealers out of my club and away from my customers,' I said, marking my territory.

The man facing me laughed. The fucking cheek of it. I felt myself bristle at the disrespect being shown to me. It was something I wasn't accustomed to. The man lifted up a bottle of clear spirit and poured some into two glasses. When he added water to the drinks, the liquid turned milky white. The man pushed back his plastic chair and stood up.

'We drink first, then we talk,' he said before he walked over to me.

The scent of liquorice wafted up my nose as I lifted the glass to my lips. I paused before I took a sip and looked suspiciously at the drink in the glass. 'Is it ouzo?'

'No, it's raki. It's much better than ouzo; it's twice the strength. Taste it. You'll like it; it's ninety per cent alcohol.' The man laughed and extended a work-worn hand towards me. 'My name is Zamir. They are Esad and Dren. They work for me.' Zamir gestured with a nod of the head to the two men sat at the table.

I stared at Zamir's dirty fingernails and reluctantly shook his hand, but my ego wouldn't allow me to introduce myself. Zamir should know who I was. Everyone knew Alfie Watson. I knocked back the aniseed-flavoured spirit and hoped I didn't catch something off the murky glass. The raki burned my throat as I swallowed it. Zamir was wrong: I didn't like it. It tasted like firewater. It was obvious I possessed a more refined palate than my new acquaintance.

A tramp sitting on a park bench drinking neat spirits from a paper bag would probably appreciate the raki, but if I ever tasted it again, it would be too soon.

I looked over my shoulder and gestured to Knuckles to release the teenagers. 'I think they belong to you.'

Zamir sat back down at the table, and he began speaking to the other men in Albanian.

'Shut the fuck up. You're getting right on my tits now,' I said, as I treated Zamir to my famous death stare. 'If you want to find yourself up to your eyeballs in trouble you're going the right way about it, my Balkan friend.'

'Relax, boss man, we don't want any trouble,' Zamir said, flashing me his untrustworthy smile.

I cast my eyes over the dark-haired, dark-eyed group. The men were all medium build, with facial hair, and weren't particularly distinguishable from each other. 'Fuck me, what is it with you lot? You all look the same. Are you related?'

Zamir let out a wheezy smoker's laugh. My intentional politically incorrect comment didn't seem to have offended him. 'I like the dry British sense of humour. You are very funny.'

'I'm not trying to amuse you; I'm merely pointing out a fact. Is having a crew cut and a beard company policy?' I smirked, but after I spoke, I knew there was a notable shift in my demeanour.

Zamir explained the uncanny resemblance the team had to one another was no accident. It was a tactic they used to make it harder for the authorities to identify them. If the men were ever arrested and ended up in a line-up, it would be very difficult for a witness to tell one of them from the other, so they wouldn't be able to say without reasonable doubt which man had committed the crime.

Even though I would never admit it, I couldn't help thinking whoever came up with that idea was a genius.

40

Alfie

After I'd paid Zamir the unexpected visit, I'd done a bit of digging and discovered that the Albanians primary business was prostitution, so they shouldn't have been any real threat to me. Unlike a lot of other criminal organisations, that wasn't an area we were involved in.

Zamir's gang trafficked Albanian girls using insider knowledge. The higher you went into the mountains in the north of the country, the further back in time you travelled. The people who lived in these remote rural areas were very poor and vulnerable, which made them easy targets. Zamir recruited many of the youngest girls from this region. In some cases, the parents sold the victims after their daughters were offered exciting propositions that were too good to turn down. The girls' parents didn't think twice about handing them over after they were given the chance of a new life with plenty of employment prospects. Opportunities like that didn't come along every day in tiny Albanian villages.

Social media was also used to target some of the girls.

Organised gangs ran fake employment agencies that posted job vacancies in childcare and hairdressing along with other professions that didn't exist. Girls were happy to leave their homes in remote parts of the country following bogus job offers. The traffickers sometimes pretended to be scouting for modelling agencies to get very young girls interested. Apparently, this tactic even worked when the girls were ugly. The prospect of making huge amounts of money that could be sent home to support the family ensured the parents were taken in by the scam.

I couldn't help thinking they should have known better, but I shouldn't judge them because I'd never been in their position. These people were desperately poor, and the young girls had been promised a better life with better opportunities. The parents had no idea what was going to become of their precious daughters.

Once ensnared by the traffickers, the unfortunate women were sold from gang to gang as commodities and found themselves in a terrifying network of underground crime. Zamir's gang used corrupt truck drivers to smuggle the women into the UK, where they would be subjected to sexual exploitation.

Zamir was the head of the highly successful illicit enterprise. His firm ran most of London's prostitution rackets in Soho and surrounding areas. The sex trade was a huge market, so he required access to a large number of women. That wasn't a problem. A vast network of criminals that operated all across Europe kept him in good supply. He ran a people-trafficking business with any surplus girls and his firm was involved in false document production, which was a big money-spinner in this line of work.

This was a male-dominated culture, and by all accounts, Zamir treated the girls who worked for him with no respect. Many of them were forced to work unpaid as prostitutes. The others faced labour exploitation, working under the radar for little or no money. The Albanians were incredibly cruel to their employees and treated the women very badly. They were made to feel they had no value. They had a reputation for brutality. The trafficked girls were terrified of them. They were plucked from their homes and were now being held prisoner by their captors, victims of modern-day slavery.

We were involved in plenty of illegal activities, but I was glad the sex trade wasn't one of them. These men were in a different league. They were animals. I was shocked by the level of cruelty and degradation Zamir subjected the women to, and it had to be said, not much shocked me. If anyone treated my sisters like that, I'd kill them with my bare hands.

41

Gemma

I'm not usually a suspicious person, but Alfie seemed to bring out that side of me. Recently, he appeared to be carrying out a campaign of flattery in an obvious attempt to win me over, but his charm offensive wasn't having the desired effect. The attention he was giving me made me feel uncomfortable. The more time I spent with him, the more it heightened my desire to put some distance between us. I could sense he had a hidden agenda.

I'd had enough of walking on eggshells around Alfie. It was time to clarify the situation. It would do more damage in the long run to sugar-coat it. The way he watched me with his blue stare left me in no doubt what was on his mind. Clinging on to my every word wouldn't persuade me to sleep with him again. That was never going to happen. I should never have cheated on my husband and bitterly regretted having a one-night stand with Alfie. It had been a stupid decision to risk my marriage for a drunken fling, but I would never make the same mistake again. The sooner Alfie understood that, the better it would be for both of us.

Nothing had happened between Alfie and I apart from on that one occasion, but I still felt obliged to let him down gently. I had to make my feelings clear, but it was going to be an awkward conversation for both of us. I thought about sending him a text, to spare myself from having to deliver the news in person. Alfie wasn't going to take my rejection well, and he wasn't the type of man you wanted to piss off intentionally. But I had to put a stop to this situation sooner rather than later. There was no point in prolonging the inevitable.

I was scared Nathan might think something was going on between us again. We'd been spending so much time together recently while Nathan was working. Alfie knew my husband could be insanely jealous at times, especially where he was concerned. It was obvious he wanted to plant the seed of doubt in Nathan's mind. His behaviour was so transparent. It wasn't going to be a difficult thing to do. Alfie and I had history, didn't we?

42

Alfie

I had agreed to be the Albanians' supplier on the condition that they didn't sell the drugs near my territory. They were a force to be reckoned with, so it was better to have them onside. Zamir's gang made the Krays look like choirboys.

'If you know what's good for you, you won't ask questions.' I handed Nathan a revolver. 'We need to be tooled up for this job in case we have to hand out a beating.'

Although he wouldn't have been my first choice, Nathan was helping to provide extra muscle when I went to deliver the shipment of cocaine. The stakes were raised on this job, so I needed extra backup.

The Mercedes pulled into the dimly lit alleyway and stopped outside unit twenty-two just before midnight. Knuckles, Nathan and I stepped out of the car. Knuckles walked around to the back and took a large black holdall out of the boot, then I led the way, being careful where I stepped. The alleyway was littered with debris and showed visible signs of drug use. Discarded needles and other drug paraphernalia lined our path to the lock-up door.

I rapped on the shabby paintwork with the back of my hand, and almost instantly, the door opened. Zamir, Esad and Dren were sitting at the table in the centre of the warehouse surrounded by a large group of men.

'Come in,' Zamir said, beckoning us with a wave of his hand to join them.

Knuckles placed the bag down on the table in front of Zamir. His eyes lit up at the sight of it. Wasting no time, he unzipped the holdall and took out a polythene-wrapped block. He ran his weathered hands over the plastic, inspecting the merchandise closely, before turning away from me. Zamir began talking to Esad and Dren in Albanian. I drummed my fingers on the table, and after a few moments, I interrupted their discussion.

'I hate to break up your mothers' meeting, but I'm sure you can appreciate it's very late, and I didn't come here for a social visit.' I wasn't used to being messed around and was frustrated by the delay.

Zamir finally turned his attention back to me. I was less than impressed at being excluded from the conversation. I knew it would be impossible to misread the look on my face. Zamir was a fool if he thought he could continue to treat me with such little respect. His consistent rudeness was beyond belief. The atmosphere in the room was already tense and awkward, but the meeting turned decidedly hostile when Esad, fixed me with his beady eyes and tried to haggle over the price. What a fucking liberty.

I had put up with enough of the gang's nonsense for one night, so I told the men I was going to walk away from the deal. Dren pushed his chair back and suddenly stood up. We locked eyes; then he calmly pulled a gun on me. I couldn't help wondering if the business at the club the other night had been a setup. Had we been deliberately led into an ambush by rival gang members?

Knuckles was surprisingly agile for such a large man. In the blink of an eye, he pulled a short link chain out of his jacket pocket, and in one smooth movement, he stepped behind Dren, wrapped the chain around his neck and began choking him. 'Drop the gun, you fucker.'

Dren's beady eyes looked like they were going to pop out of his head. He threw down his weapon and started clawing at his throat. Knuckles loosened the chain a small amount to allow the man to catch his breath, but not so much that he could cause any more trouble. Dren's breath caught in his chest when Knuckles released his hold.

'You shouldn't have done that, Alfie. Now that you've laid your hands on Dren, blood must be paid for with blood,' Zamir said. 'It's one of our deep-rooted customs.'

I shook my head slowly, unable to believe what I'd just heard. Dren pulled a gun on me, so Knuckles was acting in self-defence. Who did Zamir think he was, threatening a Watson? The man must have a serious death wish.

'I'd forget that idea if I were you unless you want to leave here in an ambulance or better still an undertaker's hearse,' I replied.

After a tense silence, Zamir began to speak. 'My street dealers tell me the price punters are willing to pay for coke has dropped.' Zamir looked over his shoulder and pointed to the dial-a-drug army standing behind him.

'I'm not negotiating on the price. If you back out of the

deal now there will be serious consequences,' I replied. I was completely unfazed by the fact that Zamir's gang hugely outnumbered us. The Albanians' treacherous behaviour could not, and would not, be overlooked.

'If I buy the cocaine at source from South America, I could reduce my overheads significantly. Then I wouldn't be forced to pay your inflated prices,' Zamir said, and a smug smile spread across his face.

'My Russian supplier won't be too happy to hear that. He has a well-organised operation set up in the Costa del Sol.'

The meeting wasn't going to plan. As there hadn't been any previous disputes between our two firms, I had very generously returned the teenage dealers without harming a hair on their heads and had merely issued the gang a warning. But instead of apologising, Zamir had thrown down the gauntlet by revealing his plan. Attempting to turn the tables on the supply chain was a bold move. Zamir was a cheeky fucker to even suggest it; I had to give him that much. The gang had originally entered the UK as refugees, and now they thought they could waltz in and take over. The UK had a five-billion-pound cocaine trade, and although a kingpin, I by no means dominated the market. I only controlled a small portion of it.

I looked down my nose at my tracksuit-clad opponent. Zamir fancied himself as the future King of Cocaine, but he was no Pablo Escobar. He was a nobody who had come to England to escape from poverty. He'd only been in the country five minutes, and now he thought he could call the shots. Zamir was about to learn the hard way. It didn't work like that in this business. He needed to earn the respect of the big players if he was going to survive in their world. The way he was going about things, I didn't reckon he'd make it until the end of the week before somebody took a pop at him.

Cocaine was usually shipped in bulk because it was too difficult to conceal. Vladimir Popov had spent years perfecting the supply chain. Corrupt Spanish port officials were on his payroll and allowed him to control cocaine importation. It was a huge operation. The drug smugglers went to extreme lengths to ensure their illegal cargo avoided detection and reached its intended destination. Cocaine, bound for the UK, was often concealed in containers of pineapples and bananas before being exported from Central and South America. The container ships docked in Spain before being moved on by Vladimir's officials to UK ports that lay along the River Thames. The huge shipments of cocaine were then offloaded from the vessel by corrupt port workers and loaded onto lorries destined for London and other parts of the UK. Because of the size of the operation, and the number of individuals involved, very few organised crime groups did end-to-end supply. It was too risky.

'I'm not in this game to make friends. I want to make money, so if you won't negotiate on the price, I'll have to cut you out of the deal and import directly from South America,' Zamir said.

I smirked, the man either had balls of steel, or he was an idiot. 'I can see where you're coming from. In theory, you'd make more money, but the risk of getting caught and banged up would also hugely increase. It might surprise you to know, there's a reason why none of us run the whole operation. Handling the drugs from shipment to distribution is virtually impossible.'

I stared at the man in front of me. I wouldn't want to be in Zamir's shoes when word of this plan reached Vladimir. Even if I didn't grass him up, the Russian mobster would find out about it. I knew from experience walls had ears, and it wouldn't take a man like Vladimir Popov long to find out there was a snake in the grass.

'Trust me,' I said, opening my arms out wide like a preacher. 'The way I operate carries the least risk. I fan the gear out to crime groups in London and Essex. Don't get too greedy, my friend. Trying to be Mr Big is the fastest way to get yourself banged up, or taken out by a rival. I'm sure I don't need to tell you, turf wars can be deadly.' I turned to look at Knuckles and Nathan. 'Gentlemen, if you're ready, we'll call it a night.'

Knuckles picked up the holdall and came to stand next to me. Nathan stood on the other side, and the three of us walked out of the warehouse and got into the Mercedes.

'Imagine trying to pull a stunt like that.' I shook my head as I looked out into the darkness. 'If Zamir and his gang know what's good for them, they'll stay in the shadows. They fancy themselves as crime warlords, but they're no threat to us. If they had brains, they would be dangerous.' I laughed.

43

Alfie

The following day, I received word that Zamir was still keen to take over the cocaine distribution in the area by undercutting all his rivals. He'd concluded, if he bought the drugs at source, he could offer a substantial discount to the end user.

The man was insane if he thought I was going to stand for that. It was time to pay him another visit. The Watsons never had, and never would compete for business. Zamir was out of line if he thought I was going to let the Albanians encroach on my territory. If he tried to, he'd soon realise the Watsons' turf was well guarded.

'You should go now,' Zamir said.

Nobody told me what to do. My stance changed in response to his comment. You didn't need to be a genius to work out that something was about to kick off. Zamir was about to find out that I thrived on intimidation and violence. It wasn't only enjoyable, it was also necessary to maintain my notoriety. The Watsons had a well-established reputation as a firm not to be messed with, so it was time to teach Zamir a lesson he'd never forget.

Zamir was a slippery character and was refusing to elaborate. He was keeping the details of his plan sketchy, but it was obvious that he had decided to forge ahead with his idea to cut the Russians and myself out of the deal. He wanted to buy his cocaine at source, but that wasn't a sensible move. Attempting to maximise his profits this way was unrealistic. Zamir was getting ahead of himself if he thought Vladimir Popov would allow him to set up an import syndicate and source the coke directly from Latin America. I'd explained that nobody ran the whole operation from start to finish, but Zamir was refusing to listen. He was testing my patience.

Greed did terrible things to a person. It made men make stupid decisions. Zamir's hare-brained idea to cut Vladimir and I out of the equation and negotiate directly with the Colombian cartels would have serious consequences. They were newcomers on the scene. They couldn't just rock up and do away with the existing supply chain. There was a long-established hierarchy in place, and they were at the bottom of the pile.

The Costa del Sol was a great networking ground for international criminals, and the Russians were there in force, so the idea of Zamir being able to oust them from the top of the rung was ridiculous. The man was delusional if he thought that would happen. He was walking a dangerous path, even considering the possibility. The drug trade generated large sums of money, so the Russians would not give up their position without a fight. They were dangerous fuckers and would not hesitate to kill if they felt they had been double-crossed. They were masters of the game and had a formidable reputation. Zamir and his tracksuit-clad army were no match for Vladimir's men. I knew for a fact that many of them were former KGB agents.

The Russians would not stand back and let Zamir take control of the drug-smuggling operation and cut them out of the cocaine trade. There was too much money at stake. They weren't known for their mediation skills. Vladimir's men were ruthless and would put a bullet in you as quick as look at you. Disregarding the rules that had been in place for generations would justify the bloodshed.

Zamir had huge balls if he thought he could rewrite the rulebook. I was certain his greed would lead to his downfall. The network was there for a reason. It was too risky for one firm to handle the operation from production to distribution. I knew the Albanians had a reputation for keeping their word. They always delivered, so this wasn't an idle threat. I wasn't looking forward to breaking the news to Vladimir.

Something would need to be done about the Albanian firm. They couldn't just cut all the links in the supply chain without bringing trouble on themselves, so I told Zamir in no uncertain terms that Vladimir would not stand for the betrayal. He would choose the best time and place, where he could be sure of getting away with the hit, and then he would get someone further down the ladder to carry out a gangland-style execution. I could guarantee it, but Zamir was too arrogant to listen to the warning.

I wasn't bluffing. If Zamir went ahead with his plan, it wouldn't be if, but when, Vladimir would get even with him.

44

Nathan

Iglanced at my watch as I sat in the front seat of the Mercedes next to Knuckles. It was close to midnight and instead of being tucked up in bed next to my beautiful wife, I was out doing Alfie's dirty work. To say that was a thorn in my side was an understatement, but I wasn't in a position to hand in my notice and apply for a job somewhere else. Unfortunately, it didn't work like that.

Alfie had instructed us to keep an eye on Zamir, and as we cruised past Wandsworth Business Park, our attention was drawn to unit twenty-two. Knuckles parked up so we could observe from the shadows. Goose pimples covered my body. I could sense something was about to kick off.

Zamir was locking up the warehouse for the evening when he was jumped by two masked men, dressed in dark clothing. One of the men smashed him across the back with a metal pole before the other forced a gun into his mouth. That muffled his cries for help and a chill ran down my spine.

Knuckles and I watched the commotion unfolding in silence. Although he resisted, the men dragged Zamir backwards towards a white Transit van. After opening the back door, one of the men pulled out a piece of rope. They forced Zamir onto the ground and bound his wrists and ankles together behind his back, rendering him immobile and helpless. Then they covered his mouth with tape before placing a sack over his head. They tossed their hogtied victim face down into the back of the van like a carcass of meat. The thought of what he was about to go through made me shudder.

'We'd best get over to Sherlock's and let Alfie know what's happened,' Knuckles said. He started the engine, and we left Zamir to his fate.

Knuckles went to have a private word with Alfie, so I took up position in the foyer of Sherlock's. Having to look for people to scan with my security wand was mind-numbingly boring, but it beat lurking outside a lock-up while some form of punishment was being dished out any day.

I was just thinking I was glad the drama of the night was over when I suddenly became aware of a large group of men shouting obscenities at the door staff. They were demanding to see Alfie and were trying to burst through the doors of the club. Curly and some other heavies were quickly on the scene. They managed to restrain the men on the pavement. When Alfie agreed to see Zamir, Curly and I escorted him to Alfie's office while his backup were forced to wait for their boss outside.

Zamir had been beaten black and blue by his attackers,

but at least he was still alive. When I saw the door of the Transit close in the deserted alleyway, I was certain the men were going to put a bullet in the back of his head.

'Listen to me, you cretin.' Alfie jabbed his finger towards Zamir's bloodied face. 'If I'd done that to you, I would own it. Get your facts straight before you start throwing wild accusations around. I had nothing to do with it. Now, unless you want to receive another hiding, get the fuck out of my club and don't come back.' Alfie got up in Zamir's face before Curly forcibly ejected the Albanian from the building.

45

Gemma

The following afternoon, Knuckles and Nathan were out running errands for the boss, so Alfie decided to escort Luca and I to Darkwood Manor. A feeling of dread came over me. I hated being cooped up in the house with Luca and Alfie while my husband was carrying out the Watsons' business. As uncomfortable as it was going to be, I was going to take the opportunity to set Alfie straight on a few things, but not while I was trapped inside the confines of the car with him. I'd wait until I could put some distance between us.

Alfie stepped behind me and began massaging my shoulders after I sat down on a stool at the breakfast bar. As his fingers dug into my flesh, I felt like slapping them away but thought better of it. To escape Alfie's wandering hands and because I suddenly felt the need to be close to Luca, I sprang to my feet and walked across the marble floor of the kitchen to where my baby was lying in his cot.

'My son looks adorable, doesn't he?' Alfie smiled. He looked down at Luca before gazing into my eyes.

Alfie's comment blindsided me and my pulse began to race. Luca was sleeping peacefully in his basket, blissfully unaware of the situation that was about to start. Even though he wasn't stirring, I decided to pick Luca up. I wasn't sure what Alfie was playing at.

'What the hell are you talking about?' A nervous laugh escaped from my lips before I could stop it. 'Luca's not your son,' I blurted out after I managed to compose myself. The room suddenly felt stifling.

Needless to say, Alfie found my comment hilarious and having closed the gap between us, he laughed in my face. 'You can say what you like, Gemma, but a blind man could see he's my child.'

My heart began pounding in my chest. 'If you believe that, you're more deluded than I ever imagined, or gave you credit for.'

'He looks exactly like me, Gemma.'

'Don't be so ridiculous. Of course he doesn't.' I couldn't hide the furious tone in my voice.

'Correct me if I'm wrong, but neither you nor Nathan have blond hair and blue eyes, do you?' Alfie's face broke into a huge smile, exposing his perfect white teeth.

'No, but my mum and sister do.' I came from a long line of brunettes, but Alfie didn't need to know that. 'Listen to yourself, Alfie. Just because Nathan and I don't have the same colouring as our son doesn't mean we're not his parents.' I shook my head to belittle his ludicrous suggestion. 'Anyway, a baby's hair and eye colour can change from birth, sometimes several times before their first birthday.

Luca could end up with dark hair and dark eyes like his father.' I spoke with confidence, but I'd just spouted some information I'd read in my pregnancy and birth book. I had no idea whether that was possible, but surely they wouldn't be able to publish information like that if it wasn't true.

'But Nathan's not his father, I am,' Alfie insisted. 'You can say what you like, Gemma, but I know Luca is my child.' Alfie looked over my shoulder and scrutinised the baby's face.

I rolled my eyes and let out a long breath. This conversation was becoming incredibly draining. 'You're very much mistaken. Luca is Nathan's and my son,' I repeated, hoping that Alfie would let the matter drop. He was like a dog with a bone. No matter how many times I told him Nathan was Luca's father, he wouldn't listen. I felt like I was banging my head against a brick wall.

'Nathan might have fallen for that, but I'm afraid I'm not quite so gullible.' Alfie flashed me a confident smile.

'Well, you'd better believe it, because it's the truth.' I stared into Alfie's blue eyes to reinforce my point.

'Deny it all you like, but the Watson family are known for their strong resemblance to each other. It's good to see the likeness has carried on for another generation.'

I felt like screaming. Alfie appeared to have tuned out to what I was saying. Every time I tried to reinforce the fact that Nathan was Luca's father, he ignored me.

'I look nothing like my parents or my sister for that matter, but that doesn't mean we don't share the same gene pool. Genes are passed down from many generations.' I knew my GCSE Biology course would come in useful at some point. I'm glad I took an interest in this topic now.

'OK, Gemma, I have a question for you. If Luca isn't my son, why is he the image of me? How old did you say he was?'

'For the last time, Alfie, there isn't the slightest possibility that Luca is your child.' I couldn't keep the frustration out of my voice.

'You seemed to have conveniently forgotten about the night we slept together, Gemma. Whereas I can recall it in great detail.'

I could feel Alfie undressing me with his eyes. He was giving me a strong non-verbal message that he still found me attractive. The way his blue eyes watched me like a hunter watching his prey was unnerving, so I glanced back at Luca to break eye contact with him.

Alfie reached forward and touched the side of my arm to get my attention. As his fingertips made contact with me, they made me jump. 'You do remember having sex with me, don't you?'

I felt my head begin to spin. As if that was something I could ever forget. It was one of the worst decisions I'd ever made, and I'd made some pretty terrible ones over the years.

Alfie took my silence as confirmation. 'That's good, so now you can stop all the bullshit.'

Alfie's tall, broad-shouldered frame loomed over me. The smug look on his face was making anger build up inside me. I couldn't hide the fury in my glare. Alfie took a closer look at Luca, and I felt perspiration break out on my upper lip.

'You know I fathered that baby.'

I shook my head and let out an audible sigh. 'On the one occasion I slept with you, you used a condom, remember?'

'So what.'

'How could I have become pregnant with your child if we used contraception?'

'That's the biggest load of bollocks I've ever heard.' Alfie threw his head back and laughed. 'If that were true, Gemma, I wouldn't be standing where I am right now. No form of contraception is one hundred per cent reliable.'

'I didn't notice the condom was damaged after we had sex.'

'That doesn't surprise me. You were in such a hurry to leave my room and scurry back to your husband before he realised you were missing, weren't you?'

Panic began rising within me, so I made a conscious effort to look as if the conversation wasn't fazing me. But as the drama unfolded around me, I struggled to keep my head and not react to the situation. I could feel myself shaking in my shoes as a wave of fear washed over me and threatened to drag me under. Alfie had walked back into my life and instantly turned my world upside down.

'The condom was intact, Alfie. Luca isn't your son,' I insisted, hoping he would let the matter drop.

'Looks like history has just repeated itself then. That's exactly what happened to my parents. I am also the product of a faulty condom. Contraception is powerless to stop the next generation of Watsons being conceived,' Alfie said before laughing in my face. The idea that the men in his family possessed some kind of super sperm clearly delighted him and boosted his already enormous ego.

I could feel my temples begin to pulsate as an agonising silence stretched out between us. As Alfie's words bombarded my brain, I couldn't think straight, and I struggled to manage the powerful emotion that had suddenly surfaced within me. Fear. A fear so tangible, I could taste it, and as I tried to swallow down the bitter pill, the acrid taste lingered in my mouth. Alfie's blue eyes bored into mine and made the hairs on the back of my neck rise and my heartbeat rapid.

'Isn't that a coincidence?' Alfie smiled as I squirmed. 'My mum was only eighteen when she had me.'

Alfie told me his mum was six months pregnant by the time his parents tied the knot. It was a shotgun wedding. Alfie's grandad insisted that Jethro marry Nora having got her in the family way. Leaving the young woman, who was pregnant with his first grandchild, as an unmarried mother was not an option as far as he was concerned. Jethro had to man up and do the right thing. Even though he protested that he didn't love Nora, his objections fell on deaf ears.

Knuckles and Nathan walked into the kitchen, and I made eye contact with my husband. He could tell by the look on my face that something was wrong, even before Alfie spoke.

'Enjoy the time you've got with Luca while it lasts.'

'What's that supposed to mean?' Nathan asked the question I'd been dreading, and a deafening silence followed.

'Pretty soon I'm going to take him away from you.'

'As if I'm going to let you take my son.' Nathan straightened his posture. His words were laced with fury.

'Gemma and I have finished our little chat now, so I'll get Knuckles to drive you home. Then your wife will be able to fill you in on what we've been talking about.' Alfie smiled and slipped his hands into the trouser pockets of his expensive suit.

Adrenaline coursed through my body and sent my pulse

racing again. The stress of the situation intensified when I realised Alfie and Nathan were waiting for me to speak, but I couldn't get my words out. My mouth was so dry when I attempted to clear my throat, I found myself gasping for air instead. I took a deep breath and tried to compose myself, but the silence dragged on.

46

Nathan

'Have you got a minute?' Dad said when he walked into the kitchen and saw I was sitting at the table alone.

'Yeah, of course. Is everything all right?'

Dad looked like he had the weight of the world on his shoulders. 'I'm really worried. I've been thinking about Alfie. You know he said he was going to take Luca away...' Dad broke eye contact with me and looked down at the floor before he finished his sentence. I could see he was distraught, so I wanted to put his mind at rest.

'It's OK. You don't need to worry. If Alfie thinks he's going to take my son in lieu of the money, he's got another thing coming.'

'I need to tell you something, Nathan. Alfie's threat might not be about the money.' Dad turned his troubled face towards me and looked at me with haunted eyes.

I bit the side of my lip; I didn't understand where we were going with this conversation. Dad wasn't making any sense. 'Trust me, it is. I know what he's like. Alfie won't go through with it, but he's threatening me to make sure I do what he wants. While his guys are in prison, he's short-staffed, so he needs me to work for him. That's all it is. Don't read too much into it.'

'Unless there's another reason you don't know about.' Dad pulled out a chair, so we were on eye level.

'Like what?'

'An eye for an eye,' Dad replied, before dropping his head in his hands.

My brows knitted together. Dad had lost me. 'What are you talking about?'

Dad looked up and let out a slow breath. 'Jethro had an older brother called Levi.'

I remembered Levi's name being mentioned a while ago when we were at Darkwood Manor, but so much had happened since then I'd put it out of my mind.

'He died a long time ago. He was killed in an accident,' Dad continued.

There was something my dad wasn't telling me about Levi's death. I could sense it. 'But what's that got to do with Luca?' I shrugged.

'Levi and I used to be friends. We went to school together. I was with him on the night he died, so Jethro and his parents blamed me for his death.' Dad suddenly revealed the cards he'd been keeping close to his chest.

Oh shit! I bit down hard on the side of my lip while I digested my father's words.

'I'm worried the Watsons are going to take Luca as payback for the family losing Levi. I couldn't bear it if something happened to the baby because of me.'

I knew there had been a bitter feud between the Stones and the Watsons for years. But up until now, I hadn't understood the reason. 'I'm not going to let the Watsons come anywhere near my son. I'll make sure he doesn't come to any harm.'

'I'm sorry, Nathan.' Dad's steely blue eyes were glistening with unshed tears.

'You've got nothing to apologise for. I'm glad you told me, but do me a favour, please don't mention this to Gemma. She'll only get stressed about it.'

My dad nodded before he walked out of the kitchen. He appeared to have aged ten years since we'd started our conversation. His words played over and over in my head. I hadn't considered Alfie taking Luca as anything more than an idle threat. I thought he just wanted to flex his muscles to scare us, but I hadn't known about Levi at the time. Men like Alfie were renowned for holding a grudge. Dad could be right. The Watsons might try to use Luca to bridge the gap between the past and the present.

Perhaps I should have taken Gemma's concerns more seriously. Since the day Luca had been born she'd been terrified that something bad was going to happen to him and no matter how many times I tried to put her mind at rest, I wasn't able to convince her. I'd considered her thoughts irrational; they would come out of nowhere and wake her in the middle of the night. She was exhausted, so I'd blamed her behaviour on her raging hormones and lack of sleep. If I was honest about it, the longer it went on, the less sympathetic I was being. No wonder she was sometimes short-tempered with me.

I felt guilty that I hadn't been more supportive. I wanted

to make it up to Gemma, so I decided to phone Mum to ask her advice, but before I had a chance to get any words out, Mum launched into an angry spiel about my dad. She wasn't happy, and wouldn't let me get a word in. Mum was very open about how much it hurt her that I was spending time with my father. I didn't understand why it bothered her so much. Mum was worried that my dad would be a bad influence on me.

The more she'd tried to poison me against my dad, the more she pushed me to fight his corner. The last thing I wanted was one of my parents suffering at the hands of the other. I wasn't going to be pressured to choose sides.

I'd finally found my dad, and all I wanted was for my mother to be as happy about the situation as I was, but instead, I felt this creeping sense of disapproval radiating down the phone line from her. I wasn't about to let her burst my bubble. No matter what she thought of Dad, the man was my father, and nothing could change that. She needed to get over the issues she had with him. They were nothing to do with me, and I wouldn't be drawn into it. But Mum's unmetabolised feelings kept coming out as barbs at my dad.

I couldn't take any more of the ear-bashing, so I reluctantly put an end to our conversation. Before I could hang up, my mum's voice broke with emotion. She was worried that I would end up having a closer relationship with my dad than her, and that would make her feel shut out. I couldn't believe what I was hearing. That was exactly what she did to Dad three decades ago when she cut him out of our lives.

*

An hour later, my mobile rang.

'I owe you an apology. I'm sorry about my outburst earlier. I don't know what came over me,' Mum said. 'We always used to be so close, but now you spend all your time with your dad, so I've been feeling a bit left out.'

I was glad she'd taken a step back. I didn't want us to be on bad terms again. 'I'm sorry too.'

I hadn't intended to make her jealous and felt a pang of guilt. I didn't want my mum to feel excluded. I'd struggled to cope with the collapse of our relationship more than I'd cared to admit. Her absence from my life had left a gaping hole behind. I wanted her to share this next chapter. This was such a special time for all of us.

'I had no right to say the things I did. I want you to know I'm happy that you and your dad are getting along and I promise I won't try to come between you.'

47

Nathan

Days had passed since Zamir had accused Alfie of roughing him up. Although Alfie had nothing to do with the beating the Albanian had received, the Watsons were convinced he would come after them to settle the score. Knuckles and I had been instructed to take up position at a discreet distance to keep watch on the warehouse.

There was little to do to occupy ourselves during the endless hours we'd sat inside the Mercedes, so I found myself mulling over my current situation. The amount of time Alfie was spending with my wife and child was really pissing me off. He saw more of them than I did, and silent resentment was building up inside me.

Luca was almost six months old now and seemed to reach a new milestone daily. I felt bitter that I was missing stages of his development because of Alfie. I was used to spending all day, every day with my wife and son and that suited me down to the ground. I loved being a dad and hated being separated from my family.

Gemma and I wanted to give Luca the kind of childhood we'd never had. We'd agreed to try and strike the right balance between showering him with love and material things, and not allowing him to become spoiled.

Gemma and I had mapped out our future together, and everything was on course until Alfie came back into our lives and put a spanner in the works. We were meant to be trying for another baby, but that was impossible due to the lack of time we spent together. I was adamant that Luca shouldn't be an only child. I'd always been desperate to have a sibling and felt cheated that my parents divorced before that became possible.

Gemma, on the other hand, reckoned she would rather not have endured the hostile, conflict-ridden interactions she'd had with her sister. She'd always maintained her run-ins with Rebecca had helped to destroy her self-esteem. My wife thought I had a rose-tinted idea of what it would be like to have brothers and sisters. I'd missed out on nothing, in her opinion. Gemma had said on more than one occasion that having a sister had only brought her heartache and drama. She used to joke that Mum and Dad had spared me from a horrible experience, and I should be forever grateful to them.

We'd already been in the car for several hours carrying out surveillance, and the boredom had well and truly set in, when Zamir, Dren, Esad and some other members of the gang came out of unit twenty-two. His men surrounded Zamir, while he locked up for the night. Out of nowhere shots rang out into the darkness as a man on the back of a motorbike wielding an automatic weapon sprayed bullets past their heads. Forming a human shield around their boss, they ran for their lives down the deserted alleyway.

Knuckles and I ducked down when the gunfire started, then peered over the dashboard to see how the events panned out. After only a few minutes, the bike roared off. The man riding pillion pointed his weapon behind him to cover any potential retaliation that might be about to come from the alleyway until they were out of sight. But there was no sign of Zamir and his gang, so whoever had carried out the hit had nothing to worry about.

48

Gemma

'Well, you couldn't expect me to stay away after I discovered your little secret, could you?' Alfie threw his head back and laughed. He was backing me into a corner. 'You have something that belongs to me.'

'If we give you back the money, will you let us go?' I said through gritted teeth. I didn't know how we were going to raise the funds, but we'd think of something.

'I'm not interested in the cash you stole, but you've got something else of mine, and I want it back.'

'I don't know what you're talking about.' The words tripped off my tongue. I hoped I sounded more convincing than I felt.

I turned and walked away from Alfie's interrogating stare. His piercing blue eyes felt like they were penetrating my brain so that he could read my thoughts. The idea of that made panic rise up within me, and once again, I struggled to stay in control.

'I'd forgotten what a good actress you are, Gemma. For

a minute, you almost had me fooled.' Alfie walked over to where I was standing with Luca in my arms. 'It's not the money I'm after. When I asked you the other day, you didn't answer my question. How old is Luca?'

Alfie's words rang in my ears.

'Come on, Gemma, what's the big secret? Surely you know how old the baby is.'

I pictured myself counting on invisible fingers while I cleared my throat. My mouth had completely dried out. 'Not that it's any of your business, but if you must know, he's almost five months.'

49

Alfie

Knuckles and Nathan drove straight from Zamir's warehouse to Darkwood Manor to fill me in on the latest events. When I heard the Mercedes approaching the house, I broke off my conversation with Gemma.

After hearing the details of the latest bit of bad luck to befall the Albanians, I decided to phone Vladimir. He immediately cleared up any speculation over who was responsible for the violent episodes. The Albanians were now officially embroiled in a feud with the Russians. Insulted by the lack of loyalty, Vladimir had issued a couple of warnings. When Zamir's beating failed to deter him, Vladimir had no choice but to up the ante and ordered a drive-by shooting.

'A close encounter with an AK-47 should do the trick.' Vladimir laughed. 'But just in case it hasn't, I want you to do me a favour, Alfie. Tell Zamir if there is any more meddling in affairs that don't concern him, this will end in a body count.'

'Keep your distance until all of this is settled. Zamir will find himself on the receiving end of an assassin's bullet if he's not careful,' Dad said. 'The Russian Mafia are very hard-headed businessmen. They're very effective at what they do. There is absolutely no way they'll risk losing face by allowing Zamir to cut them out of the deal.'

There was a pecking order in this business, and the sooner Zamir realised that, the better it would be for all of us. There was no denying I was a kingpin in the UK market, but even I had my limitations. I couldn't compete with the Russians. They were key players and wouldn't let people get away with taking liberties. The Albanians were about to find that out the hard way. If they went through with their plan, Vladimir would be forced to carry out his own form of justice before the Albanians flooded the market with cheap drugs.

'Loyalty counts for everything, doesn't it?' I said, then raised an eyebrow before flashing Gemma a bright smile.

Colour rushed to her cheeks, and she looked towards the floor while knotting her hands in her lap.

'Let Vladimir deal with Zamir. Remember you're meant to be keeping a low profile, Alf,' Dad said, breaking the awkward silence.

50

Gemma

Jethro and Alfie were deep in conversation when Luca and I arrived at Darkwood Manor the next morning. Contrary to what Nathan and I had believed, Jethro was far from retired. He might not be as involved as he used to be and had technically handed over the reins to his son, but he was still an active part of the organisation behind the scenes. More often than not, Alfie was following orders.

'You don't want to get caught up in the crossfire, Alf. It won't stop the Russians from carrying out the job even if innocent people are in the way. These men have no conscience.'

My mouth fell open. How could Jethro imply that Alfie was an innocent person? After everything the Watsons had put my family through, it was laughable that he was preaching about people not having a conscience. I was very tempted to point that out, but it would be less risky to poke a hungry bear with a large stick, than challenge Jethro about it. If I lit the fuse, there was a very good chance either Jethro or Alfie would explode.

Nathan and Knuckles walked into the kitchen a few moments later. Nathan pulled out a stool and sat next to me, whereas Alfie's right-hand man positioned himself on the far side of the room facing the windows with his back against the wall. The bodyguard was always on duty. I didn't envy his position. A lot of the time he spent long, boring hours standing around keeping watch, waiting for something to happen.

Knuckles stood with his huge hands clasped in front of him as his eyes slowly scanned the landscape for any sign of trouble. No doubt, he was carrying out a quick risk assessment of Alfie's kitchen while he was carrying out his surveillance. I found myself having to suppress a smile. This room had the potential to be the minder's worst nightmare. If a fight broke out in here, there were no end of weapons readily available, both actual and improvised, which an attacker could get their hands on.

I didn't know why I found that amusing, but a vision of Alfie being whipped with a tea towel while trying to defend himself from a frying pan onslaught suddenly came into my head. It was like a scene from an old Pink Panther movie.

My mood took a turn for the worse when Knuckles and Nathan were sent to keep watch on Zamir. Once they left the house, Jethro made himself scarce as well. Alfie stood on the other side of the granite counter grinning at me, and the look on his face sent a chill through my body. I got up and walked over to the far side of the kitchen. Luca was sitting up in his playpen chewing on one of his toys. When he saw me approach, he started babbling and reached forward with his hands. Then he began rocking back and forth on his hands and knees. This would be a huge milestone for my baby; his first step towards independent mobility, and although I had been eager to see this moment, I said a silent prayer that he wouldn't start to crawl in front of Alfie.

I could see Alfie swagger across the marble floor out of the corner of my eye, but I didn't look in his direction. When he stood shoulder to shoulder with me, my pulse began to race. For what seemed like the longest moment, he stood watching my baby with a hint of a smile on his face. His silence made my heartbeat quicken.

'Didn't you say Luca was almost five months?' Alfie tilted his head to the side and studied my reaction.

'Yes.' I didn't make eye contact with him because his gaze was interrogating.

'Fuck me, he's advanced for his age. My nieces and nephews were way older than him before they started to do that.'

'All babies develop at different rates,' I replied, brushing off his comment as though it wasn't important and not worth my consideration, but inside my old friend anxiety was bubbling under the surface. I hoped it didn't take this opportunity to make an appearance.

51

Alfie

Two days later when I'd thought the dust had settled, I paid Zamir a visit.

Knuckles, Nathan and I looked at each other when we stepped over the threshold of the dingy space. We could all feel the tension as soon as we entered the room. Although the warehouse was cavernous, the atmosphere was claustrophobic.

As we approached Zamir and his men, Dren jumped up from the table and began shouting at us in Albanian. We had no idea what the fucker was on about, but he wasn't exactly welcoming us in with open arms, so we stopped walking and stood our ground. I was aware that this could turn into a huge brawl if we weren't careful when Zamir's tracksuit-clad men quickly armed themselves with metal pipes, bats and knives.

Don't get me wrong, I love a good fight the same as the next man, and I'm usually the first one in the queue to dish out a beating, but that's not why I'd come here today.

Although it went against my instincts, on this occasion, I needed to back down from physical confrontation. I didn't want this meeting to descend into absolute chaos. But it wasn't going to be easy; being a pacifist didn't come naturally to me. I wasn't bothered about going home with a bit of blood on me, but I'd rather not be taken out of this shithole in a box.

Armed with a large kitchen knife, Dren ran over to where we were standing and tried to plunge the blade into Knuckles when he stepped in front of me. Knuckles disarmed his opponent with ease. As the knife hit the floor with a clatter, my right-hand man casually placed Dren in a headlock. I glanced over at Nathan and shook my head. He wasn't exactly an intimidating figure; the colour had drained from his face. The guy was a wimp and didn't have the presence to carry off the role I'd given him. He really wasn't cut out for this line of work, but he doubled my backup, so for now, he was an essential part of the team. I hoped he didn't let the side down and spew his guts up, or worse still, faint in a heap on the floor.

I tore my eyes away from him so that I could open up the lines of communication before Knuckles choked Dren unconscious. 'I didn't come here looking for trouble,' I said, holding my hands out in front of me, so I wasn't tempted to pull my gun out and shoot the lot of them.

'Let Dren go, and then we'll talk,' Zamir replied before lifting up a bottle of raki that was on the table in front of him and pouring some into two glasses.

I gestured to Knuckles, who instantly released his grip. Coughing and spluttering, Dren dropped onto his hands and knees. He stayed on the pigeon-shit-covered floor until he'd caught his breath. I waited impatiently until he'd stopped rasping before I continued our conversation.

'Now tell your men to put down their tools.'

Zamir's men threw down their weapons after he spoke to his tracksuited army in Albanian. He walked towards me and held out a glass with his work-worn hand. I took the firewater from him and downed it in one gulp. The stuff was disgusting, but I'd didn't want to offend him by not drinking it. The raki burned my throat long after I'd swallowed it.

'I want you to know I had nothing to do with the agro you've found yourself in recently. If you respect the boundaries, there's no reason for us to be at war. I don't have an issue with you, as long as you don't tread on my toes.'

'I understand, boss man. We don't want any trouble either. Our brush with death has spooked us,' Zamir replied.

'Believe me, if Vladimir Popov had wanted you dead, the hitman wouldn't have missed the target,' I said to reassure him. 'But you're skating on thin ice. If you don't want to find yourselves at the centre of an elaborate poison plot or some other kind of mysterious death, you'll reconsider who you buy your coke from.'

Zamir nodded. It looked like the penny had finally dropped.

'I hear what you're saying. If we want to stay safe, we'd better forget about branching out on our own.'

'Exactly.'

My face broke into a smile. I'd heard from the horse's mouth that Zamir was living on borrowed time. It was his own fault he was a target. Nobody could disrespect

Vladimir and the Russian Mafia, and get away with it. In underworld circles, looking at a rival the wrong way could be enough to leave you with a bullet planted in your brain. After the way he'd carried on, he'd have to do some serious backpedalling if he wanted to see another birthday.

'There's one more thing, I don't want to find your dealers hustling customers in my club.'

'Of course not. You have my word.'

Zamir gave me his sincerest look before he spoke in Albanian over his shoulder. Being excluded from a conversation always got my back up, and I felt myself bristle. Esad picked the bottle up from the table and walked over to join us. Zamir gestured to him, and Esad refilled our glasses.

'From now on we are allies,' Zamir said, holding his glass out in front of me.

52

Gemma

Luca was bawling his eyes out by the time Nathan, Alfie and Knuckles returned to Darkwood Manor. I had him up on my shoulder and was pacing backwards and forwards across the kitchen tiles, trying to soothe him, when my husband came in and took the baby out of my arms.

'What's the matter, mate?' Nathan asked. Luca's cheek was bright red, and he was dribbling profusely. 'Are your teeth giving you trouble?'

Nathan took the cooling ring from my hand, and Luca started gnawing on it. Within minutes he'd stopped crying. My husband definitely had the magic touch.

I walked over to the fridge and took out a glass ramekin of pureed apple I'd made up earlier. 'He might be hungry.'

Nathan placed Luca in his high chair and clipped him into the harness. 'Do you want some of this?' Nathan asked after loading a small amount onto a plastic spoon. Luca opened his mouth wide and smiled. 'There you go,' Nathan said, smiling back at the baby.

'I hate to break up this scene of domestic bliss, but you've got work to do, Nathan,' Alfie said.

Nathan handed me the dish before planting a kiss on Luca's and my cheeks. 'See you later,' he said before following Knuckles out of the door.

'Luca's on solids already. My sisters' kids were six months old before they started to wean them,' Alfie said.

'They do things differently in Spain,' I replied, not looking up from my son.

'I think it's time you cut the crap. We both know Luca's older than you're letting on.'

Even though I didn't turn around, I could feel Alfie's eyes boring into the back of my head.

'Did you know I was having you watched while you were living in Spain?'

Alfie had just confirmed my worst nightmare. The terror of feeling like I was being stalked was an experience that left me a changed person. Even in the apparent safety of my home, I felt scared and isolated. Every time I recalled the memory, it seemed to have become more frightening than it was before.

'I was kept up to date on your every move. When I heard that you were pregnant, I had a feeling I was the baby's father. I had to bide my time before I could do anything about my suspicions, but the physical similarities between myself and Luca are undeniable. Wouldn't you agree? I don't care how many times you deny it, I know Luca is my son.'

I was suddenly experiencing a full spectrum of emotions. It was time to harness them and use them to my advantage.

I couldn't let Alfie get to me. I had to pull myself together. Something told me things were about to get messy.

Luca started beaming at me, but the smile slid from my face. I was overcome with the impulse to lash out, but that would be a stupid move. Instead, I turned around and fixed Alfie with a glare. He could see the loathing in my eyes. I could feel anxiety building inside me. If he realised I was scared, it would only make Alfie's power level rise. I needed to choose my words carefully, but unfortunately, they got stuck in my throat, and the silence dragged on while I considered what to do for the best. If I let him, Alfie would take full advantage of the situation. He would prey on my weakness. I couldn't afford to let that happen.

'For the last time, Luca's not your son. He's not even five months old yet.' I reached forward and unclipped the harness. I wanted my baby close to me, so I lifted him out of the highchair and glared at Alfie while I held Luca in my arms.

'I can remember the first of September like it was yesterday,' Alfie said.

That was the day Luca was born. The pulse began pounding in my ears as I tried to swallow the lump at the back of my throat. I had to stay calm; I didn't want Alfie to sense my unease.

'It was one of the best days of my life. The game's up, Gemma.'

Alfie was backing me into a corner, marking his territory like a true dominant male, and I didn't know how to respond without making matters worse.

'I love you, Gemma, I always will. I want the three of us

to be a family.' Alfie fixed me with his blue eyes and reached forward to stroke Luca's face.

I turned my shoulder, so his fingers didn't make contact with my son. I didn't want this man near either of us. I thought I was pretty prepared for whatever life threw at me, but Alfie confessing his undying love had floored me. I felt paralysed with fear and couldn't think straight.

Alfie began grinning. 'I tell you what, I'm feeling generous tonight, so I'm going to offer you an ultimatum. You can go back to Gareth's house on the condition that you tell Nathan about Luca. You've got forty-eight hours to come clean. Otherwise, I'll tell him the truth myself.'

I had to fight back tears as my entire world started crashing down around me.

53

Gemma

Our marriage had hit rock bottom, and we hadn't had sex for over a month when Nathan and I first started trying for a baby. As we attempted to put my infidelity behind us, we'd hoped a baby would bring us closer together and help us make a fresh start.

Sitting alone on the side of the bath, I stared at my watch and tried not to look at the test on the glass shelf until the three minutes were up. They were the longest minutes of my life. They passed by like hours. When the time arrived, and I saw two lines as plain as day looking back at me, I could hardly believe it; I'd waited so long for this moment. I tore out of the bathroom, grinning from ear to ear. I didn't need to tell Nathan the outcome; he could see by the look on my face, it was good news. My husband picked me up and spun me around. He was as happy as I was. We were both over the moon. I remember the moment as if it was yesterday. Discovering that I was expecting our first child was the best thing that had happened to us in ages. This baby was going to mend our damaged relationship; I was sure of it.

The day had finally arrived. Nathan and I sat outside the room in the ultrasound department, waiting for my dating scan for what seemed like an eternity. I'd read and reread all the posters on the wall. Meanwhile, Nathan was fidgeting in the plastic chair impatiently tapping his foot on the floor while we waited for my name to be called. A huge smile spread across Nathan's handsome face when the door closest to us opened.

'Gemma Stone?' the lady dressed in blue medical scrubs asked.

'Yes,' Nathan replied in the manner of an excited child before I had a chance to speak.

Nathan was out of his chair in an instant and offered me his hand before escorting me into the dimly lit room. I lay down on the couch, and after tucking tissue paper around my clothing to protect it, the sonographer spread the cold clear gel onto my skin. As I was only in the first trimester, my stomach hadn't acquired the tell-tale bump yet, even with a bladder full of water. Nathan sat in the chair next to the couch and held one of my hands in both of his. He was taking his role as the expectant father very seriously.

When we saw the image of our child appear on the screen, Nathan and I both beamed at each other. That first glimpse of a life growing inside me was a moment I'll never forget. The heartbeat was tiny but so strong, and it brought a tear to my eye.

I confirmed the date of my last period. The information I

gave was met with stony silence. The next few moments were some of the most terrifying of my life. I thought something was wrong with the baby developing in my womb. I tried not to speculate that there was a complication, but why had the sonographer gone quiet? Maybe I was overreacting and overthinking the situation. But as my eyes moved from the screen to her face, I couldn't help noticing she was frowning. She was probably just concentrating on getting accurate measurements I reasoned, but something didn't feel right. She seemed to be repeatedly scanning the same area. I could feel my anxiety start to rise.

The sonographer worked on without saying a word, carefully examining my baby's body, until finally, she informed me that my dates appeared to be wrong. According to the ultrasound measurements she'd taken, the baby was conceived a month earlier than we had originally thought. Instead of being twelve weeks pregnant, I was sixteen weeks. This brought my due date forward from September 30 to September 2. My earlier elation had been replaced with a feeling of dread.

The sonographer's words were stuck on a continuous loop in my head. I didn't want to believe what I'd just heard and was stunned to learn I was a lot further along than I'd originally thought. When I worked out the dates again, I realised there was no chance Nathan could be the father. There was only one viable explanation. The child I was carrying was Alfie's. After just one encounter with him, I'd become pregnant. What were the chances of conceiving after a one-night stand? The situation was too awful for me to comprehend. I didn't know what to do.

I should have been relieved that the baby was healthy,

but instead, my mind felt like it was going to explode. The significance of the sonographer's findings went over Nathan's head. Having not been blessed with patience, he was delighted he wouldn't have to wait an extra month for the baby to arrive. Nathan continued clutching my hands while smiling from ear to ear. I didn't attempt to argue with her findings. She had just confirmed my worst nightmare.

Up until now, the thought had never crossed my mind that the baby might be Alfie's. Why would it? The one and only time I'd been unfaithful to my husband, I'd used protection. At the back of my mind, I was still holding on to the slim chance that the measurements were wrong, and the next time I had a scan, it would confirm that Nathan was my baby's father.

If I'd thought for one minute the condom had failed, I'd have taken the morning-after pill to prevent an unwanted pregnancy. When I glanced down at my stomach, the thought of that filled me with guilt. I was so glad I hadn't realised. I wanted this baby no matter who the biological father was.

As far as I was concerned, a baby was growing inside me. The child's paternity was irrelevant. But I wasn't sure Nathan would see it that way. He had struggled so much to get over my infidelity; if he realised the baby I was carrying wasn't his, he might not be prepared to accept it. I didn't want to take that chance, so I decided to keep my discovery a secret. That decision had now come back to haunt me.

54

Gemma

Alfie began bombarding me with text messages asking me if I'd told Nathan yet, but I ignored them all. He'd told me he'd give me forty-eight hours to come clean. That was barely twelve hours ago. I wasn't going to let him rush my life-changing decision. I needed to think things through carefully before I had the conversation I'd been dreading. It was a sensitive subject to broach. It was going to be particularly painful for Nathan, so I needed to pick the right moment, even though part of me just wanted to blurt it out and get it over with before I lost my nerve. If Alfie wasn't pressuring me into telling my secret, I wasn't sure I'd ever have admitted the truth to Nathan.

Last night, I considered every possible way the conversation with Nathan would go. Each time I pictured the scenario, the outcome was worse than the last. I had a strong tendency to overthink things, and my imagination began running riot. I reminded myself that each time I did this, the situation never unfolded the way I'd predicted it.

But that didn't stop me playing out the horrible scenes in my mind. You didn't need to be a genius to work out this wasn't going to end well.

I didn't want to tell my husband until I'd had a chance to work out a plan. The problem was I couldn't seem to come up with a solution to my dilemma. The more time that passed, the closer I got to the deadline. I knew the longer I delayed speaking to Nathan, the greater the chance I'd chicken out altogether. Things had been bad enough before, but it didn't bear thinking about what would happen if the truth was out in the open.

The inner turmoil I felt was caused by guilt, and it was having a toxic effect on our relationship. Since we'd returned from Darkwood Manor, Nathan had tried to question me on several occasions. He wanted to know what had happened with Alfie. Every time he tried to bring up the conversation, I'd bite his head off, so he'd reluctantly let it go. My anger was a mask for my fear and frustration. I was being a first-class bitch to him, I knew that, but I didn't feel ready to answer his questions. The more I tried to conceal the truth from him, the deeper I found myself sinking into the fabrication I'd created. I felt like I was wading through quicksand in a pair of concrete boots. I was in an impossible situation, and I couldn't see a way out.

The energy it took to keep my secret under wraps was exhausting, and I found it a constant drain. Would the burden be instantly lifted if I came clean? I somehow doubted that. But I knew I'd reached the end of the line. The situation had finally caught up with me. I had kept denying that Alfie was the father of my son to spare my husband's feelings. I wasn't ready to face up to what I'd done yet. I needed more time, but that was the one thing I didn't have.

The enormous amount of guilt I felt weighed heavily on my conscience. I couldn't shrug it off, and it began to eat away at me. I knew when the truth came out, it was going to cause my husband a great deal of pain and heartache. By staying quiet, I was acting like a coward. But I was frightened to open a can of worms because once my secret was freed, it would ruin my husband's life.

The way I saw it, whether Nathan was the biological father of our son or not was beside the point. He adored Luca as if the child was his own flesh and blood. If I did what Alfie wanted, I was going to take that away from him.

The voice of reason inside my head told me I should have the decency to tell Nathan myself. It wasn't right to let him hear the news from Alfie. But how do you tell somebody something that you know will destroy them? Nathan was the love of my life. I didn't want to be the one to break his heart.

55

Alfie

I'd wanted Gemma to be happy, and if that meant setting her free, so be it. At the time, I hadn't appreciated how difficult that would be. I was fully aware that the last time I made contact with Gemma, I'd told her I would let her go. But then again, I couldn't have mentioned that I was going to keep her under twenty-four-hour surveillance, could I? She would never have let her guard down if she'd realised I wasn't going to keep my word.

Soon after Gemma and Nathan relocated to the Costa del Sol, I decided to take up residence at my family's villa, close by to where the couple were living. A change of scenery would do me good after the stress I'd been through recently following my arrest in Boulogne. My dad had been desperate to take back the reins of the family business for years now, so he was more than happy to oversee the running of the firm while I had some time off. Dad knew about the situation with Gemma, and he'd given me his blessing to stay in Spain for the foreseeable future. It made good business sense. Our supplier, Vladimir, was also based in Marbella, and while I was out there, I could channel cash from our offshore bank accounts into Spanish property and businesses to expand our portfolio.

Over the years, Dad and I had fallen out on many occasions. I blamed him for my mum's death. There was never a good time to lose a parent, but it was even harder to come to terms with if it happened to a person while they were still a child. Our relationship took a nosedive after Mum's funeral. He'd treated her like shit, and I was never going to let him forget it.

It was fair to say Dad and I had our differences. We didn't see eye to eye on a lot of things, but Dad had been through an experience similar to mine when he fell in love with Rosa, so he understood what I was going through. We'd both fallen for unavailable married women. Who would have thought the situation that destroyed my family and my parents' marriage would be the thing that brought Dad and I closer together. Finally, we had something in common. The fact that we shared the same problem with our non-existent love lives gave us a new understanding of each other.

56

Gemma

When I'd discovered the true identity of Luca's father, after my first scan, I hadn't stopped to think about the consequences failing to share the details would bring. My head and my heart were in conflict as I weighed up what to do. I had to decide whether or not to come clean, or say nothing. I'd normally listen carefully to my conscience, and it was telling me that lying to Nathan was wrong whatever the circumstances. But I chose to ignore it and, instead, I focused on allowing my unsuspecting husband to believe the lie. My stomach twisted in revulsion at what I'd done. It was wrong of me to think it was OK to keep this to myself, but I panicked when I realised the baby was Alfie's, and Nathan seemed completely oblivious to the fact that my dates were wrong, so that justified keeping the news a secret from him, didn't it?

I thought I'd got away with it. Now the clock was ticking; Nathan was going to find out the truth one way or another. If I didn't come clean, Alfie was going to break the news for me. Why was I so reluctant to own up? I knew it was better that Nathan heard it from me, but the prospect of admitting what I'd done was so horrible, I didn't want to contemplate it. It was easier to hide behind my emotions, which were currently alternating between fear-filled fits of temper and floods of tears. The stress of hiding Luca's paternity was taking its toll on me.

Not surprisingly, given the pressure I was under, my relationship with Nathan had started to fall apart. I was pushing him away and had become emotionally distant from him. That was driving a wedge between us.

My worst fear had been realised. The web of lies I'd cocooned myself in was starting to unravel. The secret I'd been hiding was about to come out, and it was going to destroy Nathan. I'd never intended that to happen. I was expecting to take this information to the grave. I realised now, that was naive of me. I wasn't concealing a harmless untruth, it was a lie of monumental proportions, and staying silent was a destructive choice. It was impossible to keep a secret of this size without the details beginning to leak somewhere. The bigger the secret, the harder it was to keep. Having nobody to share it with had left me feeling incredibly isolated.

When I'd initially found out I was pregnant, I genuinely thought the baby was my husband's. He was thrilled that we were going to become parents. By the time I realised the truth, for me, there was no going back. I had a baby growing inside me and abortion was absolutely not an option for me. I made the decision not to tell Nathan the result of the scan as an act of self-preservation. I'd selfishly kept Luca's father's identity a secret in the hope it would spare Nathan immense heartache. I wanted to shield him from the suffering I knew the truth would cause.

In hindsight, I should have been honest right from the start. But I didn't know how he was going to respond. I was scared he might not be prepared to bring up another man's child, and who could blame him? I didn't know at that stage that Alfie was a free man. If he'd been behind bars like he was meant to be, I might have got away with the deception. If only I'd known then what I know now.

Fear stopped me from coming clean. I was terrified I'd have to raise my child alone. If Nathan knew the truth, he might have turned his back on me. I didn't want him to leave me. I wasn't sure I would be able to cope if I was left as a single mum. This was not a situation I ever expected to be in, not in a million years.

As I tried to reach a decision on the best time to tell my husband the truth, I lay awake, listening to every sound. Nathan was sleeping peacefully beside me, blissfully unaware of the secret I was hiding from him.

57

Nathan

Alfie had been spending an unhealthy amount of time with Gemma. I tried not to let it get to me, but it was hard for me to turn a blind eye. I trusted Gemma; and knew she was more than likely putting up with the situation, so she didn't rock the boat. But Alfie was turning on the charm at every opportunity as he tried to worm his way back into her affections. I was doing my best not to rise to the bait. I didn't want to give him the satisfaction of provoking a reaction out of me, but ignoring a man who is blatantly trying to crack on with your wife is virtually impossible.

Gemma and I needed to put on a united front. The best thing we could do to ward off his unwanted attention was show Alfie we had rebuilt our relationship and we were happy together. Then Alfie would realise he wouldn't be able to come between us, but for us to be able to do that, Gemma and I would need to be on the same page. The problem was, she'd been so distant with me recently, I was having trouble communicating with her. It was like she'd retreated into her own world. The more I tried to reach out to her, the more she was shutting me out. Something was bothering Gemma. I couldn't put my finger on what was troubling her, but whatever it was, she was keeping it to herself.

Everything I did seemed to irritate Gemma. I wasn't sure why, so I questioned her about it, but she denied she'd been snappy with me. All I wanted to do was right the wrong, but I couldn't if Gemma wouldn't tell me why she was pissed off with me. The more I thought about it, the more worried I was becoming.

The change in Gemma's attitude towards me seemed to coincide with Alfie's reappearance in our lives. Levels of trust fluctuate in a relationship, and it was normal to feel insecure, especially if you'd been burned in the past. I had a sudden sinking feeling in my stomach. It was obvious that Alfie still found Gemma attractive, but did she still have feelings for him? Perhaps something was going on between them, after all. Was I so stupid that I hadn't noticed them rekindle their romance right under my nose? If they were sleeping together, that would explain why she'd begun to push me away.

It was difficult not to be suspicious and so easy to jump to conclusions, but I had to think logically about the situation and not put two and two together and get five. I had no proof that anything was going on, so the best thing I could do was block that thought from my mind. Losing my wife, especially to Alfie, was too painful for me to contemplate.

58

Alfie

The moment I realised Gemma was pregnant, I'd had my suspicions that the child she was carrying might be mine. That gave me even more reason to keep a watchful eye on her movements and made me more convinced than ever that Gemma and I were meant to be together. I became obsessed with every aspect of her life. Absence really did make the heart grow fonder, and it soon became clear to me that I could never let her go.

In the beginning, I had to observe from the sidelines, and that was torture. I could look, but I couldn't touch. Gemma seemed to sense my presence, although I never allowed myself to get close enough so that she could see me. I wanted Gemma to think I was out of her life for good so that when the time came for us to meet again, I wouldn't have ruined the shock factor. The element of surprise always produced the best response.

I had to bide my time until I made my move. I knew Nathan wouldn't be able to resist tracking down his dad now that Rosa had told him the truth. It was only a matter of time before they came back to England. Once the family were back on UK soil, it would make my plan easier to orchestrate. Everything had fallen into place without a hitch, and when Gemma and I had eventually come face to face, she looked like she'd seen a ghost. I couldn't help smiling at the memory. Her expression was priceless. It had been worth the wait.

I couldn't believe she'd blatantly lied to me about Luca's age. It was just as well I'd witnessed her leaving for the hospital while she was in labour and returning the next day with her bundle of joy. Otherwise, I might have believed her. She was clearly desperate to throw me off the scent by pretending Luca was a month younger than he was. I was disappointed that she'd stooped to underhand tactics in an attempt to convince me that I wasn't the baby's father, but that was the behaviour of a guilty person if ever I'd seen it.

59

Gemma

When Nathan came home from Sherlock's in the early hours of the morning, he'd found me sitting alone in the dark in Gareth's living room.

'What's up, Gemma?'

'I'm terrified that Alfie's going to go through with his threat.' Tears sprang from my puffy eyes again, and I dabbed at them with a soggy tissue. The emotional roller coaster I'd recently found myself stuck on was travelling on a continuous loop at high speed.

Nathan sat down next to me. I wanted him to hold me in his muscular arms, I craved the comfort that would bring, but my husband clasped his fingers behind his head and looked into the middle distance. Then he crossed the room and looked out of the window that faced the street. 'Alfie's full of shit. As if I'm going to let him take my son over a stupid debt.'

The perfect opportunity to come clean had just presented itself to me. Nathan deserved to know the truth, but I couldn't seem to find the right words, so I kept quiet. I didn't want him to know the real reason Alfie was threatening to take Luca away. As time had gone by, the deception had increased in size, and now it had grown out of all proportion. I was carrying the weight of the world on my shoulders. It was too heavy for me to bear, and I felt myself collapsing under the strain.

'Don't look so worried. Nothing's going to happen to Luca.'

I hoped Nathan was right, but I knew he was as concerned as I was. He had always been an expert at hiding his feelings and could maintain an untroubled demeanour in the most stressful situation, but at this moment in time, his haunted expression gave away what he was thinking.

I was on borrowed time, and could only protect Luca from Alfie for so long. I didn't share my husband's optimism, but I admired his ability to remain positive in a hopeless situation. I sometimes wished I could fast-forward my life and see into the future, but I was scared of what might be waiting for me.

Nathan took hold of my hand and led me out of the living room and up the stairs. 'Let's get some sleep. Everything will look better in the morning.'

I wish I had my husband's confidence that things would turn out OK, but my mind was in turmoil.

60

Alfie

At one point, I had considered giving up on the idea of having a future with Gemma and Luca. It was proving almost impossible to come between her and Nathan, and despite my best efforts, he was still on the scene. I'd tried everything I could to convince her that she'd be better off without Nathan in her life. Although the man was a leech, she wouldn't consider leaving him, and I wasn't about to let another man bring up my child. So we were at a stalemate.

I'd spent an eternity trying to win Gemma over, and my patience had finally worn out. Gemma wasn't playing ball, so I'd had no option but to back her into a corner. I'd given her plenty of time to do the right thing. It wasn't fair on Nathan or on me that she was withholding the truth. Much as I couldn't stand the guy, I felt a bit sorry for him. He was bringing up a child thinking it was his son, and the longer Gemma deceived him, the worse it was going to be.

Gemma's unswerving loyalty to her husband was causing me problems, and I was having to fight the urge to take Nathan out of the equation. It would be easy to put a bullet in his head, but that would be too obvious, and Gemma would never forgive me. I'd have to try and divert her attention away from him, but it was hard to get through to her. Being in competition with him left a bad taste in my mouth. Nathan wasn't good enough for her; it was about time she realised that.

For Gemma and I to move forward, I'd have to make her break up with her husband. But the decision to leave had to be hers. Otherwise, we wouldn't have a future. She would always hold it against me if I intervened. Once Nathan knew the secret she'd been keeping, with any luck, we wouldn't see him for dust. He had pre-existing trust issues, and Gemma wasn't concealing a small lie. She was covering up a huge betrayal. Logic told me it would be very hard for them to stay together after she came clean.

When their relationship crumbled, Gemma would need a shoulder to cry on, and I would be waiting in the wings. I'd be more than happy to take Nathan's place. Biding my time was proving to be the hardest part of this process. One of the most important things in life my dad taught me was to be patient. If I could master that skill, rewards would follow.

Now it was time to force her hand. If I let Gemma walk away from me, I'd have to admit defeat, and that wasn't something that sat easy with me. Gemma needed to understand the message loud and clear: Luca was my son, and whether she liked it or not, I was going to be part of the child's life. There was no way I was going to stand back and let another man raise my son. So I had no choice but to play my trump card. Once Nathan knew the truth about Luca, he'd wash his hands of his deceitful wife and the problem would be solved.

61

Gemma

Although Alfie was insistent that he was Luca's father, I had never confirmed it. I hoped I'd delivered the denial convincingly enough that he would let the matter drop, and because we'd used a condom, I'd thought Alfie wouldn't realise he'd made me pregnant.

I'd always been frightened that the truth would come out if any of Alfie's family saw Luca. He didn't look a bit like me. He was a Watson through and through. Something told me, the older my son got, the more he would resemble his father and grandfather. The similarity between Jethro and Alfie was striking.

I never intended to tell my secret. Originally, I'd kept the result of the scan to myself because I was scared of what my husband would say. I'd been selfish because I didn't want to raise a child on my own, and I loved Nathan more than anything so I couldn't bear the thought of losing him. Deciding to keep the father's identity under wraps and hoping that the truth never came out was a big mistake.

Alfie was tightening the thumbscrews, and the stress I was under was causing arguments between Nathan and I. The pressure of living with this lie had driven a wedge between us and for the first time in ages we were at each other's throats. I didn't want to live like this; it wasn't healthy for Luca to grow up in an environment where his mum and dad were constantly arguing. It would be better for a child to grow up with one loving parent than a mum and dad who were fighting.

Alfie was going to make sure the whole world knew that Luca was his son and heir to the Watson dynasty. My biggest worry was that Alfie might insist on a DNA test to prove paternity. I couldn't let that happen. It would have a catastrophic effect on Nathan's and my future. Once paternity was established, it would confirm Alfie's suspicion. Luca was a Watson. There was no way to get around that. Then I would have to face a greater fear: Alfie would have rights, and he would be determined to enforce them.

Running away seemed like the only option I had. I needed to think things through. I didn't want to make a spur-of-the-moment decision, but I couldn't bear to be part of this circus. If I was going to end up a single mother anyway, instead of waiting for Nathan to leave me, maybe I should take Luca and go somewhere far away from everyone. Then I could raise my child without Alfie's interference, but where would I go? I'd need to think this through carefully. There was only going to be one chance to get this right. I'd have to try and formulate a plan, but time was running out, and I couldn't think straight.

Since Luca was born, I hadn't found things easy to cope with, and I'd had many moments where I felt close to the edge. I needed to dig deep and channel my inner strength if I was going to get out of the mess I'd created. There was nothing I could do to alter what had happened, so there was no point in dwelling on that. I couldn't change the past, but I was determined to be in control of my future. Even though I didn't want to be a single mother, I mustn't doubt my ability to raise my son alone. I could do it, and I would do it.

The last thing I wanted to do was leave Nathan, but I had no choice. Alfie had taken that away from me. I would never be able to explain my reasons for keeping the secret. The right words didn't exist to justify my actions. The thought of looking my husband in the eye and telling him that I'd lied to him was too painful to contemplate. I wished I could turn back the clock, but I couldn't, and life was too precious to be living with regrets. I owed it to Luca to make the best of this terrible situation.

62

Alfie

What I wanted more than anything was for Gemma, Luca and I to be a proper family. Because of my mum and dad's dysfunctional marriage, I felt like I'd missed out on a normal childhood. Money couldn't replace the simple things in life. We'd never had family trips to the park or the zoo like other kids. We didn't even sit around the table and eat dinner together. Dad was always out working or making himself scarce, but I was inseparable from my mum and two sisters, Dani and Sam.

When we were young, if Dad took the three of us out anywhere, Mum never came with us. She would have loved to, but she was never invited. Dad used to say it was to give her a break from us, but that was bullshit, and we knew it. He couldn't be in the same room as my mum without taking a verbal swipe at her over something or nothing. In my dad's eyes, she couldn't do anything right; from the clothes she wore to the way she made his tea, Dad found fault with everything. The worst thing about it was she never stopped trying to please him.

I hated the way Dad treated Mum, and for a long time, it poisoned our relationship, especially when she died so suddenly. I held her hand as she lay on the trolley in the ambulance, gravely ill. Mum kept asking for my dad, but we both knew he wouldn't come. I'd never forgiven him for that.

I would never get over losing my mum. I adored her; all three of us did. She would have been over the moon to know I had a son. Out of respect for her, I wanted to do the right thing and help raise my child and be the kind of father my dad never was. Mum would be proud that I'd broken the mould.

I loved Gemma, but she was determined to torture me. It was like a thorn in my side having to watch her and Nathan playing happy families from a distance, especially after my son was born. What a shame the love they had for each other was going to come to an end. It was a tragedy. My heart bled for them. If you believe that, you'd believe anything.

Gemma had another thing coming if she thought she could cut me out of my son's life. She was playing a game, but she wasn't going to win. Gemma should know from experience that I always got what I wanted in the end. Nothing would stand in my way.

I knew my name didn't appear on Luca's birth certificate, so I wouldn't automatically have parental responsibility even though I was the boy's father. Trust was one of the most important things in a relationship, and Gemma hadn't just broken Nathan's, she'd smashed it to pieces. If, by some miracle, they ended up staying together after the truth came out, I'd fight Gemma for full custody. I didn't want Nathan to be a part of my son's life. Not now, or ever.

63

Gemma

My deception had come back to haunt me, and it had finally caught up with me. I had to face the agonising dilemma of whether to tell Nathan or not. Even though I knew I had to come clean, I couldn't bring myself to do it. I kept finding reasons to put off the inevitable. Nathan deserved to know the truth so that he could make his own choice. But the truth was so awful, it made me want to continue with the lie.

Nathan didn't deserve any of this. He had always been my anchor. The rock I clung to when times got tough. He was the most loyal man you could ever meet. That was one of the reasons I couldn't picture my life without him. If I hadn't betrayed my husband, I wouldn't be in this terrible mess. But this wasn't the right time for a pity party; I had nobody to blame but myself. The sooner I told Nathan the truth, the better. I couldn't let Alfie be the one to deliver the news I knew would destroy him. I was fully aware that once something was said, it could never be taken back. With that thought still in my head, a text message came through from Alfie. It was as if he'd just read my mind.

Time is running out, Gemma. Tick tock...

My strength had deserted me at a time when I needed it the most. I'd have to pluck up the courage to talk to my husband before Alfie did it for me. As I played over the scene in my mind, my anxiety levels went through the roof. All of a sudden, I felt introverted and riddled with self-doubt. I used to be self-assured, and now I was an insecure mess, worrying about how the situation would pan out. I had to find my confidence and pull myself together.

I should have realised Alfie wouldn't keep his word and give me forty-eight hours. He was going to torment me until he got his own way. I suddenly felt like I wasn't in control of my destiny. I never wanted Nathan to find out he wasn't Luca's father. I loved my husband so much. I couldn't bear the thought of losing him.

Carrying this incredible burden of guilt was like a weight around my neck. Knowing I was about to ruin my husband's life was difficult to come to terms with. Nathan had been reluctant to start a family because he hadn't had a role model, and he was scared he'd fail at the task. Nathan had been worried about nothing; he was a wonderful dad, which made this all the harder. If Alfie got his way, he would take the opportunity away from him. But there was more to fatherhood than being a sperm donor.

Do you think Nathan's going to stay with you when he finds out the truth?

Nathan loved Luca and I unconditionally, but I could sense our future wasn't going to have a happy ending. Much as I hated to admit it, Alfie was right. Once Nathan realised that Luca wasn't his son, he would leave me for sure. Discovering a cuckoo in the nest was the ultimate way to destroy a man's pride. I'd unintentionally publicly humiliated him, and I hated myself for that. I'd let him believe that Luca was his son when I'd known all along that wasn't possible. I should have been honest about my pregnancy the moment I found out that Alfie was my baby's father. Then Nathan would have known the facts, no matter how unpleasant they were, and he could have made his own decision. It was unfair of me to have tricked him into believing a lie. Nathan never suspected a thing. It served me right that now I was trapped in a snare of my own making.

My infidelity had become a festering wound at the centre of our relationship. No matter how hard we tried to put it behind us, it kept resurfacing. Alfie was about to tear the wound wide open again, and this time I wasn't sure we'd be able to salvage what was left of our marriage. Nathan and I were destined for a lifetime of emotional pain. It was heart-breaking because everything was going so well between us until Alfie made a reappearance.

Although my aim had been to protect Nathan, nothing could justify what I'd done. I'd held on to the mistaken belief that nobody would find out about my deception, but now the shit was about to hit the fan. The revelation would floor Nathan, and I knew Alfie wouldn't be a gracious victor. He would rub Nathan's nose in it every chance he got.

I sat alone on the sofa while my baby slept in his basket, contemplating my next move. I knew if I stayed, none of us would ever be free of Alfie. He would always be hovering in the background, making his presence felt waiting for the opportunity to take Luca away from me. He was never going to sit back and allow Nathan to bring up his son.

Alfie had planted the thought in my head, and now my mind was happy to do the rest. My imagination went into overdrive as his words swam around in my head. Alfie knew his text would hit me hard. He'd wanted to hurt me and knew how to get under my skin. Stirring the pot came naturally to him. I didn't seem to have any control over this situation. I stupidly hadn't realised the decision I'd made in the act of self-preservation would have such a destructive and harmful outcome. The thought of that made panic begin to rise within me.

The last thing I wanted to do was leave Nathan, but I had no choice. Alfie had taken that away from me. I would never be able to explain my reasons for keeping the secret. The right words didn't exist to justify my actions. The thought of looking my husband in the eye and telling him that I'd lied to him was too painful to contemplate. I wished I could turn back the clock, but I couldn't, and life was too precious to be living with regrets. I owed it to Luca to make the best of this terrible situation.

Running away seemed like the only option I had. I didn't want to make a spur-of-the-moment decision, but I couldn't bear to be part of this circus. If I was going to end up a single mother anyway, instead of waiting for Nathan to leave me, maybe I should take Luca and go somewhere far away from everyone. Then I could raise my child without Alfie's interference, but where would I go? I'd need to think this through carefully. There was only going to be one chance to get this right. I'd have to try and formulate a plan, but time was running out, and I couldn't think straight.

Little did Alfie know, his latest text had just helped me make up my mind. If Nathan was going to leave me anyway, what was the point of me staying? I would leave in the middle of the night while everybody was asleep and take Luca with me. I knew that was the coward's way out, but I couldn't face the alternative.

Don't worry, Gemma, you won't have to raise my son on your own. I'll be happy to take you off Nathan's hands.

Being skilled at manipulating a situation, Alfie wasted no time offering me a solution to my problem. He was intentionally exploiting my vulnerability. I decided not to reply to his text. I'd let him think I was considering his proposition, when in fact, I was trying to work out how to get away from him. At least it would buy me some time.

Over the years, I'd had my fair share of crap to deal with, just like anyone else. But sometimes, I couldn't help feeling that life was more unkind to some people than it was to others. When I'd come face to face with Jethro in the street that day, fate dealt me a cruel blow. The Watsons were back in our lives, whether we liked it or not. I couldn't change that, but I could try and do something about it. Nobody was going to put my baby in danger.

This wasn't the right environment to raise a child in.

Luca's needs had to come first. He was the real victim in this situation. I could see where Rosa was coming from when she cut Gareth out of Nathan's life. She didn't want her son to be influenced by the bad example he'd set. I felt the same way. I didn't want Alfie to be part of my son's upbringing. Since I'd become a mother, it had changed my attitude and outlook on life.

Little did Alfie know, his latest text had just helped me make up my mind. I would leave in the middle of the night while everybody was asleep and take Luca with me. I knew that was the coward's way out, but I couldn't face the alternative. I needed to attempt to get back to Spain. If I could make it to our apartment, I could get hold of the cash I'd hidden from Nathan. I knew from previous experience that I might not be able to trust him with the money. That amount of cash would be too much of a temptation. He wouldn't be able to resist spending it. Although he was trying his best, his gambling habit was too deep-seated to give up overnight. I was glad I'd trusted my instincts now. The fact that I had a large sum of money stashed away was another secret I was keeping from my husband. But I didn't feel guilty about that one.

Once I got my hands on the money, I could take Luca to a safer location. Returning to our apartment was risky because Nathan would probably check there when he realised that I'd gone. But if I just stayed long enough to pack our things it should be OK.

'You go up to bed. I'm going to feed Luca, and then I'll follow you up.' I said before throwing my arms around my husband's neck and giving him a lingering kiss.

Knowing this might be the last time I got to touch his soft lips made sadness well up inside me, and I had to hold back my tears.

As Nathan held me in his strong arms, I rested my face against his chest. 'Don't be too long,' he said, planting a kiss on the top of my head before walking out the door.

While I watched my husband climb the stairs, I felt my heart breaking. Tears welled up in my eyes. I couldn't bear to think about losing the love of my life. I didn't want to leave Nathan, but at the moment staying with him was out of the question. When we'd decided to put our problems behind us and give our marriage another go, we promised ourselves we'd never take each other for granted again. Almost splitting up had taught us that valuable lesson.

It was hard living a double life. I hated lying to Nathan. Because of a moment of madness, when I'd had a drunken one-night stand with Alfie, we were now living a lie. I'd made a stupid mistake cheating on my husband, and I was about to pay the ultimate price. By taking the path of least resistance, I'd destroyed my relationship. My only option was to get away from here. I knew that was the right decision.

I had no intention of joining Nathan upstairs. It would be easier to slip out of the house unnoticed if I stayed down here. But I couldn't resist seeing my husband one last time. With a heavy heart, I climbed the stairs and pushed the bedroom door open. I could see Nathan's dark eyelashes fluttering as he slept. As I watched him, I felt like someone had knifed me in the stomach. The pain was too intense, so I turned and walked back down the stairs. This was going to be the hardest thing I'd ever have to do.

I returned to the living room deep in thought. As I walked, I considered leaving Nathan a note, but I didn't know what to write. Maybe I should send a text. I didn't want him to worry, but as I held my phone in my hand, I couldn't bring myself to press the keys. I was behaving like a coward, running away, so that I didn't have to face up to the consequences, but I couldn't be the one to break the news to him. He would never forgive me, and the thought of that was more than I could bear.

This seemed like the best option. Alfie's ultimatum had backed me into a corner, and this was the easiest way out, well, for me anyway. Taking my son with me, I walked out the front door and got into our Jeep.

It was just after four o'clock in the morning, so I had plenty of time to catch the 08:45 ferry from Portsmouth to Santander. I'd been up all night, but I didn't feel tired. My mind was racing at a hundred miles an hour. If I wanted to protect Luca from Alfie, I had to get as far away from London as possible.

I sat in the driver's seat, gripping the steering wheel until my knuckles turned white. I was scared to leave, but there was no going back. I'd made my decision, and now I had to go through with it. I would take care of Luca myself and build a new life for us. I didn't need to depend on a man. Plenty of women were single parents and if they could do it, so could I.

I started the engine before I had time to talk myself out of it. The roads were virtually deserted at this unearthly hour of the morning, and I made it to Portsmouth in good time for the ferry to Santander. As I waited in the queue to board, I felt an ache in my heart and wondered if Nathan had realised I'd gone yet, but then I put the thought out of my mind. There was no point dwelling on it. It wasn't going to change anything.

64

Nathan

As the early morning sunlight filtered into the bedroom, I rolled over and stretched my hand over Gemma's side of the bed. Finding it empty, I opened my eyes and looked around the room. Luca's quilted cradle was also empty. At first, I didn't think anything of it. I presumed that Gemma was feeding the baby and had taken him downstairs like she sometimes did, so as not to disturb the rest of the household.

Several hours later, when I woke again, I was surprised to see Gemma and Luca weren't back in the room. Throwing back the quilt, I swung my legs out of bed. Sitting on the edge, I reached over and picked up my iPhone to check the time. It was just after eight. I threw on some tracksuit bottoms and a T-shirt that I'd left on a chair at the far side of the bedroom.

I yawned as I walked down the stairs. First, I looked in the living room. It was empty, so I walked down the hall towards the kitchen. I was surprised to find nobody in there either, but then I realised that Luca's pram was missing.

Gemma must have taken him out somewhere. I put the kettle on and made myself a cup of instant coffee. While I was drinking it, I sent Gemma a text message.

You're up early ☺

When Gemma hadn't replied ten minutes later, I started to get worried, so I sent her another message.

Where are you?

When more time had passed, and there was still no reply, I started pacing backwards and forwards in the living room, peering out the window at the empty street. I dialled Gemma's number, and it went straight to her voicemail. A sinking feeling in the pit of my stomach told me something was wrong. I ran out of the room and started calling to my dad as I climbed the stairs two at a time.

Dad stood in the doorway of his bedroom in his boxer shorts. He was in good shape for a man of his age and had a lean, toned physique. Due to his lack of clothing, the dressing on his leg was clearly visible. It was now surrounded by a colourful bruise that covered half of his thigh.

'What's wrong, Nathan?' Dad asked as he ran his fingers through his greying hair.

'Gemma and Luca have gone.'

Dad could see by the look on my face, that I was worried sick. 'Have you tried calling her?'

'Yes, but her phone goes straight to voicemail. I've texted her twice, and she hasn't replied. Something's wrong, Dad, I know it.' I turned on my heel and paced along the hallway to my bedroom. My intuition was telling me Gemma was in trouble. 'That fucking bastard must have taken them again. I'm going after them,' I called over my shoulder.

'Let me just throw some clothes on, and I'll come with you,' Dad replied.

I was looking out of the living room window when my dad came down the stairs. 'The Jeep's gone. Why would Alfie take our car?'

Dad shook his head. 'Who knows. We can take my car, but you'll have to drive.'

A few moments later, we left the terraced house and got into Dad's Blue Ford Mondeo. I put my foot to the floor and sped off in the direction of Darkwood Manor.

'How did Alfie get into the house in the middle of the night and take Gemma and Luca without waking us?' I briefly took my eyes off the road and glanced at my dad.

'I have no idea,' Dad replied.

I stopped the car outside the wrought-iron gates, jumped out, and ran across to the intercom. I pressed the call button on the control panel above and waited for a response. Jethro's housekeeper answered the buzzer. She told me to wait a moment while she went to find Mr Watson.

When the gates started to open, I got back in the Mondeo, and with gravel spraying from the tyres, I made my way along the drive. Jethro, Alfie and Knuckles were waiting for us at the bottom of the steps when the car came to a stop.

I jumped out of the driver's seat and squared up to Alfie. 'Where are Gemma and Luca?' I could feel my nostrils flaring like a racehorse's as I waited for a reply.

A look of confusion spread over Alfie's face as the reality of my words began to register. He clenched his jaw before he spoke. 'I don't know what you're talking about.'

'Do you seriously expect me to believe that? What have you done with them, you bastard? You better not have hurt them.' I prodded Alfie in the chest with my fingers.

Knuckles grabbed my arm and twisted it back behind my body, holding me in an arm lock. I yelled out in pain, but Knuckles didn't release me until Alfie gave his bodyguard the nod.

'Don't ever put your fucking hands on me again or you're a dead man.' Alfie dusted off my invisible fingerprints from his suit jacket with his hand before smoothing down his slicked-back hair.

'Tell me where my wife and son are!' I didn't try to hide the fury in my voice.

Alfie put his hands in the pockets of his suit trousers and glared at me. 'Why did you think Gemma and Luca were here?'

Now it was my turn to look bewildered. If Gemma and Luca weren't with Alfie, where were they?

After the apathetic welcome Dad and I had received, Alfie suddenly changed at the flick of a switch. He was about to erupt; you could literally see the steam coming out of his ears as the enormity of the situation hit him like a freight train. Alfie turned on his heel and strode up the stone stairs two at a time. He burst through the double front doors, crossed the polished white marble hallway and turned into the living room. The sound of his leather shoes changed pitch when he paced across the solid wood floor. He opened up a set of double doors at the far side of the room and walked into the miniature pub. Alfie stepped behind the wood-panelled counter, reached up and lifted down a cut-glass tumbler from a shelf next to the hanging rack. He poured himself a huge measure of Jack Daniel's and gulped it down in a couple of swallows.

He was holding on to the bar with both hands having placed the tumbler on the counter in front of him when Dad and I entered the oak-beamed room. While Alfie considered his next move, he poured himself another drink. We stood in the doorway watching him.

'What are you two gawping at? You look like Tweedledee and Tweedledum. Go home, Nathan. I already told you they're not here.'

I was fuming at the way he'd spoken to me, but I could tell from Alfie's reaction that he was telling me the truth. Getting into a fight with him wasn't going to bring Gemma back. After exchanging a glance with my dad, the two of us headed back out of the door. Staying here was wasting precious time.

65

Gemma

When I glanced up and saw a tall, blond man dressed in a suit walking towards me as I tried to open my cabin door, my heartbeat started pounding.

'Would you like some help? You look like you've got your hands full,' he said as he got closer.

I held Luca's carrycot in the crook of my arm as I wrestled with the door. 'No, thank you, I'm fine,' I replied, turning my back on him, and to my relief, I felt the lock release.

As I stepped inside my cabin, I stole a glance at the man in the corridor. I couldn't believe I'd thought he was Alfie. The man bore no similarity to him at all, apart from the fact that he was tall, blond and dressed in a suit.

What the hell had happened to me? I was a nervous wreck, and my emotions were out of control. I didn't like feeling like this, but there didn't seem to be anything I could do about it. I was stuck in a rut, and an overwhelming feeling of anxiety was smothering me. I was like an empty shell, and I didn't like the person I'd become. It was as if the life had been sucked out of me. All that was left behind was a vacuum. I couldn't go on like this. Something had to change. I needed to find the strong woman who was trapped somewhere within me. I didn't want to spend the rest of my life looking over my shoulder, frightened of my own shadow.

It wasn't acceptable that fear constantly plagued my mind. It was a basic human entitlement to feel safe and secure. I had Alfie to thank for that. I was a bundle of nerves, and wouldn't be surprised if I was on the verge of a breakdown. The overwhelming feeling of paranoia undermined any rational thoughts I had and influenced every aspect of my decision-making.

Alfie was doing his best to come between Nathan and I. His presence was a constant reminder that I'd been unfaithful to my husband. It was bad enough for me; I could only imagine what Nathan felt about the situation. He hadn't mentioned anything to me, but Nathan had a habit of bottling up his feelings, so I was pretty sure it would be bothering him.

Carrying the incredible burden of guilt for all this time had taken its toll on me. I'd found myself in a dark place and knew I had a desperate battle on my hands if I wanted to regain my sense of emotional balance. But even now that I'd left London, my mind was still troubled. I was terrified, especially of strangers. That poor man was only trying to help me with the door, and I'd treated him like he was an axe murderer. I felt agitated and was being eaten up by guilty thoughts.

I was stuck on this roller-coaster ride. Every time I closed my eyes, I'd experience terrifying nightmares that Alfie was going to take Luca away, so now I was frightened to go to sleep. It was a vicious circle.

After that moment of sheer terror earlier, when I'd thought Alfie was in the corridor, I'd settled down for the night. Surprisingly, I managed to drop off on the twenty-four-hour journey and woke feeling refreshed for the first time in ages. Being in the confines of a small cabin in the middle of the ocean, surrounded by water, far away from dry land, had obviously agreed with me. I'd felt safe in the knowledge that Alfie wasn't going to burst through the door unannounced. Luca and I had made it onto the ferry. This was our first step towards freedom, and it felt good.

When we disembarked, I realised the next leg of the journey would be the worst, and I would have to be prepared to make as many stops as necessary. I couldn't expect Luca to be cooped up in the car for eleven hours straight. I'd drive while he was sleeping and take breaks when he was awake. I didn't care how long the journey took. I'd use the time constructively and decide where we could go so that Alfie wouldn't find us.

An idea suddenly came to me. Gibraltar seemed like the obvious choice. It was just a stone's throw from the Costa del Sol; you could see it from the coastline on a clear day, so the journey wouldn't be too much for Luca to cope with. Being a British Overseas Territory, it would be like home from home and a good place to bring up my son; I'd heard violence and street crime were very rare. Nathan and I had always intended to visit, but so much had happened since we'd moved to Spain we hadn't got around to it.

Finally, we reached the centre of Marbella, and my mood instantly lifted. I felt like I'd come home. I'd missed the smell of the sea and the sound of the gently swaying palm trees. The Golden Mile stretched out before me. I cruised along the coast road past the stunning beachfront villas and the pine forests before arriving at Puerto Banús, the Costa del Sol's playground for the rich and famous. The luxury yachting marina, famous for its nightlife, was still a hive of activity, even in the early hours of the morning. Fantastically chaotic, the bustling marina was a very welcome onslaught to my senses. It made me feel safe, not intimidated. Alfie's reappearance in my life had left me feeling traumatised, and I'd begun to think there was no safe place to go. I was so glad I'd come back now.

Nathan and I had been so happy here. We'd been making a fresh start and trying to put our troubled marriage behind us. We'd integrated into the community with ease, blending in with the other ex-pats while hiding out in our penthouse apartment in a large residential estate. I didn't feel exposed here hidden behind the gates with twenty-four-hour security and CCTV cameras, which for once, weren't watching me.

I couldn't help wishing Alfie hadn't made a reappearance in our lives. But there was no point dwelling on it; it didn't help matters. I had to focus on the future. Things were different now. I had Luca to think of, and his wellbeing must come first. I had to admit the prospect of being a single mother terrified me, but Rosa had done it, and so could I.

I was scared of the future, but now I was away from England, I felt mentally in a better place. I was sure I'd be able to learn to adapt to my new situation and cope with everyday stress. I had to focus on all the good things in my life. I had so much to be happy about. I finally recognised I needed to change the way I was thinking to ensure I stayed in control of my emotions. I was an independent woman, and I could handle the challenge that life had thrown me.

Now that I'd broken free of Alfie, it was time to banish the flashbacks and anxious thoughts that flooded my mind. They were a destructive force and suppressed any optimism I tried to muster. My negativity had been holding me down for too long. I needed to harness the power of positive thinking and be confident in the fact that it didn't matter how long it took, I could get my life back on track now that Alfie wasn't breathing down my neck.

66

Alfie

Fury rose up inside me as I came to terms with the news. Gemma had double-crossed me again. I couldn't believe she'd succeeded in taking my son away. Much as I loved her, the woman was making a fool of me. Now that Nathan had taken himself off, I could get down to the serious business of finding Gemma and Luca. I had to get to them before her pathetic husband did.

Zamir and his men had a lot to answer for. The beef between the Russians and the Albanians was taking up most of my valuable time. I seemed to spend every waking minute in that scabby warehouse these days. That was why I'd allowed Gemma to remain at Gareth's house for the last couple of days. I wanted her to think I was giving her and Nathan some space, but that was bollocks. I needed her out of the way so that I could make my presence felt in case Zamir considered going back on his word.

Because of all the crap I'd been dealing with recently, I'd allowed myself to get distracted. While I was acting as the mediator, I'd taken my eye off the ball and Gemma had taken advantage of that. Instead of doing what I'd told her to, she'd used the forty-eight hours I'd given her to do a runner. She needed bringing into line. It was time to remind her about the unspoken gender roles that had been handed down since the beginning of time. She seemed to have forgotten that men make the rules.

You had to admire the cheek of the woman. Gemma genuinely thought she could outsmart me, Alfie Watson, the kingpin of a notorious crime gang. She was either fearless or completely foolish. If she thought she was going to get away with this, she could think again.

Gemma was a law unto herself, and that was something that delighted and frustrated me in equal measure. She was gutsy and had a mind of her own. She didn't give a shit about the consequences her actions would bring. I admired her bravery – not that I would ever hurt her. Even in the circles I moved in, women and children were strictly off-limits. That's what separated us from men like Zamir. But I wasn't going to allow her to run rings around me either.

The more she tried to pull away from me, the more determined I was to pursue her. Surely Gemma of all people realised that when I wanted something, I didn't stop until I got it. I never could resist a challenge.

I was kicking myself; I should have known I couldn't trust Gemma. She had proved time and again that she couldn't follow orders. I only had myself to blame that she was on the run. I shouldn't have given her so much freedom. I wouldn't make the same mistake twice.

After I caught up with Gemma and Luca, I'd move them into Darkwood Manor so that I could keep an eye on them.

Initially, I'd been happy to keep them under surveillance from a distance, but now that she had violated my trust, a change of tactics was definitely in order.

Anyway, having her at the house would give me more opportunities to try and win her over. All the money and power in the world meant nothing if you had nobody to share it with. It was a Watson curse, but I was determined to break it. My dad and I had both been unlucky in love. It was about time that changed.

67

Gemma

After parking the Jeep in the underground car park, I took the lift to our penthouse apartment. It was the early hours of the morning, and I was shattered. My bed was calling. I'd get some sleep, and when I woke, I'd pack up our stuff and hit the road again. Much as I wanted to, I knew I couldn't stay here. It would be too obvious. This would be the first place Nathan would look. I was sure of it.

I put my key in the lock and opened the front door, then switched on the hall light and the corners of my mouth lifted in the smile. I breathed a sigh of relief. It was good to be home. I loved this modern, luxury apartment with its clean lines and minimal look. It was so different from the small Victorian terraced house where Gareth lived. Totally exhausted, I made my way straight to our bedroom.

'Surprise!' Alfie said.

The sudden sound of his voice made me jump out of my skin. I sprang back out of the room and panic gripped me like a vice. Alfie was sitting on the bed in the shadows waiting for me. As my chest constricted, I found it hard to breathe. I stood in the doorway, staring at him in open-mouthed horror. I felt the colour drain from my face. My fingers instinctively tightened around the handle of Luca's carrycot. Why was Alfie here? How did he know I'd left London?

'You don't look very happy to see me. You know how to hurt a man's feelings, don't you, Gemma?' Alfie laughed, then he covered his heart with his hands.

I didn't want Alfie to know I was scared, but that was easier said than done. Fear ripped through me as my eyes scanned his face. I'd have to try and talk my way out of this. But I couldn't find the right words. My mind kept time with my racing heartbeat, and I struggled to think straight. I considered running to the front door and buzzing for the in-house security, but I wasn't sure I'd make it before Alfie caught up with me. If I made him angry, there was no telling what he might do. He had a reputation as a trigger-happy gangster to maintain. The speed at which Alfie's personality could change was what scared me the most. I knew he had a vicious streak.

I heard a sound behind me, so I looked over my shoulder and saw Knuckles' huge frame emerging from the darkness of the living area. He was grinning from ear to ear. I was trapped between these two dangerous men. There was no point calling for security; they wouldn't be able to help me now.

Knuckles' presence ensured that any possible escape routes were blocked. He would make sure I didn't try and make a run for it. When I'd decided to leave London, of every possible scenario I'd imagined in my head, this wasn't one of them. I'd been worried about Nathan's reaction, but I would rather be face to face with him any day than where I was at this moment. This was the worst possible outcome. I didn't know how I was going to explain myself to Alfie. The silence hung heavy in the air between us. I felt its weight around my shoulders like I was wearing a lead cloak.

'I'm glad to see you've arrived safely. What took you so long?' Alfie asked.

I didn't understand how he'd managed to get here before me. So much for my carefully thought out plan to run away with Luca. I hadn't got very far. Alfie had tracked me down before I'd had a chance to go anywhere.

'For a minute there, I thought you were going to prove me wrong by not doing the obvious thing. But I should have known you wouldn't let me down. It was a dead cert that you'd come back to your apartment. You're a creature of habit after all.'

In hindsight, I realised I'd made a mistake. I shouldn't have come here. Although I'd thought I'd be safe at the apartment, it was too obvious. I knew if I stayed here too long, Nathan would turn up, but I never expected to find Alfie waiting for me. His presence in my home had just shattered my sense of security.

'I think you've got some explaining to do, Gemma, haven't you? Did you really think you'd get away with this? You double-crossed me, and I'm not very happy about that. I didn't think you'd be stupid enough to do that again.'

I locked eyes with Alfie, hoping he would interpret my stand as a confident gesture. A non-verbal signal that I wasn't scared of him. But I wasn't fooling anybody. Alfie could see I was bluffing. He threw his head back and laughed when he realised how terrified I was.

'If you've come here to try and snatch my baby, I'm afraid you've had a wasted journey,' I finally answered. I wanted to display a show of strength, but I hoped I hadn't just said the wrong thing.

'Knuckles, take the baby,' Alfie said.

My eyes widened as I craned my neck and stared into the face of the huge man. He placed his hands on the handle either side of mine, and I tightened my grip. I'd betrayed Alfie's trust, and now he was going to get even with me. That's the way things worked in his world. It was an unspoken rule.

'There's no way I'm going to let you take Luca,' I said, spitting out my words, in my best fighting voice.

Knuckles wrenched the carrycot out of my hands. I felt hot tears spring into my eyes, but I had to hold them back. This was no time to show weakness. I knew Alfie would thrive on that.

Channelling my sadness into fury, I straightened my posture and faced Alfie with a look of rage. 'I won't let you take Luca away from me.'

'You don't have a choice.'

I could see Alfie's white teeth shining in the darkness, and I had a sudden urge to slap him around the face. Luca was a defenceless baby, and his safety was my only concern. I was prepared to fight for him until I had no breath left in my body. But I didn't want to escalate the situation, so I managed to keep hold of my temper.

'Relax, Gemma, nobody's taking Luca away from you, but you look a mess. You need to get some rest. Knuckles is going to take good care of him while you sleep to ensure you don't slip off into the night again. I can't have you doing another disappearing act, can I? Then in a couple of days when you've recovered from the journey, we'll be going back to England.'

I knew Alfie's observation was correct. I was reeling from sleep deprivation, and the endless journey we'd just been on hadn't helped matters. But there was no way I would be able to drift off into a peaceful sleep with Alfie in my apartment. Especially if he was separating me from my son.

'As you've broken my trust again, I'm going to have to confiscate your mobile,' Alfie said, holding his hand out towards me like I was a wayward teenager.

68

Alfie

Gemma was testing my patience. I'd genuinely thought I'd made progress at wearing her down, but I'd obviously misread the situation. I was furious that she'd tried to give me the slip, but now wasn't the time to have it out with her. I'd have to wait until the morning. Hopefully, by then I'd have calmed down.

I was hopelessly in love with Gemma, so there was no way I was going to let her go. But I needed to convince her that we had a future together. Once she got used to the idea, I was sure she'd see where I was coming from. I could make her happy if she'd let me. I didn't want her to be scared of me. I saw Gemma as my equal. She was the only woman who would be capable of taking on the role of my partner. Becoming a Watson would be a lifelong commitment.

I never thought I'd be grateful to Nathan for anything, but if he hadn't turned up at Darkwood Manor, the outcome of this story might have been very different. Gemma was too smart for her own good, and if I hadn't been hot on her heels, she might have been able to get away from me. But I couldn't deny I had predatory instincts, so I wouldn't have rested until I'd tracked her down.

I was going to give Gemma a dose of sleeping tablets to make sure she didn't do a midnight flit. I knew it was an underhand tactic to give them to her without her consent, but if I'd asked her to take them, I knew she would have refused. The doctor had assured me she wouldn't come to any harm. He'd advised me to crush the tablets and dissolve them in water for two reasons. Firstly, Gemma wouldn't realise she'd taken anything, and secondly, it made the medication act faster.

I couldn't help smiling when I'd prepared the sleeping pills. A flashback of my granny crushing up a tablet before she gave it to her Rottweiler in a piece of cheese came to mind. He'd happily scoffed it down. I hoped Gemma would be as compliant.

Gemma was doing a lot of damage to herself through sleep deprivation, so this was for her own good. You only had to look at the dark circles under her eyes to see she was struggling, but Gemma was as stubborn as a mule, and she wouldn't let anybody help her. She had left me no choice but to take matters into my own hands. Gemma was exhausted, and something needed to be done about it.

69

Gemma

I woke with a start, and for a moment I wondered where I was. I tried to focus but found it hard to concentrate. My head felt fuzzy for some reason. I sat up with my back against the headboard, and as I did, I had a dizzy spell followed by a bout of nausea. What was going on? I felt strange. My breasts were painful and full. Luca must be due a feed. Then, everything started to come back to me, and I suddenly remembered Alfie had taken my baby away from me last night.

I tried to throw on some clothes, but I had a distinct lack of coordination. When I finally managed to dress, I walked out of the bedroom and into the living area. Jethro had his back to me. He was standing in front of the floor-to-ceiling windows admiring the view of the harbour, holding Luca in his arms. The sight of the two of them together made me feel uncomfortable. I spent a couple of moments taking in the scene, as I tried to control my breathing. But my efforts were in vain, and the more I looked at Jethro with my son, the more my anxiety levels increased. I should never have run away. Now I was at the mercy of the Watsons, and the thought of that made me feel helpless. I cast my mind back but didn't remember seeing Jethro last night. Then again, I seemed to have a very patchy recollection of the evening. A lot of the details were blurred.

'Hello, Gemma, you obviously slept well,' Jethro said, turning to face me.

A smile spread across Luca's face at the sight of me. I walked across the marble floor and stopped beside Jethro. 'What time is it?' I asked before I stretched my arms forward so I could take my son away from him.

Jethro smiled and the skin at the corner of his blue eyes crinkled. He handed me my baby and checked the time on his watch. 'It's just after two,' he said.

My mouth fell open. 'My God!'

Jethro threw his head back and laughed in the same way Alfie did. 'You've been asleep for twelve hours. The doctor warned us that might happen. He always advises people not to take triazolam unless they plan on sleeping for the next seven to eight hours. But you exceeded that. You must have been exhausted.'

'What are you talking about?' I stared at Jethro with eyes like saucers.

'Alfie gave you some tablets to help you sleep, but he must have given you enough to tranquillise a horse.'

Jethro laughed, but it wasn't funny, and I found myself staring at him with my mouth wide open. I couldn't believe what he'd just told me. No wonder I was having trouble remembering the details of last night. Alfie had sedated me. I could still feel the effects of the tablets. My brain seemed to be working in slow motion, and I was having trouble shaking off the grogginess. The effect I was experiencing was like coming around after a general anaesthetic.

'Why did you let Alfie drug me?'

'It was for your own good. You were exhausted, Gemma. At least he gave you prescription medication to make you sleep and not some illegal Class A drug that you could have become addicted to,' Jethro said, condoning what Alfie had done.

I should have known Jethro would justify Alfie's objectionable behaviour, so I pushed the memory of last night from my head as I tightened my arms around my son and held him close to my chest. My breasts felt like they were about to explode. It had been hours since I'd last fed my baby. But I couldn't risk giving him the milk as the sleeping tablets would still be in my bloodstream. I'd have to express it and dump it instead.

'Luca's going to need feeding.'

'Everything's under control,' Jethro replied.

When I turned around to face the kitchen, I noticed the men had found the bottles and the emergency tin of Cow and Gate I kept in the cupboard above the sink. They had made up some formula for Luca and had even managed to work out how to use the steriliser without any female assistance.

'Knuckles changed Luca and gave him a bottle about an hour ago.'

I raised my eyebrows. I couldn't picture Alfie's burly henchman in a daddy day care role. Changing my baby's nappy and giving him a bottle surely wouldn't have come naturally to him. I was used to seeing Knuckles as the brutal enforcer for an organised crime gang. Although it would appear my son hadn't come to any harm at the hands of these gangsters, and I was grateful that Luca had been well looked after, the thought of them babysitting didn't sit comfortably with me.

'Alfie's gone out. He had a bit of business to attend to, but he won't be long. When he gets back we're going to hit the road,' Jethro said. 'You must be hungry. Help yourself to something to eat. Knuckles has left some food in the kitchen for you.'

The thought of Knuckles in the role of a domestic god brought a smile to my face. I balanced Luca on my hip while I made myself a sandwich with the fresh bread and wafer-thin Serrano ham. Just as I was about to sit down to eat, the front door opened and in walked Alfie and Knuckles. He'd changed character again and was now playing the part of Alfie's bouncer. Something that suited the huge man much better than the Mrs Doubtfire role he'd assumed earlier.

'I'm glad to see Sleeping Beauty's awake at last. I've got a bone to pick with you,' Alfie said, scowling at me. 'I'm a generous man, and I gave you an opportunity to do the right thing. I was kind enough to give you forty-eight hours to tell your husband the secret you've been keeping from him for over a year. But instead of doing as I asked, you chucked it back in my face. You took the piss out of me. I don't like being taken for a mug. Did you think I wouldn't come after you?'

I could feel the hairs on the back of my neck stand up. 'I'm sorry.' My voice wobbled as I spoke. I carried my sandwich over to the table, pulled out one of the cream leather chairs and took a seat.

'I bet you are, but you're sorry you got caught, you're not sorry that you took my son away from me.'

My pulse quickened in response to his comment. I was literally squirming in my chair. The features of Alfie's handsome face hardened as he glared at me. He was right, but I couldn't admit that to him. I didn't want this man in Luca's life, and I would do everything I could to prevent it. Almost instantly, Alfie's mood changed, and he began to laugh.

'I know the doctor said to go easy with those tablets, but I didn't think two tiny pills would knock you out for as long as they did. That's a handy thing to know. I'll hold on to the rest of them.' Alfie patted his suit jacket. 'They might come in useful another time if you get out of hand.' Alfie winked.

I was tempted to respond with a barbed comment, but instead, I decided to ignore Alfie and keep my mouth shut. I didn't want to make matters worse than they already were, so I scowled at him over the top of my baguette before I picked it up and started eating.

Alfie's face broke into a huge grin. 'I'm glad to see you haven't completely lost your spiky attitude. A good night's sleep doesn't seem to have improved your mood in the slightest.'

70

Gemma

I couldn't get my head around the fact that Alfie had drugged me. Instead of reaching a place of safety, I was more vulnerable than ever. Anything could have happened to me while I was under sedation. Alfie could have taken advantage of the situation. He had a lot of undesirable qualities, but I reminded myself that being a rapist wasn't one of them. As Jethro pointed out, at least he hadn't given me addictive drugs. Thankfully, he hadn't stooped that low.

I didn't want to think about the other obvious scenario, but I forced myself to; I had to face facts. If Alfie had wanted to, he could have spirited Luca away while I was sleeping. I might never have been able to find my son if that had happened. I'd read cases in the papers where children had been abducted from their parents and never heard of again. They simply vanished into thin air, and no amount of searching uncovered the child's whereabouts. That sent a shiver down my spine.

For once, Alfie had kept his word and had taken good

care of Luca while I rested. Even though I was furious with him, the fact that he stuck to his side of the bargain counted for something.

I'd done a stupid thing by running away, but I'd been desperate for a way out of the nightmare we were stuck in, and desperation often made a person make rash decisions, didn't it? It had seemed like a good idea at the time, but now that my plan had unravelled before my eyes, I could see how reckless I'd been. I should have realised Alfie would come after us.

My thoughts suddenly turned to Nathan; he would have realised I'd gone by now. He'd be beside himself with worry. I wondered if he was trying to find us. But then something else crossed my mind. If Alfie had told my husband about Luca, I could kiss goodbye the idea of that. The trust I'd worked so hard to rebuild would have been undone in an instant. As I mulled over the events of the last few days, my eyes welled up, and my tears began to flow.

71

Gemma

Alfie walked over to the full-length windows and stood next to Jethro. It was uncanny how much he resembled his dad. When I looked at Jethro, I knew instantly what Alfie would look like in twenty-five years' time.

'How did it go?' Jethro asked, not taking his eyes off the view of the marina.

'Fine,' Alfie replied. 'But you know what the Russians are like.'

'Did Knuckles have to flex his muscles then?' Jethro asked, tilting his head to one side.

'No, not this time.'

Alfie didn't normally discuss business in front of me, so this was going to be an eye-opening experience. I sat with my back to the men, while I listened in to their conversation. I could see their reflection in the large mirror that hung above the TV.

'Where did you do the deal?' Jethro asked.

'On Popov's yacht.'

You didn't need to be a genius to work out that drugs would be at the centre of the Watsons' deal.

Jethro pulled a face. 'So Vladimir's got himself a new toy has he?'

Alfie nodded.

I wondered how Alfie and Knuckles had managed not to arouse suspicion as they boarded a yacht in broad daylight dressed in smart suits and presumably carrying a case full of money. They wouldn't exactly blend in with the yachting community or beach-loving tourists enjoying the mild Spanish weather. But the fact that he stood out from the crowd wouldn't have fazed Alfie. He oozed confidence out of every pore. The idea of carrying out his business in full view of everybody would have massaged his already enormous ego.

Alfie couldn't have picked a more public place if he'd tried. The marina was always a hive of activity. Day and night, it was bustling with people. But Alfie wasn't trying to hide what he was doing; he thought he was above the law, and although there was a police presence in the harbour, they seemed happy to turn a blind eye to the goings-on of the super-rich. No wonder Alfie didn't fear the police. In this part of the world, he didn't even have to bother outrunning them. They just looked the other way while he carried out his business right under their noses. Everyone, it seemed, was on the payroll. Cash was king.

'Business must be good,' Jethro said.

'Vladimir's got a new supplier.'

'How come?'

'Two of Vladimir's guys threw the old one over the side of their speedboat when they were on their way to collect hashish from Morocco.'

Jethro laughed. 'Did they make the poor bastard swim all the way back to Spain?'

'No, he's sleeping with the fishes. Popov told his men to put a body vest filled with weights on the Colombian, and dropped him out at sea, while he was still alive.'

Alfie and Jethro exchanged a glance.

'What had he done to deserve that?' Jethro asked.

'The dopey fucker was stupid enough to try and short-change Vladimir on a deal, and if that wasn't bad enough, he also tried to sell him an inferior product.'

'Well, he won't be doing that again will he?' Jethro laughed. 'Vladimir's a force to be reckoned with.'

'I've been trying to make Zamir understand that. But I might as well bang my head against a brick wall. He gave me his word he wouldn't try and shaft us, but I don't trust the guy. He's a slippery bastard.'

'If everybody plays by the rules, everything runs smoothly.'

'I know, but you always seem to get one greedy fucker who'll try to bite the hand that feeds it,' Alfie said.

'Then they deserve everything they get. Scores need to be settled quickly,' Jethro replied. 'In our line of work, you can't afford to lose face, or your rivals see it as a sign of weakness.'

Were Jethro and Alfie having this conversation for my benefit? It certainly felt like they were letting me know the lengths criminals like them went to if somebody crossed them. Removing a person's teeth with pliers and cutting off someone's fingers one by one with bolt cutters, barbaric as it seemed, was all part of the job description. Their casual chat reminded me of the danger Luca and I were in. When I'd left England, I'd intended to take my son to safety, not lead him into the lion's den.

'Have you got the shipment?' Jethro stood toe to toe with his look-alike son.

'Yeah, the gear's in the car,' Alfie replied.

Jethro nodded. 'In that case, we should make tracks.'

A mixture of fear and intense fury flooded my veins. If Alfie was expecting me to travel in a car with my son when he was transporting drugs in it, he was putting us both in great danger.

'I'm going to head home for a bit. Phone me when you're ready to leave,' Jethro said.

My ears pricked up. Jethro had said he was heading home, so he must have a property in the area. The thought of that rang alarm bells within me. Nathan and I had thought we'd given the Watsons the slip when we moved into this apartment, but we'd been very much mistaken. Everything was starting to make sense. Alfie told me he was having me watched while we were living in Spain, but I hadn't realised the family had a base here. No wonder I'd spent months feeling like eyes were following me wherever I went – and to think Nathan was convinced I was imagining it.

I suppose it made sense for the Watsons to have a place here. This part of Spain was renowned for being a criminal's paradise and had attracted all manner of villains over the years. The Costa del Crime, as it was affectionately known, on the southern coast of Spain was home to some of Europe's most dangerous criminals. Puerto Banús was a playground for the rich and famous. There were so many wealthy people floating around here that Jethro would easily blend in.

The profit from the Watson family's non-legitimate businesses needed to be lost somewhere, and this was the perfect place to carry out money laundering on a huge scale. Spending large amounts of cash in Marbella wouldn't be something that would draw attention to a person. It was an everyday occurrence in a resort packed with owners of luxury villas, sports cars and big boats.

'Gemma, you've got five minutes to pack up your belongings. You won't be coming back to this apartment ever again.'

My heart began pounding. I could feel my dream of moving to Gibraltar slipping through my fingers but now wasn't the right time to panic. I needed to keep a clear head. I didn't want to go with Alfie, but there wasn't another option. I felt completely powerless. If I didn't do what he told me to, something terrible might happen to us. Alfie had a violent temper that he could unleash in the blink of an eye. If he thought I was scared, it would only make him want to exert his dominance even more. One of his favourite pastimes was exploiting a person's weaknesses. So I'd have to put on a brave face and play the game.

Alfie checked the time on his watch. 'Four minutes and counting...'

I freaked out any time Luca was out of my sight, so I took him with me and went into the bedroom. Closing the door behind me, I pulled out the suitcase from the bottom of the wardrobe and placed it on the bed, then ripped the clothes from the hangers and bundled them into the case. I tore around the room, pulling open drawers, firing the contents into the bag from the other side of the room like I was shooting a ball through a basketball hoop. I sat Luca in the middle of the bed and surrounded him with pillows, to keep him from moving around and falling off the bed. Then I gave him a toy to keep him occupied while I pulled the bedside cabinet away from the wall and lifted the piece of loose laminate flooring. Thank God, the huge bag of money I'd stashed some time ago was still there. After lifting it out, I placed it at the bottom of my case and arranged the clothes back over it. I was doing up the zip when Alfie opened the door. He swaggered into the room and stood next to the bed, towering over Luca. A smile spread over his face as he watched his son.

'It's time to go,' Alfie said.

'But I haven't packed Luca's things yet.'

'Well get a move on. We haven't got all day.'

Knuckles came into the bedroom and lifted my case off the bed.

'Take that down to the car, and then come back and give us a hand with the rest of the stuff,' Alfie said.

I wanted to make sure I had everything of importance with us, in case, at some point in the future, the opportunity presented itself for us to disappear. Stashed at the bottom of Luca's wardrobe were mine and Nathan's collection of bogus passports and the jewellery from the heist at the Antwerp Diamond Centre. I decided to bring it all with me. It might come in handy. Alfie told me before that if somebody wanted to successfully disappear off-grid all they needed was to have one decent piece of ID. Once you had that, you could get hold of anything else you might need.

Making a fresh start wouldn't get off the ground if I didn't have any identification or money.

I packed up Luca's clothes, but I couldn't get the idea of moving to Gibraltar out of my head. I don't know why I hadn't thought of it before. It seemed like the obvious choice now. Its official language was English, so communication wouldn't have been an issue. That would have been one less thing to worry about. As I prepared to go with Alfie, a new beginning seemed like a pipe dream, but I had to have faith that one day Luca and I would be free of him. Otherwise, I wasn't sure I could find the strength to carry on.

The thought of being held by Alfie sent a flood of emotions racing through my body. I didn't want to spend my days walking on eggshells again, worrying that I might say or do something that would set him off.

'Gemma, we need to leave now, or we're going to miss our flight.'

The sound of Alfie's voice made me jump. I was a nervous wreck. Because my mind was on other things, for a moment, I wondered if I'd misheard him.

'We're flying?' I questioned.

'Yes.' Alfie smiled. 'Don't look so surprised.'

But I couldn't help it. Alfie always avoided airports like the plague. There was far too much security for his liking. I felt the corners of my mouth turn up.

'You look happy,' Alfie said, smiling back at me.

I looked up at him with a grin pasted on my face, and on this occasion, my delight was genuine. Fingers crossed, we might get detained by immigration.

I felt a lump form in my throat as I looked around the apartment one last time. Nathan and I had been so happy here. I didn't want to leave, but I didn't have a choice at this moment in time. I could see The Rock in the distance outside the window, rising out of a glittering blue sea, and tempting as it was, there was no point trying to make a run for it. I'd never be able to get away from Alfie. Instead, I was going to have to pin all hope on being stopped by airport security.

I put Luca in his car seat, and Knuckles carried him out of the living area and down the hallway. Alfie and I followed him. Just before he opened the front door, Alfie stepped in front of me and looked me in the eye. I tried not to give away how I was feeling, but it was difficult to remain calm as the intensity of his stare bored into me.

'When we go outside, don't try anything stupid. Do I make myself clear?'

I nodded, to acknowledge that I understood what Alfie meant. Much as I was desperate to get away from him, I had to pick the right time, and this wasn't it.

I felt like an A-list celebrity surrounded by a team of bodyguards as we made our way to the underground car park. I was being flanked on each side by Knuckles and Alfie. When we got to the black Mercedes, Knuckles opened the back door and placed Luca's carrycot on the leather seat.

Alfie took hold of my elbow and led me to the other door. 'Get in,' he said, resting his hand of the small of my back.

I reluctantly took my seat, and with trembling fingers, I tried to fasten the seat belt. A moment later, a middle-aged man, wearing dark sunglasses and dressed in a short-sleeve shirt and smart trousers got out of another Mercedes parked next to ours. He walked around to the back of the car and opened the door. Jethro got out and had a brief conversation with Alfie. Although I tried, I couldn't hear what they were saying. When Jethro got back in the car, the man closed the door behind him. I wondered why he wasn't travelling with us. There was plenty of room in the car. Maybe they were copying royal protocol and preserving the line of succession, I thought. It would never do if two heirs to the Watson dynasty were wiped out in a tragic car accident, would it?

Once Alfie got into the car and sat next to Knuckles, he began reversing the Mercedes out of the parking space.

'Isn't your dad coming back to England?' I asked.

'Yes, but he's going to meet us at the airport.'

'Why does he need to travel in another car? Is it a security measure?' I was trying to gauge the level of danger we were in. Alfie had just done a business deal with the Russians, and it was very likely there was a shipment of cocaine in the boot of our car. If it wasn't cocaine, I could guarantee whatever we were transporting was something illegal.

Alfie laughed. 'You've been watching too much TV.'

'So why is he travelling in another car?'

Alfie paused. He was famous for dodging the answer to a question, so I wasn't expecting a response. Then he pulled down the sun visor and looked at me in the mirror. 'Nobody wants to sit in the middle seat, do they, Gemma?'

I squinted when we came out from the dark underground car park into daylight. The afternoon sun shone brightly above us in a cloudless blue sky. Glancing out of the car window, I stole one last look at Puerto Banús. Framed by the dramatic Andalusian mountains and the calm turquoise water of the Mediterranean that lapped at the sand, it was idyllic.

The further away from Marbella we drove, the crowds of tourists thinned out dramatically, and by the time we reached the airport, there wasn't a single pedestrian to be seen. Knuckles followed the signs to the terminal used solely by private jets. I should have realised we wouldn't be one of the millions using the main terminal. It was obvious we weren't going to be boarding a standard flight.

To my amazement, we didn't have to wait in the customs queue. That dashed my hopes of being detained by Spanish officials. Our party and all our questionable luggage had been pre-cleared, so we were ushered through the VIP charter terminal and onto the private jet. Ryanair could learn a thing or two from the smooth running of this operation, I thought. Now I understood how Alfie had got to Puerto Banús before me. He'd broken his no flying rule and had travelled by private jet. My heart sank at the thought of returning to UK soil.

72

Nathan

On the long journey from England to Spain, I had plenty of time to think. I wondered what had happened to make Gemma act so out of character. Why would she disappear like this without saying a word? I understood my wife wanted to get away from Alfie, but why did she go without me?

I breathed a sigh of relief, and my mood instantly lifted when I pulled into the underground car park and saw the Jeep parked in our space. My hunch that Gemma would come back here had paid off. I'm glad I trusted my instincts now. Turning to face Dad, I let out a long breath.

After letting us in, I went straight to mine and Gemma's bedroom. It was six o'clock in the morning, so I expected to find her asleep, but the room was empty. I pulled back the quilt and ran my hand over the Egyptian cotton sheet; the bed hadn't been slept in recently; it was stone cold.

When I looked around the apartment, I soon realised Gemma had cleared out all of her and Luca's belongings.

She hadn't just packed for a couple of days; everything had gone. My heart sank. I knew that meant she wasn't planning on coming back. Gemma and I had promised to stick by each other for life. Those vows seem to have meant nothing to her because she'd left me. I felt like this had come from nowhere without warning, but maybe I just hadn't picked up on the signs. I should have realised something was wrong; Gemma had been so cold and unapproachable lately. She'd emotionally detached herself from me, and like a fool, I'd put that down to her depressive state of mind.

I walked into the living room, biting the nails on my left hand. 'Gemma's gone. She's taken all her stuff.'

Dad glanced over at me, so I went to stand next to him. I looked out at the incredible view, struggling to understand what had caused my wife to behave like this. I knew she hated Alfie being back in our lives, but I didn't for one minute think that she would do something as extreme as this. Why hadn't she confided in me? She obviously didn't trust me. The thought of that left a bad taste in my mouth like I'd been sucking on a sweet made of battery acid.

'Are you OK?' Dad asked, squeezing the top of my shoulder.

I turned to face him. Overwhelmed by the amount of stress I was under, I felt my face twist in agony, mirroring what was going on inside my body. 'I feel like somebody's just punched me in the gut. I can't make sense of the situation; it's too confusing to try to sort through.'

Dad didn't reply, but he slapped the top of my arm to show his support.

'This is all my fault. If I'd known Gemma was that

worried about being in London, I would have brought her and Luca home. Anything would be better than this.'

'You can't blame yourself, Nathan. You weren't to know this would happen.'

I clasped my fingers behind my head and fought to hold back the tears that were threatening to make an appearance. The thought of being separated from my wife and child was more than I could bear. They meant everything to me. Growing up without my father had left me with a fear of rejection and abandonment. I didn't want to go through that experience again. Gemma's departure had floored me.

Guilt gnawed away at me. Why hadn't I taken Gemma's concerns more seriously? She was terrified that Alfie was going to harm Luca. I'd seen how edgy she'd become. It was impossible not to notice her uneasiness, but I'd chosen to ignore it. I was convinced Alfie was just throwing his weight around. I didn't think for one minute he'd hurt our son, but he needed me to work for him while his guys were doing time. Even if we could have given him back the money we took from the yacht, he wouldn't have wanted it. It wasn't about the money; Alfie wanted to control us.

I knew I'd been selfish insisting that we go back to England, but I was so desperate to meet my dad after all the years we'd spent apart. I'd put my own needs before that of my wife and child. Their happiness was just as important as mine. If I hadn't insisted on going back to London, we wouldn't have bumped into the Watsons again.

I hated to admit it, but my selfish streak ran deep. My behaviour stemmed from being an only child. I was used to getting my own way and wasn't good at compromising. I'd taken Gemma for granted again, and this time she wasn't prepared to put up with it. I promised myself I wouldn't stop until I found her. I didn't want to consider the possibility that I'd pushed her back into Alfie's arms. That was too painful to contemplate. But I needed to know the truth for my peace of mind. I had so many unresolved questions.

'I know I haven't been there for you in the past, but I want you to know you can rely on me now. I've got your back,' Dad said.

I smiled to acknowledge my dad's words of support, but I remained quiet. There was a huge lump in my throat, preventing me from answering. Gemma's leaving could easily send me into a downward spiral.

'Don't worry, Nathan, we'll find them.'

I ran my fingers through my hair before letting out a loud sigh. 'I've been trying to work out where Gemma might have gone, but I haven't got a clue.'

'She can't have got very far without the car,' Dad pointed out.

I turned away from the windows and faced my dad. I'd been considering what to do when his comment gave me an idea. 'The underground car park has CCTV cameras. I think I'll go down and talk to security and see if they'll let me have a look at the recent footage.'

'That's a good idea. It's got to be worth a try,' Dad agreed.

I walked into the foyer on the ground floor of the building and caught the two overweight guards having a snooze behind the front desk. Why would the management company employ people like that? There was no way they would be able to catch someone who was up to no good, so they were paying them to do nothing. Unless sleeping on the job was one of their duties. I cleared my throat to get their attention before explaining that my wife and son had disappeared. At first, I asked for their help, but they were reluctant to trawl back over the tapes as it would have interfered with their siesta.

Thinking on my feet, I added that I was worried my wife and baby had been kidnapped by a stalker. I told the men my wife had noticed somebody following her a few days ago. I wanted to see if the footage held any clues to their whereabouts before I contacted the police. When one of the guards stood up and stretched, the buttons on the front of his shirt only just managed not to pop open as the fabric gaped widely.

The men had a phobia of work, so I was going to have to make this easy for them if I wanted their co-operation. 'I'm not asking you to go through the tapes – I appreciate that's very time-consuming. Would it be possible for me to look over them instead?'

The guard who was still seated ran his fingers down each side of his thick black moustache before he glanced up at his colleague. 'What do you think, Miguel?'

The standing guard folded his arms across his enormous stomach and then shook his head. 'Not possible,' he replied in a thick Spanish accent.

Tensing my jaw, I leant over the counter. 'I tell you what, I won't report you for being asleep when you're meant to be working if you let me see the footage.'

Dad put his hand in the pocket of his jeans and produced two twenty-euro notes. The sight of the money persuaded the men to give me access to the recordings. Dad and I began scanning through the frames. I soon noticed two black Mercedes parked adjacent to my Jeep. Neither of the cars were in the car park now. When I looked further back, I found the camera had captured pictures of the cars when they entered the car park in convoy. I scrutinised the next images. They showed the occupants getting out of the blacked-out cars. Cold sweat began seeping from my pores when I saw the clear pictures of Alfie, Jethro and Knuckles.

I'd told the guards I thought Gemma and Luca had been kidnapped to appeal to their better nature and encourage the men to help me. I didn't think they had been kidnapped until I saw the Watsons had visited the building. When I scanned more of the footage, my worst nightmare was confirmed. Gemma and Luca left the apartment block yesterday in Alfie's Mercedes.

My chest tightened when I saw my wife and child getting into the car, and a feeling of regret washed over me. I had let them both down, and now Alfie was holding the two people I loved most in the world. All I could think about was getting them back.

I blew out a breath then began pacing towards the lift. While I waited for Dad to catch me up, I impatiently pressed the up arrow multiple times. 'Where do you think Alfie has taken them?'

Dad paused for a moment. 'My guess would be Darkwood Manor. The place is like a fortress.'

Dad and I didn't waste time mulling over our options. I grabbed the car keys from the grey granite worktop, and we took the lift back down to the car park. Leaving the Jeep in its parking space, Dad and I got into the Mondeo. Only hours after arriving, we were travelling back to Santander and would take the first available ferry to Portsmouth. Now we knew Alfie was holding Gemma and Luca, we didn't have a moment to lose.

73

Gemma

I still couldn't work out how Alfie knew I'd gone. If he'd been watching Gareth's house, I wouldn't have made it this far. My curiosity got the better of me, so I asked him the question.

'How did you know I'd left England?' I tore my eyes away from the cotton wool clouds that were rolling past the window and looked him in the eye.

Alfie laughed. 'I wouldn't have done if Nathan hadn't unintentionally raised the alarm. He turned up at Darkwood Manor in a right state looking for you. For some reason, he thought I'd kidnapped you. What a terrible thing to accuse me of,' he replied.

My heart sank; I shouldn't have put Nathan through that; it was cruel. If I'd done the decent thing and told my husband I was leaving, he wouldn't have gone to Jethro's house looking for me. My plan had backfired in spectacular fashion, and I'd inadvertently tipped Alfie off to my disappearance.

'Poor Nathan was beside himself with worry when he turned up at my dad's house.' A huge smile spread across Alfie's face. 'He'd got it into his head that I'd broken into Gareth's dump of a place and spirited you away in the middle of the night without anybody noticing. It was almost impossible to convince him that your disappearance had nothing to do with me. He seemed to find it difficult to accept that his wife had left him for no apparent reason. But you have got a reason, haven't you, Gemma? A very good reason, in fact.' Alfie flashed me a bright white smile.

Alfie had me over a barrel, and he knew it. He was going to milk the situation for all it was worth. The walls on the private plane appeared to be closing in on me. I suddenly felt lightheaded as I broke eye contact with Alfie and stared into space. The pulse began pounding in my temples. I had to hold it together, but I could feel myself beginning to lose the battle.

I'd thought running away was the answer, but I hadn't got very far. Alfie had eyes and ears everywhere. He was a dangerous man and a respected figure in the underworld. It was stupid of me to think I could disappear without a trace. If I had managed to get away, I'd have spent the rest of my days living in fear.

74

Nathan

When the people-tracing service found my dad, I'd decided it was the perfect time to return to the UK. Gemma had made it clear she didn't want to go, but I brushed her concerns to one side and forged ahead with my plan to leave Spain. If I'd known at the time Alfie wasn't behind bars, I would have taken her protest more seriously.

I'd waited years to make contact with my dad and Gemma made no secret of the fact that she was missing my mum. I knew my wife was struggling with the demands of motherhood, and in a bid to support her, I thought if we went back to England, my mum would be able to help her with the baby. Even though, at the time, I hadn't felt ready to make peace with my mum, there was no reason for Gemma not to see her.

If something had happened to Gemma and Luca, I would never forgive myself. I should have protected them from Alfie. I knew more than anyone what a maniac the man was. When I'd first got involved with him, I'd been blissfully unaware of the feud that existed between our families. It had been bubbling under the surface for years. The Watsons had been waiting for an opportunity to stir up trouble again. When I'd borrowed the money from Alfie, I'd kick-started the grudge and became involved in the feud myself.

Jethro and Alfie both wanted revenge on my family. Both the men felt they had scores to settle. There were more twists and turns to the story than a country lane. Jethro despised my dad because he blamed him for his brother's death and Alfie credits my mum for splitting up their family, even though she had nothing to do with it. It wasn't my mum's fault that Jethro and Nora had a miserable marriage. If Alfie wanted to accuse anyone, the finger pointed firmly at Jethro. But they would never hold one of their own accountable. They were professional blame-shifters.

When all of this started, both of my parents were completely innocent of any wrongdoing, but that didn't stop the Watsons holding a vendetta against them. There was no escape from the bitter legacy. The war between our families had already spanned generations, and there was no sign of the conflict being resolved any time soon. The bitterness continued to fester, and it had the potential to impact generations to come. By taking my wife and son, it was another way for the Watsons to make my family suffer.

I'd always known Alfie was pure evil, but I didn't have any real knowledge of Jethro. That was before Dad enlightened me. The whole family were responsible for making our lives a misery, and now that I had my dad by my side, I wasn't sure I was prepared to turn a blind eye to that. We had all been made to suffer at their hands. I had a growing urge to get back at them, but I'd have to try not to give in to temptation. It would be better to practise moving on than staying trapped in the past. I knew I shouldn't waste time planning how to get even with the Watsons, but I couldn't seem to get the thought out of my head.

I'd have plenty of time to do some much-needed soul-searching on the long journey back to England. Grudges hurt everyone involved. Dwelling on what had happened wasn't a healthy thing to do. It was destructive and didn't change anything, but when somebody wronged you, the desire to get even was a natural reaction. Even if Alfie didn't harm Gemma and Luca, I would want to get him back for putting me through this nightmare.

I knew that thought was toxic. At this rate, the scores would never be settled. Holding on to a grudge was draining. It was time-consuming and counterproductive to carry around hatred. If I had any sense, I'd banish it and move on with my life, but Jethro and Alfie were never going to let that happen. Forgiveness wasn't a word either of those men understood.

75

'Did you think I was going to let you walk away from me?' Alfie's laugh echoed around the room.

Alfie was not going to let me take his baby without a fight. He was determined to be part of Luca's life whether I liked it or not. Even though I was no pushover, I knew I was no match for him, and without Nathan by my side, I was at my most vulnerable. Alfie was the type of man who was going to use this situation to his advantage.

I'd weathered life's storms before, and managed to come out the other side. I had to find the strength to do it again, but my resolve seemed to have disappeared overnight, and I knew I was a shadow of my former self. Right now, I had to be brave in the face of adversity. Otherwise, my weakness would be my downfall.

'I'm disappointed that you didn't keep your side of the bargain. I underestimated you. I didn't think you'd have the guts to double-cross me again.' Alfie got to his feet and walked across the room with a self-assured swagger. He pulled back the sleeve of his suit and checked the time on his Rolex. 'It's getting late.'

'Is Knuckles going to drive me home?'

Alfie laughed. 'No, you're staying here tonight.'

I let out an involuntary groan, which brought a smile to Alfie's face.

'I'll show you to your room; you need to get some sleep.'

As if that was going to happen. Knowing there was a psychotic gun-toting lunatic under the same roof, I'd be too stressed out to close my eyes. I'd be tossing and turning all night. I didn't want to stay at Darkwood Manor, but there was no point arguing about it, so I stooped down and picked up Luca's carrycot.

'Allow me,' Alfie said as he went to relieve me of the burden.

'It's fine. I can manage.' I forced out a fake smile. Luca's basket wasn't heavy, but it was awkward to carry. Even so, I wasn't about to let Alfie get his hands on my son.

Alfie shook his head, then rolled his eyes at me. I dutifully followed him across the marble floor of the hallway and up the grand sweeping staircase. My shoes sank into the deep pile of the pale grey carpet as we walked along the landing. Alfie opened the door to the vast bedroom with the dressing room and en-suite bathroom I'd used before to feed Luca in. It was one of the guest suites.

'I'm assuming I can trust you to do what I've asked this time. You're not going to attempt another moonlight flit, are you?'

Alfie's question was met with silence. I broke eye contact with him when his stare became too intense and walked over to the enormous circular bed covered in lilac silk bedding and scatter cushions. When I turned around to face him, a slow smile spread across his handsome face.

'In that case, we'd better keep hold of the baby, so we can ensure you don't do another disappearing act.'

My grip tightened on the handle of the Moses basket, as a mixture of fury and fear flooded my body. I looked up and glared at Alfie when he swaggered across the room and took the carrycot containing my sleeping baby out of my hands. 'Where are you taking Luca?' I kept my eyes on Alfie because I didn't trust him.

'We're not taking him anywhere. Knuckles is going to watch him while you get some rest. Don't worry, Gemma, he'll be perfectly safe. He's in good hands. Knuckles loves babies.'

The idea of this enormous ogre-like man liking babies was so alien. He looked like he ate small children for breakfast. I wanted to banish that thought from my brain as soon as it appeared. Now I was being ridiculous, thinking Knuckles might have cannibalistic tendencies. But that's what my irrational mind did when I was scared. It took my thoughts and rather than come up with a logical explanation, it twisted them into something that ended up terrifying me even more. Instead of listening to the voice inside my head, for once, I decided to ignore it.

Alfie took a set of handcuffs out of his jacket pocket and went to place them on my wrists.

'Do you think that's necessary?' I asked. I was horrified that he'd go to such lengths.

Alfie smirked. 'I'm not sure I can trust you, Gemma, given your track record.'

'You don't need to lock me up. I promise I won't try to escape.'

Alfie considered my answer for a moment.

'I'm not going to go anywhere while you're holding Luca, am I?'

I didn't want to see my baby come to any harm. Tempting as it was to say that, I kept the thought to myself. The slightest thing could antagonise Alfie. He was fully aware of the effect his verbal intimidation was having on me. He could see from the look on my face, I was terrified of what might happen if I disobeyed him. The feeling of his threat hanging over me was enough to curb my desire to run. Alfie was prepared to go to any lengths to ensure I didn't try to leave, even holding his son hostage.

Alfie put the handcuffs back in his pocket. 'Now take these – they'll help you sleep.' Alfie took a pot of pills out of the other pocket of his suit jacket. He opened the lid and shook two tablets into the palm of his hand before offering them to me.

I shook my head. 'I'm not taking those. I don't want them.' A defiant tone crept into my voice.

'I didn't ask you if you wanted to take them. Do yourself a favour and follow orders for once.' Alfie walked over to the bedside cabinet and picked up a glass of water. He brought it over to where I was standing. 'We can do this the easy way or the hard way. The choice is yours. Now swallow the pills like a good girl. You need to rest, and they'll help you sleep.'

When I looked into Alfie's eyes, they were cold and expressionless. They say the eyes are the windows to the soul, and I didn't want to imagine what Alfie's was like. For Luca's sake, I knew I had to do what he said. But when Alfie slid his hands around my waist and kissed me on each cheek. I had to stop myself from recoiling. His embrace lingered too long for comfort. I wanted to push him away, but I couldn't afford to annoy him at this stage. Thankfully he took his hands off me and stepped back.

'Goodnight, Gemma, sweet dreams, darling,' Alfie said before walking out of the door.

76

Gemma

Nathan and Gareth followed the housekeeper through the dining room and into the huge kitchen. I was sitting on a stool in front of the granite breakfast bar and spun around on my seat when they entered the room.

Nathan rushed towards the central island and threw his arms over my shoulders. I burrowed my face into his chest and wrapped my arms around his waist.

'Are you OK?' Nathan pulled away from me and his dark eyes gazed into mine.

Instead of replying to him, I burst into tears. Up until that moment, I'd managed to hold it all together, but the minute Nathan put his arms around me, I let my guard down and turned into a needy, insecure person. In the blink of an eye, I totally fell to pieces and my emotions went into overdrive. I was so relieved that Nathan was pleased to see me after everything I'd put him through that I became overwhelmed and loud, uncontrollable sobs escaped from my lips.

'What's with the waterworks?' Alfie asked.

The sound of Alfie's voice stopped my river of tears instantly. I'd allowed myself to show weakness. I didn't want him to use that against me. He was a master of psychological torture.

Alfie's shoes echoed as he walked across the kitchen floor with an air of confidence. When he came face to face with my husband, they locked eyes. He pulled a gun out of the inside pocket of his suit jacket and pointed it at Nathan. 'I've had enough of this bullshit. You need to tell Nathan what's been going on or I'll be forced to do a spot of target practice.'

That was the moment I realised Alfie hadn't told Nathan about Luca. I was shocked and more than a little relieved. I should have known Nathan didn't have any idea. I'm not sure he would have bothered to come looking for me if he knew what I was keeping from him.

'You look surprised, Gemma. Did you think I'd let Nathan in on our little secret?' Alfie winked then flashed me a smile. 'Believe me, I was tempted to, but I was too preoccupied with tracking you down.'

Running away hadn't solved anything in the long run. It might even have made matters worse. I should have stayed and faced up to what I'd done.

'It's time to come clean. Either you tell him, or I will.' Alfie put the gun back inside his jacket, walked around to the other side of the breakfast bar and stood opposite us. He eyed me with a smile on his face. He was enjoying watching me squirm.

I knew that wasn't an empty threat. He had been itching to tell Nathan the truth, and now that he had the opportunity, he was going to use it. The best I could hope for was damage limitation. I needed to buy myself a bit of time so that I could choose my words carefully. Once they were out, I could never take them back.

The pleasure of owning up to my husband had fallen back into my hands. Bracing myself for the inevitable backlash, I felt a sense of impending doom. Keeping secrets of any size from your partner is an act of betrayal. But the skeleton in my closet was of such monumental proportions, it was going to create seismic shock waves like a tsunami. As I plucked up the courage to come clean, I knew I'd failed in my attempt to protect Nathan from the agony the truth would bring. As he stared at me, the pain in his eyes was so intense, I felt like I'd taken a knife and plunged it into his heart.

Even with Alfie's threat hanging over me, I couldn't bring myself to say the words. I knew how much Nathan loved Luca, and even though he'd been reluctant to start a family, he was a brilliant dad. He adored the baby. It would break his heart when he found out the truth. I didn't want to be the one to have to do that to him. Nathan was the only man I'd ever loved. He was my soulmate, and the thought of having to destroy him was more than I could bear. The guilt was eating away at me. I knew I needed to own up to my husband, but I just couldn't bring myself to do it.

I should have known this would happen. Lies bred lies. It would have been a lot easier if I had told him the truth in the beginning, instead of tricking him into believing that Luca was his child.

Nathan looked at me with a haunted expression on his face as a muscle twitched in his jaw. He knew something bad was about to happen. Buckling under the weight of his accusatory stare, the tears I'd tried desperately to hold in began to flow. I glanced over to Alfie. He was staring at Nathan as a faint smile played on his lips. I saw the colour drain from Nathan's face before he spoke.

'You don't need to explain; I understand what's going on. You two have been sleeping together again, haven't you? How could you do this to me, Gemma? After everything we've been through. I was a fool to ever think I could trust you again.'

I had trouble digesting Nathan's words, and my reply got stuck in my throat. Before I had the chance to say anything, my husband turned on his heel and stomped off across the kitchen floor. I jumped off of the stool and ran after him, but he quickened his pace as I tried to close the gap between us. I was suddenly aware of loud footsteps coming up behind me, one, two, three, four. They speeded up before I had a chance to react. I was ploughed into from behind, and I found myself immediately immobilised. Alfie's arms wrapped around me and stopped me in my tracks. I fought him with everything I had, but he was too strong. All I could do was watch as my husband disappeared out of sight.

Gareth glanced over in my direction as he hobbled after his son. The look of disgust on his face was clear.

'Please tell Nathan he's got it all wrong. I'm not sleeping with Alfie. I need to talk to him so that I can straighten this out.' I hoped my father-in-law would pass on the message.

Gareth stopped walking and turned towards me. 'I'll tell him, Gemma, but I'm not sure he'll want to speak to you at the moment. You need to give him time to calm down.'

77

Nathan

My head felt like it was going to explode as I drove out of the gates of Darkwood Manor. Gemma had betrayed me again. I couldn't bear the thought of her with another man. To block out the pain, I put my foot down and floored the Mondeo. As the car raced through the forest, I sat behind the wheel in a trance-like state. Dad sat beside me in the passenger seat, gripping the handle on the door as the Ford sped along the twisty country lane. I knew I was driving dangerously, but I was so full of adrenaline I couldn't seem to stop. To convince myself this situation was real, and I wasn't experiencing a nightmare, I needed to feel the danger of the white-knuckle ride.

The rain was pelting against the windscreen and visibility was poor. Dad suggested I slow down, due to the adverse weather conditions, but I was in no mood to listen to reason until I almost crashed the Mondeo into another car when it sped past us on one of the narrowest stretches. Neither of us were prepared to give way, and we narrowly avoided colliding with each other. Dad winced at the sound of the hedgerows scraping the windows and paintwork of his car. I braked heavily, and the Mondeo came to an abrupt stop. Almost having an accident was the shock I'd needed to bring myself back to reality. If I wrapped the car around a lamppost or we ended up in a ditch, it wasn't going to solve anything. I was behaving recklessly and had put our lives in danger. That was a selfish thing to do.

Realising I wasn't in the right frame of mind to listen to a lecture, Dad stayed quiet when I put the car into gear and drove off at a sensible pace. A few minutes earlier, he'd told me that I was going to crash if I wasn't careful, but he didn't rub my nose in the near-miss. He'd had the good grace to stay silent for the rest of the journey and left me with my thoughts.

Once my rage had subsided, it was replaced with a gut-wrenching feeling of despair. I had to fight the urge to break down in tears. Not many men would have been bothered to stick around if they found out their wife had been unfaithful to them. But like a fool, I believed Gemma when she'd told me she'd never cheat on me again. I should never have given her another chance. If I hadn't, I could have saved myself a lot of heartache. The old wounds had resurfaced. Gemma and I would never be able to come back from this, and the thought of that made a feeling of utter devastation come over me.

I stomped into the kitchen once we were back at Dad's house, pulled open the fridge door, and got out two bottles of Stella. I opened them and handed one to my dad as he hobbled into the room.

Dad took a seat at the wooden table. 'Do you want to talk about it?' he asked.

After taking a large gulp of my beer, I pulled out the chair opposite him. I slammed the bottle down on the table in a fit of rage before clasping my hands behind my head. 'She's totally fucking heartless. How could she do this to me again? She knows how strongly I feel about cheating.' My tone of voice conveyed my fury. I didn't try to keep a lid on my volcanic temper. I needed to let the anger out.

'For what it's worth, Gemma said you've got it wrong. Nothing is going on between her and Alfie.'

Dad was doing his best to pacify me, but my world was falling apart.

'She's bound to say that, isn't she?'

Dad shrugged. 'She seemed pretty convincing.'

I ran my fingers through my hair and looked into the middle distance as I digested my dad's words.

'You can tell me to mind my own business if you like, but what happened between Gemma and Alfie?'

I brought my eyes back to Dad's, took a deep breath and exhaled it slowly through my nostrils. 'They had a one-night stand about a year ago. Gemma promised me if I gave her another chance she'd never be unfaithful again, and like a fool, I believed her. How come the people you love the most hurt you the worst?' I locked eyes with my dad and tears began rolling down my cheeks. Having my heart broken again by the woman I loved was soul-destroying.

'Seeing you in agony like this has made a lump form in

my throat. I wish I could do something to take your pain away.' Dad's steely blue eyes misted over when he spoke.

I slumped forward and rested my elbows on the table. The feeling of being betrayed by Gemma for the second time weighed heavy on my shoulders. I was becoming trapped in a downward spiral of negativity. I didn't want to think about breaking up with my wife, but I had to face the fact it was on the horizon. If she'd strayed again, I knew that was my only option. There would be no coming back from it this time. Our marriage would be over. I would never be able to trust her again.

'What am I going to do?'

Dad blew out a long breath. 'You're asking the wrong man. I don't exactly have a great track record with women. Look at what happened to my marriage. It ended in divorce before it even got started. Whereas you and Gemma have been together for a long time.'

'I feel like going around there now and beating the shit out of Alfie. He only wants her because she's with me. He's doing the same thing Jethro did to Mum.' My lips thinned as I clenched my jaw.

'I'm sorry, Nathan, you'll have to rewind a little bit. I don't know what you're talking about.' Dad looked at me with a puzzled expression on his face.

I bit the side of my lip. It was obvious from the look on my dad's face that he knew nothing about this. I'd unintentionally let the cat out of the bag. 'I'm sorry, I thought you knew.'

'Knew what? I think you better tell me what's going on.' Dad's expression changed. His words had a cold edge to them.

After more than thirty years apart, we had become close recently. I was reluctant to do anything that might change that. Much as I didn't want to be the bearer of bad news, I knew I had to finish what I'd started.

'Jethro set you up when you went to rob that Securicor van,' I began, choosing my words carefully.

'Yeah, I know the bastard did. From the day Levi died, my card was marked. It was only a matter of time before the family got even with me. They got me sent down as payback for Levi's death.'

I started biting the nails on my right hand. How was I going to break this to my dad? If Alfie's version of events was correct, there was another reason entirely why Jethro wanted to see my father locked up.

'That's not what Alfie told Gemma.' My face was expressionless.

Dad stared at me with hollow eyes. 'What did Alfie tell her?'

I took a deep breath. 'Alfie said, Jethro wanted you behind bars, so he'd be free to make a move on Mum. He was obsessed with her.'

Dad pushed his chair back from the table and stood up. I could see the unexpected news had shocked him to the core. He looked like I'd slapped him across the face. His normally placid demeanour was replaced with fury. Dad's lips thinned, and he began to shake his head. He was unable to believe what I'd just told him.

'I'm going to kill that fucking bastard.' Dad spat out his bitter words. 'I've dreamt for years about bringing Jethro Watson to justice, and making him suffer for everything he did to me, but you mellow as you get older and I'd pushed that idea out of my head. After what you've told me, it's reignited my desire for revenge.'

I could see anger burning in Dad's eyes. He was struggling to stay calm and keep his temper under control. It was horrible to see him like this; he was normally so easy-going.

Dad covered his tormented face with his hands, then he clasped his long fingers together in front of his chest. 'Even though I might not like what you're going to say, you must tell me the truth. What did your mother do?' Dad asked the question, but I could see he wasn't sure he wanted to know the answer to it.

'She turned him down, of course. Mum didn't want anything to do with him.' I gave Dad a half-smile.

'Thank God for that.' Dad breathed a sigh of relief, and I noticed his forehead unpucker.

Dad had broken my mum's heart, so she didn't want to ever be in a relationship again. I became Mum's main focus in life. She poured everything she had into raising me. The thought of that made me feel sad. I'd given her such a hard time when I'd found out she'd lied to me. She was only twenty-two when Dad was sent down and didn't know what to do for the best. I should have been more understanding. I wished we'd never fallen out over it. Not being on speaking terms had been a horrible experience for both of us. But I was glad to say I'd gradually come to terms with my mum's decision to withhold the truth from me, and I'd finally let go of my resentment.

'By all accounts, Jethro was furious when Mum knocked him back,' I said after a lengthy pause.

'I bet he was.' That brought a smile to Dad's face.

'Alfie told Gemma that Jethro never gave a shit about

Nora the whole time they were married because he was in love with Mum.'

Dad shook his head and mulled the thought over before he replied. 'Jethro did treat Nora appallingly, but I never suspected it was because he was harbouring feelings for your mum. Back in the day, he was a cocky little wanker, and I think it made him feel like a big man to trample all over his wife. Everyone could see she was terrified of him.'

Now I was questioning Alfie's version of events. Had Jethro really been in love with Mum, or did he just want to take her away from my dad as another way of getting revenge? Jethro made no secret of the fact that he hated Dad and had a long-held grudge against him. But I thought it was because the two of them were in love with the same woman. I hadn't known about Levi. I wondered if Alfie knew that part of the story. It certainly added another dimension to their feud.

'Jethro set me up big time. I was charged with attempted murder, armed robbery, possessing a firearm with intent to endanger life or injure property. I'm not proud of what I did. I was young and stupid, so I had to pay my debt to society.'

'And you did. We all had to pay the price for your mistake.'

Dad's mouth fell open, and he stared at me with a horrified look on his face.

I lowered my eyes to the floor. 'I'm sorry, Dad, I shouldn't have said that. It was insensitive of me.'

'Your mum hadn't worked since you were born and we were short of cash,' Dad said by way of explanation. 'Jethro said it was easy money, and his family would look favourably on me for carrying out the job. In return for my involvement, the slate would be wiped clean.'

I shook my head. That sounded familiar; Alfie had done the same thing to us. He'd told Gemma if she visited a jewellery shop for him and did a bit of shopping, he'd clear my debt. Of course he hadn't kept his word.

'I was keen to make peace and Jethro led me to believe our feud would be forgotten. It's never a good idea to fall out with such a powerful family, so I stupidly agreed to do the job as a one-off. I should have known Jethro would set me up. He despised me.' Dad ran his fingers through his greying hair before interlocking them at the back of his head. Although he felt the need to explain the situation, he was struggling to tell the story. 'After I got sent to prison, I lost my wife and the chance to watch you grow up.' Dad shook his head; the emotion in his voice was evident.

'Jethro changed the whole course of our lives,' I added through gritted teeth.

'While I was paying the ultimate price, everyone else's lives moved on.' Dad channelled his sadness into anger. 'The judge handed me a life sentence, and I had to serve a minimum of twelve years before being considered for parole.'

'When did you get out?'

'Eight years ago. I should have been out a lot sooner, but I had trouble adjusting to prison life. I knew I had to behave myself if I wanted to be released early, but it's a tough environment. Your mum washed her hands of me. I don't blame her for that, but I found it hard to accept, and that made me easy prey. Other inmates provoked me to pass the time, and I couldn't control my temper.'

That surprised me. I'd always thought I'd inherited my fiery side from my mum. I would have thought Dad was a model prisoner. It must have been a difficult time for him. I could see it had left its mark on him.

'Being released on parole isn't an automatic right, and I was declined by the board repeatedly,' Dad continued. 'Every time they reviewed my case, they didn't recommend me for release or to be moved to an open prison because I continued to be a violent prisoner. As they considered me a risk to society, it justified keeping me imprisoned, and I had to serve a total of twenty-four years. That's a lifetime.'

Dad's eyes misted over when he finished speaking, and I felt a sudden pang of guilt. I'd grown up resenting my dad for abandoning me because Mum had kept the truth from me. The experience had a powerful effect on me and filled me with insecurity, but now it was obvious Dad hadn't come out of it unscathed either. Jethro had a lot to answer for.

'You know what they say, Dad, don't get mad, get even!'

78

Gemma

This mess was getting worse by the day, and it was all my own making. If I'd just been honest with Nathan in the first place, none of this would have happened. I should have realised there was a chance he might form his own conclusion, but I hadn't thought for one minute he'd decide something was going on between Alfie and myself.

'If Nathan thinks we're sleeping together anyway, it almost seems a shame to waste the opportunity. I'm game if you are.' Alfie laughed, leading me back over to the breakfast bar. He rested one hand on the top of my shoulder as I took a seat on one of the stools. 'It would be lovely to give our son a little brother or sister, don't you think?' Alfie walked around the island and winked a blue eye at me.

This was another one of Alfie's attempts to get under my skin. I shot him a look of pure contempt before I turned towards him with a frenzied look on my face. 'The thought of sleeping with you makes bile rise in my stomach.' A mixture of fury and worry coated my words.

Alfie threw his head back and laughed. 'That's more like it, Gemma. You're regaining your feisty spirit. You know I love the spiky side of your personality. You're a strong woman, and you're not afraid to stand up to me.'

Regardless of what he believed, I was most definitely afraid to stand up to Alfie, but I was glad he hadn't realised that.

'You and Luca will be living at Darkwood Manor for the time being.'

'I don't want to stay here. I want to go back to Gareth's house.'

Alfie didn't reply, and I felt suffocated by the silence. Although my surroundings were luxurious, it didn't change the fact that I was a prisoner within these four walls, no matter how nicely decorated they were. The secluded location of Darkwood Manor, nestled within the heart of Epping Forest, added to the isolation.

'Given the situation, that would be a bit awkward, don't you think? Anyway, once you break the news to Nathan, he'll be out of the picture for good. Then we can make plans for the future.'

I had to stifle a laugh that wanted to escape from my lips. Alfie was deluded if he thought we had a future together. I had every intention of doing a disappearing act at the first opportunity. I was just waiting for the right time. It was the only thing I could do.

'We'll live here for the moment until we get our own place. There are plenty of nice houses in the area. We'll need to stay somewhere local so that I can continue to run the business until my son takes over from me.'

The idea of that sent a shiver down my spine. I couldn't let

Luca grow up in this environment. It was too unpredictable and dangerous.

Alfie rambled on about the three of us setting up home together as though it was the most natural thing in the world. He seemed to have conveniently forgotten that I was married to Nathan and had no plans to divorce him. I had every intention of staying with my husband, but the ball was in his court. Nathan might not be prepared to stay with me when he found out what I'd been keeping from him.

I couldn't change the fact that Alfie was Luca's father, but we weren't going to become a family. I wouldn't be able to stop Alfie having visitation rights, but the two of us being together wasn't part of the deal.

The whole situation was so unjust. Nathan and I had waited years to start a family because he was worried he wasn't up to the job. Nathan might not be Luca's biological father, but he was a fantastic dad. I couldn't help feeling that Alfie only wanted to be part of Luca's life so that he could take him away from Nathan. It was another way for him to assert his power over us. Alfie was a control freak.

'There's something about you, Gemma. You fascinate me, and because of that, I'll never lose interest in you.'

Alfie flashed me a smile. He was the master of superficial charm and switched it on and off at will. His behaviour was erratic and unpredictable. That's what was so frightening about him. I had to admit, not knowing what he might do next was absolutely terrifying.

'Don't be put off by my tough exterior. If you scratch beneath the surface you'll find I'm a big softie at heart. My mum brought me up to respect women. If you don't believe me, ask my sisters. We're very close. If you give me the chance, I'll treat you like a queen, Gemma.'

Alfie had been droning on for ages, so I was only half-listening. My eyes had glazed over, but at the mention of my name, I looked towards him and met his cheerful gaze with expressionless eyes. The idea of this violent gangster being a big softie was hilarious, but I didn't dare laugh. I knew better than that.

'Even though you're not looking your best at the moment, I'm more than prepared to take you off Nathan's hands. In fact, it would give me great pleasure to do so. The winner takes it all, so they say.'

What a cheek! The way his words tripped off his tongue like I had no say in the matter. I had to stop myself laughing out loud. This conversation was getting worse by the minute. Was Alfie trying to make me feel insecure, so his manipulation would be more effective? Well, if that was the case, it wasn't having the desired effect. Instead of making me feel needy, I could feel the anger building up inside me. It was reaching boiling point, but I wouldn't give Alfie the satisfaction of blowing my top. I didn't want him to think his insult had bothered me, so I shrugged away his hurtful comment.

It was just as well I had a thick skin. If Alfie was going to continue down this route, it would no doubt come in very handy in the future.

I had more important things on my mind than to be worried about Alfie's slap in the face. How did he know the dark circles around my eyes and my grey complexion weren't a strategic move? I'm glad he didn't approve of the way I looked. At least I wouldn't have to ward off his unwelcome attention. My world had become a spiral of dirty nappies and breastfeeding. I was still adjusting to the new schedule a baby brought with it. My external appearance wasn't high on my list of priorities at the moment. I would gladly continue to rock the dragged through a hedge backwards look, especially now that I knew Alfie didn't rate it.

At this moment in time, my main concern was Nathan. I needed to see him and tell him the truth about Luca. I didn't want to stand here playing games with Alfie. I had more important things to do.

'I want to go and see Nathan.'

'I bet you do.' Alfie's eyes penetrated through me, and I felt my pulse quicken in response.

'Can Knuckles take me to Gareth's house?'

Alfie fixed me with a death stare. 'No, he can't. Knuckles and I have some business in Southend to attend to.' His words hung in the air long after he walked out of the kitchen, and closed the double doors behind him.

79

Alfie

Zamir had decided to ignore my warning and was stupidly attempting to sidestep the Russians. He'd set the wheels in motion to do a deal with the Colombian cartel instead. Vladimir wasn't pleased when the news reached him.

On the way to meet the Colombian cartel, Zamir, Esad and Dren became the victims of a contract killing when the car they were travelling in exploded. A bomb, concealed underneath the vehicle, was detonated by remote control. All three men died instantly, so the deal never went ahead.

'Vladimir must have been in a good mood when he gave the order to take Zamir and his guys out,' I said.

'How do you work that out? I thought you said the men were dead,' Gemma pointed out.

'They are, but it could have been so much worse for them.'

Gemma stared at me like I had two heads. I could tell she didn't understand the logic behind my comment.

'Why are you looking at me like that?' I laughed. 'Would you like me to fill you in on the finer details of a gangland turf war?'

She looked taken aback by my suggestion.

'Vladimir can be a nasty bastard when he wants to be. I witnessed him open up someone's stomach before dousing them in petrol and setting them alight. The unfortunate guy who'd pissed Vladimir off squealed like a pig while he burnt alive.'

'Oh my God, that's barbaric.'

I gave her a wry smile before I continued. My account had left her ashen-faced. 'Popov must be going soft. I've never seen him let people off so lightly before. He didn't make Zamir and his guys suffer at all – being blown to pieces would have been quick. They wouldn't have known anything about it. There are much more painful ways to die.'

Gemma shook her head. The horrified look on her face made me smile.

'I wouldn't have been so lenient if those Albanian fuckers had tried to double-cross me. I warned them time and time again, and they took no notice. Disrespectful men like that deserve to die screaming.'

The Albanians had been taking the piss, so Vladimir put them in their place. If you were stupid enough to double-cross a rival gangster, especially one more powerful than yourself, you'd expect to get what you'd deserved. The Russian mob used a variety of killing methods; a timed car bomb was a favourite within their repertoire when they had a score to settle. Zamir should have seen it coming. No self-respecting villain was going to die in their sleep.

Knuckles and I were keeping a close eye on the lock-up. There was no telling what they might do now that Zamir was out of the picture. The remaining Albanian crew might be stupid enough to try a revenge attack. Even though it was the Russians who had taken out their guys, we'd also had a run-in with Zamir, so we couldn't rule out some form of retaliation. It was a deep-rooted Albanian custom that blood had to be paid for with blood and Zamir's bearded gang were quick-tempered and considered themselves invincible. That was a dangerous combination.

But I wasn't overly concerned. We were the main criminal family in the area, and although we were a bit thin on the ground at the moment, the Watson name was a fear factor in itself, and that was usually enough to defuse trouble before it even started.

For now, business continued as usual, but Vladimir Popov wouldn't allow the Albanians to rise up the ladder after they'd tried to shaft him. If they had any sense, the best thing they could do was relocate to a different part of the country before something serious kicked off. If they thought I was going to stand back and let them muscle in on my territory again, they had another thing coming. They'd be wishing Vladimir had taken them all out by the time I'd finished with them. That wasn't an empty threat.

80

Gemma

'Alfie's asked me to keep you company,' Jethro said when he walked into the living room. His shoes echoed on the solid wood flooring as he approached the fireplace where a real fire was roaring.

The room was warm and cosy, and I was deep in thought, but the sound of Jethro's voice brought me back to reality. I was sitting on the dark purple velvet sofa opposite the fire, so I lifted my eyes to meet his, and my lips stretched into a false smile.

'You two are a good match, you know. You're not frightened to stand up to Alfie. He doesn't want a woman who hangs on his every word. He saw what that did to his mum.'

So that was what this was about. Jethro wasn't here to prevent me from feeling lonely or bored. I'd imagined we were going to spend the evening making small talk, but I should have known he'd have another agenda. The way Jethro had suddenly begun watching me intently made my pulse rate quicken, so I cast my eyes downwards to escape from his stare.

Then, without me commenting, Jethro carried on where he left off. 'I know my son loves you. I can see it in the way he looks at you. There could be worse things in life than the two of you ending up together.'

Could there? I sincerely doubted that. Jethro was getting carried away with his romantic notions, and I became rattled by his line of thinking. I didn't want him meddling in my love life. Anyway, Alfie didn't need Jethro to become his biggest cheerleader; he already had an inflated opinion of himself as it was. What did he want me to say? Knotting my hands in my lap, I agonised over how to respond. I wanted to remind him that I was a married woman, but I was scared of his reaction. Jethro had always treated me with respect, but I knew he could be violent, and I didn't want to provoke him.

Even though the room was spacious, all of a sudden, the deep purple colour of the walls made me feel claustrophobic. They felt like they were closing in on me as an oppressive silence dragged on. In an attempt to end the awkward atmosphere, I settled back against the plump feather cushions and regained eye contact with Jethro. I couldn't bring myself to challenge him, so I decided to let him ramble on instead.

'I want my son to be happy,' Jethro said. 'He's had a lot of sorrow in his life. Alfie was only fifteen when he lost his mum. He never really got over it. Her death affected him very badly. Nora was great with the kids. She adored all of them, but she had a special bond with Alfie. He was the apple of her eye. They were always together.'

Jethro giving me the low-down on Alfie's heartbreaking childhood was obviously a ploy to win me over, and I had to resist the urge to get my violin out and accompany him as he set the tragic scene. I wasn't sure whether they'd hatched the plan together or not. Either way, it made no difference.

The more Jethro tried to sway my opinion, the more he was getting my back up. I desperately wanted to tell Jethro he could spare me his matchmaking service but thought better of it. If he was half as unpredictable as Alfie, it would be safer to keep my mouth shut and my opinions to myself. But by staying silent, I was probably giving him the wrong idea. I didn't want him to think he'd talked me around.

Jethro smiled. 'Alfie loves you, and I hope one day, you will learn to reciprocate the feeling.'

They were the last words I wanted to hear. I cast my eyes to the floor so that I could break away from Jethro's intense stare. I couldn't understand why Jethro was trying to force me into a relationship with Alfie. He knew from first-hand experience what it was like to be married to a woman he didn't love. This conversation was going from bad to worse, and I found myself wishing Alfie would return so that I could put an end to it. I wasn't sure Jethro would be speaking as freely if his son was in the house.

'Who would have thought Alfie would end up in the same position as me? The Watson men seem to find the Stone women irresistible. Your husbands have good taste.' Jethro flashed me a calculated smile.

I felt the colour rush to my cheeks, and a sudden wave of embarrassment washed over me. Right now, I would give anything to be somewhere else. I didn't know how to respond, so I started laughing. It was a nervous habit.

'I'm being serious, Gemma. That was meant to be a compliment.'

'Thank you,' I replied, but I still wasn't convinced Alfie's feelings for me and Jethro's for Rosa were genuine. Maybe I was cynical, but it was much more likely they were part of the elaborate revenge plot that had been running for decades. Stealing your arch-enemy's wife would be the perfect way to get them back, wouldn't it?

No matter how much Jethro tried to convince me, Alfie and I were never going to be together. I'd made a huge mistake when I'd slept with him. I felt awful admitting that because I loved my son more than anything, and if I hadn't had sex with Alfie, he would never have been conceived. I didn't for one minute regret having Luca. I just wished Alfie wasn't his father. That was my punishment for being unfaithful to Nathan. I wouldn't be in this situation now if I hadn't betrayed him.

'Think about what I've said. Don't throw the towel in before you give Alfie a chance. Nora and I hadn't planned to start a family either when she fell pregnant, but sometimes it's better when fate takes the decision out of your hands.'

Alfie and I were in an entirely different position to his parents. When I became pregnant after a one-night stand, I was married to Nathan, and right from the start, I'd always been clear with Alfie that as far as I was concerned sleeping with him had been a mistake. He knew Nathan and I had decided to put my infidelity behind us. Much as he'd tried to come between us, we were putting on a united front and staying together.

I realised that might be about to change. If Nathan and I split up as a result of my deception, one thing was certain:

I wasn't about to set up home with Alfie. No matter how much the Watson family seemed to want me to, it wasn't going to happen. I could literally feel Jethro's eyes boring into me, so I lifted my head and looked at him.

'I never expected to lose my wife when I was forty.' Jethro laced his fingers together and rested them on his chest. 'After Nora died, I went off the rails for a while. I channelled my grief into aggression and took it out on my rivals. I came to my senses when I nearly got sent down for gouging out the eye of a bent copper.'

My stomach flipped over. I was surprised he'd told me that. Perhaps he had a feeling I'd underestimated him, and he was giving me an insight into what he was capable of. To be honest, I wouldn't have thought Jethro had it in him. It just goes to show how appearances can be deceptive. Like Alfie, he was difficult to read. I would never have imagined a violent maniac was lurking inside this softly spoken man. He had that side of his personality well concealed.

'In my defence, he deserved it. The guy kept poking his nose into my business. There's nothing worse than a cop who's happy to accept bribes and live on the edge of the criminal underworld but still tries to lay down the law. It's a liberty. I pay the Old Bill to clear up our mess and keep us out of trouble. I don't pay them to have opinions.'

Jethro glanced down and adjusted the sleeves of his suit jacket before he turned his attention back to me.

'I can still see my old mum's face, pleading with me to get a grip of myself for my kids' sake. They needed me, and if I was behind bars, I wouldn't be any good to them. Her lecture made me realise I needed to run the business with a less hands-on approach.'

The Watsons had avoided being sent down for a very long time because they had people in high places on the payroll. That nugget of information was important; I wouldn't forget it.

The sound of the front door slamming made me freeze. My wish had been granted. Alfie was back. Then a thought crossed my mind; you should be careful what you wish for, shouldn't you?

Alfie walked into the living room, and he flashed me a bright smile. 'What have you two been talking about then?'

'Let's just say your ears must be burning,' I replied.

'Excellent.' Alfie winked.

He undid the button on his grey suit jacket and began talking business with Jethro. My eyes were initially drawn to the holster he was wearing over his crisp white shirt, but then I found myself absentmindedly studying the contours of his muscles through the thin fabric before I managed to snap myself out of it.

What the hell was I doing? There was no denying Alfie was a good-looking man and bore a strong resemblance to his father, but that wasn't the only thing they shared. They were both psychotic lunatics. I hoped for my son's sake he'd inherited the Watsons' good looks but not their temperament.

81

I'd never found a woman I wanted to settle down with before. That was until Gemma walked into my life. She was the one. I'd never been more certain about anything. We were a perfect match. It frustrated me that she refused to see it. Her misplaced loyalty to Nathan was clouding her judgement. Was I pinning my hope for a future with Gemma on a lost cause? Only time would tell.

I hadn't gone blind. I'd still notice an attractive woman if she walked into the room, but nobody compared to Gemma in my eyes. She was the most beautiful woman in the world and was in a league of her own. I couldn't stop thinking about her. I loved everything about her, especially the way she'd start fidgeting with her hair when she felt uncomfortable or when she flashed me a look of contempt with her incredible green eyes. I even loved the torrent of verbal abuse she gave me when she was trying to wind me up.

There was an art to picking up women, which I was

happy to say I'd mastered over the years. I'd never needed to go on a Tinder date. My line of work and bank balance ensured I had a never-ending supply of potential partners. The opposite sex literally threw themselves at my feet, and I'd be lying if I said I didn't enjoy that. I liked having the freedom to sleep with different women whenever I felt like it. In the past, I'd even been guilty of juggling a few at the same time. That was one of the privileges of being single.

But since I'd spent the night with Gemma, I hadn't been interested in sharing my bed with anyone else. I think it was my body's way of telling me that I'd found my other half, even though I hadn't been looking for it.

I realised being part of a couple shouldn't mean you lost your identity, but because I had a fear of dependence, I'd never felt the need to be in a committed relationship before. Why would I? It made you vulnerable, and that was something that didn't sit comfortably with me.

82

Gemma

I'd been suffering from insomnia for some time now, but ever since Alfie had made Luca and I move into Darkwood Manor, so he could keep an eye on us, it had reached another level. Alfie wanted to know my every move, and that in itself was stressful.

The world Alfie lived in was unsafe. The war with the Albanians was far from over. How could it be? Somebody still needed to pay for the loss of lives they had endured, and it would be easier to target Alfie than Vladimir. I was petrified that something awful would happen to Nathan while we were estranged. I didn't want my husband to suffer at the hands of one of Alfie's enemies.

I never wanted Nathan and Luca to become involved in this mess. The clock was ticking; I knew the truth would be revealed very soon; I had almost run out of time. If I could get away, I wouldn't have to be the one to tell my husband the details of the secret I'd been keeping from him. But no matter how hard I tried, I couldn't come up with a plan.

Even if I did manage to escape, would we ever really be free of Alfie? I knew the answer, but it was too depressing to contemplate. Because of my stupidity, our lives would always be tangled together.

When the bedroom door opened and I saw Alfie standing in front of me, my heartbeat went into overdrive. He cast an eye over my state of undress, I was aware that the thin fabric of my pyjamas was slightly see-through, but I hadn't been expecting company. I was on my way to bed.

'You look beautiful, Gemma.' Alfie smiled, saying plenty with his eyes.

As I turned my back on him and went to walk away, Alfie closed the gap and slipped his hands around my waist. I felt myself freeze. Keeping my back to him, I tried to push Alfie's hands away, but he grabbed hold of my wrist, and he swung me around, so I had no option but to face him. He pulled me towards him, and his mouth was on mine before I had a chance to protest.

When one of his hands skimmed over my breast, I felt rage erupt inside me. It was bubbling under the surface like molten lava. Who did he think he was? It was about time Alfie realised he couldn't paw me whenever he felt like it. I put both of my hands on his chest and pushed him backwards, then looked up at him. My face was like thunder. Alfie looked stunned by my sudden outburst. It was just as well I'd caught him off guard. Otherwise, I would never have been able to overpower him.

'What's the matter, Gemma?' Alfie laughed.

I clenched my fists as I glared at him, hoping to compose myself before I had to speak.

'Why the long pause?' Alfie's eyes twinkled as he waited for me to reply.

'Get out of my room,' I finally blurted out. My words were loaded with hate. I crossed my arms over my chest when I noticed Alfie's blue eyes sweep over me and linger on my cleavage.

'I take it you're turning me down again, are you? Not even a maybe?' Alfie winked, openly flirting with me. 'That's a shame. Things were just about to get interesting.' Alfie smiled, and charm oozed out of his pores.

He took a step towards me and ran his fingers across my lips. Panic ripped through me, and acting on instinct I sprang back to put some distance between us.

'My offer still stands. I'd be happy to take you off Nathan's hands. So if you change your mind, you know where to find me.' Alfie winked again. 'I'll leave you with that thought,' he said before he walked out of the room and closed the door behind him.

A moment later, I found myself leaning against the back of the door listening to the muffled sound of his footsteps as they retreated down the hall. I finally let out the breath I'd been holding. There was no lock on my bedroom door, so I knew I wouldn't be getting much sleep tonight.

83

Gemma

'I think it's about time you and Nathan had a little chat,' Alfie said. 'Knuckles is going to drive us over to Gareth's house, and you're going to tell your husband about Luca No excuses this time, Gemma.'

I felt my stomach contents somersault at his suggestion. Thoughts were racing around in my head so fast I was having trouble concentrating. I'd have to force myself to focus. I wanted to see Nathan more than anything, but I wasn't ready to tell him the truth. I somehow doubted I ever would be. I could see Alfie meant business, so there was no point stalling any longer. I could do with some liquid courage before I faced my husband, but we'd only just had breakfast, so I didn't think it was appropriate to ask Alfie if I could have a stiff drink before we left.

As I prepared my son for the journey, a sense of guilt washed over me. It was time to face up to what I'd done. When I looked back at the terrible decision I'd made keeping Luca's paternity a secret, I wondered what I was thinking of. There was more than a chance I wasn't thinking at all. I must have been acting on emotion, not logic. I'd been selfish and stupid lying to Nathan about Luca because I was scared of the outcome. That was ridiculous. There was no justifying what I'd done.

It was impossible to know how Nathan was going to react when I dropped the bombshell. I'd been playing out what-if scenarios in my mind for long enough now. As I tried to muster up the courage, I reminded myself that Nathan and I had overcome huge hurdles before, and this latest crisis wouldn't necessarily spell the end of our marriage. A catastrophe had the potential to make a relationship stronger. I had to believe that was possible. Otherwise, I'd never be able to go through with it. It was time to stop torturing myself and get this over and done with. I kept hoping that once I'd revealed my secret, it would ease my troubled mind, but until my confession was set free, I was stuck in a state of limbo.

'You only get the chance to fuck up once, Gemma. I don't give second chances, so be a good girl and let's get this over with,' Alfie said.

I sat in the back of the car sandwiched between Alfie and Jethro; Luca was in the front next to Knuckles. The atmosphere was tense, and anxiety flowed through my body like an electric current. I stayed silent for the entire journey to Whitechapel.

I began wringing my hands as Jethro, Alfie and I approached Gareth's terraced house. Knuckles was going to wait in the car with Luca.

'Hello, Gemma,' Gareth said after he opened the front door.

'Can I see Nathan please?' My lip quivered as I spoke.

'I'm not sure he'll want to talk to you, especially as Alfie and Jethro are with you.'

'Well, we're not going anywhere, and if Gemma has to ask you again, you're going to be sorry,' Alfie replied, throwing his weight about as his eyes bored into Gareth's.

Gareth blew out a breath and shrugged. 'You'd better come in then.'

Gareth turned on his heel and walked down the hallway towards the kitchen. Alfie, Jethro and I followed behind.

I'd become tangled in a web of lies of my own creation, and the only way to escape was to tell my husband the truth. It was a moment I'd been dreading for so long, but now it was time for me to come clean and put an end to the deceit once and for all. I stood staring at Nathan, contemplating how to begin this awkward conversation.

'What do you want, Gemma? I'm sure this isn't a social visit.'

Biting down on my lip, I glanced at Alfie out of the corner of my eye, as I prepared to speak. He was scratching the side of his cheek with immaculately clean fingernails while eyeballing Nathan.

'How nice of you to bring Alfie with you. Have you come to rub my nose in it? By the way, where's Luca?'

I left his question unanswered. I needed to focus on the purpose of my visit and not allow myself to get distracted. Otherwise, I was going to chicken out.

'I've got something to tell you, Nathan.' My tears rolled silently down my cheeks.

I could feel every pair of eyes in the room watching me.

'It's OK, Gemma, you can save your breath.' Nathan put his hand up to silence me.

I looked into my husband's eyes, but I didn't recognise the man standing in front of me. I never imagined Nathan had this callous side to his personality. It was as though he'd already accepted our marriage was over. He didn't even want to discuss it. Nathan was prepared to let me go. I felt myself start to crumble at the thought of that, but I had to get a grip and finish what I'd come here to do.

'Please don't interrupt me, just let me say my piece.'

'Maybe you should save it for somebody who gives a shit. You two are welcome to each other.' Nathan was shaking with fury, and his voice was laced with venom.

Alfie pushed his face right into my husband's, and the atmosphere in the room changed. 'Wind your neck in and stop trying to dominate the conversation, you prick.'

When Alfie smirked, Nathan clenched his teeth, and a muscle twitched in my husband's jaw. I'd have to get a move on before anger got the better of him.

I took a deep breath, then the words tumbled out of my mouth. 'There's no easy way to say this.' I tried to keep my voice steady so that I could gauge his reaction, but when I continued to speak, tears started to pour from my eyes as emotion welled up in me. 'Luca's not your son, he's Alfie's.'

Nathan stared at me with a look of horror on his face. He couldn't believe what he'd just heard. I could see my words were floating around in his mind. Nathan swallowed hard, then steadied himself on the back of the kitchen chair. He'd had the wind knocked out of his sails. The news had blindsided Nathan. It hit him like a tonne of bricks, and he flew into a jealous rage. When Nathan's fist made contact with Alfie's face, the sound resonated in the room around us. There was no way he was going to get away with that, I thought. I was right.

Alfie looked into Nathan's eyes before he grabbed him by the throat and pushed him back against the wall. Nathan hooked him with a jab to the side of the head, and a fight broke out between them. When Gareth and Jethro finally dragged them apart, Nathan's knuckles were bruised and bleeding. Although he'd taken multiple blows, Alfie didn't have a mark on his face, or a hair out of place and his suit still looked immaculate.

I should have realised they would end up resorting to violence. Nathan had an incredibly short fuse and was prone to sudden eruptions of volcanic rage, and Alfie's temper was legendary. This latest episode did nothing to dispel the rumour.

I don't think I would ever have come clean if Alfie hadn't forced my hand. I found myself crying hysterically, pleading for one more chance between sobs. I promised I'd never do anything to hurt my husband again and rambled on, wallowing in self-pity, but my grovelling fell on deaf ears.

Nathan was still trying to take in the news. As my words began to register, he stared at me. His dark eyes suddenly misted with tears as they searched mine. He was waiting for me to speak, but I had nothing more to say and felt suffocated by the silence. I had to get out of the room. I couldn't bear to look at the shell of the man standing in front of me. The feeling of guilt was overwhelming. I'd hurt him so badly.

Nathan had a vulnerability about him that usually

brought out my protective side, but I'd just obliterated him by sharing my secret with him. I might as well have picked up a gun and blown his brains out. Nathan was broken. Watching the man I loved crumble in front of me sent my mind into turmoil.

I glanced over at Alfie. He didn't try and suppress his satisfied smile, and that made anger rise up inside me.

84

Nathan

My wife had shattered my dream and pain seared into my body as if I'd been kicked in the stomach. What Gemma had done was incredibly cruel, and now so many unanswered questions whirred around in my mind. How could the woman I loved betray me like this?

I wondered how long my wife had known that Alfie was Luca's father? Did Gemma know she was already pregnant when we'd started trying for a baby? I hoped not. That would make matters so much worse.

Since I'd found out that Gemma was pregnant, I'd become preoccupied with finding my dad. When I'd finally met up with him, our reunion couldn't have gone any better, and now that I'd repaired my relationship with my mum, I'd thought everything was going to be rosy. Even though my parents were divorced, I wanted them to be part of my son's upbringing. I hoped we could have a happy future together after all the years we'd spent apart.

Having a close family network meant everything to me.

I wasn't sure Gemma fully appreciated how strongly I felt about that. She had never had much of a bond with her parents or her sister, Rebecca, and I very much doubted she would ever make peace with them. As far as Gemma was concerned, they were toxic, and she was better off without them.

I wished Gemma had told me the truth, instead of letting me believe Luca was mine. It was going to break my heart to walk away from my wife and the child I thought was my son now that I'd bonded with the baby, but what choice did I have? Alfie wasn't going to allow us to continue to live as a family, so there was no point in even considering that option. Not that I wanted to. Gemma had broken my trust again, and I was struggling to deal with her betrayal. I couldn't believe she'd been so deceitful keeping something as important as this to herself. That was such a selfish thing to do.

When the thought had crossed my mind that Gemma and Alfie had rekindled their affair, I didn't think my mood could sink any lower, but I was wrong. The pain I was experiencing now was on a different level. I felt empty and hollow like Gemma had slashed a knife across my stomach, and my insides had spilt out.

Luca wasn't my biological son, but I'd been the only father he'd ever known and now, thanks to my wife's deception, I had lost my child. No parent should ever have to experience the pain that caused. I couldn't even begin to describe the devastation I was feeling. It was the ultimate tragedy. The gaping hole Luca's presence would leave behind would be impossible to fill. I felt like I'd suffered a bereavement.

Gemma had robbed me of my parenting role, and that left

me feeling numb and disconnected. I couldn't just switch off my emotions. I loved Luca, and now I'd have to learn to live without him, but it would be torture. I wouldn't wish this pain on my worst enemy.

I couldn't believe Gemma had hidden this from me. I felt like I didn't know her at all. How could she have maintained the lie for so long? My wife clearly didn't have a conscience. If Alfie hadn't forced her hand, I wondered whether she would have ever told me the truth. In the blink of an eye, Gemma had destroyed the trust we'd worked so hard to rebuild.

Suddenly, without warning, Gemma had turned my life upside down, and her selfish actions had destroyed my whole world. I asked myself if our relationship was worth trying to salvage. Now that I knew the truth, I didn't think there was any way we could work things out. I would never be able to trust my wife again, so I wasn't sure I wanted her to be in my life any more.

Gemma's confession had left me with a wound so raw, I wasn't sure it would ever be able to heal. I couldn't help thinking there were some things you were better off not knowing. I wished Gemma's secret had stayed under wraps and spared me the pain of this unbearable heartache.

85

Alfie

Nathan's suffering gave me great satisfaction. His face was a picture when Gemma broke the news to him. What heightened my enjoyment of the situation even more, was that at the start of their conversation, he'd thought he had the upper hand. He'd had no idea his wife was keeping such an enormous secret from him, so the pleasure had been all mine when she floored him with the news. Gemma hadn't tried to sugar-coat it; she'd dropped a bomb and delivered the facts in her usual no-nonsense manner.

Although it had been a long time coming, it had been worth the wait. Seeing the devastation on Nathan's face had made my day. Gemma's betrayal had hit him every bit as hard as I knew it would. Stage one of the demise of their marriage was complete, which left the door wide open for me. Now I had Gemma right where I wanted her. She could live with me in the lap of luxury or struggle on her own as a single parent. Staying with Nathan was not going to be an option for her, and the sooner she accepted that, the better it would be for all of us. When I'd fathered her child, it had been the kiss of death for her marriage.

I'd been kept at arm's length for long enough as Gemma confidently batted away my insistence that I was Luca's father. She'd blatantly lied to me about his age in a desperate attempt to throw me off the trail. Gemma was stupid to think she could keep her secret without anybody finding out. I had to admit I'd enjoyed backing her into a corner. I was intrigued to see how far she'd be prepared to go to conceal the fact that I was Luca's father. She didn't disappoint me. Gemma would have taken this to the grave if I hadn't forced her to come clean.

But now that the truth was out, I wanted to get to know my son. It was funny how things worked out. I'd never seen myself as a family man, but now that I'd been given the opportunity, I was determined to throw myself into the role one hundred per cent. It might be a good thing for Gemma to see the softer side of me. I did have one, but I didn't show it to many people.

I wasn't completely inexperienced with babies, I had nephews and nieces, which was unfortunate for Gemma, because I was able to pick my sisters' brains about child development, and that definitely helped me catch her out.

86

Gemma

I'd made the decision to bring a child who wasn't biologically my husband's into the world without consulting him. In hindsight that wasn't the smartest move I'd ever made. But I stood by my decision. Even though our relationship had been strong at the time, if Nathan had known I was carrying Alfie's child, it would have destroyed him, and the last thing I'd wanted to do was hurt him.

It was naive of me to think I was going to get away with keeping Luca's paternity to myself. That wasn't fair on Nathan, Luca or Alfie. It was a selfish thing to do. They all had a right to know the truth. But the truth was so awful, I didn't want to think about it. Life was cruel. This whole experience was emotionally draining.

All I could think about was whether our marriage would survive now that my secret was out in the open. Breaking up with Nathan would feel like the end of the world. If he left me, he would take my heart with him. The thought of losing him was terrifying. My decision to lie came from fear. I did it because I thought it would be easier to live with the consequences of the lie than face the pain of the truth. By concealing the facts, I'd hoped to minimise the damage and keep my husband's pain at bay. This was the most difficult emotional trial I'd had to go through for some time, but that didn't justify the way I'd handled it.

Nathan was the most loyal person you could meet, and I kept hoping he wouldn't bail on me now that the shit had hit the fan. But there was only so much a man could take. I had wounded his pride at the deepest level and destroyed his masculinity by telling him that Luca wasn't his son. When I'd delivered the news, I saw it suck the life out of him.

87

Nathan

I sat alone at the kitchen table with my fingers clasped around a mug of coffee, mulling over the drama of the night before. Gemma's confession had come out of the blue. I couldn't believe what she'd told me. My instinct was to bury my head in the sand and pretend none of this had happened, but I knew that wasn't an option.

Keeping a secret this size had caused the death of the dream, and now, not for the first time, our marriage was on its last legs. It was wrong of Gemma to let me believe Luca was my child. How could the woman who claimed to love me be so cruel? In order for a relationship to thrive, trust had to be present, and that was something that had to be earned. I should never have given her a second chance, but I was a glutton for punishment.

Looking back, I should have realised something didn't add up. If I'd been given a pound every time somebody asked, 'Who does he take after? Is he the milkman's?' when they saw the blond-haired blue-eyed baby, I'd be a very rich man. But I was so delighted in my new role that the penny didn't drop, and we weren't the only dark-haired parents in history to produce a fair-haired child, so I didn't think anything of it. Gemma always glossed over the issue of our son's colouring with some spiel she'd read in a book. She spoke with such confidence, so I didn't suspect a thing. That was no doubt to cover up her guilty conscience.

My emotional stability was a distant memory. I didn't know what to do for the best. My mind was all over the place. The bombshell Gemma had dropped had changed our lives forever. Now the truth was out in the open, I couldn't ignore it. For once, I couldn't brush the issue under the carpet. The problem needed to be dealt with.

88

Gemma

I put my phone down on the blue pearl counter, let out a slow breath and stared into space. I frowned as I struggled to work out the logic behind Nathan's suggestion.

'Why the long face?' Alfie smiled.

'It's nothing.'

Alfie knew something was wrong, and he didn't try to hide his enjoyment. He was like a pig in clover savouring every moment of my despair. The fact that my marriage was once again in trouble filled him with delight. 'What did Nathan say?'

As I turned to face Alfie, I noticed Jethro watching me. He was observing our exchange from the sidelines, but it was a private matter, and I'd rather not be discussing it in front of an audience.

'Come on, Gemma, don't keep me in suspense. What's the big secret?' Alfie raised an eyebrow.

'Nathan wants us to do a DNA test.'

Alfie's eyes blazed, and he slammed his fist down on the

counter next to where I was sitting. The sound of the impact made me jump as Alfie's mood suddenly shifted.

'Calm down, Alfie,' Jethro said when he realised his son had startled me. 'Are you OK, Gemma?'

I could see Jethro's concern was genuine as he looked deeply into my eyes. 'Yes,' I replied, nodding my head.

'Who the fuck does he think he is demanding a DNA test? Nathan's got bigger balls than I gave him credit for. Phone him back and tell him to get his ass over here right now. We've got things to discuss.'

Alfie balled his right hand into a fist and began punching his left palm with it as he paced backwards and forwards in front of the full-length windows.

I was surprised Nathan had asked for a DNA test too. There was no doubting Luca's paternity. But knowing Nathan, he was probably in denial and didn't want to accept what I'd told him. I didn't know what he was hoping the test would prove. It wasn't going to change anything, but maybe he needed to see the result in black and white to be able to accept it. In reality, he was putting off the inevitable.

Alfie returned to where I was sitting. He put his hand under my chin and tilted my face towards his. 'I'm sorry I scared you.' When he kissed the side of my cheek. I felt the hairs on the back of my neck stand up, and I recoiled from his touch. Alfie laughed. Then he turned away and spoke over his shoulder. 'Thanks for the slap in the face. I should have known you wouldn't let me down gently.' Alfie paced across the kitchen floor and disappeared out of sight.

★

When Nathan and Gareth arrived, Alfie swaggered back into the room, and the scent of trouble wafted in behind him. Clutching a tumbler of Jack Daniel's in his hand, he went to stand next to Jethro.

'So I hear you want a DNA test?'

Nathan ignored Alfie's question. 'I want to speak to my wife in private,' he replied.

'This matter concerns all of us, so you either talk to Gemma here or not at all.' Alfie glared at Nathan while he swirled his drink around in his glass.

We'd left Gareth's house abruptly, so I hadn't offered Nathan an explanation. Now that my husband was standing in front of me, it was time to find my voice. 'I'm so sorry I kept the truth from you,' I began, hoping my apology would pave the way to a peaceful resolution. 'I should have been honest and come clean when I first...'

Nathan interrupted me before I'd finished my sentence. 'How long have you known?'

'Since I went for the dating scan.' I looked down as I spoke, so the tears in my eyes wouldn't be visible. I didn't want this to turn into a pity party. Nathan was the one who'd been wronged, so I had no right to cry.

'Naughty, naughty, Gemma, you realised ages ago the child was mine.' Alfie's face broke into a slow smile. 'And to think you were so insistent that Nathan was Luca's father when I confronted you about it.'

Nathan's mouth fell open when he realised how long I'd been keeping the secret. He stood opposite me, staring blankly into space.

After listening to Alfie stir the pot with his big wooden spoon, I couldn't help myself, and I took a thinly veiled swipe at him in retaliation. 'Fascinating as your running commentary is, I'd appreciate it if you could do us all a favour and pipe down for a minute. You're not helping the situation.' I felt like I'd just scolded a naughty child, but Alfie threw his head back and laughed, taking no notice of my reprimand, so I scowled at him, before eyeing him with disgust.

'Why are you looking at me like that? Anyone would think I'd just said, do me a favour and show me your tits, love.'

I exhaled louder than I'd intended. Alfie was being an arsehole, so I wasn't going to waste time engaging with him. 'Part of me thought I should tell you the moment I realised there was a chance Alfie was Luca's father, but the other part of me knew, if I wanted us to stay together, I shouldn't ever tell you.' I locked eyes with my husband and tried to block everyone else out of my mind.

Gripped by guilt, I continued to talk, rambling on as I tried to come up with a justifiable reason for keeping the information a secret. But there was nothing I could say. The only excuse I had was that my heart had overruled my brain. I made the best decisions when I used a careful balance of emotion and logic. At the time, my emotions were running high, so my logic must have been low. I was sure that was what led me to take the irrational decision to cover up the truth.

At one point, I saw Nathan's eyes glaze over. I knew by the spaced-out look on his face that he wasn't listening to me. His attention was on a different commentary that was going on inside his head. Nathan had zoned out because it was too much for him to take in. He started staring into space with dead eyes.

A blind person could see the hurt I'd inflicted, and I knew there was a chance that Nathan's wounds might never heal. I was ashamed of myself. I shouldn't have treated my husband like this. Once again I'd broken his trust, and now I was going to pay dearly for the betrayal. A feeling of devastation came over me. I looked into my husband's dark eyes, then went to hold his hand, but he pulled away.

Alfie laughed. 'Now you know what it feels like, Gemma. Rejection stings like a bitch, doesn't it?'

89

Nathan

When I'd first found out Gemma was pregnant, I'd shouted it from the rooftops. I'd told anyone who was prepared to listen that my wife was expecting our first child. It was an exciting time in our lives, and I wanted to enjoy every minute of it. Now Gemma had pulled the rug out from beneath me, and I wasn't sure I'd ever be able to forgive her.

I had boundaries, and Gemma had well and truly overstepped them. Under the circumstances, I didn't think I could raise another man's child. Luca was the product of Gemma's infidelity, so it would be hard to look at him and not be reminded of what my wife had done. It wasn't easy to repress the jealous thoughts that kept surfacing within me.

When I'd discover what Gemma had been hiding from me, my gut instinct was to walk away from her and Luca and save myself from a lot of suffering. Something I'd learnt over the years was that I should never ignore my intuition.

Its ultimate purpose was to protect me. But it wasn't as simple as that. I still loved them both, so it was going to be torture to face a future without them.

While I was agonising over my decision, Dad was doing his best to support me. But I found it hard to talk about and was overcome with a host of different emotions every time I tried. One minute I felt angry, and the next I was drowning in despair. This was a humiliating experience. I hadn't even told my mum yet; it was too embarrassing. As far as I was concerned until I had the official result, the fewer people who knew the better. Then Dad offered me some advice. He told me it wasn't fair to make Luca suffer. None of this was his fault.

Although I knew deep down what the outcome of the test would be, I was clinging to the hope that Gemma was mistaken and Luca was my son after all. Until I saw the proof in black and white, I wasn't prepared to accept it. I'd spent the last six months caring for that baby as if he was my own flesh and blood, and I wasn't going to walk away from him that easily. It was my name that appeared on Luca's birth certificate, not Alfie's, so Gemma was going to have to prove to me without a doubt that he wasn't my son.

The sooner we took the DNA test, the better. This matter needed to be settled once and for all. I was keeping everything crossed that it would prove Luca was mine, but if it didn't, hopefully, it would help me come to terms with the fact that the baby I'd been raising wasn't my son.

90

Gemma

Thanks to the growing trend in people tracing their ancestry, DNA testing had become a simple procedure. But this genetic test wasn't going to be harmless fun; the outcome had the potential to split my family up for good and leave us traumatised by the emotional fallout.

I fired up my laptop and found a company that provided a confidential DNA testing service using state-of-the-art technology. I scrolled through the information on the website to see what was available. A standard DNA test took about four days. That was quicker than I was expecting. We weren't taking the test out of casual curiosity; it was to resolve the issue of paternity, so the sooner we had the result, the better.

I was just about to fill in the online form to request the testing kit when Alfie breezed into the kitchen. 'What are you doing?'

'I'm sending off for the DNA test.'

'Don't bother. The doctor's going to carry out the test so

the results will be court admissible. We can't use a do-it-yourself kit; it needs to be a legal one.' Alfie smirked.

Alfie summoned Nathan, and the three of us gathered in the dining room. When Jethro's doctor arrived to collect the samples, a sudden fear gripped me. What if I'd made a mistake and Nathan was Luca's father after all? Could we trust Jethro's doctor not to tamper with the results?

The doctor put on his gloves and opened up the first kit. 'Let's get started,' he said.

'Ladies first,' Alfie replied, prodding me in the back with his index finger.

'Wash your mouth out three times with warm water and then take a seat,' the doctor said.

I was a bundle of nerves, and my mouth was as dry as the Sahara desert, but I did as instructed.

'Open wide.'

When the doctor removed the first swab from the sterile packaging, I leant back in the leather high-backed chair and gripped onto the seat. He rolled the buccal swab firmly on the inside of both of my cheeks and under my tongue for about one minute to collect the cells that would provide my sample. He repeated the process another three times, as four swabs had to be submitted.

'Next,' the doctor said when he'd finished the procedure.

Nathan looked me in the eye before the doctor placed the swab in his mouth, and I got goose pimples all over my arms and legs. I knew the result of this test would seal our fate. I'd have to prepare myself that I might have to venture into the uncharted territory of single parenthood any day.

Alfie sat down with a smug look on his face, so I wandered

over to the windows and pretended to be admiring the view. I couldn't bear to watch.

Luca was due a feed and wailed at the top of his lungs as the doctor tried to collect the sample. It wasn't easy. He was wriggling like an eel, but the doctor eventually managed to run the swap around the inside of his mouth and his lower lip. I put my baby up on my shoulder to comfort him then glared at Nathan for making me put the poor child through this. It was completely unnecessary. I would hardly have admitted to him that Alfie was Luca's father if I was in any doubt.

Having allowed the swabs containing our DNA profiles to air dry, the doctor placed them in the sample collection envelopes before sealing them. 'I'll be in touch when I have the results. The clinic releases the reports at four o'clock on the designated day,' he said. Then he left us with our thoughts.

91

Gemma

'I'm glad to see you haven't lost your silver tongue.' Jethro smiled, before relaxing back in the velvet armchair next to the fire.

The sound of Jethro's voice recaptured my attention, so I glanced up from my lap, and he caught my eye. I'd zoned out for a moment. I was sitting on the sofa swirling my pink grapefruit gin and tonic around in the glass while doing my best to ignore Alfie's flattering commentary. He'd been laying the compliments on with a trowel all evening, in a blatant attempt to win me over and I was bored of listening to him drone on.

'Has Alf managed to sweet-talk his way into your heart yet?' Jethro paused momentarily to gauge my reaction, so I stared at him with a deadpan expression. But despite the look on my face, he continued talking. 'It doesn't look like Gemma has fallen for your charms yet. I think you'll have to try a bit harder son!' Jethro took a sip of his drink before steering the conversation onto a touchy subject. 'Alfie

adored his mum. You never got over her death, did you?'
Jethro glanced at Alfie, but Alfie looked straight through
him. 'It's time to let go of the past, Alf. Otherwise, you'll
always have trouble forming relationships with women.'

'Since when did you become a counsellor?' Alfie asked in
a sarcastic tone. 'Thanks for the words of wisdom, but you
won't be offended if I don't follow your advice, will you?
Anyway, you're a fine one to talk. You didn't set me a very
good example, did you?'

Jethro looked taken aback as though he'd been punched
in the face by Alfie's words.

'The truth hurts, doesn't it?' Alfie added.

Jethro turned his attention back to me and continued
talking as if his son wasn't present. 'Alfie needs a strong
woman like you, Gemma. He doesn't want someone to
go along with everything he says. His mum was a people
pleaser. She was weak, and he saw what that did to her.'

'My mum wasn't weak. If she had been, she'd never have
been able to put up with the shit you put her through. You
destroyed her because you were out shagging anything with
a pulse. You weren't even discreet about it. I would never
treat my wife like that.' Alfie spat his words straight into his
father's face, and the energy in the room shifted.

Their conversation stunned me to silence. Tensions were
running high. Was it all about to kick off? I sat there for a
moment, lost in my thoughts. To speak or not to speak, that
was the question? But as I suffered from an incurable case of
foot in mouth disease, I thought it was probably best to stay
quiet for the time being. Even though I wanted to intervene,
I decided it wasn't my place to say anything. I couldn't trust
myself not to make the situation worse by blurting out the

wrong thing. Sometimes my words came out like a runaway train, and I didn't always filter what I said efficiently. I could be impulsive. That had sometimes enabled me to make the best decisions ever and sometimes the worst. So instead of trying to pacify the situation, I stayed tight-lipped and hoped they didn't perceive my silence as rudeness.

'I can see why you're besotted with Gemma. Make sure you treat her well,' Jethro continued, undeterred by Alfie's outburst.

'That's rich coming from you after what you did to Mum.' Alfie put his tumbler of Jack Daniel's down on the mantelpiece and locked eyes with his father. He was spoiling for a fight.

Jethro smiled at his son. 'I'll hold my hands up and admit I was a lousy husband, so learn from that and don't make the same mistakes I did.'

Jethro hadn't risen to the bait, but Alfie must have hit a nerve because his face became expressionless. This had always been a sensitive issue in their house. He'd had to live with the guilt that he'd been responsible for his wife's untimely death. He'd treated her so badly; he drove her to drink. Knowing it was his fault, his three children had grown up without their mother was a huge burden for Jethro to carry.

Alfie downed the drink in his glass before he stormed out of the room.

'Women come and go all the time, but you'll only ever have one mum in your lifetime,' Jethro said as soon as Alfie was out of earshot. 'It broke his heart when Nora died. Grief is a powerful emotion, and we all react differently, so don't think badly of the way he's just behaved.'

For once, I didn't think Alfie was out of order. It made sense that he'd feel strongly about his parents' relationship. But I could also see Jethro was a prisoner of his past wrongdoings and it was something they were never going to see eye to eye on.

Jethro fixed us both a refill and began telling me about his youth. It was almost as though he wanted to tell me the background to his troubled relationship with Nora to justify the way he'd treated her. By all accounts, he'd been instantly attracted to Rosa the moment he saw her shortly after she arrived from Italy when she was eighteen years old. She'd come to England with her sister and brother-in-law to find work and was living away from home for the first time.

'My dad gave Bernardo the opportunity to run a new Italian restaurant that he was opening in Southend on the condition that the ownership stayed a secret. Dad wanted everyone to think it belonged to Bernardo. Even Rosa and Donatella were kept in the dark. I assume the reason behind that was because Dad was cooking the books.'

Jethro explained that Rosa was young and shy and used to blush every time he came into the restaurant. He was sure she was attracted to him, but he took too long to make a move on her and his old rival Gareth got in first and stole her heart.

Jethro broke off when he heard Alfie's footsteps approaching. His attraction to Rosa wasn't the best subject for us to be discussing under the circumstances. Alfie breezed through the living room and fixed himself a drink at the bar.

'I don't think I ever told you that Levi and Gareth used to be friends,' Jethro said when Alfie put his glass down on the mantelpiece and stood with his back to the fire.

I'd found myself hovering nervously on the edge of the sofa and wondered if I should excuse myself so the two men could talk in private, but decided against it as the conversation was about to get interesting. There was no better way to bond than by sharing an old family secret, I thought. Was this Jethro's way of apologising to his son, without actually having to say sorry?

'No, you didn't, because you never speak about your older brother,' Alfie replied in a frosty tone, but it was clear Jethro had his full attention.

Jethro composed himself before he recounted the story of the night his brother died. Gareth and Levi were walking home after a house party when a car mounted the kerb and rammed into them. Gareth escaped unscathed, as Levi took the full force of the crash. The high-speed hit-and-run left Levi with severe head injuries. According to Gareth, he phoned for an ambulance, but Levi drifted in and out of consciousness as they waited for help to arrive. Levi was rushed to hospital but died as a result of his injuries. He was only twenty. Jethro looked visibly moved when he finished speaking and paused while he took several sips of his gin.

'The police searched for the driver, but he'd fled the scene. Gareth was the only witness.' Jethro's lip curled as he spoke. 'He told officers that he'd been drinking heavily and was so shocked by what happened he couldn't remember many details. My family felt he knew more about the circumstances that surrounded Levi's death than he was letting on. They thought the car that mowed my brother down was driven by someone from a rival family. My dad wanted Gareth to name names. But no amount of torture provided him with any information.'

A shiver ran down my spine. Poor Gareth. I couldn't begin to imagine what they'd put him through.

'Did they ever catch who was responsible?' Alfie asked.

Jethro shook his head. 'Nobody was ever charged with Levi's murder. Gareth reckoned he felt guilty that his friend died, while he'd escaped unhurt. He told Dad he would do anything he could to make amends with our family. As far as Dad was concerned, Gareth's card was marked. He blamed Gareth for Levi's death. It was only a matter of time before Dad would seek revenge. Getting even with a person who crossed the firm would usually follow the same pattern. Their target's abduction would end with a dead body bearing the signs of torture rather than a negotiated release. But this time, Dad didn't want Gareth dead; he wanted to prolong his suffering.'

Alfie nodded in agreement. 'Being the victim of a contract killing would have let him off too lightly.'

'Gareth soon showed his true colours. The coward moved to London for his own safety after the beatings became too much for him to handle.' Jethro smiled.

Alfie stood looking into space as he mulled over what had happened to his uncle. 'So how did Gareth end up with Rosa?'

'Gareth had to move back because he couldn't afford to live in London. He dossed around doing odd jobs to get by before becoming a delivery driver. He met Rosa when she signed for an order he'd just dropped off at the restaurant.' As Jethro spoke his lips visibly thinned.

'I'm surprised Grandad allowed him to come back. Gareth was taking the fucking piss. Talk about rubbing salt into the wounds,' Alfie said.

'Gareth tried to stay under the radar and by the time we realised he was back, he'd already hooked up with Rosa. We reluctantly left Gareth alone because she was part of the restaurant's cover. But revenge was still bubbling under the surface. We hadn't been on good terms with him since Levi died. It was only a matter of time until we'd get even. I was delighted when I finally got the chance to stitch the bastard up.'

92

Nathan

Although I knew the DNA test would confirm that Alfie was Luca's biological father, I wouldn't be able to accept the outcome until I saw the findings on the report. I could tell Gemma was pissed off with me for insisting that we were all tested, but I was desperately clinging to the remote chance that Luca was mine even though, now I thought about it, the baby was the image of Alfie.

It was hard to describe how I was feeling. Anger, hurt and disappointment were all jostling for the place at the top of the list. Life was complicated. Trust was a double-edged sword. It was painful when someone you loved betrayed you but equally hurtful when the same person didn't trust you enough to confide in you in the first place.

Moving forward, our marriage wouldn't survive without it. But since I'd discovered that Gemma had lied to me again, she'd destroyed the peace and harmony we'd worked so hard to rebuild. There was a thin line separating what secrets were acceptable to keep and which ones would haunt your partner for life. Gemma hadn't mastered the art of knowing which was which yet. By withholding something so important from me, I felt an enormous sense of betrayal. It would be hard for us to come back from this.

I lay awake, staring at the ceiling as I tried to process my thoughts. Gemma had lied to me about Luca's paternity, so my self-esteem and ego had taken a battering. Having come to terms with the fact that she'd cheated on me, I now had to accept that my wife had got pregnant by another man. That wasn't an easy thing to do and felt like the final insult.

But at least she hadn't been unfaithful to me again. Loyalty counted for a lot in my book. Now that I'd had time to absorb the information, I knew I didn't want things to turn toxic between Gemma and I. She was my soulmate. There had only ever been one woman for me, and that was Gemma. I didn't know how we were going to get over this, but I didn't want to lose her.

I still loved Gemma with all my heart, so I'd have to try and sort things out with her. I'd regret it if I let her go. I knew what the outcome of the test was going to be, and despite the absence of blood ties, I still wanted to be part of Luca's life. He might not be my biological child, but I could never reject him. In my mind, I would always be his father. I loved him the same now as I did before Gemma confirmed my worst nightmare. You can't just switch off your feelings. They hadn't changed at all. Alfie might be Luca's biological father, but I was his real dad. I'd bonded with the baby, and loved Luca as if he were my son.

Gemma was Luca's mother, and I was pretty sure she would get custody of the baby if Alfie took us to court, even if she had to allow him visitation rights. He might be Luca's father, but that didn't mean he could take away my opportunity to be Luca's stepdad.

A huge weight suddenly lifted from my shoulders as I made my decision. I wasn't prepared to give Gemma or Luca up without a fight. The problem was neither was Alfie. I'd have to consider my next move carefully. Once the storm had passed, I was going to pick up the pieces and salvage what was left of our marriage. I was determined that Gemma and Luca would always be a part of my life. If we could get through this, we could get through anything life threw at us.

93

'Why have you got the hump?' Alfie asked with an amused look on his face.

Although he didn't know it yet, he was about to bear the brunt of my bad mood. I didn't even try to keep some civility in my tone, and my words came out barbed like angry flesh-tearing thorns. 'I think you know the reason.'

'I'm sorry, Gemma, you're not making any sense. You'll have to elaborate.'

'OK, if you want me to spell it out, I'm fed up of listening to you and Jethro prattling on. You both seem to have conveniently forgotten that I'm married to Nathan and I have no plan to change that, so I'd appreciate it if you didn't keep suggesting that it was only a matter of time until the two of us became a couple.'

'I hate to point out the obvious,' Alfie said, his voice laced with sarcasm, 'but you're forgetting one important factor. The decision to stay together isn't yours to make.

There are only so many times a man will stand by and let a woman make a fool of him before he'll throw the towel in. I know Nathan's a bit of a doormat where you're concerned, but even he must have some pride. You've completely humiliated him this time. You must have a very high opinion of yourself if you think he'll still want to be with you after the way you've treated him. Once the test confirms he's not Luca's father, I very much doubt he'll want anything to do with you.'

Alfie's words were designed to hurt me, and he'd achieved that goal, but I wouldn't give him the satisfaction of letting him know that. He didn't need to plant a seed of doubt in my mind, though, it was already there. I'd intended to give Alfie a piece of my mind, but he'd dominated the conversation and turned it on its head, to the extent that I'd barely been able to get a word in. This was a prime example of Alfie at his best. He couldn't resist trying to control and manipulate the situation while preying on my vulnerability. I couldn't be bothered to continue speaking to him. The harsh reality of what lay ahead was causing me to feel stressed without Alfie trying to wind me up.

'I don't have the energy to humour you any more. I'm going to check on Luca,' I said before I breezed out of the kitchen.

I crossed the hallway and began climbing the stairs to the guest suite, with my heart thundering against my ribcage. My head was reeling from the painful things Alfie had just said.

'Have I upset you?' Alfie called after me.

His words made me stop in my tracks, and I stole a glance

at him over the edge of the sweeping staircase that curved back around on itself. 'No,' I replied, but that wasn't true. I was so grateful my voice didn't crack with emotion.

'You probably won't believe me, but I'm sorry.'

Although what Alfie had just said was positive, he stood gazing up at me with a smug look on his face. He didn't even try to hide it. His facial expression undermined any good intentions his apology might have had, proving the point that it doesn't matter what you say but how you say it.

Luca was sound asleep, so I sat on the window seat and stared out at the floodlit manicured lawn. No matter how much Alfie tried to exploit my weakness and use it against me, I couldn't let him succeed in wearing me down. But it was virtually impossible to stay strong. Our conversation had left me feeling very insecure. Alfie always managed to find subtle and not so subtle ways to make me feel like this.

I mustn't waste time feeling sorry for myself. The most destructive vice a person could have was self-pity. If I allowed myself to get in that mindset, it would destroy everything around me. I couldn't afford to give my misery an inch, or it would take over, and that would leave me feeling more deflated than I already did. It was time to harness the power of positivity and regain my fighting spirit. I had to focus on the good things in my life, not the bad. The only person who could make my situation better was me. I couldn't change the fact that Nathan wasn't Luca's biological father, and there was a very real chance my husband would never be able to forgive me for keeping that from him.

The best thing I could do was accept the outcome, even if that meant us going our separate ways. I should have the dignity to move on without him. I knew that was going to test the strength of my character, but I'd have to summon every bit of determination I had. Once Alfie realised I was going to raise our son on my own, that would wipe the smile off his face.

I decided to turn in; it would do me good to get an early night, and I couldn't face spending the rest of the evening with Alfie. I threw the scatter cushions onto the floor, then pulled back the lilac silk bedding and climbed into the centre of the enormous circular bed. My eyelashes felt like they had lead weights tied to them, and my eyes closed almost as soon as my head sank into the feather pillow.

But I couldn't sleep; I lay in the darkness, tossing and turning; the silence outside seemed deafening. I wasn't used to the sound of tranquillity and longed to hear the familiar rhythmic thud of Puerto Banús nightlife. I loved nature, but there was something creepy about the forest at night. The rustling of the leaves and the owl hooting were enough to give me a full-blown panic attack. I tried to convince myself there was nothing to worry about; the nocturnal noises just belonged to woodland creatures going about their business. But the thought of what might be lurking in the darkness would ensure I kept one eye open.

I would never get used to living in a remote location, but I'd have to bide my time for the moment and do what Alfie told me to. I'd need all my wits about me if I was going to outsmart him. Alfie's polished exterior camouflaged what truly lay beneath his Savile Row suits. The man was a monster. I was almost certain he only wanted to be with Luca and I so he could get back at Nathan.

Alfie lived in a man's world. He loved nothing more than

celebrating his criminal behaviour. I didn't want myself or Luca to be part of that life. I was desperate to disappear to a place of safety. But I'd have to watch my back. If I crossed him, Alfie would track us down like he was hunting an animal. I played the thought over in my head. No wonder I was having trouble sleeping at night. It wasn't just the sounds of nature that were keeping me awake.

94

Alfie

Call me two-faced, but I couldn't let Gemma know what I was planning. It was true that I'd been instrumental in the demise of her marriage, but I couldn't afford to gloat about that, much as I wanted to. Nathan wasn't right for Gemma; so it was time I took his place. That had always been my goal, and it had become even more important to me since Luca had been born. Whatever she might think, it wasn't an act of vengeance; I was in love with Gemma. I'd got it bad.

I'd have to have a word with my dad; we'd have to tone it down a bit; Gemma was getting narky with us. How dare we talk about her marriage to Nathan in the past tense? Speculating that the star-crossed-lovers fairy tale would end in tears was very unkind of us. We should be ashamed of ourselves. I couldn't help smiling when I thought back to our earlier conversation. Gemma was outraged; she'd been stomping about the house in a foul mood for hours waiting for the opportunity to let rip at me. But I cut her down and sent her packing before she had a chance to. Gemma was no match for me, but I loved the fact that she thought she was. You had to admire the woman; I was seriously impressed; even hardened criminals were terrified of me.

Gemma thought I hadn't noticed that her green eyes were filled with tears when she'd gone off to sulk in her room. I hated seeing her upset, but it would do her good to stew for a bit. She might appreciate what I was trying to do for her when she'd had time to calm down. Anyone would think I was offering her a dose of genital herpes, not a life of luxury.

Our plan was backfiring, so Dad and I would need to ease off for a bit. I was meant to be winning Gemma over, not pushing her away. I knew my future with her was hanging in the balance. Dad was as keen for us to be together as I was, but Gemma was stubborn as a mule and was resisting heavily. The decision to set up home with me had to be hers; I couldn't force her into it. I was used to calling the shots, but I'd have to handle Gemma differently to get the desired outcome. Frustrating as it was, I'd have to let her do things at her own pace.

I couldn't make demands. It was lucky I was a patient man. At this rate, I'd be old and grey before I convinced her we were meant to be together.

95

Gemma

Alfie and I had spent a tense couple of days, awkward in each other's company, while we waited for the DNA test results to come back. We both knew what the outcome would be; I couldn't change that no matter how much I wanted to, but until I saw the result in black and white I kept hoping the test would reveal that Nathan was Luca's father after all.

Although the doctor had taken our samples, he had set me up an account with the clinic that was carrying out the test. About every twenty minutes or so, I kept logging in to track the progress of our case, even though the expected completion date wasn't until tomorrow. I couldn't help myself. Waiting for life-changing news was proving to be incredibly stressful. I wished there was something I could do to lessen the anxiety. It wasn't as if I didn't already know the outcome of the test, but that somehow made matters worse. It made me feel powerless.

The best thing I could do was try to take my mind off

things. But that was easier said than done. My greatest weapon against the long wait was distraction, but distracting yourself was almost impossible when you couldn't concentrate on anything. The dreaded DNA test result was the only thing my mind would focus on.

The past ninety-six hours had dragged by in slow motion as the clock's hands inched agonisingly towards the day we'd receive the results. Finally, it had arrived. As I fired up my laptop, a debilitating feeling came over me. I entered my password with shaking fingers while my heartbeat pounded against my ribs. I let out a loud groan. Talk about an anti-climax; there was no update. Now I'd have to spend another twenty-four hours walking on eggshells in the Watson mansion.

96

Gemma

It was no secret that I'd struggled with the pressure of being the perfect mother. Inwardly I was in turmoil but to the outside world, I always pasted on a smile. Only Nathan knew the full extent of my anguish because, for all his faults, he never judged me.

Nathan was my rock. He broke down my barriers and made me face my demons and all the things I tried to hide from everyone. My disastrous relationship with my family had made me develop a tough exterior, but behind it, I'd always had a deep-seated fear of not being good enough. Motherhood was proving to be harder than I'd ever imagined.

By pushing me out of my comfort zone, Nathan had encouraged me to deal with my insecurities and everything I'd attempted to suppress for so long. Although facing up to my issues was challenging, it was also strangely therapeutic, and over the years, my husband had inadvertently become my therapist. He understood me on such a deep level. We shared a special connection. I'd always thought it was unbreakable.

Cobwebs of despair were busy spinning themselves around my heart, ensnaring it. There was a good chance the love Nathan and I shared was going to come to an abrupt end. I didn't want to contemplate a future without my husband. I knew I should force myself to consider it, but at the moment, my emotions were too raw. I was grieving for something that hadn't happened yet. I couldn't seem to stop myself. The intense feelings of sadness and grief were overwhelming.

I wasn't sure I'd ever be able to get past the pain of losing Nathan. The situation was almost too horrible to think about. The worst part about it was that I had nobody to blame but myself if he walked away from me.

97

Gemma

'How much longer are we going to have to wait,' Nathan said. 'The doctor told us four days, so we should have had the result yesterday. Do you think there's something wrong with the samples?' he asked in an optimistic tone of voice.

'How do I know!' I snapped. I shouldn't have bitten his head off, but I couldn't help it. Tensions were running high, and he was breathing down my neck. It was driving me insane.

Maybe Nathan was right, but the last thing I wanted was for him to get his hopes up. You could cut the atmosphere in the room with a knife. Even Alfie's normally super smooth exterior looked ruffled.

'Knuckles, get the quack on the phone and ask him what the fuck's going on,' Alfie said before he ran the palm of his hand over his slicked-back blond hair.

Knuckles stepped outside to make the call. Then several minutes later, he delivered the message. The lab had been snowed under, having received an unusually large number of samples last week, so they were running behind schedule. The doctor had already chased the clinic up and had been assured that the result would be uploaded this afternoon.

'If you hadn't slept with Alfie in the first place, none of us would be in this position,' Nathan said under his breath.

My husband had his back to me, so I wasn't sure whether he'd intended me to hear what he'd said, but I had, and his words stung like the venom from a thousand angry wasps. He seemed surprised when he turned around and saw the look on my face. I was furious. My pent-up anger was threatening to make an appearance. It was bubbling inside me, and I knew any minute now I was going to let rip. I'd made a stupid mistake, but Nathan had also made plenty. I could hear the sound of my pulse pounding in my temple as I tried to control my breathing.

'You were the one who insisted on having the DNA test done.' I had to dig deep to stop my voice from wobbling. Emotions were running high.

'Don't try and pass the blame my way. This is all your fault, Gemma.'

'Thanks for your support.'

The words kept spilling from our mouths in an endless stream. We couldn't seem to stop them as Nathan and I pointed the finger at each other. Neither of us wanted to take responsibility for the chain of events that had led us into this situation. Alfie observed us in silence with a satisfied smile playing on his lips. I broke off from our heated exchange when I heard the sound of a new notification coming through on my phone. I'd received an email informing me that the Paternity Report had been uploaded. This was the moment we'd all been waiting for. While I read it, it would give Nathan and I some temporary respite from being at each other's throats.

I walked over to the table, fired up my laptop and opened the email. Based on the analysis of fifteen independent autosomal DNA markers, Mr Nathan Stone has been excluded as the alleged biological father of Luca Stone, because more than two of Mr Nathan Stone's DNA components are absent from the DNA profile of Luca Stone. In summary, Mr Nathan Stone is not the alleged biological father of the child, Luca Stone.

My head began to swim, and a wave of nausea engulfed me as I read the words on the screen. Based on the analysis of fifteen independent autosomal DNA markers, the probability of Mr Alfie Watson being the biological father of Luca Stone is ninety-nine point nine per cent. In summary, the DNA results conclude that Mr Alfie Watson is not excluded as the biological father of Luca Stone.

The report's findings didn't come as a surprise. It was the outcome I had expected. The test proved that Nathan couldn't be Luca's father, but seeing it in writing somehow made it feel more real. The DNA test had also confirmed my worst fear, and that threw me into a panic.

Now that paternity had been established, Alfie would have legal rights to Luca. He wasn't going to allow another man to raise his son, even if Nathan still wanted to be part of Luca's life. Alfie wouldn't be denied his parental responsibility. He would insist on visitation rights and possibly even take me to court to fight for custody. He'd also insist that Luca's birth certificate was amended. I was almost certain he could obtain a court order to force me to name him as the father.

My mind was racing with possibilities. I knew it was natural to fear the worst and think your whole world was about to end, but preparing for the worst might not be the best solution. I needed to stay positive. I could be worrying about nothing. Who was I trying to kid? Alfie Watson was not going to let Nathan and I skip off into the sunset with his son.

As I prepared myself to break the news to Nathan, I became a boiling cauldron of emotion. I loved my husband; even if I didn't like him very much at the moment. I'd never intended to hurt him, but the test results were going to break his heart. Nathan demanding a DNA test to resolve the paternity issue once and for all had opened a can of worms. Our lives could have been so different if the truth hadn't come out.

I knew the outcome of the test was going to crush Nathan. I felt panic rise within me. I needed to take a deep breath and pull myself together. It was time to take a step back and refocus. Catastrophising the situation wasn't going to help. I didn't know exactly what Nathan's reaction would be until I told him. There was no point in second-guessing how he would respond. Our goal had always been to grow old together. I was about to find out whether that was going to happen now.

I closed the lid of my laptop and stared into space for a moment while I tried to choose the right words. I felt terrible that I hadn't been honest with Nathan from the start. If I had, this situation could have been avoided. But I'd taken the coward's way out and lied to my husband. Maybe if I explained my reasons, Nathan would be understanding, and that would absolve me of any guilt. But that would only prolong the agony for him and wouldn't change anything. It was time to stop being selfish and cut to the chase.

Taking a deep breath, I got up from the table and went to stand in front of Nathan. I felt numb as I looked at his handsome face.

'There's no easy way to say this, but...'

Nathan interrupted me before I'd finished my sentence. He obviously didn't want to hear me say the words he'd been dreading. 'I was over the moon when you told me you were pregnant.'

I could remember that day as if it was yesterday. I stared into my husband's haunted eyes before casting mine to the floor. I couldn't bear to look at the shell of a man in front of me.

'When Luca came into the world, he made me feel complete. I have such happy memories of that time, but now I want to block them out. They're too painful to think about. This has got to be the worst day of my life.' Nathan shook his head. The pain I'd caused was written all over his face.

'I'm sorry, Nathan.' Tears filled my eyes and threatened to spill down my cheeks. I needed to strengthen my emotional muscles to stop myself from spiralling into a state of despair. I had no right to cry.

'Can you imagine how I feel? You lied to me and let me think Luca was my son when you knew all along he was Alfie's.'

I couldn't imagine how he was feeling. I wanted to tell

Nathan how sorry I was and take away his pain, but how could I find the right thing to say, when there were no words? I took hold of both of his hands and went to kiss the side of his face. He pulled his hands out of my grip, turned on his heel and walked out of the house.

98

Nathan

My wife's display of emotion stirred nothing within me. I felt hollow inside. Moments ago, when I tried to vent my anger about the situation she'd put me in, Gemma had given me an ear-bashing and blamed me for pushing her into Alfie's arms in the first place. I'd had to sustain a dose of verbal abuse from someone who was supposed to love me. Now she was expecting me to be sympathetic towards her because she'd opened the flood gates. I couldn't muster up any compassion. I was the wronged party. Did she seriously expect me to feel sorry for her?

Alfie had the upper hand now. You could almost see the power pour out of him. He'd looked so smug as he watched Gemma and I exchange hurtful comments. I could see him enjoying my suffering and couldn't trust myself not to unleash my fury on him. There was only so much I could take. I needed some space to clear my head, so I'd walked out of Jethro's house and left my wife in the kitchen, sobbing into a tissue. Gemma had broken my heart, and it felt like the end of the world, and yet, she was the one who was shedding the tears.

I wished I could cry, but at the moment, I was too angry. I felt like lashing out and destroying everything in my path, but I knew that wasn't the answer.

I jumped in the Mondeo and clutched the steering wheel with both hands. Tears of frustration started to stream down my face as my anger and sadness overlapped. Gemma had pushed me to the edge, and much as I'd thought I'd wanted us to stay together, I wasn't sure I'd be able to recover from this betrayal after all. I thought I'd made my decision, but now I was doubting it again. I didn't know what to do. Should we stay together or go our separate ways?

Dad hobbled down the steps and climbed into the passenger seat. He reached across and put his hand on my shoulder to try to comfort me, but nothing he could do would make any difference. My world was falling apart. I wasn't surprised by the outcome of the test, but it was still difficult to accept it. I felt like the hope that I'd been clinging to like a life raft had been smashed to pieces by a giant wave, and I was sinking to the bottom of the ocean.

It had taken me a long time to come to terms with Gemma's infidelity. I'd had an uphill battle to banish the mistrust and suspicion it left me with. When I thought back to the day Luca was born, I genuinely thought we'd put the bad times behind us. As a couple, we were stronger than ever, but bad luck and circumstances had conspired against me and dealt me another blow. Life could be cruel.

With trembling hands, I started the car and drove along Jethro's driveway as fast as the tyres would allow. Gravel sprayed up and hit the doors as we made our way towards the road. Once the wheels touched the tarmac, I put my foot to the floor. I needed to put as much distance between myself and the Watsons as possible. Driving on the winding country lanes, with no regard of the speed limit, I was vaguely aware of Dad's voice telling me to slow down, but there wasn't another car in sight, so I dismissed his concerns.

My mind was on other things. I was preoccupied with the damage my wife's secret had caused, so I ignored common sense, and instead of taking my foot off the accelerator, I went around a blind bend far too fast. The car skidded, and that led to disaster. I wasn't a stunt man, but what happened next was like an action sequence in a James Bond film.

I somehow thought if I steered frantically, the Mondeo would be able to defy the laws of physics like cars did in the movies. The events that followed took place in slow motion. One minute we were hurtling along the narrow country lane, approaching a corner, and the next the car was flipping upside down. That was the last thing I remembered.

99

Gemma

I'd hoped Nathan and I could put everything behind us and start over, but he'd taken the results of the DNA test worse than I'd expected. So I wasn't convinced my husband thought our marriage was worth saving. He'd stormed out of the house before we'd had a chance to discuss anything. Everything was still hanging in the balance.

'Before you try and absolve me of my parental responsibility, I think you should know I have no intention of allowing another man to raise my son.'

The sound of Alfie's voice brought me back to reality, and as I glanced over at him, I saw him looking at me with calculating eyes. He gave me an insight into how he was feeling. He was Luca's biological father, and even though I didn't want him in my son's life, I couldn't stop them from having a relationship.

Why had I let Nathan interfere? The reason I'd been reluctant to have a DNA test done was I knew it would prove without a doubt that Alfie was Luca's father and now that meant he had rights. The DNA test would stand up in court, so there was no point being uncooperative.

'By the way, I don't like the name you chose for our son. If I'd have been consulted, I'd have chosen something completely different. Obviously, we will need to take Nathan's name off the birth certificate, and while we're at it, we can change Luca's name to Alfie Watson Junior.'

Over my dead body, I thought, but I decided to keep that to myself just in case Alfie got any ideas. It wouldn't be the first time he disposed of somebody if they didn't toe the line. I didn't want Alfie to be involved in the upbringing of my child, yet thanks to the result of the legal DNA test, I couldn't stop him from amending the father's details on Luca's birth certificate, but I wasn't going to give my consent to changing his name.

'We belong together. You're the mother of my child. Nobody in their right mind would try to come between us,' Alfie said, and the corners of his mouth lifted. 'I want us to be a family, Gemma, but if you won't agree to that, you can kiss your son goodbye.'

I faked a laugh to hide my fear, but I knew this was no idle threat. Alfie's words echoed around in my head. I should have seen that coming, but sometimes signposts are clearer in the rear-view mirror, aren't they?

'You might be the head of a criminal empire, but I'm Luca's mother, and if you try to take him away from me, you're going to wish you hadn't bothered.' Nobody could protect their offspring better than a mother could. I'd never been a pushover, so if Alfie wanted a fight that was exactly what he was going to have. He was not going to take custody of my son.

Alfie threw his head back and laughed. 'Are you threatening me, Gemma?'

For a moment I had to replay in my head what I'd said out loud. 'No, but you're deliberately manipulating the situation. Stop trying to take advantage of me.'

'I'm not taking advantage of you, Gemma. You won't let me.' Alfie winked before I broke eye contact with him.

Alfie had another thing coming if he thought I was going to give up Luca that easily. I'd waited years to fulfil my dream of becoming a mother, and even Alfie Watson wasn't going to be powerful enough to take my child away from me. If he tried to, he was going to see a different side of me. Alfie might be used to playing the role of the alpha male, but he was underestimating the lengths I'd go to, to keep my baby safe. I loved my son with a ferocity that only a mother could understand and I would go to the ends of the earth to protect him.

Alfie lived in a world ruled by violence, and his behaviour was so unpredictable, there was no telling what he might do. My imagination began running riot. I couldn't think straight. Luca was the centre of my universe and nobody, not even Alfie, was going to come between us. The feeling of anxiety began to ebb away like the turning of the high tide when I reminded myself that no court would take a child away from its mother without a very good reason.

I wasn't an expert on family law by any means, but I was Luca's biological mother, and I was almost certain that meant I automatically had parental responsibility for him. But Alfie wouldn't care if I was Luca's legal guardian. He didn't need a reason to challenge me over it, he had judges on the payroll, and I knew how determined he could be. I couldn't afford to get into that position. If I did, I would be powerless to stop him.

I didn't want to leave Nathan, and despite what Alfie had said, I wasn't going to let him take my baby. I wanted to find a peaceful resolution to the situation we were in. I didn't want us to be at war. That wouldn't be a healthy environment for Luca to grow up in. The feud between the Watsons and the Stones needed to end. I didn't want the poison to seep into the next generation. It was time to put things behind us and not look back. I didn't want my son to be exposed to the age-old hatred that was dominating our lives. It was destructive and had the ability to spiral out of control if it wasn't curbed.

We all needed to learn to manage our emotions better. Some of us were guilty of being quick-tempered, but as long as we vented our frustration, I was confident we could stop issues building up. The Stone and Watson families lives were tangled together now whether we liked it or not. But instead of that being a problem, we should see Luca's birth as a building block for the future. Everything happened for a reason. Hopefully, my son's presence in this world would put an end to the trouble that had raged for years. I didn't want the spirit of vengeance to contaminate another generation.

Luca began to cry, so I walked over to his cot and lifted him out.

'If you think I'm going to step aside and let another man bring up my son, you're mistaken. Luca will follow in my footsteps whether you like it or not. As soon as he's old enough I'll groom him and then one day I can hand over the baton. I'll teach him the tricks of the trade so that he can take the reins of the family business.'

In the event of Alfie's retirement or untimely death, Luca would be the natural successor. But I wouldn't allow him to be the one to step up and take over his father's position as head of the family firm. Alfie's legacy would not live on through Luca even though he was heir to Alfie's criminal empire.

'There's no way I'm going to let you take my son away from me and cut me out of his life. Like I said, I want us to be a family, Gemma, but if you're not prepared to leave Nathan, things will get ugly. Don't try to fight me on this.'

I would stop at nothing to protect Luca. I didn't want my son to have a father he was scared of. It was every mother's worst nightmare that somebody might take their baby away or harm them in some way. But this wasn't a bad dream; it was a reality. Alfie meant everything he'd said. His words hung over me like a dark shadow. I was terrified of what he would do, and knowing how Alfie had behaved in the past, it was probably a valid fear.

Alfie flashed me a bright smile. 'Now give Luca to me – I want to hold him.'

Alfie reached his hands out towards Luca, and I instinctively tightened my grip on my baby. I wasn't about to hand him over.

100

I sat in the living room looking up at the ceiling, mulling over Alfie's ultimatum. I didn't want my son to become part of the Watson family firm and inherit the criminal empire, not now, or ever. I couldn't allow Alfie to be involved in raising my son, so I knew I had to get away before Luca's birth certificate was changed.

I loved my son with all my heart and soul, and it was my job to keep him safe. The Watson family had a reputation for being violent and dangerous. Nobody in their right mind messed with them, so I'd have to watch my back, but I had to get Luca away from here. I didn't want him to be exposed to their way of life.

I'd have to find the strength necessary to take control of the situation. Luca was my son, and I would decide who could be part of his life. I couldn't change the fact that Alfie was his father, but we were never going to be a family. Nathan was great with Luca. Any man could be a biological father, but it took a special person to be a dad. But after everything that had happened, I wasn't sure Nathan and I would be able to save our marriage. My heart was in his hands. I hoped he'd be gentle with it.

If we ended up going our separate ways, I knew I could survive the fallout a divorce would bring. I wouldn't let myself go to pieces. I owed it to my son to dust myself off and start again.

The future of my relationship with Nathan was out of my hands, so there was no point spending my time thinking about it. No good ever came from dwelling on the past. I should channel my energy into something more constructive. I needed to find a way out of this situation. There had to be one. Even though it didn't seem possible at the moment, Luca and I would get away from Alfie's clutches. I was certain of that.

101

Gemma

I had just finished feeding Luca and had put him down for a nap when my mobile began ringing. My heart skipped a beat when I saw it was Gareth's number. He told me that he and Nathan had been involved in an accident. Any thoughts of Luca and I vanishing into thin air disappeared from my mind. Even before I knew the details of the crash, I had a gut feeling that Alfie was behind the accident. He had always maintained that things would be so much easier with my husband out of the picture. I felt a shiver run down my spine.

Police, paramedics and firefighters attended the scene because Nathan was trapped in the car, but firefighters had managed to cut him free, and he'd been flown by air ambulance to the Royal London Hospital. Gareth stayed incredibly calm as he relayed the information. He didn't know the extent of Nathan's injuries; all he could tell me was that he was in a bad way. Gareth had also been injured and was being taken to the Princess Alexandra Hospital by road ambulance.

When I put down the phone from Gareth, I rushed into the bathroom and vomited into the toilet. The news had come as such a shock. I had trouble taking it all in. For the paramedics to transport my husband by air ambulance, he must be seriously injured. What if he didn't survive? I had to push that thought from my mind; it wasn't going to help the situation if I went into meltdown.

Gareth didn't go into details about what caused the crash, but the circumstances surrounding it seemed mysterious to me. There was no way I could prove anything, but that didn't mean I wasn't going to confront Alfie about it. Gangsters had a habit of disposing of people they didn't want around any more. Alfie was on the running machine in the indoor gym when I burst into the room.

'I need to go to the hospital. Nathan and Gareth have been involved in an accident, but you already know that, don't you?' The words were out of my mouth before I could stop them.

'I don't know what you're talking about.' Alfie stopped the machine. He walked over to a chair in the corner of the room, picked up a fluffy, white towel and mopped the sweat off his forehead with it.

'It seems like a bit of a coincidence that two of your family's enemies have been badly hurt in an accident, doesn't it?'

'What are you implying, Gemma?'

Alfie looked furious. I was beginning to wish I'd kept my mouth shut now. He wasn't a man to cross. Even though I thought it, I couldn't accuse Alfie of tampering with their car. I wasn't prepared to go that far.

'You didn't answer my question.' A huge smile spread across Alfie's face.

102

Alfie

I had to admit I felt ecstatic when Gemma broke the news of Nathan's accident to me, but that didn't mean I was guilty of causing it. I genuinely had nothing to do with it, but that didn't stop her throwing accusations around. Gemma thought I was behind the crash that put her husband teetering on the brink of death, but if I had been, he wouldn't be breathing now. She was furious with me. She'd burst through the door of the gym with her green eyes blazing like an avenging angel.

Don't get me wrong, I'd wanted to take Nathan out of the equation on many occasions, but I'd always managed to resist the urge. Much as Gemma wanted to pin the blame on me, I was completely innocent for once. I'd be lying if I said I wasn't delighted to hear that Nathan was wired up to machines and fighting for his life, but I wasn't responsible for putting him in a hospital bed. For once, my conscience was clear. I couldn't take the credit for landing Nathan in intensive care; it was his dangerous driving that had done that. Not for the first time, his reckless behaviour had come back to haunt him.

I can't say I wasn't tempted to pay Nathan a visit and switch off the machines that were keeping him alive, but I was prepared to let nature take its course. The doctors had given him such a slim chance of survival; waiting a few more days would make no difference. It was a shame Gareth hadn't endured life-threatening injuries too. That would have put an end to our vendetta once and for all. Then Gemma and I could get down the serious business of raising our son.

Dad would be elated when he found out. I couldn't wait to give him the good news, although his happiness might be tinged with sadness. Years ago, my grandad and his brother were killed in a car crash, so this could stir up bad memories for him. Police never discovered what caused their car to crash through the central reservation, and veer out of control, in good driving conditions on a straight stretch of road. A head-on collision with a car on the other carriageway followed, killing all four of the occupants at the scene.

Dad was the only male heir, so he took over the family business. Since my grandad and his brother started the firm, none of the men in the Watson family had made it to old age. I couldn't help wondering if that was a coincidence or not. Running a business of this nature was fraught with danger. The moment you chose this path, you had to be aware that your life could end suddenly. Your enemies might snuff you out, or worse still, you could end up in the clink. But just for the record, I had no intention of either of those things happening to me.

103

Gemma

Today was a dark day. Nobody went through life unscathed by trouble, but I'd had more than my fair share of it. I hoped there would soon be an end to the downward spiral of grief I'd found myself in. Being cooped up in the hospital was pure misery.

I sat by my husband's bed, clutching his hand, listening to the beat of the heart monitor. I couldn't allow myself to lose hope, so I willed him to regain consciousness. It was agonising watching him fight for his life, but I couldn't give up on Nathan. It was hard to stay positive seeing him hooked up to the wires of a life support machine, with an oxygen mask covering his face, and a drip standing guard by his side. I had to fight back the tears as Nathan hovered close to death, the doctor offered me a sympathetic smile.

'Why don't you go home and get some rest. I'll stay with him,' Rosa said in a low pitch when she walked into the intensive care unit. She could see the effect this was having on me.

'Thanks for the offer but I want to be here when he wakes up.'

My mother-in-law came over to where I was sitting and put her arm around my shoulder. 'We must be strong for him,' she said as she held back a river of unshed tears.

After a few moments, Rosa went to sit in the chair on the other side of the bed. I didn't make eye contact with her; I was being eaten up by guilty thoughts. This was all my fault. As Rosa's eyes scanned her son's battered body, she clasped her hands in front of her lips and began muttering something under her breath before she made the sign of the cross. But Nathan needed more than her prayers; he needed a miracle.

While Nathan was in the hospital, I'd had to leave Luca in his father's care. I hoped he didn't use the opportunity to spirit Luca away somewhere. But it was a chance I'd have to take. It wasn't an ideal situation by any means, but I didn't have another choice. Although I was reluctant to let Alfie have access to his son, I didn't have the energy to fight him at the moment. The custody struggle between us would have to be put on hold for the time being. I hoped my decision wouldn't come back to haunt me.

On the third day of my bedside vigil, Gareth came to visit. He'd been released from hospital after being kept in for observation and was desperate to see Nathan. I had been by my husband's side since the accident. My father-in-law told me about his terrifying brush with death. Nathan had been driving too fast on the narrow country lane, and he lost control of the car on a bend. The Mondeo skidded off the road and flipped upside down. Although he was dazed, Gareth managed to climb out of the broken window and raise the alarm. Nathan was stuck inside, unconscious and bleeding heavily from a wound on his head.

Amazingly, Gareth had walked away relatively unscathed. He had broken his shoulder, collarbone, and two ribs as well as puncturing his lung. The numerous cuts and bruises over his face and arms would remind him of the near-miss every time he looked in the mirror.

'I got off lightly in comparison,' Gareth said as he looked at his son's body wired up to machines. 'The police said we were lucky to get out of the smash alive. The car's a crumpled wreck.'

Gareth's words made me more certain than ever that Alfie was behind the crash, which had left my husband in a coma, fighting for his life. It seemed like too much of a coincidence. Alfie had made no secret of the fact that he wanted Nathan out of the picture.

To help myself cope with the grief as the days dragged by, I thought about how life always managed to find a way to move us past terrible events. Even though at this moment in time, I was finding it hard to believe that I would get through this, I knew I would. I had to stay positive for Nathan's sake. But dark thoughts kept filling my mind. Nathan might not come out of the coma. If he did, would he be able to forgive me for keeping my secret, or would he hold it against me for the rest of my life? The questions were on my lips, but I might never get a chance to ask them.

So I sat on the hard plastic chair, holding my husband's hand and hoping for a miracle. I thought I was dreaming when the doctor told me Nathan was showing signs of improvement, but he wasn't out of the woods yet.

'When a person wakes up from a coma, they usually come

round gradually. They may be very agitated and confused, to begin with, so don't be alarmed if that happens,' the doctor said.

Nathan was taken off the ventilator and was able to breathe unassisted for the first time since the accident. Even though he was taking baby steps, they were going in the right direction, and that was the most important thing. It was encouraging to see him following simple commands. As he began to regain consciousness, he seemed very confused by his surroundings, but thankfully he recognised me.

Nathan didn't remember being in the accident. The doctor told me it was too soon to know if the rest of his memory had been affected.

Nathan was still very weak but continued to make good progress over the coming days, and when he was well enough to talk, he told me he'd felt me holding his hand. Before he woke up, he thought he'd been standing in a white room, like a doctor's surgery, waiting for something to happen, but he didn't know what. He'd heard things going on around him, but he'd been trapped in his body and was unable to move or speak. It had been a terrifying experience for all of us.

'I love you, Gemma.' Nathan clutched my hand and smiled at me. 'I want us to stay together.'

Nathan's words made me break down in tears. My husband still wanted to be with me despite everything I'd put him through.

'Being in this accident has made me realise I should appreciate the gift that's been given to me. Life is precious, Gemma, so none of us should take it for granted.'

I leant forward and kissed my husband on the lips.

Nathan looked into my eyes while holding on to my hand. 'I can't imagine my life without you and Luca in it. When I get out of here, we can go back to Spain if you like.'

'I don't think Alfie would be too happy about that.'

'Don't worry about Alfie. We'll work something out with him.' Nathan squeezed my hand before he held it up to his lips and kissed it.

Surviving his brush with death had obviously given Nathan a new zest for life, and while I had to admire his optimism, he was underestimating how difficult it would be to take Luca away from the Watsons. I didn't want to upset Nathan, so I wasn't going to point that out. He had enough on his plate at the moment and needed to concentrate on getting better.

I smiled at my husband to hide what was going on inside my head. Alfie was never going to sit back and allow us to skip off into the sunset with his son. The DNA test had confirmed he was Luca's father, so he would insist he was part of our baby's upbringing. The best I could hope for was that he didn't fight me for full custody.

I'd have to put those thoughts out of my head before my mood darkened. Speculating on the result of a battle that hadn't happened would cast a shadow over an otherwise perfect day. I had so much to be grateful for, not only was Nathan alive, he was also expected to make a full recovery. I thanked my lucky stars that we'd been given another chance to be together. I wasn't about to waste the opportunity – life was for living.

Acknowledgements

Thank you to Hannah Smith, my amazing editor. It has been an absolute pleasure working with you again.

Thank you to Vicky Joss and the team at Aria Fiction for all your hard work.

Thank you to the members of the Romantic Novelists' Association for your words of wisdom and for welcoming me into the fold.

About the Author

STEPHANIE HARTE was born and raised in North West London.

She was educated at St Michael's Catholic Grammar school in Finchley. After leaving school she trained in Hairdressing and Beauty Therapy at London College of Fashion.

She worked for many years as a Pharmaceutical Buyer for the NHS. Her career path led her to work for an international export company whose markets included The Cayman Islands and Bermuda.

Stephanie took up writing as a hobby and self-published two novels and two novellas before signing a contract in March 2019 with Aria Fiction.

Hello from Aria

We hope you enjoyed this book! If you did let us know, we'd love to hear from you.

We are Aria, a dynamic digital-first fiction imprint from award-winning independent publishers Head of Zeus. At heart, we're committed to publishing fantastic commercial fiction – from romance and sagas to crime, thrillers and historical fiction. Visit us online and discover a community of like-minded fiction fans!

We're also on the look out for tomorrow's superstar authors. So, if you're a budding writer looking for a publisher, we'd love to hear from you. You can submit your book online at ariafiction.com/we-want-read-your-book

You can find us at:
Email: aria@headofzeus.com
Website: www.ariafiction.com
Submissions: www.ariafiction.com/
we-want-read-your-book

�n @ariafiction
🐦 @Aria_Fiction
📷 @ariafiction

Printed in Great Britain
by Amazon

38821503R00245